ACCLAIM FOR THE SUSPENSE NOVELS OF SEAN FLANNERY

The Zebra Network

"A masterpiece of escapist entertainment!"
—*Library Journal*

"The pace never lets up!" —*Indianapolis Star*

Broken Idols

"A cracking good thriller!"
—Alfred Coppel, author of *The Apocalypse Brigade*

"Tightly drawn intrigue." —*Denver Post*

False Prophets

"An elaborate . . . exciting spy novel."
—*Publishers Weekly*

"A staple of [the suspense novel] genre."
—John D. MacDonald

SEAN FLANNERY

NETWORK

ST. MARTIN'S PAPERBACKS

Published by arrangement with William Morrow and Company, Inc.

THE ZEBRA NETWORK

Library of Congress Catalog Card Number: 88-29138

ISBN: 0-312-92104-7

Printed in the United States of America

William Morrow hardcover edition published 1989
St. Martin's Paperbacks edition/April 1990

10 9 8 7 6 5 4 3 2

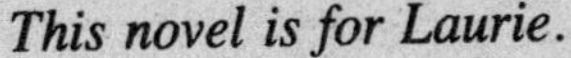

This novel is for Laurie.

Preface

WASHINGTON—Accused Russian spy network kingpin James Franklin O'Haire, 42, pleaded guilty Monday to charges of espionage and income tax evasion.

Along with his younger brother, U.S. Air Force Captain Liam Casey O'Haire, 37, who pleaded guilty to the same charges last week, James O'Haire will likely be sentenced to life imprisonment. Both brothers would be eligible for parole in 25 years.

The O'Haires were indicted in July after a two-year investigation by the U.S. Justice Department, the Federal Bureau of Investigation and the U.S. Internal Revenue Service. Investigators charge that James O'Haire headed the spy ring that included seven other men and women besides his brother to hand over U.S. technical and military secrets to the Soviet Union.

The other seven, who also pleaded guilty, will be sentenced in U.S. District Court next month.

Investigators say the full extent of the damage the O'Haire spy ring inflicted on U.S. interests may never be known. But they say it is "extensive" and includes information about the so-called Star Wars, Strategic Defense Initiative.

The last similar spy case in this country involved the Walker family in 1986.

Part One

Chapter 1

October had come early to Moscow. A few minutes after ten on an evening late in the month, the air was January-crisp. Snow lay everywhere in big dirty piles. Moscow was an eastern city; dark, brooding, mysterious. The onion domes of St. Basil's on Red Square seemed a natural counterpoint to the Kremlin's Spassky Tower. A trollybus rattled by. Two soldiers, drunk stupid on vodka, paused beneath a streetlight to pass their bottle. An official Zil limousine raced along the right-hand lane, ignoring the stoplights.

A tall, well-built American stepped from the doorway of a dumpy apartment building on Yelizarovoy Street, just around the corner from the Embassy of Chad. He hunched up his coat collar, looked both ways up the deserted street, and started on foot to where he had parked his car two blocks away. He was just a little disgusted with himself, and nervous. From time to time he looked over his shoulder as if he knew that someone or something might be coming after him.

At the end of the block he looked back once more to the second-story apartment window still lit with a dull yellow glow. He was never going back. No reason for it. *Look to Washington. Look to Moscow. Zebra One, Zebra Two.* They were Voronin's words. Cryptic. Spoken in a self-pitying drunken haze. Spittle had run down the cripple's stubbled chin, his rheumy eyes hazed with cataracts, his fists pounding on his useless legs.

This is the end then, the American thought turning once again and heading the last blocks to his car. "When they start talking claptrap, boyo, it's time to get yourself free lest you get caught with your paws up some girl's panties." For six months he'd worked Viktor Voronin, who had until eighteen months ago been an officer in the KGB. A stupid, senseless automobile accident had crippled the man for life. The KGB had retired him, of course, and he'd begun drinking on the same evening he got religion. No more wars, he rambled. A world state in which everyone is equal. The perfect socialism. But Voronin had been a gold seam. The mother lode. Some of what he had provided them had been stunning, hadn't it? Worth the risks. But tonight the clock had run down. Voronin had finally slipped into a fantasy world in which he began to mix the truth with his wild imaginings. He could no longer be considered reliable.

Look to Washington. Look to Moscow. What the hell was it supposed to mean? *Zebra One, Zebra Two.*

He decided that his final report could wait until morning. It would go out with the daily summaries to Langley by four in the afternoon, Moscow Civil Time. Operation Look Back was finished, and he was glad of it. From start to finish it hadn't been his sort of project. "Listening to old bitter men vehemently denying their own countries, spewing out their hate and vindictiveness is like digging through someone's rotting garbage looking for a decent meal," he'd said.

At thirty-nine, David McAllister—Mac to his wife and friends—did not like hiding in closets, skulking around dark corners, opening other people's mail, or listening to their personal telephone conversations. An unlikely combination for a spy, he supposed, but then he'd never known a spy who was—likely. He was a cautious man, which came from his Scots' heritage, though the nearest he'd ever come to his distant past was an admitted enjoyment of bagpipe skirling and a pride in his grandfather, Stewart Alvin McAllister, who'd come down to London from Edinburgh to straighten out the fledgling British Secret Intelligence Service during the first world war. His father, who had immigrated to the States in the early twenties, had joined the U.S. Army, had risen to the rank of brigadier general, and had been one of the shakers and movers of the OSS during the second world war, and the CIA afterward. The military, spying, and tradecraft . . . all these things were in McAllister's blood. Not babysitting old bitter men with an axe to grind.

McAllister's little Fiat was parked half up on the curb in the middle of a narrow, deserted block. He took out his car keys as he reached it at the same moment a pair of headlights appeared at the end of the street. He stopped and looked over his shoulder as another pair of headlights appeared from behind. Both vehicles stopped.

They'd blocked off his only exits. McAllister forced himself to remain calm as he stepped back and put his hand in his coat pocket, his fingers curling around the grip of his Beretta 9 mm automatic. Carrying a gun around Moscow is madness, his station chief had argued. "Until you need it," he countered.

An amplified voice, speaking English, came from the end of the street. "Put your hands up, please, in very plain sight."

McAllister hesitated. Two men stepped out of the doorway of an apartment building across the sidewalk from his Fiat. They were dressed in civilian clothes, but they were armed with Kalashnikov assault rifles. In unison they drew back the ejector slides.

"Do not be foolish, Mr. McAllister. Do as you are told," the amplified voice instructed.

Two other men appeared on the opposite side of the street. There were no lights in any of the apartments. The street-lights were out as well. He should have noticed. Above, on the roofs on both sides of the street, he could make out the shadowy figures of at least a dozen marksmen. They'd gone through a lot of trouble to get him. Because of Voronin? He doubted it. They would have arrested him there.

Slowly he took his hand out of his pocket and then raised both hands over his head.

A short, very thin man dressed in a fur hat and bulky sheepskin coat came up the street. He was dark, in a Georgian sort of a way, and intense, his motions quick, birdlike. He stopped a couple of feet away.

"David Stewart McAllister," he said, his English thick with a Russian accent. He smiled. "At last. You are under arrest."

"Charged with what?" McAllister asked, keeping calm. He'd be reported missing within a couple of hours. Gloria would call the Embassy.

"Spying against the Soviet Union," the little man said.

The morning came cold and dark gray as General Aleksandr Ilyich Borodin stepped from the elevator on the fourth floor of KGB's Lubyanka Headquarters and charged down the corridor to his office, like a one-man freight train. He was a tall man, by Russian standards, thick of neck and broad of chest, with a nearly bald head and deep, penetrating eyes. Except for a certain overzealousness when it came to some of his projects, it was rumored that he could have risen to director of the Komitet. For the moment, it was said that wiser heads prevailed in the Kremlin which held him as director of the First Chief Directorate's Special Counter-intelligence Service II, charged with penetrating foreign secret intelligence operations.

On the way in from his dacha on the Istra River outside of town, the general had run through the morning reports his driver had brought out. And now he was angry that he had not been included in last night's operation.

"Good morning, Comrade General," his secretary said as Borodin charged through his outer office and into his own private domain with its view of Dzerzhinsky Square.

"Get me General Suslev on the telephone," Borodin bellowed, throwing off his great coat and lighting a cigarette.

How could one hope to run an overseas operation without knowing what was happening in one's own back yard? All the years of work could easily be escaping like a puff of smoke. Once it was away and dissipated no science in the world could reconstruct it. Like acid rain it could even spread destroying everything in its path. Coordination, was all he asked. Not so much. Even the CIA had its oversight committee to make certain their people didn't step on each other's toes. It made sense, damnit. He had argued until he was blue in the face, first with Andropov and then with that fool of a successor.

He sat down, inhaling smoke deeply into his lungs, then closed his eyes. "With care, Aleksandr," he told himself. "It is time to move with care."

His intercom buzzed. "It is General Suslev, sir," his secretary said. Suslev was head of the First Chief Directorate, charged with watching Americans in Russia.

Borodin picked up the telephone. "Nikolai, now what exactly was it you did last night?"

"My job, Aleksandr Ilyich," Suslev said. "Arresting spies."

"Who is he?"

"Come down and see for yourself, if you're so anxious."

General Borodin rode the elevator down to the basement and strode through the broad stone-walled corridor to the interrogation center where he was immediately passed through to Chief Interrogator Miroshnikov's office. General Suslev was already there. They were watching the American in the interrogation chamber through a one-way glass. He'd obviously been here since they'd arrested him shortly after ten last evening. His coat was off, his tie loose and at that moment he was seated in a straight-backed chair, smoking a cigarette as he faced his two preliminary interrogators.

"Who is he?" General Borodin asked.

"David McAllister," General Suslev said, looking up. The general, who had changed his name from the Georgian Suslevili, was a small, intense man whom Borodin hated with a passion. Suslev, however, would probably become the KGB's director one day. "He is a special assistant to the Ambassador."

"CIA?"

"You're particularly astute this morning, Aleksandr. Actually he's deputy chief of station."

Borodin ignored the sarcasm. He stepped a little closer to the window so that he could get a better look. McAllister seemed weary, his complexion pale in the harsh white light reflecting sharply off the stark white tiles. He looked nervous, perhaps even concerned, but he did not seem like the sort of man who would give in easily. It was something about the American's eyes that Borodin found fascinating. He could see in them, even from this distance, a hint of power, of raw strength. It was a look he saw in his own eyes each morning in the mirror. A look he admired. This one would be tough to break.

"You have an interest in this case, Comrade General?" Chief Interrogator Miroshnikov asked. He was a big, oily man, nearly as large as Borodin. But his eyes were small and narrow and close set. They reminded his subordinates of pig eyes. No one liked him. Even his wife, it was said, waited for the day her husband would be struck down by a bus. But he was very good at his job, which was finding out things.

"Is there a possibility of turning him?" Borodin asked, masking the real reason for his interest.

"I do not believe so," Miroshnikov said wistfully. "Perhaps, given the time . . ."

"You are on the wrong side of the ocean with this one, Aleksandr," Suslev said. "Your job is penetrating the CIA in Washington, not Moscow."

"He will not remain in the Rodina forever, Nikolai," Borodin said, gesturing toward McAllister. "Not unless you mean to kill him." He looked at the American again. His eyes narrowed, as if he had thought of something else. "Where was he when you picked him up?"

"Just off Lyalina Square," Suslev answered.

"What was he doing there at that hour of the night? Meeting someone? Passing secrets?"

"We don't know, yet. But he was armed," Suslev said.

"Perhaps we'll find that out this morning, Comrade General," Miroshnikov said.

Borodin looked at him, and then in at McAllister. He nodded. With Miroshnikov across the table from you, anything was possible. He shuddered inwardly. With Miroshnikov the coming days would not be very pleasant for McAllister.

Colonel Petr Valentin Miroshnikov switched off the tape recorder and laid the headphones on his desk. He sat back and stretched, temporarily relieving the pressure on his lower spine. The day had not been entirely satisfactory. The American had refused to give them anything, anything at all, and General Suslev had called every hour wanting to know what progress had been made. Yet the interrogation was going as it should. As he expected it would. There was a certain symmetry to these things. First came the shock of arrest which led to a timidity between the prisoner and his interviewers. It was up to the good interrogator to make the prisoner understand, as soon as possible, that his very existence was no longer in his own hands. Someone else controlled his destiny. From that moment on, the prisoner would become the interrogator's friend. They would become allies. Confidants in the end.

Miroshnikov looked at the tape recorder, then glanced into the empty interrogation chamber: its stainless steel tables, its sturdy chairs, the instruments, the white tiled floor and walls gleaming like an operating theater beneath strong overhead lights, excited him. With McAllister the symmetry was there, but Miroshnikov knew that the process would be long and drawn out and painful. From the first moment he'd laid eyes on the American he'd instinctively sensed a strength in the man, well beyond the men who had passed this way before. And for that Miroshnikov was grateful. Breaking a man's will, his spirit, was the real joy. If it was too easily accomplished, if it came too quickly, there was little or no satisfaction. "The world is *my* will and *my* idea." It was bad Schopenhauer philosophy, but one which Miroshnikov had embraced early as a young exile growing up in Irkutsk in Siberia. He was an outsider. The foreigner in a land of displaced persons, and he had to fight his way through school. His father had never learned to fight or even cope and he had died out there, as had Miroshnikov's mother. But Petr had learned that the key to the domination of any man was in first understanding his will and then making it yours.

The pitiful little Jews they sent to him who wanted to emigrate so badly to the West, or the poor farmer boy turned soldier who was guilty of nothing more than perhaps a moment's indiscretion were of no consequence. Boring actually. Just hauling them into the Lubyanka was often all the impetus they needed to spill their guts. For a few others, a few *sluzhbas,* Soviet political officers, who had become just a little too enamored of life in the West, the challenge was somewhat greater, though intelligence was not necessarily the mark of a man who could withstand an interrogation.

With this one, however, Miroshnikov sensed the biggest challenge of all. McAllister was as intelligent as he was strong. Miroshnikov sensed in the American an extremely well-developed instinct for survival. Challenging. Challenging indeed.

The interrogator got up and went into the tiny bathroom just off his office where he closed and locked the door. He looked at his face in the mirror over the sink and liked what he saw, because he could see beyond mere physical appearance. The eyes are windows into the soul. Looking into his own eyes he could see no soul. Nothing. Only a deep, smoldering hate for Great Russians. Hate for what the Soviet Union had done to him, for what he had been made to endure as a boy, for what he had become. He took a bottle of cognac and a glass from his medicine cabinet, poured himself a stiff measure and drank it down, the liquor warming his insides, straightening out the knots in his stomach. He splashed some water on his face, then tipped his head back, stretching the muscles at the base of his neck, releasing some of the tension that had been building. He took a deep breath, held it for the count of five, and then let it out slowly, forcing all the air out of his lungs, before he turned and went back out to his office.

They'd started with McAllister last night the moment he had been brought in, and had not let up until three this afternoon. Four interrogators, rotating on two teams, had begun the softening up process, the opening acts. McAllister had been allowed a few hours rest, and now it was time to begin in earnest.

Miroshnikov took McAllister's files, left his office and next door let himself into the interrogation chamber. The tape recorders and video cameras would run automatically.

He allowed no one to watch his work. It was his way. And his staff respected his wishes.

He smiled. He'd been waiting for this for a long time. A challenge that he intended savoring slowly, and with delicacy. He pressed the intercom button.

"Bring him in now," he said, his voice as soft as wind through a graveyard.

McAllister was dressed in a pair of thin coveralls and paper slippers. His eyes were red from lack of sleep, but he seemed alert. He sat erect in the thick, unpadded steel chair.

"Your name please," Miroshnikov said, studying the open file on the steel table in front of him.

"David McAllister."

"Your occupation, Mr. McAllister?"

"I am employed by the United States Department of State. At present I am a Second Secretary under Ambassador Leland Smith."

"You are not a spy?"

"No."

Miroshnikov looked up. He smiled gently. *"Do you speak Russian?"* he asked in Russian.

McAllister did not reply.

"I asked if you spoke Russian," Miroshnikov said in English.

"No."

"I think you are lying to me. I think you will be doing a lot of lying at first. But there is time. All the time in the world."

"I'd like to speak with a representative of my embassy," McAllister said. His voice was clear, but held just a hint of an East Coast accent.

Miroshnikov sat forward and glanced at McAllister's file. "An odd job, wouldn't you say, a Second Secretary? Odd, that is, for a man who graduated first in his class at West Point. Quite an achievement, I might add."

"It happens."

"What I don't understand, however, is why you resigned your commission after only two years. I am under the impression that upon graduation from West Point you are required to serve six years. Your father, the general, must have been terribly disappointed in you."

McAllister held his silence.

"Or was he, I wonder," Miroshnikov said.

McAllister had lost all sense of time, though he suspected that it might be after midnight. He was tired, hungry, cold, and stiff from sitting so many hours in the steel chair.

"I wonder if you are aware of Soviet law in regards suspected foreign agents," Miroshnikov said.

"Only vaguely," McAllister replied. He was thinking about his wife. By now she would be safely at the embassy. She would light a fire under Ambassador Smith himself, if need be.

"Unfortunately for the individual there is no right of habeas corpus here. I can keep you like this for as long as I want. For as long as it takes to find out what it is my superiors are so anxious to learn."

"I am not a spy." He had been through this training at the Farm. It was called Progressive Resistance Under Interrogation. Give nothing at first, they'd been taught. Only later should you admit to bits and pieces, nothing important at first. In the end, of course, they all knew that a man's will could be broken. Torture or drugs. Sooner or later it would come, and with it the possibility of mental or physical damage. But with this one, he thought, damage would not matter. It was in the interrogator's eyes. The man was not human.

"Oh, but you are, Mr. McAllister. We knew that from the very moment you set foot on Soviet soil twenty-three months and eleven days ago. We have been watching you. Waiting for the proper time to arrest you. And it has come.

We are now in what can be considered the pretrial phase. Are you listening to me?"

"I'm listening," McAllister said. By now Langley would have been notified that he was missing. The first stage of the search was called Pre-Comms, in which his haunts in Moscow would be quietly visited. Perhaps he was having an affair, and he was at the home of his mistress. Perhaps he was involved with one of his sources and could not break free. Perhaps he was with friends. Later, the Ex-Comms stage would be initiated. Hospitals would be contacted, as would the Moscow Militia—equivalent to American civil police. Perhaps McAllister had been injured in an auto accident. Perhaps he had been arrested for drunken driving, or running a stoplight. In Moscow it took very little to land in jail, especially for a foreigner. But all that took time.

"Very good," Miroshnikov was saying. "Because believe me, your life depends upon your complete understanding."

"I demand to speak to a representative of my embassy."

"Let's talk, for a moment, about your grandfather . . ."

"Let's not."

"Stewart Alvin McAllister. A Scot. Very important man in Great Britain in his day. Did you know, by the way, that your grandfather came here to Moscow in 1920? He was sent to study the Cheka—the forerunner of our KGB. He was looking for ideas for his own Secret Intelligence Service. And he was quite effective, from what I gather."

"I never knew him."

"More's the pity," Miroshnikov said. "It's an odd thing about us Russians, but don't you know that in one respect we are very much like the German peoples. We have a propensity for keeping records. We write things down in triplicate, and then file the bits and pieces in little cubbyholes. Someday you will have to see the great pile of records we've amassed since 1917, awesome."

"I'm sure it is."

"Your father, for instance, is in our files. He immigrated to the United States in 1923, joined the army and became a general. Another amazing achievement. In fact it was your father, along with Alan Dulles, Bill Donovan, and a few others, who created your secret intelligence service. So I imagine he was actually quite proud indeed when you resigned your army commission to work for the Company."

"I work for the State Department."

"It is too bad your father isn't alive now to see this. He was a good man. A brave man. A straightforward man. A soldier. He knew who his enemies were, and he met them head on. He didn't have to sneak around back alleys talking to dissidents."

McAllister held himself in check. Had it been because of Voronin after all? If they got to that old man he would fold and they would have all the evidence they would need for a conviction. He began to have his first doubts that this would turn out so good after all. He sat a little forward. "May I have something to eat?"

"No."

"Something to drink, at least?"

"I think not. There is more ground to cover here. For instance, why didn't you make a career of the military service? You were raised in an officer's household, you attended military boarding school—the Thomas Academy in Connecticut—and you graduated West Point. Class of '71."

"I was tired of the military."

"I haven't seen your complete service record yet. But I am sure that you distinguished yourself in Vietnam. Or did something happen in 1973? Did you feel the sense of shame that you had lost your little war? Is that it? Are you a dropout?"

"The State Department was hiring."

Miroshnikov smiled again. "You thought you could do more for your country with words than bullets, is that it?"

"Something like that."

"Are you a Democrat or a Republican, Mr. McAllister? A registered party member?"

"What about it?"

"You're not. Curious that you are willing to fight, or talk, for your freedom, but you are not willing to register with a party. In this country we take our government much more seriously."

"You don't have the choice."

"Neither do you now," Miroshnikov said softly.

"Only because I'm here in this place for the moment."

"For the moment, yes, Mr. McAllister. But a moment that could stretch to the end of your life. It depends on you. Upon how willing you will be to cooperate. And in the end you will talk to me. They all do."

"If I don't?"

"You will."

"If I'm damaged you'll have a hard time explaining it."

"I think not."

"Drugs, is that it?"

"Perhaps," Miroshnikov said. "But I am glad to see that you are beginning to have a healthy curiosity about your future. It means to me that you will not be so tough, though from what I understand the CIA's training camp outside of Williamsburg—the Farm, isn't that what you call the place?—is staffed with some of the very best instructors in the business. I've often found myself wishing I could see it."

McAllister allowed himself a smile. "With my connections at State, I'm sure something could be worked out. Perhaps a tour of the headquarters building at Langley, Colonel . . . I didn't catch your name."

Miroshnikov glanced at the file again. "I suspect you were trained at the Farm in 1974, did your desk duty at Langley and then received your first overseas posting shortly afterward. I show you in Greece in 1975."

"As a Special Assistant in the Political Affairs Section."

"Your cover."

"I am not a spy, I don't know how many times I have to tell you that."

"No?"

"No."

Miroshnikov smiled gently, indulgently, as a father might at a child who has been naughty. "Then a dreadful mistake has been made here, Mr. McAllister. A letter of apology will have to be sent, of course. This sort of thing has never happened before. You understand?"

"No, I don't."

"Just a few more questions, I think. You can manage just a little longer?"

"A mistake has been made. So release me. Now. Short of that let me speak with a representative from my embassy."

Miroshnikov's eyebrows rose. "Dear me, my good fellow, I believe you don't understand after all."

"What?"

"A mistake has been made, but not by us. By you, sir. By your government. By your ambassador."

McAllister glanced up at the video camera mounted on the ceiling, its lens staring implacably toward the center of the room. He looked back at Miroshnikov. "What are you talking about?"

"The gun. The Beretta automatic that you were carrying in your pocket. Your ambassador must write us an immediate letter of explanation and apology. Second secretaries, even assistants to the ambassador, do not run around Moscow armed with deadly weapons. Only spies carry weapons, don't you see? And in Moscow we execute spies."

Chapter 2

The method of interrogation was as simple as it was effective. The Russians had been perfecting the art for many years, and Chief Interrogator Miroshnikov was very good at it.

In the first place, McAllister was denied sleep or even any proper rest. The interrogation sessions, sometimes lasting up to ten hours each, came at any time of the day or night. He would often be brought back to his tiny cell with its strong overhead light that was never switched off, where he might be allowed to lie on his bed which consisted of nothing more than an unpadded stainless-steel shelf hanging off the wall. Sometimes this bed was wet, at other times it was too hot even to touch and he would have to squat against the wall because the floor constantly had water running over it.

As often as not his rest period only lasted ten or fifteen minutes, when he would be hauled to his feet, dragged out into the corridor where he was made to undress and stand, shivering in the cold, at attention, until it was time to return to the interrogation room.

"There will come a point where I will be useless to you," McAllister said, running a hand across the stubble of beard on his face. "It's a delicate balance for you, colonel, between wearing me down so I become cooperative, versus wearing me down so badly that I'll collapse on you. Maybe my heart will stop."

"Time, I believe you are beginning to understand, is on my side," Miroshnikov said, sipping his tea, steam rising from the glass. "For you, of course, the actual hours and minutes are of little consequence." He smiled. "And yes, I agree with you. Your heart might stop. It is something to think about."

"Then I would be dead, and of no further use to you."

"On the contrary. We might not let you die. Not yet. But even in death you would be of some use to us. We Russians are frugal with our resources. And you, my dear McAllister, are most definitely a resource."

"I would like to speak to a representative of my embassy."

"Such comments are counterproductive at this point," Miroshnikov said. He opened a file folder on the steel table between them. "Let's return to Greece, August of 1975. As we see it your cover was as a special assistant in the embassy's political section. You were the new kid on the block, as they say, but nevertheless you were given the responsibility for product management of a very successful agent network that operated across the border in Bulgaria."

"I was a political officer, nothing more. We were having trouble with the Greek government at the time, as you may recall. I was a troubleshooter."

"The network was called Scorpius, which we thought at the time was quite imaginative. In fact your little nest of spies was quite effective, until the woman—Raiza Stainov—fell out of love with her control officer, in this case a man we learned was Alfred Lapides, with whom you had regular contact over a period of thirty-three months."

"I've never heard the names," McAllister said.

"It's of no mind to me now. Lapides is dead, killed in an unfortunate automobile accident in Sofia. We need, however, information on two other men—Thomas Murdock and Georgi Morozov. They were part of your Scorpius Network. Where exactly did they fit, can you tell me at least that much?''

The extent of Miroshnikov's knowledge was bothersome, but they had known finally that the network had been blown, though they had never suspected Raiza. She had been one of their gold seams. Her husband had been chief of Section Three of the Bulgarian Military Intelligence Service, serving directly under General Ivan Vladigerov. Through Raiza they had learned about troop movements, about the new Soviet-Bulgarian missile pact in which Soviet SS-18 nuclear missiles were placed very near the Greek border, and on the failing health of Bulgarian Defense Minister Petko Dimitrov. How much of that information had been legitimate and how much had been disinformation now was seriously in doubt. Miroshnikov had provided him with a stunning piece of intelligence. Information, however, that was of absolutely no use in here.

''I've never heard their names either,'' McAllister said.

''You are lying, but there is time, and I have no doubt that we will finally hit upon a subject of which you will be willing to speak about with me.''

''We can talk about my work with the Greek government.''

Miroshnikov looked up from the file folder. ''I want nothing more than the truth here, Mr. McAllister. Not so terribly much to ask, you know. I have all of the facts, or at least most of them. I'll admit this much to you; in all honesty we think that your work has been absolutely tops. Just first class. It is, in fact, the very reason you are here now. We don't arrest second-rate spies.''

''I'm not a spy.''

''Oh, but you are, Mr. McAllister. Of that there can be no doubt. But let's go back to your record. I show you in West Berlin from June of 1978 until June of 1980. In

Czechoslovakia from July of 1980 until June of 1982. Poland from July of 1982 to December 1984. Afghanistan for nine months until August 1985, and then here to Moscow in September of that same year." Miroshnikov looked up again. "Including your year at the Farm and on the various foreign desks at Langley, a quite remarkable fourteen-year career."

"With the State Department."

"With the Central Intelligence Agency." Again Miroshnikov consulted his file and read off a number. "Your agency identification number, is it not?"

It was. "I've never heard that number before."

"There is no use belaboring that point for the moment. Let's go back to Athens, and the Scorpius network. Specifically to Thomas Murdock, an elusive man by all accounts. Last we heard of him he was running an airline out of Panama. The drug connection. But in this we are not one hundred percent certain. Can you tell me about him? A very large man, isn't he?"

Murdock had been one of the best, though McAllister had no fond memories about him. He was a large man, six-feet-six at two hundred fifty pounds. He smoked Cuban cigars, drank black rum, and had been really out of place with Scorpius. In those days it was still possible to operate light planes or helicopters across the border well under Bulgarian radar. His job was as network resupply and drop officer, as well as a safety valve should they need to get their people out in a big hurry. He had been a man with absolutely no fear.

"Thank you," Miroshnikov said respectfully. He wrote something in the files. "Go on."

McAllister looked at the Russian. Had he spoken out loud? He rubbed his eyes. His stomach was rumbling, his gut tight, and there was a heavy, disconcerting feeling in his chest. He searched the edges of his awareness, mentally exploring his mind and body. It could be drugs, he thought, though he felt nothing, no tingling around the edges as he had been taught might be the case. Miroshnikov, he decided, was playing with him. Testing him.

"Go on with what?" he asked at length.

"With what you were saying about Murdock, naturally. We were finally getting somewhere. You knew him, and you admitted it, though you did not like him. No personal friendships there, such as with Lapides. But can you tell me what he is doing these days? Just a station name. Or even a simple confirmation of my information that he is in Panama. Just anything, Mr. McAllister."

"I don't know what you're talking about."

"But you do, my dear fellow, you do." Miroshnikov was beaming earnestly. "We're making progress and I feel very good about it." He closed the file folder. "And so should you. We have finally broken down the first barrier which is always the most difficult." He stood up. "Really quite excellent," he said.

McAllister looked up at him, his head suddenly very heavy, his eyes burning. What in God's name had he said? Had he actually given voice to his thoughts?

"I will now give you a piece of information. A bit of stimuli for you. Today is Wednesday, Mr. McAllister, and do you know what that means?"

"No."

"You have been with us for one week and a day," Miroshnikov shook his head in amazement. "A record, I think. We usually come to this first stage much sooner. Sometimes within hours, certainly never in my memory as long as a week."

In the second place McAllister was denied proper food. His meals, when they came, consisted of little more than tepid water, a very thin gruel or sometimes a potato soup and occasionally a slice of dark, stale bread. It was enough nourishment to keep him alive, barely, and of course his food was laced with chemicals which at times caused him severe stomach cramps, at other times nausea so that he would vomit what he had just eaten, and at still other times, diarrhea. There was no toilet, or even bucket in his tiny cell. Water constantly ran over the concrete floor, draining through a hole in the corner. He was forced to take care of his bodily functions while leaning against the cold wall, sometimes remaining in that position for an hour, the thin, watery stool running down his legs. He would then cross to the opposite side of the cell where he would wash himself as best he could.

Once, after one of these sessions, when he was hauled out of his cell and made to strip and stand at attention in the corridor, his legs would no longer support him, and he had collapsed on the floor. They had allowed him to lay there, resting for a few minutes, until one of the guards came back with a big Turkish bathtowel which he soaked in a bucket of ice water. For the next twenty minutes he proceeded to beat McAllister on the back and legs, and even the bottoms of his feet with the towel, the pain exquisite without the danger of inflicting serious injury.

His interrogation sessions seemed to come more often then, and with greater intensity, as if Miroshnikov sensed that time was finally running out for him. During these sessions he often thanked McAllister for various bits of information, until McAllister began to seriously doubt his own sanity. Was he speaking when he believed he was merely thinking? Or was it simply another of Miroshnikov's techniques? Through it all, McAllister began to have a respect for the Russian that at times bordered frighteningly on friendship and even gratitude. His only stimuli became the interrogation sessions and the occasional beating, so that he came to look forward to his time with Miroshnikov.

"We have come a long ways together, you and I, Mac," Miroshnikov said. "Although it has taken an inordinate amount of time."

"How long have I been here?" McAllister asked, shocked at how weak and far away his voice seemed in his ears.

"Twenty-seven days," Miroshnikov said proudly. "And now the first phase of our work together has finally been completed." He took a cigarette out of his tunic pocket, lit it, and held it out across the steel table.

Without thinking, McAllister took it and brought it to his lips, inhaling the smoke deeply into his lungs. His stomach turned over and he threw up down the front of his thin prison coveralls, his head spinning so badly that he nearly fell off his chair.

Miroshnikov was smiling again. "Very good. It is time now for us to begin the second phase for which it will be best if your system is completely purged. It will be easier for us, and certainly far easier for you. In some extreme cases our subjects have even choked to death on their own vomit. We wouldn't want that to happen to you. Not now, not after we have come so far together."

"What are you talking about?" McAllister asked after a long time. It seemed nearly impossible for him to focus on anything but Miroshnikov's face. When he tried to look elsewhere across the distance of the suddenly large room, nausea rose up again, bile bitter at the back of his throat.

"We have completed the first level. You have been cooperative, but there is nothing else, at this stage, you will be able to tell me. Your very fine conditioning precludes that. It is time, then, as I was saying, to probe deeper, much deeper, and for that another method is indicated."

"I won't be able to take much more of this," McAllister heard himself saying.

"Oh, but I think you can and will. You are a very strong man, Mr. McAllister, and for this I greatly admire you."

"Fuck you."

Miroshnikov was momentarily startled, his eyes wide. But then a huge smile crossed his face, and he threw back his head and laughed so hard that tears began to stream down his cheeks. "Oh, my," he gasped. "Oh, dear, that is rich, Mr. McAllister. I love it, I honestly love it and you."

"Let me speak with my embassy."

"It's time now," Miroshnikov said rising. He came around the table and took McAllister's hand, helping him up. "It's not far in distance, Mac, but it will be light years in conception. Believe me, we are going to have a splendid time together, you and I. Simply splendid."

The torture chamber was a very small room, laid out much like a hospital's operating theater. A steel table with stirrups for his feet and leather straps for his arms and legs, was situated beneath a large, focused light fixture in the center of the spotlessly clean room. Electronic instruments were clustered around the head of the table. A stainless-steel roll-about cart held several trays, each covered with crisp white towels. Video cameras were set on each wall so that not one single aspect of a prisoner's interrogation could possibly be missed on tape.

Two stern-faced nurses in starched white uniforms removed McAllister's coveralls and slippers and helped him up on the table, where he was strapped in place, his legs bent at the knees, open as if he were a woman about to give birth. There was no value, at this point, for active resistance, he had been taught at the Farm. Now is when you will need all of your strength. The course of training was called Pain Management. Cancer specialists were on the staff, instructing them how to "go with the flow." Allow the pain to wash through your body. Don't resist it. Don't fight it. Scream your bloody head off, in fact, because when you consider the alternative to pain—death—you'll learn to endure.

The nurses placed an electroencephalogram headband around his forehead, EKG pickups on his chest, a pulse counter on his left wrist, and a blood-pressure cuff on his biceps. They also attached metal clips to his nipples, and soft, almost sensuous suction cups on his testicles. When they were finished they left the room, the door closing quietly after them.

Miroshnikov sat on a tall stool behind and to McAllister's right. He leaned forward and adjusted a knob on one of the electronic instruments, and immediately McAllister could hear the sounds of his own heartbeat and respiration over a loudspeaker. He willed himself to relax, to accept whatever would come.

They will break your will sooner or later, of course, his instructors had told him. So one might rightly ask: What is the value of resistance of any sort? Simply that the enemy knows we will treat his captured spies exactly the same as they do ours. Treat ours with respect and we will do the same. Treat ours with punishment, and we will respond in kind. The more you take, the more they know will be inflicted on their people.

So where was the twin of this room back home? *Look to Washington. Look to Moscow. Zebra One, Zebra Two.*

"What?" Miroshnikov asked, his face overhead.

McAllister smiled. "Fuck you," he said good-naturedly.

"Thomas Murdock, let us begin with him. It is all that I want this evening."

McAllister closed his eyes, the faint traces of a smile at the corners of his mouth. It was very possible, he told himself, that he would not come out of this alive. It was ironic that they wanted him to tell them about Murdock, of whom he knew nothing. Voronin, on the other hand, had been the gold seam. Had been, that is, until their last evening together. When? Had it been days, or weeks . . . or had it been only hours ago . . .

A blindingly massive pain reached up from his groin, raced through his body, and rebounded in his armpits. From a long ways off he heard someone screaming, the sound animal, not human. As the pain receded he could hear his own heartbeat coming from the speaker, fast but still strong.

A second pain came, this one across his chest, and although the hurt of it was much less than the first, it was more frightening in that while it was happening he could clearly hear that his heart had stopped. When it began again he nearly cried in relief.

"Do you know Thomas Murdock, Mr. McAllister?" Miroshnikov's voice was close in his ear.

No he did not. In the old days of Scorpius, of course, he had worked with Tom, but not afterward. Not in ten years.

The pain at his groin came again, this time more intensely, as if hot pokers had been rammed into his armpits, penetrating all the way inside his skull. Once when he was a young boy he had hit his finger with a hammer, and he couldn't understand why the pain had been the most intense and most lasting in his elbow.

Again the pain shot up from his groin, followed almost immediately by the more exquisite torture across his chest, his heart stopping, then beginning raggedly, and frighteningly weaker than before.

Tom had been a womanizer, a boozer, the network's resident high roller. McAllister decided that he wouldn't put it past the man to be involved down in Panama as a mule—a delivery and drop man. The cocaine connection, the pipeline back to the States, supposedly measured in the billions of dollars. Tom would be drawn to it, yes. But was there an Agency connection? We needed the hard currency, beyond the prying eyes of Congress. But how far? . . .

Again the pain came, this time unbelievably bad and his heartbeat stopped again. He listened. He was reminded for some insane reason about the guillotinings during the French Revolution. The man whose head had just been cut off had a few seconds to look up from the basket at his own mutilated torso flopping in the stock before the dark veil of death descended over him. McAllister found the same thing happening to him; the lights in the room began to fade, faster and faster . . .

"Mr. McAllister, Mr. McAllister," someone was calling to him from an impossibly long distance. "Mac."

He opened his eyes to find that he had been unhooked from the electronic instruments, and had been unstrapped from the table. He was sitting up. There was little or no pain remaining, only a detached feeling, as if he were floating a few inches off the table. Miroshnikov stood at his side holding his arm, a big grin on his face.

"Splendid, really quite splendid, you know," he was saying.

Everything was coming back into focus for McAllister, and in some strange, almost indefinable way he felt even better for his experience. As if he had been cleansed. It was the same feeling, he supposed, that a marathon runner must feel after completing his race. Terribly tired and strung out, but with a feeling of inner strength coming from a Herculean accomplishment. They'd not told him about this at the Farm.

He also felt an exceedingly odd bonding with Miroshnikov. As if they had been, until just this moment, Siamese twins. The connecting tissues had been severed with the removal of the electronic probes and the electrodes from his chest and testicles, but he still felt as one with his interrogator.

"You should have felt the pain," McAllister heard himself say, and he was no less astonished by his statement than Miroshnikov was.

"But we've made progress, my dear fellow. So much wonderful progress that there cannot possibly be any animosity," Miroshnikov said. "Here, let me help you down."

McAllister allowed himself to be helped down from the table at the same moment the two nurses from before entered the room. He stood for a second or two, wavering slightly on his feet, then he leaned left away from Miroshnikov, as if he were about to fall.

The Russian stepped forward, his legs spread at that moment, his right hand outstretched, when McAllister turned back, bringing up his right knee with every ounce of his strength into Miroshnikov's groin. A look of pain and disbelief spread across the interrogator's face, and he started to rear back, his mouth opening in a bellow of pain.

The two nurses started forward, giving McAllister just enough time to roll left, then right again, the side of his right hand driving into Miroshnikov's throat, then they were on him, shoving him roughly back against the tall torture table.

"Bastard," one of them hissed.

"*Fuck your mother,*" McAllister replied in Russian.

Chapter 3

The cell was clean, warm, and reasonably well furnished. For the last three evenings the lights had been extinguished so he had been able to sleep. Solid, if plain meals had been brought at regular intervals. The Soviet attorney looked up from his reading.

"A substantial case has been built against you, Mr. McAllister. I don't think a lengthy trial would be of much value. In fact, because sentencing in these kinds of matters is left entirely to the discretion of the judges, the easier you make it for them, the easier they will make it for you."

"What about my defense?"

Yevgenni Tarasenko, the court-appointed attorney, shook his head and smiled. "Under the circumstances, I frankly don't think you have a defense."

"Why have I not been allowed to speak with a representative from my embassy?"

"We have been in communication with them," Tarasenko said. "In fact, I personally have spoken with Mr. Lacey, your chargé d'affaires, and his concern goes out to you with all sincerity. He too wishes for a speedy conclusion."

"Will I be able to speak with him?"

"Before your trial?"

"Now, immediately," McAllister said. He felt much better than he had for days, and yet he still had the sensation of detachment. He supposed his food was still being drugged.

"I am sorry, Mr. McAllister, but in these matters we must adhere to Soviet law. Our constitution clearly outlines our rights as well as our responsibilities. It is the same in Washington, I assure you."

McAllister had wondered about Miroshnikov. After that first night of torture, the interrogation sessions had ended. That very night he had been moved to this cell. The next morning he had been allowed to shower and shave, and had been fed a huge breakfast. It all had been confusing. "Formal charges have been filed against me?"

"Yes, they have. You are accused of spying for the United States against my government. Very grave, very serious charges."

"And you are to be my attorney?"

"Yes, that is correct."

"Are there other charges?"

The attorney shrugged. "You were armed with a deadly weapon at the time of your arrest. And there is the matter of the assault on Colonel Miroshnikov in front of witnesses."

"Was my torture witnessed?"

The attorney looked again at the bulky files he had brought in with him. "Those charges may be dropped, Mr. McAllister, but it depends upon you."

"On my cooperation."

"Yes, exactly."

McAllister thought about the chief interrogator and their sessions together. Never once had Voronin been mentioned. Most of their time had been spent going over the Scorpius Network, and Tom Murdock's whereabouts these days. Evidently the Russians were still feeling the effects of the Bulgarian operation. For that, at least, he was thankful. He sat forward. "Then what evidence is there against me?"

The attorney's eyes were round. "Your confession, of course. We wouldn't have dreamed of going to trial without it."

"May I see it?"

"There is no need, believe me, it is very complete. You spelled out in very complete detail how you, at the orders of your government of course, operated a successful nest of spies in Sofia in the late seventies. Really, Mr. McAllister, there can be no doubt in anyone's mind."

"I don't remember making any such confession . . . of my own free will, that is."

The attorney's lips compressed. "You signed the transcript."

"Under duress."

"Please, Mr. McAllister, believe me when I advise you to plead simply guilty before the judges. It will be much better for you, much better indeed."

"Thanks for the advice," McAllister said. "I suppose I'll get your bill in the morning."

It took a moment for Tarasenko to realize that McAllister had made a joke, and then his face split into a wide grin. "Very good," he said, gathering up his papers and rising. "Yes, very good, Mr. McAllister. My bill in the morning."

With lunch they brought him a blue pin-striped suit, a white shirt and tie, underwear and socks, and freshly polished black shoes, all of which fit well, though the cut wasn't very good by Western standards.

He had been here for a long time. Certainly weeks, possibly more than a month, yet his memories were hazy and indistinct, partly because of the drugs he had been given and partly because of the lack of sleep and proper food. Yet he didn't feel terrible. There was no real pain, only a weakness and the slight feeling that he was floating. When he stood up too suddenly sometimes, he would experience a little nausea and light-headedness, but even those feelings had slowly begun to pass, over the past few days.

After he got dressed he began pacing his cell, five steps to the steel door, turn, five steps back. If indeed Bill Lacey had been contacted at the embassy the wheels in Washington would be in motion. At the very least they would stave off any possibility of a death penalty. It was likely that he would be sentenced to a few years imprisonment, probably even here in Moscow. But even Francis Gary Powers had been quickly released. Spies were exchanged on a regular basis.

It could be months, or possibly even a couple of years, but he was definitely going home to the desk, because from this point on he would present too high a profile for field-work. Langley had many such men forever denied sensitive foreign postings.

He stopped. They had his confession, according to the attorney, which meant they had broken him. Or had they? Was it all a big ploy? Was this just another of Miroshnikov's little tricks? Was this simply another of the interrogator's phases? Perhaps there wasn't going to be a trial just yet. Perhaps he would be taken instead back to Miroshnikov, or perhaps back to the torture chamber.

The Scorpius Network was a long time ago. The information by now was outdated. What was of more immediate importance was Voronin, and yet his name had never come up. He searched his memory, but he could not recall being asked, other than in a superficial manner, exactly what he had been doing out so late on the streets the night of his arrest. Had they operated with blinders on, so excited by the prospect of catching an American spy, that they had missed the obvious? Or had he missed the obvious?

Look to Washington. Look to Moscow. Zebra One, Zebra Two.

What the hell did it mean? Thinking about it now, he was no longer certain that those words had simply been the ravings of a man gone finally mad. They were cryptic, yes, but they had cadence, they hinted at some abbreviated message, there was meaning. Some sort of a connection between Washington and Moscow? How was that possible, he wondered. And what was or were Zebra One and Two? Obviously code words. Zebra One, a man in Washington and Zebra Two, a man in Moscow? Or was he chasing a will-o'-the-wisp after all?

He began his pacing again, five steps to the steel door, turn, and five steps back again, as he tried to get himself ready for whatever would be coming next.

The two armed guards came for him early in the afternoon, and he fell in between them as they marched wordlessly down the broad, stone-walled corridor. At the end they entered an elevator. On the way up both guards stared at McAllister as if he were a wild animal who at any moment might try to run. The flaps of their holsters were undone. One of them rested his hand on the butt of his pistol.

It was to be a trial after all.

He was in the Lubyanka, that much he knew, which was located on Dzerzhinsky Square downtown. In the old days, before the war, this building had housed the All-Russian Insurance Company. Nazi POWs had been made to build a big new addition to the building which was then used to house the NKGB and NKVD which were the forerunners of the modern-day Soviet Secret Service.

The elevator opened onto another corridor, this one like the one below, deserted. They turned right, marched to the end and suddenly they were outside in a narrow lane that led up from a broad courtyard. It was very cold. A black windowless van was waiting for them, and McAllister was hustled inside, and the doors slammed shut before he had a chance to savor the frigid air and bright afternoon sun, his first for a very long time.

As on the elevator, his guards carefully watched him as the van lurched forward, turned, slowed, turned again, and then accelerated, the driver crashing through the gears.

He hadn't really expected to stand trial at the Lubyanka. It would have been like holding a trial for an accused Russian spy at CIA headquarters in Langley. Where exactly he would be tried, however, would depend upon how important they thought he was, and how out of the eyes of the foreign press they wanted to keep it.

His answer came fifteen minutes later when they finally stopped and the back doors were opened. McAllister instantly recognized the place from his briefings. It was the Lefortovsky Military Prison in Moscow's northeastern district. The most ominous of any trial location for him. Security was tight here, and in the rear courtyard they executed people.

Here, he realized, his life could very well end.

They entered through a back door, walked down a short narrow corridor and took one flight of stairs up, where they were made to wait in a large office at which a half a dozen military clerks were busy at their desks. None of them bothered to look up. McAllister watched the secondhand on the clock above the door, suddenly fascinated with time. It had been weeks since he had had any notion of the hour or minute. It was a few minutes before three now. In the afternoon. He tried to imagine what was happening at the embassy, and what Gloria would be doing.

The door opened and Tarasenko, his attorney, beckoned to them. McAllister's guard accompanied him inside. At the head of the large room was the raised bench for the three judges, called tribunals in the Soviet judicial system, flanked by the Soviet flag and the State Prosecutor's flag, and backed by a photograph of Lenin. The Moscow District Prosecutor was seated on the right with Chief Interrogator Miroshnikov and General Suslev, the man who had arrested him. William Lacey, the American chargé d'affaires, was the only person in the gallery. When McAllister was ushered in he jumped up.

"You have just a moment or two before it begins," Tarasenko said.

Lacey was a tall, slightly built, angular-faced man, with thinning gray hair, who always dressed impeccably in three-piece suits. His overcoat and Russian fur hat were lying on the bench beside him. He made no move to come over. McAllister tried to read something in the man's expression, but he could not.

Tarasenko moved off to the defense attorney's table to the left of the bench, and McAllister stepped over to where Lacey was waiting.

"Christ, am I glad to see you, Bill," McAllister said, keeping his voice low.

"How are you, are you all right?" Lacey asked, searching McAllister's face.

"I've been better. How about getting me out of here?"

"We're working on it, Mac. But listen, Langley says for you to plead guilty to whatever you're charged with."

McAllister stiffened. This wasn't what he had expected at all.

"Listen to me, goddamnit. Plead guilty, and you'll probably be sentenced to immediate expulsion from the Soviet Union. We grabbed one of their people two weeks ago in New York. He was operating out of the UN, and they've been making all the right noises to get him back. They'll trade. You're going to have to trust us on this one. With luck we can have you out of here within the next twenty-four hours."

"My ass is hanging out there," McAllister said. His stomach was tight. He glanced over at the defense attorney who was watching them. "They say they have my confession."

"It doesn't matter, Mac. Just plead guilty and we'll get you out of here in one piece. Soon. I promise you."

McAllister looked at Lacey. He compressed his lips and nodded slightly. "You're the boss," he said. "How's Gloria?"

"Worried," Lacey said. "She's back in Washington. We thought it best under the circumstances, to get her the hell out of here."

"Good . . ." McAllister started to say, when a door at the head of the chamber opened and the three tribunals filed in.

"All rise," a clerk intoned.

"This will be over in a couple of minutes," Lacey whispered. "Hang in there."

"Sure," McAllister said, and he moved with his guards to the rail for the accused, directly in front of the bench. A set of headphones hung on a hook for the translation. He didn't bother with them. By now they knew he spoke Russian.

The tribunals looked down sternly at him as the clerk read out the charges specified against him before the Moscow Northeast District People's Special Court. Spying against the People's State of Bulgaria, the German Democratic Republic, the People's States of Czechoslovakia and Poland, Afghanistan, and the Union of Soviet Socialist Republics. He was also charged with carrying a deadly weapon, and with assault on an officer of the KGB who was, at the time of the assault, conducting lawful business of the State.

The tribunals sat down, and then everyone else sat except for McAllister and his guards.

"In the matter before the court, comrades," the District Prosecutor said getting up, "the State has prepared several items of evidence including the accused's sworn confession, the accused's deadly weapon which he was carrying at the time of his arrest—sworn to by Comrade General Suslev

—and of course Comrade Colonel Miroshnikov's own testimony of the assault made on his person.''

Attorney Tarasenko got to his feet. ''If it pleases the court, we would like to make a brief statement before we proceed.''

All three tribunals had shifted their gaze from the prosecutor to Tarasenko.

''My client wishes to plead guilty to all of the charges specified against him, without mitigating circumstances.'' The attorney turned and dramatically pointed a stern finger at McAllister. ''There, comrades, stands an American spy. An agent for the Central Intelligence Agency, by his own admission. A puppet of a State gone terribly . . . oh so terribly bad.'' He turned back to the tribunals, a new respect in his voice. ''Acting on orders from his masters, he has admitted that since 1975, when he began spying against the People's State of Bulgaria, he has engaged in the systematic assault on all good Soviet peoples . . . in fact upon all peace-loving peoples of the world. By his own admission, comrades . . . and with remorse, I might add . . . the accused stands humbly before this court begging understanding and forgiveness for his heinous crimes against mankind.''

''Are you pleading guilty to these crimes, Comrade Tarasenko?'' the chief tribunal asked. He was an older man, his voice as dry as winter grass.

''Yes, comrade, I am, with the fervent wish that compassion and mercy will be shown here.''

''The District Prosecutor's office has no animosity toward this unfortunate man,'' the prosecutor said.

''What of you, Comrade Colonel?'' the chief tribunal asked.

Miroshnikov smiled sadly as he glanced at McAllister. He shook his head. ''No, comrade, I hold no animosity toward Mr. McAllister. In fact he has become my friend. Believe me when I tell you that I genuinely care for this man. I see a good and kind person beneath the trappings of his profession—a load, I might add, that he no longer wishes to carry.''

''You are a generous man, Comrade Colonel,'' the chief tribunal said.

McAllister felt as if he were in a very bad high school play parodying a Russian kangaroo court. The kids couldn't have done a worse job than the real participants.

''May I speak?'' McAllister said in very good Russian.

The tribunals seemed genuinely surprised. The chief tribunal's eyes knitted. ''Only if you wish to contradict the very fine words that have already been spoken on your behalf.'' He leaned forward. ''Everyone in this room is on your side, young man.''

McAllister glanced back at Lacey who sat without expression.

''Well?'' the chief tribunal demanded.

McAllister turned back. ''I wish to enter a plea of guilty.''

''That has already been done,'' the chief tribunal said impatiently. ''Have you anything else to add?''

''Nyet,'' McAllister said after a moment.

The chief tribunal continued to stare at him for several long seconds, then he leaned over and said something to the other two tribunals. He nodded and straightened up again.

''The death penalty is indicated for a crime so vast as yours,'' he said, addressing his remarks to McAllister's attorney. ''But even the prosecutor has had very kind words to say about you. However, it cannot be forgotten that you carried a deadly weapon—here in Moscow of all places—and that you assaulted the body of a good and just man while he was engaged in the performance of his lawful duties.''

McAllister might not have been there. His attorney was the object of the chief tribunal's mounting wrath. Only Bill Lacey's presence behind him buoyed his spirits.

''It is the unanimous opinion of this court that you be

sentenced to life imprisonment at hard labor in the Autonomous Republic of Yakutsk. It is also the unanimous opinion of this court that your imprisonment shall commence immediately, and shall be without possibility of parole or exchange.'' The chief tribunal rose up a little higher in his seat, and now he looked directly at McAllister. ''Here you shall live out the rest of your days as a reminder to all foreign interventionists and adventurers that the Soviet peoples are a peaceloving peoples who want nothing more than to live without interference.''

Yarasenko and Miroshnikov were smiling. When McAllister turned around Lacey was gone from the courtroom.

Evening had come to Moscow, and with it the first few flakes of an approaching snowstorm whipped by a building cold wind. General Alexandr Borodin sat alone in his Lubyanka office, his ashtray filled, his mouth foul from too many cigarettes, and his uniform tunic off, his tie loose and his shirt collar open. He pressed the earphone more tightly against his left ear as he worked the tape recorder controls with his right hand.

At first he could hear the sounds of a door opening and closing, and then footsteps. He could hear the rustling of fabric as McAllister was undressed.

He had listened to all of these sounds over and over again a dozen times or more in the last two hours since the edited interrogation tapes had finally been sent up to him.

He leaned forward and closed his eyes as if by these actions he could hear better. He turned the volume up as high as it would go.

''Look to Washington. Look to Moscow. Zebra One, Zebra Two.''

There it was again. No mistaking the words this time. No mistake at all.

''What?'' Chief Interrogator Miroshnikov had asked.

A pause.

"Fuck you," McAllister's words again.

General Borodin reached out and savagely snapped the machine off. He was reminded of an old Russian proverb: Once a word is out of your mouth, you can't swallow it again. Had Miroshnikov heard? Had he understood what McAllister had babbled in his delirium?

Look to Washington. Look to Moscow. Zebra One, Zebra Two.

Fuck your mother, but this wasn't going to turn out so good. He reached out for the telephone on his desk, but then stayed his hand. There had to be a way out. But how? Where? To whom could he turn without starting in motion the machinery of his own destruction?

Chapter 4

It was very late at night, but they were flying west so that the dawn for them would be delayed. They were seated alone in the first-class section of Air France's nonstop service to Paris. Behind them, in coach class, the other passengers were quiet, most of them sleeping, their seat backs reclined, their overhead lights switched off. There was nothing to be seen below, in any event. Since this was an overnight flight out of Moscow a regular meal had not been served; snacks had been made available, and of course drinks. In coach class passengers were served in plastic cups, in first class they were served in crystal. The first-class stewardess stepped around the corner from the galley and smiled.

"Care for another drink, Monsieur McAllister?" she asked, her pretty white teeth flashing.

"No. Thanks," McAllister said tiredly. "I think I'll try to get some rest. How soon will we be in Paris?"

"A little more than an hour."

McAllister glanced across the aisle at his two escorts. Langley had sent them out from Washington last week and they had waited around the embassy until he was released. Other than introducing themselves at Sheremetyevo Airport when he had been turned over to them, they'd said little or nothing to him. Now, as before, their reticence was bothersome.

Mark Carrick, seated on the aisle, glanced up from the magazine he'd been reading. "It probably would be for the best if you got some shut-eye, sir."

McAllister looked up. The stewardess had returned to the galley. "What the hell happened back there? One minute I'm on my way to Siberia, and the next thing I know I'm handed over to you two at the airport. I couldn't believe it."

"Believe it, sir. You're going home."

The other agency legman, Thomas Maas, turned away from the window and stared across at McAllister. His expression, like Lacey's yesterday afternoon in the courtroom was unreadable. But it wasn't friendly. "Are you feeling all right now, sir?"

"They were drugging my food. It'll probably take a little while for the stuff to work itself out of my system."

"They'll take care of that in Washington," Carrick said. "They're all set up for you."

"But what happened back there? Was a trade made after all?"

Carrick shrugged. He was a heavyset man, with short-cropped gray hair, steel-blue eyes, and a no-nonsense air about him. "I couldn't say, sir. Our orders were to wait for your release and then get you home."

"You knew about my trial?"

"No, sir," Carrick said.

"Then who sent you out here? Was it Bob Highnote?"

"Why don't you try to get some rest, Mr. McAllister," Maas said. "There'll be a layover in Paris, and again in New York before we can catch the D.C. shuttle. It's going to be a long trip."

"You're probably right," McAllister mumbled laying his head back and closing his eyes. He wasn't thinking straight. Everything had happened so fast, with so much finality.

After his trial he had been taken back to the Lubyanka where after dinner the clothing he had been wearing the night of his arrest had been returned to him, freshly laundered and pressed. No one came to see him, or even to remove the dishes from his meal, or the suit he'd worn to the trial, until very late.

He had felt betrayed. Lacey's disappearance at the end of the trial had deeply shaken him, so when his guards came for him around midnight, he was convinced that this was one predicament that wouldn't be so easy to get out of. All of his life he had relied on his own abilities; he was responsible for his own well-being and safety. Only this time he had absolutely no control over what would happen to him next.

Walking up the familiar corridors and out into the waiting van, he had gone meekly. You can't fight the whole Russian Army, boyo. The words came to his mind in a familiar yet distant voice. Survival, that's the name of the game. Hang on, maybe the cavalry will be coming after all. He wondered what his father would have done in the same circumstances, or how his grandfather would have reacted. They'll break your will sooner or later, he'd been taught at the Farm. It is inevitable. Your job is to hold out for as long as you possibly can.

But they had his confession. Miroshnikov had won after all. The Soviet system had won. They had finally ground him down to nothing, so that he was even incapable of helping himself or offering anything but a token resistance. Attacking Miroshnikov had been nothing more than the pitiful last-ditch stand of a man totally overwhelmed by the odds.

He managed the slightest of smiles. But, damn, it had been worth it.

Voronin's face swam into view, and McAllister knew that he was drifting now, half in and half out of sleep, the muted hum of the jetliner's engines lulling him. Voronin had been the gold seam after all. The mother load, in the parlance.

Look to Washington. Look to Moscow. Zebra One, Zebra Two. What did it mean? Where was the logic? Why hadn't they asked him about Voronin? Why?

He'd been to Moscow, so now the answers were waiting for him in Washington. Did he want to pursue them? Or was it time to step down?

Someone touched his arm and he opened his eyes and looked up into the smiling face of the stewardess.

"We're coming in for a landing, monsieur," she said. "*S'il vous plaît,* fasten your seatbelt."

Charles de Gaulle Airport had always resembled, to McAllister's way of thinking, a space station of aluminum, glass, and acrylic elevators and moving walkways and brightly lit notice boards directing passengers to the various functions and shops. The airport was divided into two sections: Aérogare 1 which served mostly foreign airlines, and Aérogare 2 which was for the exclusive use of Air France.

They carried no luggage, so customs and passport control were accomplished in a few minutes. The airport was very empty at this early hour and what few French officials were on duty were sleepy and inattentive.

McAllister walked with Carrick and Maas across the terminal where they got on one of the moving sidewalks that took them up into the circular Aérogare 1, for the Pan Am flight to New York. They had a little more than an hour to wait. Most of the shops and restaurants were closed, so they went into a small stand-up café near the boarding gate and ordered coffee. Maas went off to make a telephone call leaving McAllister and Carrick alone for a few minutes.

The heavyset CIA legman hunched over his coffee, avoiding McAllister's eyes. Alone now he seemed somewhat ill at ease, nervous.

McAllister studied the man's profile for a moment or two.

Something was going on. Something was definitely wrong. He had felt it at the airport in Moscow, and on the plane, but he had put his apprehensive feelings aside as simple paranoia; a mild form of drug-induced hysteria. He wasn't so sure now.

"Excuse me a moment," he mumbled, stepping away from the counter. "I have to go to the bathroom."

Carrick looked up startled. "I'll go with you."

McAllister stopped and looked directly into the man's eyes. "What the hell is going on here, Mark?"

"What do you mean?" Carrick asked. He glanced over McAllister's shoulder into the broad concourse, evidently searching for Maas to return.

"I'm getting the impression that I'm not returning home the conquering hero. What are your orders?"

"I don't know what you're talking about, Mr. McAllister. Shit, I'm just doing my job."

"Which is?"

"Fetch you home from Moscow."

"And deliver me to whom?"

"We'll be met at the airport."

"What else?" McAllister demanded. He was beginning to feel mean. "What else were you told?"

"Nothing."

"Do you know what I've gone through over the past few weeks?"

A hard look came into Carrick's eyes. He nodded, his jaw tight. "You're in one piece."

"What's that supposed to mean?"

Carrick shook his head. "Look, I don't want to get into it with you, Mr. McAllister."

"Go ahead, get into it."

Still Carrick hesitated. Again he looked out into the concourse for Maas.

"If I turn around and walk out of here, are you going to stop me?"

"You're damned right I'll stop you. So don't push it."

"Then what's going on?"

"It beats the hell out of me, McAllister. All I know is that you were with the Russians for a goddamned long time, and there are some people back home who'd like to know what you talked to them about, and why you came out in one piece, and why they decided at the last minute to release you—without a trade. They released you straight up."

"So you think I'm a traitor?"

Carrick's lip curled into a sneer. "Just don't try to walk away from me. I've got my job to do, that's all."

McAllister actually got a couple of hours' sleep on the transatlantic flight, though it wasn't restful. After his talk with Carrick in the café, his two escorts had become almost surly, dropping any pretense of friendship or respect. He was a traitor returning home under arrest. As on the Air France flight out of Moscow they had first class to themselves, and McAllister sat by himself, confused and angry.

He had given everything to the Agency over the past fourteen years. A legion of cities and faces and dark alleys and letter drops and one-time codes, and nights waiting at some border crossing for one of his madmen to show up, passed through his mind. He could picture each place and each incident in perfect clarity.

At first it had been exciting. Only later had he begun to wear down, tiring at last of the lies big and little, of the betrayals and of the fact that it had been simply impossible for him and Gloria to have real friends. They'd been able only to maintain sham relationships that if he could be honest with himself (and even that began to come apart at the seams) had begun to erode the fabric of his marriage as well as his own mental well being.

Perhaps he had been ripe for an arrest. His tradecraft had been slipping.

He opened his eyes, his heart pounding, a slight sheen

of perspiration on his forehead. He was returning home to what? To questions for which he had no answers. For accusations to which he had no defenses. He had been in the hands of the KGB for more than a month (God, could it have been that long?) and he had resisted to the best of his ability. But it hadn't been enough. Not enough.

What are you doing to yourself?

He had to do something, move, anything. Unbuckling his seatbelt he got up and before Carrick or Maas could come after him he went forward to where the two stewardesses were seated across from the galley. They looked up.

"Can't sleep," McAllister said.

"May I get you something, sir?" one of the girls asked, concerned.

"Maybe a drink. Brandy?"

"Sure," the stew said. She got up and stepped into the narrow galley where she opened a cabinet and took out a couple of small bottles of brandy, and from another cabinet a glass.

"No ice," McAllister said, taking the drinks from her. "May I take them up to the lounge?"

The girl looked over his shoulder. Carrick stood right behind him. "Sure," she said.

"Thanks," McAllister mumbled, and he turned, brushed past Carrick and went back to the circular stairs that led to the 747's upper level.

The lounge was deserted and dimly lit at this hour. During the daytime and early evening transatlantic flights it would have been filled with first-class passengers drinking and talking. McAllister slumped down at one of the tables as Carrick appeared at the head of the stairs. Opening one of the small bottles, he poured it into the crystal glass, then sat back.

"What are you doing up here?" Carrick asked.

McAllister raised his glass. "Care for a drink?"

"No. And with the shit that's probably still in your system, you shouldn't have another either."

"Your concern is touching," McAllister said.

"Look, McAllister . . ."

"No, you look. If you want to talk to me straight, then go ahead. Otherwise keep your mouth shut."

Carrick said nothing.

McAllister swirled the liquor around in his glass. "I've had enough bullshit thrown at me over the past thirty days to last a lifetime. And I'm going to get more of it when I get home, so I don't need yours now."

"I didn't ask for this job."

"But I did," McAllister said softly. He took a deep drink, the brandy rebounding in his stomach, and then settling, warmth rising up into his head. "It's like Nam all over again. No returning hero this time either."

"None of us were," Carrick said. "I know what you mean."

In the distance McAllister could hear the mob screaming below on the streets as they tried to break down the embassy gates. There was a lot of small-arms fire through the city, and all night the rockets had come in from every direction. One by one the choppers came in, touched down on the roof and took a load. McAllister and some of the others were among the last to leave. They'd spent most of the night destroying papers and crypto equipment, trying to swallow, as best they could, their deep sense of shame that they were leaving, that they were giving up. God, what a waste. What a terrible waste.

"What happened back there?" Carrick was asking.

McAllister focused on him and shrugged. "They say they extracted a confession from me, and I signed it, but I don't remember doing it."

"Shit."

"Have you ever been on an interrogation team?"

Carrick shook his head. "No."

"Neither have I," McAllister said. "I wonder how we handle the poor bastards we haul in."

"Better than they treated you," Carrick said, studying McAllister's face. "I hope."

McAllister managed a tired smile. He'd been overreacting again, of course. The KGB had had him for a month, Langley would have to know what went on; how much information had the Russians been given—inadvertently or advertently. He knew so many names and dates and places; knew about so many operations current as well as past. All of Moscow operations would be in a shambles now, everything would have to be changed. The fallout would already have been tremendous. It would still be happening. Someone was going to have to answer for it. The problem was that there was very little he could tell anyone because he simply could not remember the details of his questioning. They said they had his confession, but what exactly was it he had confessed to? How much information had he given them? The only things he could remember in detail were Miroshnikov's persistent questions about the Scorpius network, and about Tom Murdock's whereabouts these days. There'd been nothing about Voronin, or about current Moscow operations, so far as he could remember.

Had Miroshnikov been clever enough to read his mind? They'd released him without a trade. A Soviet court had found him guilty of espionage. Why hadn't he been sent to Siberia? They'd sent a message to Langley by handing him over to Carrick and Maas at the airport, but what exactly was that message?

McAllister opened the second bottle of brandy and emptied it in his glass.

"Maybe you should cool it on that stuff," Carrick said. He glanced at his watch. "We'll be touching down at JFK pretty soon."

"It'd be a hell of a deal if you delivered me drunk."

Carrick sat forward. "I didn't mean it that way," he said earnestly. "We both know that you're going to be in for a bad time."

"I'll need all my wits about me."

"Well I'll be damned if *I'm* going to deliver a drunk," Maas said at the head of the stairs, a scowl set on his face. He came across the lounge and reached over the table for the glass. McAllister held it out of his reach.

"How badly do you want it?"

"Enough to take you apart, you sonofabitch," Maas hissed.

"Then come and get it, otherwise stay the hell away from me."

Maas started around the table, but Carrick jumped up and shouldered him aside. "What the hell's the matter with you, Tom?"

"The bastard is . . ." Maas cut himself off. He was shaking with anger.

"Is what?" McAllister asked. He didn't know why he was goading the man, except that he felt battered and he wasn't going to take much more of it.

What was happening? Where had it gone wrong?

Look to Washington. Look to Moscow. Zebra One, Zebra Two.

He could accept his arrest and his interrogation. He could even accept the inevitability of his trial and conviction. But after that everything had been turned upside down. Had he become a traitor? Is that what had happened to him in the Lubyanka?

"You know," Maas said, backing off.

Yes I do know. And yet I know nothing.

McAllister sat back and raised the glass of brandy to his lips as he stared up into the hate-filled eyes of Tom Maas, and the concerned face of Mark Carrick.

At altitude the eastern sky was already beginning to lighten with the dawn, but when they touched down at New York's

JFK Airport it was still dark, the white runway lights giving way to the blue as the giant airliner turned onto the taxiway, Manhattan beyond Queens glowing with a million pinpoints of light.

He was home. It seemed like such a terribly long time since he had been here last, and now he was anxious to get down to Washington to straighten everything out and get on with his life. He was worried about Gloria; how she had been holding up these past weeks, what she had been thinking, and what, if anything, she'd been told. It must have been hell for her. He resolved that he would try again to work on his marriage, to make it better for her. It was time, in any event, for him to get out of the Company. Time to try normalizing his life. Time, as she'd often said, to join the human race.

When they reached the Pan Am terminal, the aircraft's cabin lights were switched on, the curtain separating first class from coach was pulled aside, and the other passengers began streaming tiredly by. Carrick motioned for McAllister to wait. From his window he could see the boarding tunnel that led into the terminal. A pair of ground crewmen dressed in white coveralls stood at the base of the stairs. One of them was smoking a cigarette, which McAllister found odd.

After all the passengers were gone, McAllister fell in between Carrick and Maas as they got off the plane. Instead of going down the boarding tunnel, Carrick opened the outside door and they took the stairs down to the tarmac. The air was very cold and smelled strongly of burned jet fuel. The 747's engines had been shut down. On the opposite side of the plane the baggage handlers had opened the cargo bays and were off-loading the luggage, the engine of the baggage train clattering noisily in the crisp air.

"We have a car coming for us," Carrick said over his shoulder.

"What about customs?" McAllister asked.

"Forget about it," Maas said from behind him.

When they got to the bottom of the stairs, McAllister looked for the two ground crewmen he'd seen from the plane, but they had disappeared.

Carrick looked at his watch. "They were supposed to be here by now," he said. "What the hell are we supposed to do, stand out here freezing our balls off?"

McAllister glanced up at the terminal windows. Two New York City cops stood talking, their backs to the window. Something was not quite right. It was the cigarette the one crewman had been smoking. Tiredness, or his internal warning system?

He turned to say something to Carrick when the legman started to swing left as he reached inside his coat. McAllister caught a movement out of the corner of his eye, and he began to turn at the same moment the two crewmen he'd seen before, came out of the shadows, big pistols in their hands, silencers on the barrels.

Both men opened fire at the same time, the noise of the silenced gunshots lost to the sounds of the baggage train's engine.

Carrick was shoved violently back, off his feet, his head bouncing on the pavement. Maas had pushed McAllister aside, and was pulling out his gun when he went down, taking at least three bullets to the torso, his body crumpling in a heap on the boarding tunnel's stairs.

McAllister, on his hands and knees, scrambled to Carrick's body and pulled the dead agent's gun out of his hand, then rolled left, snapping off two shots as he came around.

He was sure that he had hit one of the assassins, but then they disappeared into the maintenance basement of the terminal.

It had all happened in a second or two, and as McAllister jumped to his feet he glanced up at the window. One of the cops was looking down at him, a walkie-talkie raised to his lips, a frantic expression on his face.

McAllister stepped back a pace, realizing that he was

holding Carrick's gun, and what it must look like to the cop who could not have seen the two gunmen who had never stepped out from beneath the overhang.

His head was spinning from the remnants of the drugs still in his system, and from the alcohol he had consumed on the flight.

They thought he was a traitor, and now there was at least one witness who would swear that he was a killer.

Chapter 5

The cop with the walkie-talkie disappeared from the window; the other one was already on his way down here, probably through the boarding tunnel, and they would shoot before they stopped to ask questions.

McAllister moved quickly away from the aircraft and hurried beneath the overhang to the broad service doors leading into the Pan Am baggage handling area. He was in time to see two crewmen in white coveralls heading away in a small electric-driven cart. His eyes swept past them toward two other crewmen busy loading out-going baggage onto a train. Nothing seemed out of the ordinary. No one was rushing away. No sounds of alarm had been raised.

He looked again down the broad corridor in time to see one of the crewmen in the retreating cart slump forward and hold his shoulder. It was them. The assassins. And he had wounded one of them.

Stay or run? The situation here would only last for a few moments longer. He could put down the gun, raise his hands and wait for the police. Or he could go after the killers.

Carrick and Maas had thought he was a traitor and now they were dead. At least two New York City cops knew that he was a murderer. They had seen it with their own eyes.

What the hell was happening?

McAllister stepped the rest of the way into the baggage-handling area, and concealing the pistol behind his leg edged away from the brightly lit central corridor into the shadows, and then raced after the slowly retreating service cart, careful to make no noise, or expose himself to the other crewmen at work.

The killers were professionals who understood that to rush away would mark them as out of the ordinary, a force to reckon with. Because of this McAllister was able to gain on them. No doubt they had a car parked somewhere outside the international terminal area. There was possibly a driver waiting for them. The operation had been smooth. They had waited for the flight knowing that their targets would be getting off the plane last and would come down the stairs from the boarding tunnel. But Carrick had said they would be met by a car. Had the signals been crossed innocently, or had their pickup's absence been arranged?

By whom? How? Why? A dozen dark possibilities, each more ominous than the last, crowded into McAllister's head as he darted in and around piles of boxes and tow carts filled with baggage.

The assassins passed through the Pan Am baggage area into Eastern's, crossed a broad, well-lit tarmac, then turned sharply left through the big service doors that led back outside.

McAllister pulled up short, ducking behind a large crate as someone shouted something from behind him. The two cops had raced into the Pan Am baggage area and were questioning the two crewmen. They were obviously frantic, gesticulating and pointing first in the opposite direction, and then this way. Getting out of here was suddenly impossible. The moment he moved out of hiding he would be spotted.

The baggage train from the Pan Am flight came noisily through the service doors, passing directly in front of the two cops, momentarily blocking their view. McAllister stepped out of the shadows and walked at a normal pace into Eastern's baggage area. To move any faster would be to attract attention to himself. So far the alarms had not spread, only the two cops behind him had taken up the hunt. So far.

Reaching the service doors, he stepped outside. A big Eastern Airlines jet was getting ready for departure. There was a lot of activity around the aircraft; last-minute fueling, baggage loading, provisioning through a rear hatch. He hung back for a few moments, searching for the killers. He thought they would be moving directly away from the terminal, so he didn't immediately spot the service cart parked off to the right in the shadows beyond an empty baggage train. They had stopped. He stepped forward out of the shadows as two men, dressed in dark jackets and trousers stepped around from behind the baggage train, and climbed into the back seat of a black Chevrolet sedan.

McAllister knew that he could not use Carrick's gun. It was not silenced and the noise of the gunshots would mark him immediately. He could feel blind panic rising up inside of him. Already a crowd had gathered around the Pan Am aircraft, and in the distance he could hear the sounds of the first sirens. He was going to have to get out of here now, or else he would be trapped.

He shoved the gun in his pocket as the big car turned and headed off into the night, its taillights winking. He had caught enough of a glimpse of the license plate to see that it was a New York tag; nongovernmental, nondiplomatic.

Even more people were racing to the Pan Am plane as McAllister forced himself to walk calmly to where the service cart was parked. Two sets of coveralls were stuffed behind the seats. One of them had a lot of blood on the shoulder, the other was clean. Airport identification badges were still clipped to the pockets. Looking around to make certain that no one had noticed him yet, he took the clean set of coveralls out of the cart and stepped around behind a big truck where he hurriedly pulled them on. By the time he walked back around to the service cart the two cops from the window had raced up from the Pan Am baggage area, and had emerged from Eastern's service area. Too late McAllister realized that they might recognize his face. He averted his eyes.

"Did you see anybody coming out of here?" one of the cops shouted. The other was speaking into his walkie-talkie.

McAllister nodded over his shoulder the way the car had gone. "Some guy got in a car," he said, doing the best he could with a New Jersey accent. "What's going on?"

"Where?" the cop shouted. "Just now?"

"Yeah," McAllister said, climbing behind the wheel. "Just now. Headed outta here in a big hurry. Wasn't wearing no badge either."

The cop's eyes strayed to the badge on McAllister's pocket. Airport security lived and died on such open identification. If you had such a badge you were legitimate. If you didn't, you did not belong.

Another car was drawing up between the Eastern and Pan Am planes as McAllister started the service cart's motor and backed out. This one he recognized. The plates were United States government, the series the FBI used.

The two cops hurried back to the growing commotion around the Pan Am plane. McAllister swung the service cart around and headed in the opposite direction. The FBI had come to pick up him and his Agency escorts. They would be expecting three men. Once they realized that McAllister was missing, they would seal the airport, although the report from the cops that a ground crewman had seen a man getting into a car and driving off, might confuse them for a little while. Long enough, McAllister hoped. It was his only chance at this point.

He drove down the line of planes and around the international terminal, finally angling across the tarmac to where the domestic flights were serviced as the sun began to lighten the eastern sky in a grayish-pink haze. Getting out of the international terminal without going through customs would have been impossible for him. Only his apparent status at this moment as a ground crewman intent on some airport business allowed him to cross the ramp without being stopped and questioned. Nevertheless it wouldn't be very long now before the entire airport would be closed. Unless he got out before that happened he would be stuck here, and slowly but surely the noose would be tightened and he would be taken.

Washington. The answers were in Washington, and so was his safety. Home base. The free zone where he could surround himself with friends who knew and understood that he of all people could not be a traitor or a murderer. Once he was allowed to tell his side of the story, Langley would understand. But what story was it he could tell them? About the ramblings of a vodka-crazed old bitter Russian? A former KGB officer? Or, of his own interrogation under torture and drugs? There were, in reality, no concrete answers he could give them. Nothing solid other than the fact the Russians had suddenly let him free with no apparent motive.

Even more sirens were converging on the international terminal as McAllister parked the service cart in a row of others and hurried through Piedmont Airlines' baggage area and out into the passenger terminal, nearly deserted at this hour. No one saw the ground crewman in white coveralls enter the men's room, nor did anyone notice the tall man in civilian clothes emerge moments later and head for the main concourse and the taxi ranks outside.

He was going to have to get down to Washington. To safety. Some sort of a message had been sent from Moscow to Langley: McAllister was the mark, kill him at all costs. He mustn't be allowed to live.

But by whom? And why?

* * *

The Soviets had not returned his gun, of course, but they had been meticulous in returning his passport, wallet, credit cards, a few hundred dollars in American currency, and other things just before he had been handed over to Carrick and Maas at Sheremetyevo. The cabby dropped him off in front of Eastern Airlines at LaGuardia Airport in plenty of time for him to ditch the gun he had taken from Carrick's body, and then purchase a roundtrip on the eight o'clock shuttle to Washington's National Airport, with a return on the five o'clock shuttle under the name G. Thompson. A one-way ticket would have been a dead giveaway to the first inquiries the FBI undoubtedly would begin making this morning. It was just one more bit of tradecraft designed to buy him a little extra time.

A couple of minutes before he was to board, he found a pay phone just down the corridor from the gate and direct-dialed his house in Georgetown. Bill Lacey had told him that Gloria was back in the States. He assumed she had reopened their house.

He let it ring ten times before he hung up. If Langley believed that he was a traitor, they might have isolated her either in an Alexandria safehouse, or possibly even down in Williamsburg at the Farm. Nevertheless, he would have thought they'd have placed a monitor on his phone line with automatic switching to bring all incoming calls out to Langley.

Nothing that had happened to him since his arrest seemed to add up. He thought with a twinge that by now Gloria would have been informed that something was wrong. What exactly had they told her, and how she had taken the news was bothersome. Their marriage wasn't on the strongest of grounds, though they had both been trying very hard to make it work. They wanted different things; it was as simple and as terribly complex as that. She wanted Washington on a regular basis, and he wanted . . . what? Exactly what was it he wanted?

He glanced down the corridor as the first boarding call for his flight came over the speakers. Maybe he didn't know what he wanted. Maybe he never would. And part of the problem was that she couldn't stand his searching.

He picked up the telephone and started to dial a second Washington number, but then decided against it and hung up. In the last analysis, boyo, you can't trust anyone in the business, he'd been told. Which is too bad, because people like us need and demand just that; a trust in something or short of that, a trust in somebody.

But not over the telephone lines, he decided. He would have to tell his story face-to-face so that he could gauge reactions from the other man's eyes. Other *men,* he corrected himself. How many were there whom he could trust? One, two, a handful? No more than that. But would they believe him? Could they possibly believe him against the weight of evidence that had already been built against him?

Traitor. Murderer. You've gone over to the other side. Not an uncommon failing. It was the business that did it in the end. Turn a man, make him sell out his country, take his secrets from him, and on your side of the border he is a hero, but back home he is a traitor. What did that do to such men, and more important at this moment, what did such work do to the agent runner? How did it warp their sense of right versus wrong, of justice, of fair play?

McAllister ran a hand over his eyes. He was sweating slightly, even though the corridor was chilly. The effects, still, of the drugs he'd been given during his captivity, or something else? Fear? Confusion? Shame?

We're making progress and I feel very good about it. And so should you. We have finally broken down the first barrier . . . really quite excellent. You have been cooperative . . . Mac.

Bits and pieces of Miroshnikov's words came back to him, like gentle whispers in the darkness, like water moving softly on a sand beach. Frightening and yet oddly comforting. They were reassurances from a source that should not have provided him assurances.

God, what had happened to him in Moscow? What was happening to him now? What did they want? Why him?

McAllister stepped away from the pay phone, realizing that the boarding-gate area which had minutes earlier been filled with passengers was now empty except for the airline clerks, one of whom was looking up the corridor toward him. Another, behind the counter, picked up the telephone.

"This is the final boarding call for Eastern's shuttle service, 1411, to Washington, D.C.," the clerk's amplified voice came from the speakers in the ceiling. "Passengers holding confirmed reservations, please board now."

The answers were in Washington. Pulling his ticket and boarding pass out of his pocket, he hurried down the corridor to the gate. His answers were there, if he could survive long enough to find them.

His flight touched down a few minutes after nine, and twenty minutes later he was heading up the Washington Parkway, in heavy traffic in a rental Ford Escort, the day bright and warm in contrast to Moscow, the city with her parks and monuments gleaming green and white, and at this distance clean and somehow safe. This was the capital. Home base. The reason for his existence, for his life, in fact.

He had decided that whoever was trying to stop him, for whatever reason, would not suspect that he would run here, and so he openly rented a car in his own name. For the moment speed would be more effective than stealth.

Robert Highnote.

McAllister's mouth was dry, his stomach rumbled and his peripheral vision was still slightly blurry from the cumulative effects of the drugs, the lack of sleep, and the lack of decent food. But he understood his tradecraft at a deeper, instinctual level; covering his tracks, making the proper moves at the proper times, knowing when to hesitate and when to act, were almost like knee jerk reactions to him. Before he approached his old friend, mentor and boss, he needed to know the extent of the Agency's concern over him.

Crossing the river on the Key Bridge into Georgetown, he reached M Street and turned right, merging with traffic. He stopped for a red light across from the Rive Gauche, a restaurant he and Gloria frequented each time they'd been reassigned briefly to Washington between foreign postings. It gave him an odd feeling to be here like this now.

He turned left up Wisconsin Avenue, the sights and sounds and smells coming back to him like an old familiar jacket one has rediscovered in his closet; oddly out-of-date, and out-of-fashion. Yet oh so comfortable and friendly. New York and especially Moscow seemed like a long way away now, not only in distance but in time.

Highnote would listen to him, would help him, if anyone would, or could. But first he had to know one thing.

A couple of blocks past the Georgetown Theater he took P Street over to 31st, that ran at an odd angle up toward Montrose Park, then slowed down two blocks later, passing the intersection with Avon Lane. This was a neighborhood of three-story brownstone houses each attached to the next. His was six doors from the corner on the upper side.

McAllister had participated in enough surveillance operations over the past fourteen years to know what he was looking at. A Toyota van, its windows blocked with reflective film, was parked twenty yards beyond his house. A yellow cab was parked at the far corner. Behind it the cabby and a big burly man in shirtsleeves were looking at something beneath the raised hood of a Mercedes.

They were waiting for him. Expecting him to come here. Two hours ago when he had telephoned from New York there'd been no answer at his house, no switching equipment. If they'd been waiting for him two hours ago, the telephone would have been manned.

This surveillance had been ordered up because of what had happened on the ramp at JFK. A traitor is loose; a dangerous lunatic who has killed two of our own is heading our way.

McAllister realized that he was shaking. Violently. Sweat had popped out on his forehead and yet he was freezing cold. He turned east on R Street and a couple of blocks later pulled over across from the Oak Hill Cemetery.

Life was going forth at an ordinary speed all through the city. McAllister felt as if he were a tree limb snagged in a swiftly moving stream, the waters swirling around him. He was helpless. Once he was caught up in the swift current he would drown. There was no avoiding it.

They were waiting for him.

God in heaven what was happening? What did they think he had become?

Look to Washington. Look to Moscow.

He had been to Moscow, and here he was in Washington. But look for what, for whom?

He was driving through Arlington National Cemetery across the river from the Lincoln Memorial, and there was very little traffic. It was early evening and behind him the city lights were beginning to mingle with the darkening star-studded sky. Being here likc this now, he was struck with a sense of unreality, not only with what he was doing, and why, but with the fact he was doing anything at all. He was on the outside looking in. It was very strange.

If anyone had the answers it would be Highnote.

Earlier he had driven out to Dulles International Airport where he had left the rental car in the long-term parking garage, because if they were expecting him to come to

Washington they'd be checking with all the car rental agencies and his name would turn up.

It had taken him less than a half hour in the busy air terminal to find a man about his own height, general build and age, lift his wallet as he stood at one of the cocktail lounge bars, and using the man's driver's license and credit card, rent a car from the Hertz counter.

By the time he had hurried back to the cocktail lounge, the man—Thomas Hobart from Muncie, Indiana—was still at the bar. McAllister dropped his wallet on the floor, then turned and left, retrieving the Ford Taurus from where he had left it out front.

In the afternoon he had had a late lunch at a roadside restaurant south of Alexandria where he had searched the Washington and New York afternoon papers for a story about the shootout at JFK, but there'd been nothing. He would have been surprised if there had been.

At first he had watched in his rearview mirror each time he turned a corner, switched lanes, or changed speeds. But so far as he had been able to tell, no one was on his tail. They might suspect, at this point, that he was in Washington, but so far he had not been spotted. That wouldn't last, of course. It couldn't last. Sooner or later someone would see and recognize him, especially if he kept moving around. As it began to get dark he had driven back up past National Airport and into the cemetery where he had slowed his speed. If they got to him now and shot him to death, would he be buried here at Arlington with his father? It wasn't likely. He was a traitor and a murderer. But was there any peace for him, could there be any peace for him even in death? Somehow he doubted that as well.

He passed through the western edge of the vast cemetery, crossed Washington Boulevard and was in Arlington Heights, a nice but unpretentious neighborhood of pleasant homes. It was dark by the time he reached Astor Avenue, parking in the middle of the block, and shutting off his lights and engine.

Highnote's house was located at the end of a cul-de-sac. Except for a light over the garage door and another on the front porch, the place was dark.

McAllister got out of his car, walked the rest of the way down the block, and crossed the lawn between Highnote's house and his neighbor's, also dark. Somewhere in the close distance a dog started barking, and McAllister stopped a moment in the darkness. After a few seconds the dog stopped, and he continued around to the rear through a tall hedge, and across the patio past the swimming pool.

The kitchen light was on, but Highnote's study was in darkness. At the study window, McAllister put his ear to the glass. He could vaguely hear someone talking, or a television set playing, and through the curtains he could see that the study door was closed.

Stepping back he took off his jacket, wrapped it around his right elbow, and using as little strength as possible, broke one of the small square windowpanes just at the lock. The noise seemed very loud in the still night air, and for several seconds McAllister held his breath waiting for the sounds of an alarm to be raised. But there was nothing. He reached inside, undid the lock, slid the window open and crawled through.

McAllister had been in this room before. Quite often. He and Gloria had been friends with Highnote and his wife Merrilee for years, despite the age difference of fifteen years. He knew the layout well. The desk was directly opposite the window, a leather couch and coffee table were to the right, and on the left was the door to the tiny bathroom. Books lined two walls, and a third held framed photographs and certificates of achievement. With the curtains open he could see well enough in the dim light coming from outside.

Sitting down at the desk McAllister opened the bottom left drawer and took out Highnote's Walther PPK. The flat automatic, which at one time had been the weapon of choice among British Secret Intelligence Service field operatives, had been a gift from Kim Philby when the Brit was stationed here in Washington. Highnote always said the gun gave him a lot of ironic pleasure. He'd been one of those, even as a young man, who'd thought Philby was too good to be true.

He checked the action of the gun. It was well oiled and loaded.

There were two telephones on the desk; one was the house line, and the other was Highnote's private number. McAllister picked up the second one and dialed the house number. The connection was made and he could hear the telephones in the rest of the house ringing. Highnote picked it up on the second ring.

"Yes?"

"Hello, Bob," McAllister said. The gun was on the desk in front of him. He was watching the door.

"Jesus," Highnote whispered. "Where the hell are you?"

"Are you alone?"

Highnote said something away from the phone. "Just Merrilee and me. Are you in the city? Can I come and get you?"

"I need some answers, Bob."

"So do I. Where the hell are you?"

"Here," McAllister said. "At your desk in your study."

"Good Lord," Highnote said after the briefest of hesitations. "I'll be right in." He hung up.

McAllister put down the phone and picked up the Walther. Whom to trust? He didn't know any longer. Perhaps he never really knew.

The door opened seconds later and Robert Highnote, deputy director of operations for the Central Intelligence Agency, entered the study. He was a man of medium height, with a mostly bald head, wide honest eyes, and a manner of speaking and bearing that were almost old-worldly elegant. He was a Harvard graduate, a Rhodes scholar, and a deeply religious man. Every evening of his adult life he had spent at least one hour studying the Bible. He was something of an expert on it. His life was a story, but then so was everyone else's in the Agency; the business seemed to attract them like flies to honey. His eyes went to the gun in McAllister's hand. "Do you mean to shoot me too, Mac?" he asked softly.

"I didn't shoot Carrick and Maas. I think ballistics will bear me out," McAllister said.

Highnote came the rest of the way into his study, closing the door behind him. He was coatless, but he still wore his tie. He'd probably just returned from his office. He sat down across from McAllister and reached for the desk light.

"No," McAllister said.

Highnote stayed his hand, hesitated again, then sat back in his chair. He shook his head. "You *have* come as a surprise, Mac. A very big surprise."

"They were waiting for us when we got off the plane. Two of them, in ground-crew uniforms. Our pickup car was late. Carrick and Maas never had a chance."

"But you did," Highnote said.

"I was lucky."

"You were seen with a gun."

"Carrick's. I managed to wound one of them."

"But they got away."

"They had a car waiting for them, Bob," McAllister said. He leaned forward a little. "They were waiting for us, goddamnit. How did they know?"

"I can't answer that. . . ." Highnote pursed his lips, his eyes suddenly wide. "What are you trying to say?"

"Who knew that I was coming in on that particular flight?"

"A lot of people. Smitty and his crowd. They made the actual arrangements. Finance. The crew chief."

"And the FBI office in New York?"

Highnote nodded. "They were supposed to take you over to the shuttle terminal right there at JFK."

"How, Bob? What was my status?"

"I don't know what you mean."

"What were the FBI told about me? And why bring them into it? I could have walked with Carrick and Maas over to the shuttle."

"We wanted to avoid customs."

"You didn't need the FBI for that . . . not unless I was being brought back as a criminal and you wanted no publicity."

Highnote reacted. McAllister could see it in his old friend's eyes. Was it fear? Disgust?

"Is that it, Bob?" McAllister asked, softening his voice. "Do you think I'm a traitor because I caved in? They had me for a month, and they're very good. Even better than they taught us out at the Farm."

"We suspected that from the beginning," Highnote said. "Because of . . . what started to happen. What's still happening."

"Our networks?" McAllister asked, the words catching in his throat because he knew the answer even before Highnote gave voice to it. He'd known it instinctively. Miroshnikov was more than good. The man was the devil.

"Our foreign operations are in a complete shambles. Years of work gone down the drain. A lot of good men have fallen. There've been a few killings, but mostly arrests, exposures, expulsions. Under the circumstances not much of a public fuss has been made, but we've been devastated. You can't believe how bad it's become."

"Because of me."

Highnote nodded sadly. "They went to extraordinary lengths to keep you. The President even canceled his meeting with Gorbachev in Zurich, over it. Still they didn't budge."

"I was a gold seam."

"The mother lode," Highnote said, nodding. "Once we realized what was happening, we began pulling our people out of the way, but it was already too late."

"Christ, you can't know how sorry I am, Bob. I tried. God help me, I tried."

There was no compassion in Highnote's expression, only a distant coolness and something else. His eyes went again to the gun in McAllister's hand. "Let's go back to the office. See what we can put together. If we know what you told them, we might be able to minimize some of the continuing damage."

"I don't know what I told them," McAllister said. "But that's not it, anyway, is it. They released me. That's what has you worried. No exchange, no concessions, nothing, they just handed me over to our people at the airport and let me leave."

"It worried us," Highnote said dryly.

"Then who tried to kill me in New York and why?"

"Maybe they weren't gunning for you, Mac. Maybe they did exactly what they set out to do."

"That doesn't make any sense," McAllister said with frustration.

"No, it doesn't," Highnote agreed, the same odd look in his eyes.

It suddenly dawned on McAllister what Highnote had to be thinking. "You don't believe me," he said. "About the two men in New York."

"No one saw them," Highnote said patiently.

"I fired back and hit one of them. You'll find a pair of bloody coveralls in a service cart at the Eastern baggage handling area." McAllister explained exactly where it had been parked. "Has a ballistics check been made on the bullets that killed Carrick and Maas?"

"I haven't seen the report."

"Well do that much at least for me."

Highnote nodded. "We'll do that and more if you'll come in with me. I'm on your side, Mac. So is Gloria. I talked to her again this morning. She told me that no matter what happens, no matter how it turns out, she'll stick with you if you'll just turn yourself in. Before it's too late, Mac. For God's sake."

The words stung worse than the wet Turkish towel his Soviet guards had used on him in the prison corridor. "What was Gloria told?"

"Under the circumstances, I couldn't do anything but tell her the truth. Surely you can understand that."

"What truth?" McAllister asked, his voice rising.

"That there was a very good possibility that you'd been turned. That they were sending you home in the hope that you would somehow come through your debriefings with a clean bill of health. That there was a possibility you would actually become operational again. They'd gotten everything they needed from you, and now they were hoping for a little gravy, a little frosting on the cake."

"Is that what you think, Bob?" McAllister asked.

Highnote looked at him for a very long time. "What else can I think?"

McAllister pushed back his chair and got heavily to his feet. Highnote started to rise too, but McAllister motioned him back. "Check with ballistics, and find the coveralls, and you'll see that I didn't kill Carrick and Maas. I'll call you in the morning."

"I can't let you leave here."

"I'm sorry, but you don't have a choice in the matter right now."

Highnote bared his teeth. "Goddamnit, Mac, I trusted you! We all did. But it's not your fault. Those bastards pumped you so full of drugs you didn't know what you were doing. We can fix it for you. Trust me, Mac, for God's sake . . ."

McAllister yanked the two phone cords out of their wall

sockets. It would only take Highnote a few seconds to get to one of the other telephones in the house, but it was something. Highnote had watched with narrowed eyes. At the window McAllister looked back at him.

"I'm not a traitor, and I didn't kill those two in New York, Bob. But until we find out who did, and why, I won't have a chance in hell of convincing you, let alone anyone else, that I'm innocent. Find those coveralls, and look at the ballistics report. I'll call you in the morning."

As he raced across the lawn back to the street he pocketed the Walther. If Highnote didn't believe him, who would? Worst of all it hurt that Gloria thought he had been turned. What was happening?

The police would be here very quickly, but they didn't know his car. Getting away would be difficult, but not impossible.

As he reached the curb, an automobile's headlights raced up from the end of the block, and someone stepped out from behind the hedges. He started to turn when something very hard smashed into the back of his skull and he fell forward, his head bouncing off the pavement.

"*Kill him,*" someone said above him, in Russian.

"*Not here, you fool.*"

Chapter 6

McAllister kept thinking about Highnote's gun in his pocket, but he couldn't seem to get his arms or legs to work. He felt like a big dishrag, limp, without any strength. But he could see and hear and feel.

The car had pulled up in front of him. The car door opened and the driver jumped out and hurried around. Strong hands pulled McAllister around, then lifted his body up, shoving him through the open door into the back seat, the smell of leather instantly surrounding him.

There were three of them. Two had been hiding in the bushes waiting for him to come from around back, and the third waiting in the big Mercedes at the end of the block. It meant that despite his earlier precautions they had managed to follow him here. Had his tradecraft been that sloppy?

"*Hurry,*" one of them said. In Russian. That fact finally began to penetrate McAllister's brain. They were Russians. He'd been recaptured by the KGB, but it was ludicrous; such things did not happen in Washington, D.C., not in front of the house of the deputy director of operations for the CIA.

The driver and one of the others got in the front seat together, and the third Russian piled in the back with

McAllister. *"There's blood all over the place back here, fuck your mother."*

"Is he dead?" one in the front asked.

McAllister was crumpled in a heap, half on the seat, half on the floor. The car had made a U-turn in the street and was speeding back toward Washington Boulevard. His head was splitting and his stomach turned over each time the car swayed, but his strength was coming back. He'd been dazed by the blow, but not knocked unconscious. The Russian's hands were on his body, pulling him up onto the seat. He willed himself to go completely limp, his mouth slack, his eyes open and unmoving.

"I don't know," the Russian said above him.

"Is he breathing, you fool?"

McAllister's left arm was jammed awkwardly beneath him, but his right hand had fallen naturally over his jacket pocket. The car swung around a corner, causing the Russian in the back seat with him to lurch. It was all the opening McAllister needed.

He screamed, rolling with the motion of the car, getting his left arm free at the same time he reached in his right pocket, his fingers curling around the Walther's grip, and he pulled the gun out of his pocket.

"Watch out," the one in the front seat bellowed, clawing inside his coat for his own gun.

McAllister thumbed the Walther's safety off at the same moment the Russian in the back seat regained his balance and kicked out. He fell back, firing at point-blank range, the bullet catching the Russian high in the chest, the noise deafening in the close confines of the automobile.

He switched aim, firing a second time and then a third through the back of the front seat, shoving the second Russian forward into the dash panel, his head crashing into the windshield.

The driver slammed on the brakes sending McAllister tumbling off the seat, losing his grip on the gun. Split seconds later he managed to shove himself upright in time to see a big, silenced Makarov automatic in the driver's left hand coming over the top of the seat, the man's face split in a grimace of fear and grim determination. One moment the American was possibly dead, certainly unconscious, and in the next moment he had killed two men.

There was no time to find the Walther. McAllister lunged left as the Russian fired, the shot creasing the side of his neck with an incredibly hot stitch. He grabbed the man's gun arm and yanked it sharply downward over the back of the seat, the bones breaking with an audible pop as the big car jumped up over the curb and came to a stop.

The Russian screamed in pain, dropping the gun. But he was a professional and very well trained. His right hand was suddenly in McAllister's face, his blunt fingers gouging at Mac's eyes in a last desperate attempt to save his own life.

McAllister shrugged out of the man's reach, then grabbed him by the back of his skull and his face, and twisted his head as far to the left and backward as it would go, and then jerked it sharply beyond the breaking point. The big Russian reared up, trying to lever his body over the seat in the same direction McAllister was twisting, but the angle was all wrong for him. He gave one final massive heave when his neck broke, and his body shuddered once, and then went limp, blood pouring out of his mouth where he had bitten through his tongue.

They were in a quiet neighborhood, still in Arlington Heights a couple of blocks away from Highnote's house, and less than a quarter of a mile from the western entrance to Arlington National Cemetery and the Tomb of the Unknown Soldier. A car came slowly past, a man driving and a woman in the passenger seat. They looked over, their eyes wide as they passed, and then the car speeded up, turning the corner at the far end of the block.

They'd seen that something was obviously wrong. The

car was up on the curb, two men were slumped over in the front seat, and one man with blood all over his face and neck was sitting up in the back. They would call the police as soon as they could find a telephone. He was going to have to get out of here, and now. Immediately.

It took him nearly a full minute to pull the driver's body from behind the wheel and manhandle it into the back seat. He was weak, and his head was pounding. At times he was seeing double. He supposed he had received a slight concussion from the blow to the back of his head.

Climbing behind the wheel, he slammed the car into reverse, backed down off the curb, and then, dropping it into drive, raced to the corner and turned left. The next few minutes were going to be crucial.

Highnote would have called someone by now; possibly the police or the FBI, or possibly someone from the Agency. They'd be on their way by now. But to drive around Washington in a car filled with dead bodies and a lot of blood would be to invite certain arrest. Someone would be sure to spot him.

Chances. His life had always been filled with risk. He was going to have to take a very large risk now, because he still needed answers.

Highnote's street was still dark as McAllister pulled up and parked the Mercedes behind his rented Ford Taurus. It had been minutes since he had left his friend's house, but he had expected at least to hear the sounds of sirens converging here by now. But no one had come. Yet.

Jumping out of the car he yanked open the rear door, retrieved the Walther, and quickly searched the three bodies, coming up with their Soviet Embassy diplomatic credentials and nearly a thousand dollars in cash.

Hurrying back to the Ford he got in behind the wheel, started the engine, and pulled away.

Answers. He needed more answers.

* * *

This time he took the more direct route back into town, past Fort Meyer, up through Colonial Village, then Rosslyn and finally the Key Bridge into Georgetown, the city glittering with lights and traffic. As he drove he had used his handkerchief to clean off some of the blood from his forehead and from the gash in his neck. Neither wound was serious, his luck had held, but his head was on fire, he was sick at his stomach and his vision kept coming in and out of double.

They'd been sent to the airport in New York to kill him, and again to Washington. But how had they known his whereabouts? He was certain that he hadn't been tailed. It would have taken a team of at least four vehicles to pull it off. He'd been part of the drill for too long, and too often to be taken in by a single car behind him.

His presence in New York could have been supplied by air traffic control at Moscow and in Paris. But here in Washington? Would they have figured that he would run first to his old friend and mentor Bob Highnote? It was logical. The question was, how many other people were looking for him at this moment? And what other places would they be watching?

Still, he told himself, he was going to have to take this risk now, no matter what the odds. He was going to have to see his wife; tell her his side of the story. She would understand and believe him. She, of any person on this earth, would *have* to believe in him.

I'm on your side, Mac. So is Gloria. I talked to her again this morning. She told me that no matter what happens, no matter how it turns out, she'll stick with you, if you'll just turn yourself in.

Instead of turning up 31st Street, McAllister drove another block, turning left on 30th, and a half a block later left again on Cambridge Place which was a narrow lane that led back over to Avon. It was the back way to his house. There was no traffic here at this hour, though there were a lot of cars parked on the upper side of the street. He stopped, backed into a driveway and then pulled out again, parking twenty yards down the lane, the car now facing back out toward 30th.

He checked the Walther's clip. There were five bullets left, including the one in the breach. Too late he realized that he should have taken one of the Russians' weapons; the Makarov was a much heavier weapon, with far more stopping power than the lightweight Walther. The Russians' weapons had also been silenced.

Mistakes. He was making too many of them. One piled on top of the other. Sooner or later they would cost him his life.

Getting out of the car, he pocketed the gun, crossed the street and keeping to the shadows as much as possible, hurried up to Avon Place. This was an area of smart brownstone homes, some of which had window boxes on the second story windows that in summer were alive with flowers, but were now barren. A chill, damp wind was blowing up from the Potomac with odors of river mud, diesel fumes and city. Familiar smells. Home smells. But very strange now for him, coming here like this.

The cab and the Mercedes that had been here earlier were gone now, but the Toyota van with reflective film over its windows was still parked just down the street. A dim light shone from the second floor living room windows of his house. As he hung back by the corner, he thought he saw a shadow moving up there, but then it was gone.

Would they expect him to come here like this now? Had they pulled away everyone except the Toyota van in an attempt to lure him in? It's safe now. We've pulled our people out. But who was upstairs in his house? Gloria, or someone else? Someone with the orders from Moscow: A maniac is on the loose, kill him on sight.

Hunching up his coat collar McAllister walked silently on the balls of his feet toward the van, never taking his eyes off the windscreen. The interior of the vehicle was in darkness, but as he got closer he could see that no one was sitting in the front. If anyone was inside, they were in the back, in the darkness.

He stopped twenty feet away and glanced up toward the living room windows of his house. Nothing had changed, the light still illuminated the curtains, but there was no movement.

Taking out the gun, he held it in his right hand, out of sight at his side, and cautiously approached the van. A half a block away traffic passed normally along 31st Street. But here nothing moved. It was one of the reasons they had bought this place. The neighborhood was quiet and safe.

This close he could see all the way inside the van, over the backs of the front seats. No one was inside. The van was empty. Nor did it seem now like the vehicle was used for surveillance. He could see no communications radio. Unless they used walkie-talkies they'd be out of touch here.

He tried the passenger door. It was locked. Even if it was a surveillance van, they'd never leave it locked like that. Seconds spent fumbling with keys, unlocking doors could be crucial seconds wasted in a developing situation.

A message may have gone out from Highnote. McAllister is here in Arlington Heights. The search would have been shifted to the other side of the river. Plausible? Or was he chasing again after will-o'-the-wisps?

Stepping around behind the van, he hesitated a moment longer, then walked across the street, mounting the steps to his front door. He listened at the frosted-glass pane, but could hear nothing inside. He tried the doorknob and it gave easily in his hand, the door opening a crack. Whoever was upstairs had not locked up. He and Gloria used to have bitter arguments about it. She always forgot to lock the door at night, and he would get angry with her over it.

This now was another of her lapses, or was it a trap? His internal warning system was in high gear. This was all wrong. Everything was wrong. No outward signs of a surveillance team. The Toyota van as . . . what? A dummy, a decoy? The light in the upstairs window, inviting him: everything is all right here, Mac. No trouble here. Only your good and patient wife waiting for you; your good and patient and *forgetful* wife waiting for you with the front door unlocked.

Standing there at the partially opened door he thumbed the Walther's safety off, and then back on. Had he come to the point that he would fire on an Agency security officer, or a Bureau agent? Christ, had he been reduced to that?

He pushed the door the rest of the way open with his right foot, waited a moment longer, and then stepped into the dark stairhall.

He could hear music playing upstairs, softly. It sounded classical. Gloria had hated Moscow, but she'd always loved Tchaikovsky, Rimsky-Korsakov, Prokofiev. She was upstairs waiting for him? Or was the message too clear?

The house was typical of most in the area; three stories, long and narrow. On the ground floor were storage rooms, a nursery for the child they'd never had, and a servants' apartment for the servants they'd never hired. The second floor contained the living room, dining room, kitchen, and a bathroom. And the top floor contained two bedrooms and another bathroom. In back was a courtyard garden area and a garage in which his Peugeot was parked.

McAllister closed the door and moved silently to the foot of the stairs. The upper stairhall was in darkness, but now he could more clearly hear the music coming from above. It was definitely Tchaikovsky; the violin concerto, Gloria's favorite.

He started up, his right foot on the first tread when a woman's voice came to him from the darkness to his right. In the storeroom.

"Please stop right there, Mr. McAllister. I don't want to shoot you, but I will."

McAllister froze where he was. She sounded young and frightened. Frightened people made mistakes. But was she alone? "Who are you?"

"Albright. Office of Security. We've been waiting for you."

He carefully turned his head left and looked toward the sound of her voice. She had to be just within the storeroom which was in pitch blackness. He couldn't see her. "The others must be in Arlington Heights."

"We just got the word," she said. "But no one thought you'd be coming back here."

McAllister stepped back and turned toward her. He didn't think she'd seen the gun at his side. A lot of what had been happening suddenly became clear to him because of her presence here. The Company's Office of Security usually handled background checks on prospective employees. Only rarely was it called in on this kind of a surveillance operation. They wanted to keep this contained. The FBI was most likely involved too, but it would not have been told the entire story. Agency security officers rarely carried weapons. They didn't have the training for it.

"Raise your hands please," the woman said.

"Look, before this gets out of control, why don't you call Bob Highnote. He'll explain everything to you."

"Put your hands up. . . ."

"No," McAllister said, keeping his tone reasonable. "I think you'd better call someone, or shoot me, but don't let's just stand here." She was an amateur. He was waiting for the mistake.

She stepped out of the storeroom into the dim light filtering through the frosted-glass window in the front door. She was young, perhaps thirty, about five-feet-six, very slightly built, with a thin face, a round but slightly crooked nose, and medium-length brown hair. She held a small .32 automatic in her right hand and a walkie-talkie in her left. She seemed extremely nervous.

"I came here to talk to my wife," McAllister said. "Have your people get in touch with Highnote. Tell him that I'm here and won't give anybody any trouble. Can you do that much for me?"

The young woman glanced up the stairs.

"My wife is up there, isn't she? Waiting for me?"

"Yes," the young woman said.

"Good," McAllister replied. "Call your team leader. I'll just go upstairs now." He turned again and made as if he were going to start up the stairs.

"Wait," she said, moving toward him.

It was the mistake he'd been waiting for.

McAllister started to raise his hands, the sudden motion confusing her, then he stepped directly into her, swiveling on his left foot so that his body was inside her extended gun hand. She tried to step back, to get away from him, but it was too late. He grabbed her gun hand with his left, twisted it sharply outward, and he had the little automatic.

She let out a cry and started to bring the walkie-talkie to her lips. McAllister raised his pistol so that the barrel was inches from her face.

"Key that thing and I'll kill you." He spoke softly, but with urgency.

"My God . . ."

"I don't want to hurt you, and I won't if you do exactly as I say. I have to talk to my wife, and then I'll be getting out of here. Once I'm clear I'll release you. But for the moment you're going to have to stay with me."

"Don't do this. . . ."

"I won't hurt you, I promise," McAllister said. He pocketed her gun, then took the walkie-talkie from her and stepped back away from the stairs. He motioned for her to go up first.

She was terrified, but she did as she was told, stepping past him and starting up the stairs. He quickly unscrewed the walkie-talkie's antenna, pocketed it, and then laid the unit on the hall table. Above, the music got louder. The woman stopped. The upper landing was suddenly bathed in light.

McAllister was just below the woman when his wife appeared at the head of the stairs. She was dressed in slacks and a light sweater. Her feet were bare.

"Who is that?" she called down. "Stephanie?" Her voice was husky. It sounded as if she'd been crying.

McAllister moved aside so that he was in the light spilling down from above. "It's me," he said.

Gloria's reaction was sudden and startling. She stepped back a pace as if she had just received a stunning blow, her face screwed up in a grimace, her teeth bared. "You," she hissed.

"Gloria . . . ?" he said, confused. This wasn't making any sense.

"You bastard! Why did you come here?" his wife shrieked.

Her words were like battering rams, the blows physical.

"You're a traitor! Murderer! What do you want? There's nothing here for you!"

"Listen to me. . . ."

"Get out!" she screamed. "Get out . . . traitor! Go back to your Russian friends! Get out before I kill you myself!"

This was impossible. It could not be happening. Not like this. His vision was blurred again, and the pain in his head caused him to reel backward, almost losing his balance on the stairs.

"I'll kill you myself . . ." Gloria was screeching. She'd turned away and was fumbling at the small table on the landing.

Stephanie Albright had stepped back a pace too. "Mrs. McAllister . . . ?"

It was the gun. They'd kept a .38 revolver in the table drawer. She was actually going to try to kill him. He simply could not believe what he was seeing, what he was hearing. His entire world had suddenly been turned upside down.

Gloria's body filled the landing, the pistol held in both outstretched hands, and she fired, the shot going wide and high, shattering the mirror on the wall halfway up the stairs.

Stephanie Albright was scrambling back down the stairs, trying to get out of the line of fire. On instinct alone, McAllister stepped to the side and backward, trying to place himself in the shadows, twisting his body sideways so that he would present less of a target.

Gloria fired a second time, and a third, this shot catching McAllister high on his left side, just beneath his armpit, the pain exploding in his chest.

He lurched away from the stairs as Stephanie reached the front door, tore it open with a crash and disappeared into the night.

Chapter 7

Gloria fired two more shots, one of them shattering the frosted-glass pane in the door and ricocheting off the pavement outside with a high-pitched whine.

McAllister stood in the darkness holding his left arm tightly against his side to staunch the flow of blood. He could see his wife's legs halfway up the stairs. She'd stopped. He stepped out of the shadows.

"Gloria?" he said.

Her eyes widened at the sight of him. She raised the pistol so that it was pointing directly at his face and without hesitation pulled the trigger. The hammer fell on an empty cylinder. For safety he'd never loaded more than five bullets into the gun. She'd forgotten or had miscounted. Either way it was of no matter; she definitely wanted him dead.

"Why?" he asked softly. His heart was pounding.

"Bastard!" she screamed, spittle flying from her lips. She spun around and raced back up the stairs. For a second he thought about going after her. But everything was changed now. The skids had been knocked out from under him. He was no longer sure of anything, including himself.

He stepped back, turned and looked outside. Stephanie Albright was clawing open the Toyota's door. It had been a mistake on her part, locking the van. The thought registered automatically in McAllister's brain. But it seemed impossible that he could or even should do anything other than wait right here to be taken. She would get help. They would come for him, and it would be over. He wouldn't have to fight any longer. He was confused and hurt; it was even worse now than it had been at the Lubyanka when he'd lain, strapped to the steel table in the torture chamber, listening to his heart stopping.

The vision of Miroshnikov standing over him, smiling, telling him that they had come so far together, that he was so proud of their work, came to him and he shuddered. If he gave up now they would have won . . . whoever *they* were, and whatever *they* wanted. He wasn't built that way. He'd never been that way, not from the beginning.

Stephanie Albright was just climbing behind the wheel of the Toyota van when McAllister finally roused himself out of his daze, spun on his heel and without a backward glance raced out the door, down the stairs and across the street.

The van's engine came to life. He jammed his gun against the window, aiming directly at her head.

She looked up, one hand on the steering wheel, the other on the gearshift lever.

"I need your help," he shouted.

She was shaking. Her mouth was opening and closing but no sounds were coming out. Traffic was passing normally on 31st Street. It was unreal.

"Just a little longer. Then I'll let you go, I promise."

"No," she moaned.

McAllister yanked the door open. "I won't hurt you, I swear to God I won't."

"What do you want?"

"Just get me out of here, that's all I ask."

McAllister sat directly behind Stephanie Albright as she

drove. They'd crossed the Key Bridge on his instructions and headed northwest up the Washington Parkway that paralleled the river.

Once they were away from the bright city lights, he laid the gun on the seat beside him, undid his shirt and probed the wound with the fingers of his right hand. The .38-caliber bullet had entered his chest at an oblique angle a couple of inches to the left of his left breast, nicking a rib, and emerging below his shoulder blade. It hadn't done a lot of damage, and already the bleeding had slowed to an ooze, but his entire left side was numb from his shoulder all the way down to his hip, and he felt light-headed not only from his latest wound, but from the severe blow to the back of his skull. He stuffed his handkerchief under his shirt.

He needed medical help, he needed sleep and food, but more than that he desperately needed answers.

"We can't drive around all night," Stephanie Albright said. "They've got to be searching for me and this van already."

"Just hope they don't find us too soon," McAllister said.

"Too soon for what?" she asked, looking in the rearview mirrow at him. "Are you going to kill me?"

"Not if you do exactly as I tell you."

"Then tell me something," she said, her voice rising.

"Keep driving," he said tiredly. He picked up the gun, and holding it on his lap laid his head back on the seat.

Robert Highnote and Gloria. The two people he most trusted in the world had turned against him. They had called him a traitor, a murderer. He couldn't get the image of Gloria's face twisted into a grimace of hate and revulsion from his mind. It hurt him more than his wounds. *You can't trust anybody in this business, boyo.* The words came back to him again. He had never understood their real significance until this moment. Despite his dangerous occupation he had led a relatively safe life. There was always Gloria, and always Langley for him to turn to for help, for comfort, for understanding, and backing. Now the very people who had loved and trusted him, meant to hunt him down and kill him.

He could run, of course. He was an expert at hiding out. Somewhere in Europe, on a Greek island in the middle of nowhere, perhaps in the Caribbean. But how long could he stay hidden? Sooner or later they would catch up with him. If the Agency or the KGB wanted it badly enough they would find you. Too many people knew his habits, knew more importantly his failings. The old sage of the Company, Wallace Mahoney, had once lectured at the Farm that ". . . by your tradecraft shall you be known." Like so much in the Agency, the litany once learned dominated your life.

In Washington were the answers. But to whom could he turn now?

In this business you can't trust anybody . . . unless it's someone without an axe to grind.

But he needed answers, which meant he needed someone who knew . . . what?

He was drifting. His brain making associations, rejecting connections. Passing over names and places and dates.

Janos Sikorski. He was the man with the answers.

He sat forward. "We're going to Reston."

She looked at him again in the rearview mirror. "Reston?"

"It's on the way to Dulles."

"I know where it is," she said. "Why Reston? What's there?"

"Answers," he said. "I hope."

"You're crazy," she snapped. Her fear was being replaced by anger. "Why don't you let me take you to Langley?"

"Because someone is trying to kill me."

"Your wife included."

"Yes," McAllister said softly, the pain intensifying. "Just drive me to Reston."

"Then will you let me go?"
"We'll see."

Sikorski's house was actually a large cabin at the end of a long dirt road outside of Sunset Hills southeast of the town of Reston. It took them nearly an hour in the darkness to find the place. McAllister had only been here twice before. Once with his father about fifteen years ago, and a second time six years ago when Sikorski had retired from the Agency and he'd had the crowd up for what he called a "go to hell" party.

He'd come out of Poland in the summer of 1939, a couple of weeks before the Nazi invasion, where he'd set up shop with some of the other émigrés who were working with the British SIS. After the war he'd gone into semi-retirement—he'd had enough guns and fighting and killing to last ten lifetimes. But he'd been recruited in the late forties into the fledgling CIA by McAllister's father. For twenty-five years he had run the Agency's Records Section with an iron hand and a razor-sharp mind. It was said that whatever Sikorski *didn't* know wasn't worth knowing. McAllister hoped it was true.

"What is this place?" Stephanie Albright asked nervously as they bumped slowly down the very dark, very narrow lane. The trees grew very close on both sides of the road here, forming a canopy overhead.

"Turn off your headlights," McAllister ordered. He'd seen a flash of light at the end of the road.

"What?"

"Goddamnit, turn off your headlights. Now!"

She did as she was told, the road disappearing in front of them. She stabbed the brakes hard, bringing them to a sudden halt. "I can't see anything."

McAllister could. About fifty yards farther down the road he could just make out the dim lights from the cabin. This was close enough. There was no telling who could be waiting for him.

"Shut off the engine."

"What?" she cried, suddenly alarmed. Her face was twisted into a mask of fear.

McAllister brought the Walther over the back of the seat, pressing the barrel against her cheek. "I'm tired of arguing with you. Shut off the engine!"

"I don't want to die here like this," she moaned.

"Nor will you if you do as I say," McAllister said. "There's a cabin at the end of this road. Someone is there who I have to talk to. We're going to get out and walk down to it. Together. Now shut off the engine and give me the keys, and I promise I won't hurt you."

"Oh, God . . . oh, God . . ." she sobbed, but she did as he told her.

McAllister pocketed the keys, opened the side door and got out. At first he nearly collapsed, and he had to lean against the side of the van for support until he got his balance. Stephanie Albright was staring at him through the window.

He opened the door for her, and when she got out she stumbled against him, until he took her arm and together they started down the dirt road.

Sikorski's cabin was located in a narrow clearing at the edge of a steep wooded hill. In the distance to the north they could see the lights of the town of Reston. It was a scenic spot. An old Chevrolet pickup truck was parked at the side of the house beneath a carport. A light was on in the kitchen, the rest of the place was in darkness.

McAllister angled across the driveway to the opposite side of the cabin where he'd spotted the telephone line coming in. Reaching it, he yanked the wires out of the small junction box. Whatever happened next, help could not be so easily summoned.

Around front McAllister knocked on the door and then stepped aside, shoving Stephanie Albright forward. "If he asks, tell him that you've come from the Agency. There are some questions."

Moments later the front light came on. The door opened and Janos Sikorski was standing there. He was an old man, at least in his early seventies, with long, startlingly white hair, slack blue-gray skin that hung like a hound dog's pelt around his neck and jowls, and broad, coal-black eyes. He was dressed in an open-collar white shirt and iron-gray workman's trousers, slippers on his feet. "Hi-ho, my luck has just taken a bloody big turn for the better," he hooted, his accent, even after all these years, Polish, but his expressions British.

"Hello, Janos," McAllister said, stepping into the light before Stephanie Albright could speak.

The breath went out of the old man, and he staggered backward, grabbing the edge of the door so he wouldn't fall. His complexion had turned white. "You're a surprise, kid."

"I need some help," McAllister said.

"I'd guess you do," Sikorski replied. He shook his head wryly. "I'll take it back, the bit about my luck." His eyes strayed to the gun in McAllister's hand, and the blood over his neck and at his side. "You'd better come in, then, before you fall down."

The cabin was furnished pleasantly if rustically. There were a lot of books everywhere; on shelves, on the fireplace mantel, stacked in piles here and there, on chairs, on tables, on the floor in the corners.

"I've already taken care of the telephone line," McAllister said.

"Naturally," the old man replied. He eyed the woman. "What's with her?"

"He's kidnapped me," she said woodenly.

Sikorski shrugged, turning his attention back to McAllister. "So, kid, what brings you out here? You do remember that I'm retired. Six years now."

"I need some answers, Janos," McAllister said. He stood with his back to the door. The old man had moved across the room to stand in front of the fireplace. Stephanie stood to the right, near the entry to the kitchen. She looked like a frightened doe, ready to bolt at any moment.

"I don't know if I can help you. Have you talked to Highnote?"

"He thinks I'm a traitor."

Again Sikorski shrugged. "I've heard something about it. The Russkies gave you a pretty rough bash-up, in the Lubyanka. Lots of good people have fallen by the wayside."

"Drugs," McAllister said.

"I also heard that you wasted a couple of our boys up in New York this morning."

"I didn't do it."

"Have you talked to Gloria yet?"

McAllister nodded.

The old man's thick eyebrows rose. "I see," he said. "So what in bloody hell are you doing out here like this? I'm no doctor, though from what I can see you sure as hell are in need of one, nor is this the bloody monastery—no refuge from the Philistines here."

"Someone wants me dead, Janos, and I don't understand why. It's the Russians. I killed three of them in Arlington Heights a couple of hours ago. They'd been waiting for me to show up at Bob's."

"Pardon me, kid, if I seem a bit skeptical, but from what I understand the Russians are your pals. Too bad, 'cause your old dad was first rate, and I always thought you were too."

"Then why did I come out here?" McAllister snapped. He trusted Sikorski as his father had, from the very beginning. Totally unaffected by the partisan politics of the Hill,

Sikorski was the Rock of Gibraltar at Langley. Always had been. A man of rare judgment, insight, and honesty, was how he'd been described.

"You tell me," the old man said harshly.

McAllister slowly lowered his gun and slumped back against the door. He was exhausted, and he was seeing double again. It was becoming increasingly difficult for him to keep his thoughts in any semblance of order. He'd been operating on adrenaline for so long that he had very little strength left. He raised his head and looked at Sikorski. He was being given his hearing. It's all he had wanted from the start; simply to be listened to. If anyone could or would understand, it would be this one.

"I was arrested by the KGB in Moscow on October twenty-eighth," McAllister began, and in the retelling he was acutely aware of how little he could actually recall of his interrogation. Bits and pieces of his treatment, snatches of his conversations with Miroshnikov came back to him through his drug-hazed memories. But it wasn't enough. He could see in Sikorski's eyes that the old man was not believing him.

We're making progress and I feel very good about it, Miroshnikov said. And so should you. We have finally broken down the first barrier . . . really quite excellent.

How much had he told them? Perhaps Highnote had been correct after all, perhaps the Russians had sent him back to work as a double agent. But why then had they tried to kill him?

Sikorski was talking, but McAllister was finding it difficult to concentrate.

"Again, kid, why did you come here?" the old man asked, his voice rising.

Stephanie Albright had turned her head and was looking at something in the kitchen. She was shivering.

McAllister pushed himself away from the door, and stood there wavering on his feet, the gun held limply at his side.

His body seemed remote. Looking at Sikorski across the room it was hard to focus.

"Look to Washington. Look to Moscow. Zebra One, Zebra Two." They were Voronin's words. What did they mean?

Sikorski stepped forward, his entire manner changed, his face contorted into a mask of hate and fury. "What did you say?" he growled.

McAllister's stomach was turning over. "I heard it in Moscow. One of my madmen . . . I was working him. . . ."

"Who else have you spoken these words to?" Sikorski demanded, barely in control of his rage.

"Nobody . . ." McAllister started to say when he caught a movement out of the corner of his eye. He turned. Stephanie Albright had disappeared into the kitchen. "Wait," he shouted, when the kitchen lights went out, the only illumination now in the cabin from the flickering embers in the fireplace. Sikorski had stepped over to a cabinet, yanked open a drawer, and he was turning around, a big automatic in his hand. McAllister dove to the left, below the level of the couch between them, as the old man fired, the shot smacking into the thick wood of the door.

"Traitor!" Sikorski screamed in animal fury. "They'll give me a medal for your body!"

Stephanie Albright was outside, racing away from the kitchen door when she heard the shot, and moments later Sikorski's ragged cries. She wanted ' stop, but she was professional enough to understand that unarmed there wasn't a thing she could do for the old man. McAllister had to be stopped before he killed even more people.

As she ran full tilt back up the dirt road she fumbled in her pocket for the van's keys that she had lifted from McAllister when she'd stumbled against him. At that instant she had known that she had been closer to death than she'd ever been in her life. He hadn't felt a thing, but all the way up to the cabin, and inside as he was telling his insane lies, her heart had been in her throat.

Reaching the Toyota, she tore open the door, got in behind the wheel and started the engine. She had listened for more gunshots, but the cabin had been silent. Ominously silent. She imagined McAllister racing up the dark road behind her, crazy with rage.

It took her precious seconds in the darkness to get the van turned around on the narrow dirt track, and when she did she flipped on the headlights and floored the accelerator, dirt and gravel spitting out from behind the rear tires, as she careened toward the main road.

Her mind was racing to a dozen different possibilities. There wasn't enough time for her to drive all the way back into Washington. She needed to find a telephone. Immediately, before the monster got loose again. She fixed her thoughts on Reston. It was a town of about forty thousand. There would be a service station on the highway. A telephone. Help.

She found what she was looking for less than ten minutes later on the outskirts of town. Pulling off the highway she screeched to a halt in front of the pumps, shoved open the door and leaped out.

A young man in dark-blue coveralls came running out of one of the service bays, wiping his hands on a rag.

"This is an emergency!" Stephanie screamed, racing past him toward the office. "I need a telephone!"

The attendant came after her. "You need the cops?" he shouted.

She rushed behind the counter and picked up the telephone on the desk.

"Hey, you can't go back there . . ." the young man was saying, but Stephanie waved him off.

She dialed a Langley number which was answered on the

first ring. ''This is Albright,'' she said, forcing herself to calm down. ''McAllister is on the loose. Outside of Reston.''

''Stand by,'' the Security Section OD said with maddening calmness.

The attendant was staring at her, open-mouthed.

''Stephanie, is that you?'' Dexter Kingman, director of security, said.

''Yes,'' she cried in relief. ''I'm at a Texaco station just outside of Reston. McAllister brought me out to a cabin nearby. He spoke with an old man. Janos . . . something.''

''Sikorski,'' Kingman said. ''Where is he now?''

''When I left he was still with the old man. There was a gunshot.''

Kingman said something away from the telephone. When he came back he seemed out of breath. ''Are you all right, Stephanie?''

''I'm fine.''

''Stay where you are, we're on our way.''

Chapter 8

McAllister had been lying in a heap behind the couch for how long? He realized with a terrible start that he had no idea. The sudden movement and fall had jarred something in his head. He must have blacked out.

He still had the Walther, though. He tried to push himself over with his left hand, but his arm collapsed beneath him, his entire left side ablaze in pain. He could feel blood trickling down his side.

"Janos?" he called out.

There was no answer. The only sounds in the house were the crackling of the flames in the fireplace.

"Janos, let's talk," he called into the darkness. "It's not what you think. I swear to God. . . ."

There was a noise. Off to his right. In the kitchen. The scrape of something soft against the floor. Sikorski's slippers?

"Janos?" McAllister shouted, scrambling as best he could to his feet.

The kitchen door banged open.

McAllister tottered across the room as fast as he could make his legs work, his head spinning, his heart thumping raggedly in his chest. At the entryway into the kitchen he held up, listening for sounds, any sounds. There was something in the distance. Outside. Someone running.

Stepping around the corner, he rushed to the open kitchen door and stepped out into the night. At first he could make out nothing except the dark woods rising up from the clearing in front of the cabin, the dirt road leading back over the hill, and to the north the lights of Reston in the far distance. And then he saw Sikorski's frail form disappearing over the edge of the hill, his white hair flying behind him.

Standing in the darkness McAllister wavered, trying to decide what to do. It was hard to make his thoughts come straight. The old man had lived alone up here for the past six years. He almost certainly knew his way around these hills in the darkness. To go after him now like this would be to invite suicide. There would be any of a dozen places within a hundred yards of the cabin where Sikorski could stage an ambush.

He turned and staggered around to the front of the cabin, searching the darkness up the narrow dirt road. Stephanie had to be here someplace. She couldn't have gone far on foot. He patted his pocket where he had dropped the van's keys, but it was empty, as were his other pockets. The keys were gone. He still had her .32 automatic, but the keys were gone. He looked back toward the cabin. He hadn't dropped them. But how . . . ? Then it came to him. She had fallen against him getting out of the van. They had been in close contact with each other long enough for her to have stolen the keys.

Christ. A part of him had to admire her courage. She had taken a big risk. By now she could have reached a telephone. Other men would be coming. Professionals with orders to kill him. There would be no way out for him.

The fact of Sikorski's pickup truck parked under the carport suddenly penetrated. He'd been lucky so far, too lucky. There was no reason for it to hold much longer. It was possible that the old man had the keys in his pocket, or had placed them in some obvious spot in the house that could take minutes to find—minutes he did not have.

His luck held. The keys dangled from the ignition.

McAllister got painfully behind the wheel, pumped the gas pedal a couple of times and turned the key. The engine roared to life with a noisy clatter. Switching on the headlights—now was no time to run off the road in the darkness—he backed out of the carport, his left foot so numb that he jerked the clutch, nearly stalling the engine. His head was spinning badly, and it was becoming increasingly difficult for him to keep his head up, let alone see much more than faded double images.

Somehow he got the old truck straightened out and headed back up the dirt road. Time. He had to get as far away from this place as quickly as possible before his escape routes were completely cut off.

But where?

At the base of the hill he turned left on the secondary highway, away from Reston. Traffic was light, but each time he met an oncoming car the headlights temporarily blinded him, making it almost impossible to keep the truck in a straight line. Minutes later he passed under the Dulles Airport access road, and continued south into the Virginia countryside, traffic almost nonexistent now. He drove with the window down, and at one point he thought he could hear the sound of sirens, a lot of sirens, in the distance to the southeast toward Washington. He pulled over to the side of the road, shut off the truck's engine and lights, and stepped out, cocking his ear. It was there again, faintly on the night breeze. Sirens. And low in the sky toward the east, he thought he could pick out slow-moving lights, though it was hard for him to focus his eyes. Probably helicopters. They wanted him in a very big way, and once they understood he was gone the search would fan out.

He looked at his watch: It was nearly eleven. He had been running continuously since early this morning when the insanity had begun at JFK Airport in New York. There was nothing much left inside of him. He needed a place to hole up; a first-aid kit, food, and sleep, in that order. He climbed back into the truck, started the engine, flipped on the headlights and pulled up onto the highway.

He could see the glow of Washington to his left, fifteen miles away. The Potomac was between him and the city. That fact stuck in his mind. The river flowing south past Alexandria and Woodbridge and a dozen quaint little towns all the way down to the Chesapeake Bay had some significance for him at this moment.

Look for the anomalies. The irregularities. The bits and pieces that don't seem to fit the mold. Down those avenues you will find the answers.

The Potomac. A first-aid kit. Food. Rest. The river.

He was free-associating again. Each time, his thoughts came back to the river. Something about it, something remembered from a time past.

An afternoon of warmth in the sun. Drinks, food, good company. Gloria had scraped her knee on a deck fitting. They'd been on a boat, sailing down the river. Her knee had been inexpertly bandaged. They'd all laughed about it . . . especially Bob Highnote. She was called the *Merrilee*, and she was docked at a small marina somewhere south of the city.

In Dumfries. He remembered the name of the town now, because of the jokes they'd made about it, and about Gloria's silly accident.

By your tradecraft you shall be known. Do the unexpected. Run inward when they expect you to run away. It's the principle of the children's game: hide-the-thimble.

He desperately needed to rest. Even more important, he needed time to think, to reason it out. Sikorski's reaction to Voronin's cryptic words had been immediate and swift, lending a terrible credence to the message. At this point, he knew that his only hope for survival would be in unraveling its meaning. But it was only a slim hope.

A damp cold wind was blowing directly across the river raising whitecaps in the narrow bay that fronted the tiny town of Dumfries. McAllister had left the truck in a public parking lot a block from the Marina. He'd taken the tire iron from behind the seat, stuffed it in his belt beneath his coat, and walked back along the quay to the half-empty yacht haven. At this time of the year many of the owners had pulled their boats out of the water until spring, but there were still at least fifty vessels of all sizes and descriptions left. Halyards slapping in the wind against the aluminum masts of the sailboats set up a tinkling, almost musical racket. All the boats bobbed in the wavelets crossing the harbor.

The town was very quiet. He kept to the shadows as much as possible, and the occasional car that passed paid him no attention.

There was no security guard in the marina, and the dockmaster's office was closed. It took him less than five minutes to find Highnote's forty-five-foot sailboat securely tied between a pair of finger piers two-thirds of the way out from the main dock. He clambered silently aboard and huddled out of the wind at the main hatch, waiting for an alarm to be raised, for someone to come out of the darkness and demand to know what he was doing aboard.

But no one came. The marina was deserted.

He pulled the tire iron out of his belt, inserted it in the loop of the combination lock and yanked down with all of his strength, putting his weight into it. The lock held, but the hasp broke with a loud snap, the entire mechanism falling to the fiberglass deck with a huge clatter.

Again McAllister crouched in the darkness waiting for someone to investigate the commotion, but after a full minute he was satisfied that he had not been heard simply because there wasn't another soul in the place.

Below, he closed the hatch, made sure the curtains were tightly drawn over the windows, and searched for the electrical panel, finding it after a couple of minutes by feel. He turned on the battery switch, the cabin lights breaker, and then the small gooseneck light over the chart table, the interior of the big sailboat's salon suddenly bathed in a soft red glow.

His knees were shaking from fatigue. He had to hold on to the chart table for support until he could catch his breath. The simple action of walking one block and forcing his entry in here had completely drained what little strength he had left.

After a minute or so, he went looking for the first-aid kit, finding it in a cabinet in the forward head. It took him another ten minutes to find the valves for the propane stove (one of which was outside in a locker with the tanks), and put on some water to boil. Laying Highnote's Walther and Stephanie Albright's .32 automatic on the salon table, he took off his jacket and peeled off his blood-soaked shirt. The handkerchief had stuck to the wound in his chest, and he had to yank it off, blood oozing again out of the angry-looking hole. A huge bruise had formed on his shoulder and down his side, but he understood that he had been very lucky. Again. If he'd been hit just an inch farther to the right he would have been dead.

He soaked a big wad of paper towels with hydrogen peroxide from the first-aid kit and gingerly daubed both the entry and exit wounds in his side, and then the gash on his forehead.

Working carefully and deliberately because he could move no faster in his present condition, he pulled off long strips of adhesive tape from the roll, sticking them to the edge of the table, and then folded up two big squares of gauze from one of the sterile packets.

When the water was nearly at a boil, he soaked a clean towel and carefully washed both wounds, and then the rest of his side and chest, cleaning off as much of the crusted blood as he could reach.

When he'd dried off, the wounds were seeping quite a lot of blood, and it took him nearly a half an hour to daub disinfectant cream on the gauze pads and tape them in place, his fingers thick and numb, and his side so stiff and painful that when he moved wrong, he nearly passed out.

He began to hallucinate then as he forced himself to fix a packet of dried soup. His father helped him find a can of beer in the locker, and a package of crackers in another. He also found one of Highnote's old sailing sweaters.

The old man had not aged very much. He was still dressed in a natty houndstooth hunting jacket with a sweater vest beneath it and a silk cravat around his neck. But sitting across the table from him, McAllister could see that his mustache had begun to turn gray, and he wondered why his father wasn't wearing his uniform. He loved wearing it, and he loved being called *the general*.

He told a story while McAllister ate his soup.

"Back in the late forties we hosted a high-ranking British intelligence service officer in Washington. He was an expert on the Soviets and was a natural to set up the lines of liaison between the CIA and FBI on this side of the Atlantic, and the SIS and MI5 in England. We were just getting started in the business and he was a godsend. You know how it was, you read the histories. There was so much going on in those days none of us could understand, that the one hand didn't know what the other was doing. It was like drowning, let me tell you. The chap tossing out the life ring was the one to rally 'round. Problem was, of course, that this fellow was a hard one to fathom. Rather like the blind Indians and the elephant. The man cut a damned dashing figure in a tuxedo, flitting here and there to every Washington function. He was a socialite. But he also was a one-man blizzard with the paperwork and organization. He had our sections humming within six months of his arrival. He was a genius at administration. He was a friend of the U.S., too. Used to drop in on you any time of the day or night with one of his brainstorms for making whatever it was you happened to be doing, easier. He was sort of a repayment for all the years of lendlease. But finally he was a Russian spy. Sold us and the British down the river. For years this went on. And even up to the end his own people convinced Hoover to back down, close the files. Wasn't till he disappeared from his posting in Beirut in sixty-three and turned up big as life in Moscow, that we knew that side of him. But don't you see, Philby was all of those things . . . all at the same time . . . and more. He was just a man, though. Put his trousers on one leg at a time every morning just like the rest of us. Don't be blind, boyo, see it all, this time."

"Thank you," McAllister said out loud, but his father wasn't there.

He got up weaker than he imagined he was, and stumbled into the forward cabin where he fell into bed, his eyes closing immediately.

Look to Washington. Look to Moscow. Zebra One, Zebra Two. Voronin's words.

Traitor!

All the way back into town from Janos Sikorski's hilltop cabin, Stephanie Albright had been troubled by something. By words spoken . . . or, rather by a phrase not repeated.

"*Look to Washington. Look to Moscow. Zebra One, Zebra Two.*" McAllister's words, spoken in a pained whisper, almost as if he had been in a trance. She had heard them, and so had Sikorski. But the old man had not mentioned it. He had not said a thing about the exchange, or his reactions. McAllister had shown up with her in tow, had asked for help, and in the confusion Sikorski had grabbed a gun and opened fire. That was his *entire* story.

The FBI was involved now. An APB had been put out on the pickup truck McAllister had used for his escape. They'd find it sooner or later.

"Looks as if he's running to all his old pals," her boss, Dexter Kingman had said.

"Some friends," she'd murmured. The woods had been crawling with agents from the Bureau and from the Company's Office of Security. Three helicopters had been brought over from Andrews Air Force Base and were following the highways leading away from Reston.

"We're probably too late from this end," Kingman had said. "But he won't get far if he's in as bad a shape as you say he is. He's going to have to find a rat hole, some place to tend to his wounds. We'll find him."

Kingman was a big southerner with a barrel chest and a ruddy, outdoors complexion. He'd been trained as a psychologist, but had risen rapidly in Security to head the section. All of his people, Stephanie included, had a good deal of respect for him, though sometimes he tended to get a bit stuffy and overbearing.

"You were lucky, Stephanie," he said.

She looked up at him.

"He could have killed you. It's a wonder he didn't."

Yes, she thought, as she drove. It's a wonder he hadn't killed her. He could have, perhaps even should have. Once they had reached the dark woods above Sikorski's house he could have shot her and left her body somewhere off the road. They wouldn't have found her until morning, and perhaps not for days.

It would have made his escape much easier.

Nor had he killed the old man. Sikorski had admitted that McAllister had not returned his fire. Only the one shot, his own, had been fired. He had crawled into the kitchen and then had escaped down the hill into the woods.

"It doesn't make any sense to me," Kingman had told her just before she left. She was off duty. He was sending her home for a few hours' sleep.

"He kept saying that someone was trying to kill him, and that he needed the answers."

"I'd like a few answers myself," the security chief said, shaking his head. "We found his pals in Arlington Heights."

Stephanie looked at him. The place was crawling with Agency and Bureau people. They were alone for the moment, however, out of earshot from the others. "Russians?"

Kingman nodded. "A half a block from Highnote's house. All three of them dead. Wasn't a pretty sight from what I'm told. Two of them died of gunshot wounds, the other had his neck broken."

"Then why . . ." Stephanie started to ask the obvious question, but Kingman held her off.

"I don't know. But if we can take him alive, we might find out." He shook his head again. "It beats the hell out of me, Stephanie. It surely does."

She had an apartment in Alexandria which she shared with a girl from State. But instead of taking the Capital Beltway south, she stayed on the highway back into Washington, crossing the river on the Key Bridge into Georgetown. It was late, nearly one in the morning, and she was dead tired, but not the least bit sleepy. Her mind was seething with a dozen conjectures. Something about McAllister, his manner, his actions, the words he had spoken, disturbed her. He hadn't acted like the demented agent turned double she'd been led to believe he was. He'd acted more like . . . what? A terribly confused man who was desperately seeking something. A solution to some deadly riddle.

And what about the Russians in Arlington Heights? He'd told the truth about that much at least.

Looks as if he's running to all his old pals, Kingman had said. *He's going to have to find a rat hole someplace to tend to his wounds.*

Traffic was almost nonexistent on 31st, but when she'd turned down Avon Place she was stopped by a Washington PD roadblock and had to show her Agency identification.

"Your people are inside," the cop said, passing her through.

She parked across the street from McAllister's house and went inside. Two Bureau agents wearing baseball caps and dark-blue windbreakers, FBI stenciled in yellow on the back, were talking with Hollis Winchester, one of the Agency's security officers.

"Any word yet?" he asked when she came in.

"I just came from Reston. He's still on the loose." She glanced toward the head of the stairs. "She still upstairs?"

"Mr. Highnote came for her an hour ago."

Stephanie looked at him. The news was bothersome to her, yet she couldn't really say why. It just struck her as odd that the deputy director of operations should be taking a personal hand in caring for the wife of an agent gone bad. A killer. A traitor. But then she'd had a rough night. She wasn't thinking straight. What was she doing here anyway?

"I'm going up for a minute," she said.

"Anything I should know about?" Winchester asked, his eyes narrowing. The Bureau agents were looking at her.

"No," Stephanie said tersely, and she went upstairs.

All the lights in the house were on, which also struck her as odd. Gloria McAllister had cooperated with them completely. They'd hastily gone through the house searching for anything that might help them track down her husband. A half a dozen technicians had come over from Technical Services and had taken the place apart this morning . . . yesterday morning, actually. But they'd found nothing and had left by early afternoon. Everyone was gone. Why the lights?

It was obvious at first glance that the place had been searched, though Gloria had made an attempt to straighten up. The living room was furnished pleasantly modern with a white couch and loveseat, glass and brass tables, some artwork on the textured walls, and a lot of books and bric-a-brac from all over the world. The McAllisters had done a lot of traveling; this place had been their home base. It was a refuge, the thought came unbidden to Stephanie. As was Gloria a refuge. It's why McAllister had come here, even though he had to know that his house would be watched. What a shock it must have been for him when Gloria had turned on him.

She moved through the living room, passing the bookshelves, glancing at some of the titles, at the bits and pieces from the McAllisters' lives: a handmade vase that looked Greek and very old, a brass sailboat on a polished granite base, an elaborate wax figure of a medieval wizard, a beer stein with a silver hinged lid, and several photographs in acrylic frames . . . smiling faces, happy times with friends . . . winter scenes, summer scenes on the water.

In the kitchen two coffee cups, a spoon, and a coffee pot sat upside down on the drain board. Gloria had rinsed them out before she'd gone off with Highnote. Stephanie stared at them. Everything was striking her as odd now. It was the lateness of the hour, and the ordeal she'd gone through. *You're lucky. . . . He could have killed you. . . . It's a wonder he didn't.*

The woman had shot at her husband. She had wounded him. She had screamed at him. Called him a traitor. And then she had come back here and rinsed out her coffee things.

Looks as if he's running to all his old pals.

First Robert Highnote. Next his wife. Then Janos Sikorski. Where was he going next?

He's going to have to find a rat hole someplace . . . tend to his wounds.

Stephanie turned suddenly and hurried back to the bookshelves in the living room. To the photographs. To one in particular.

She took it down from the shelf and stared at it. The McAllisters were seated in the cockpit of what appeared to be a large sailboat. Gloria had a clumsy bandage on her knee. Highnote was just coming through the hatchway with three glasses of wine, a big grin on his face. They were tied up at a dock, and whoever was taking the picture was standing off to the side. On the opposite side of the slip was a big signboard attached to a piling. She could just read the words. DUMFRIES YACHT HAVEN. She knew the place.

A rat hole? A place to hole up, to tend to his wounds?

The boat rocked and settled very slightly to port. The motion was subtly different from the wave-induced movements. An anomaly. McAllister opened his eyes, for just a moment disoriented.

Someone had gotten aboard the boat. As the cobwebs cleared he could hear the very slight scuffling of shoe leather on the fiberglass deck. Whoever was above was taking great pains to move in silence.

McAllister sat up, the sudden movement causing a wave of dizziness and nausea to pass through him, sweat popping out on his forehead. They had found him. Somehow they had tracked him here.

Christ, was there no peace?

They'd spotted the truck, of course. And he had forgotten to turn off the light over the chart table. The conclusions were obvious. Check all the possibilities. His tradecraft is good. Expect the unexpected with him.

McAllister started to crawl out of the V-berth. The guns were in the salon on the table. The main hatch suddenly slid open and the figure of a man was outlined in the opening.

No time now! He reared back and frantically undogged the Lexan hatch just over the bed. It sprung open with a crash at the same moment thc man at the main hatch fired.

"Watch out," someone shouted.

McAllister levered himself out of the hatch onto the foredeck, mindless of the damage he was doing to his wounds. The night wind was suddenly terribly cold.

He started to turn when two more silenced shots were fired, the first catching him in his side, and the second slamming into his head, the impact sending him backward. The lifeline caught his legs just above the knees and he flipped over, plunging into the river, the dark swirling waters closing over him, a billion stars bursting in his eyes.

Chapter 9

The sounds of the silenced shots were clearly recognizable for what they were, even at a distance of twenty-five yards.

A moment later McAllister fell into the river with a loud splash.

Stephanie Albright stepped back into the shadows behind the dockmaster's office at the end of the quay, hardly able to believe what she had just witnessed. *Watch out,* the one in the cockpit had shouted, in English. These were no Russians. The two of them held a hurried conference on the boat, then one of them went below while the other moved slowly up the length of the deck, searching the water.

Stephanie had no gun. But even if she had been armed she didn't think she would have gone in and opened fire.

The boat light went out, and the first man came up from below and closed the hatch. He joined the other man searching the water.

After a minute or so they both climbed up on the dock and began searching the water on both sides, between the other boats, along each finger pier, and even beneath the dock, getting down on their hands and knees.

They worked quickly and efficiently. Watching them,

Stephanie knew that they were professionals. But from where? The Agency or the Bureau?

We don't work this way. We don't shoot people in cold blood. She'd seen McAllister's hands when he'd come up through the forward hatch. He'd not been armed, yet they had shot him.

After a long time, the two men said something else to each other, then holstered their weapons and headed back up the dock without a backward glance. They passed within ten feet of where Stephanie had edged around to the opposite side of the small building, and then crossed the street and got into a dark Ford Thunderbird. She had spotted the car parked on the street when she'd come in, but she had attached no significance to its presence. Other cars were parked nearby, and the plates were not of any government series that she knew of.

They left, making a U-turn and heading back toward the Washington highway, their job finished.

McAllister was dead. There could be little doubt of it, he'd been hit at least once in the head. She'd seen that much very clearly.

She stepped out from behind the dockmaster's building, walked to the end of the dock and looked out across the narrow bay. The wind was biting cold, raising whitecaps on the dark water. He was dead, so what was she doing here like this? Turn around and go home, get some sleep. Forget about it.

Something is going on here that you don't know about, something that you are not supposed to know about, something that you don't *want* to know about.

Yet she had just witnessed a murder. It was her job . . . her duty to report what she'd seen. Telephone Kingman, tell him everything, including why she had come down here. She cursed her own stupidity, but it was happening so fast, it was so unexpected.

She looked down at how the water swirled around the

dock pilings. It was the river current, eddying here in the narrow bay. Sweeping everything out toward the Chesapeake Bay and beyond to the ocean.

Stephanie's thoughts stopped in mid-stride. Everything would be swept downriver. At least as far as the south side of the bay. Everything. Everybody . . .

But he was dead, she thought as she hurried back off the central dock, then over to the next pier south. The two professionals who had tracked him here and shot him had been certain enough of their work to leave after only a cursory search. They knew what they were doing. They had fired at him from a distance of less than twenty feet. Impossible to miss. Impossible to be misled into believing he was dead.

At the end of the pier, she flopped down on her stomach and hung way over the edge so that she could see along the line of pilings. The choppy water was barely two feet beneath the bottom of the dock. Even if he had somehow survived the gunshot wound to his head, he would have been knocked unsconscious, and surely would have drowned by now. The water was very cold. Hypothermia would make it impossible to move his arms and legs so that he could stay afloat.

She scrambled to her feet and rushed back to the quay and out the final pier to the south. Halfway to the end she heard a soft groan under the dock. She dropped to her hands and knees and looked over the edge.

McAllister, blood streaming into his eyes from a wound in the side of the forehead just at the hairline, was clinging to one of the fat wooden pilings just behind a low-slung power boat, its big outboard motor tilted up out of the water. His mouth was opening and closing, his eyes fluttering.

"McAllister. Can you hear me?" Stephanie called softly.

He reared back as if he were going to try to swim away from her voice, and he lost his grip on the piling, his head sinking beneath the water.

"Oh, God," Stephanie cried. She scrambled down into the back of the powerboat, and was about to jump into the water when McAllister's head surfaced a couple of feet away, pushed closer to the boat by the current.

She grabbed a handful of his sweater and hauled him closer.

"No," he mumbled. "Enough . . . no more . . . please . . ."

"It's all right," Stephanie said, pulling him around the motor to the boat's swim platform just at the water level. "You've got to help me. I don't think I can pull you out of the water myself."

"No," McAllister mumbled, trying to pull away from her. "Go away . . . leave me alone . . . they'll come back . . . impossible . . ."

Stephanie managed to get him turned around, his back to the boat, and bracing her legs against the transom heaved with all of her might, getting him into a sitting position on the teak grating of the low swim platform.

"Put your arm up here," she said, pulling his right arm up over the edge of the transom. She climbed over the back of the boat onto the swim platform with him, the water coming up over her ankles. She pulled his legs out of the freezing water, and then turned his body around so that his right side was up against the back of the boat.

"Pull yourself up," she said, heaving his body over the edge. "Now," she grunted with an effort. "Pull."

He did as she told him, finally, and with a sudden heave he was up over the back of the boat, and tumbled loosely into the open cockpit, blood everywhere from his wounds.

Stephanie clambered back onto the dock and hurried back to the quay, then across the street to the next block where she had parked the Toyota. So far her luck was holding. The streets were deserted at this hour. Only the local police would be out and around. Sooner or later they would be cruising past. If they spotted her, she had no idea what she would say to them.

She got the van started and drove back down to the marina, backing up to the quay, and dousing her lights, but leaving the engine running.

Just a few minutes longer, she told herself jumping out. She opened the side door, then glancing both ways up the street, hurried back onto the dock.

McAllister had come around again, and by the time she reached him, he had somehow managed to pull himself up on the back of the boat, and was halfway up onto the dock.

"You," he said looking up when she reached him.

"I'm going to get you out of here," Stephanie said, pulling him the rest of the way up.

"Why . . . ?" he mumbled. "Why are you doing this . . . ?"

"I don't know," she said, helping him to his feet and starting back to the van. "I just don't know . . . yet."

McAllister's first conscious thoughts were of a dry, stationary bed, blankets covering him, warmth, and of bandages around his head, and tightly binding the wounds in his side. There had been lights and voices and movements around him, but he wasn't at all sure he hadn't been dreaming that part.

He was in a small bedroom, with a sloping ceiling. He could see city lights outside the single window. It was night.

"How do you feel?" a voice came at him from the left.

McAllister turned his head as an older man with a kindly face and a thin, hawk nose came from the door. "Weak. Hungry, I think."

"That's good," the man said. He wore thick, horn-rimmed glasses that made his eyes seem huge and vulnerable behind the lenses.

"Where am I?" McAllister asked. His voice sounded distant to him.

"Baltimore," the man said. He'd been carrying a white enameled tray. He put it on the table next to the bed, and did something with the bandages at McAllister's head. His touch was gentle.

"Are you a doctor?"

"In a manner of speaking. I'm a veterinarian. Nicholas Albright. Stephanie's father."

McAllister tried to digest that news. The last thing he could remember was the boat . . . Highnote's sailboat in Dumfries . . . and then the shots, and the cold, dark water. "What am I doing here?"

Albright smiled gently. "Stephanie brought you here." He shook his head. "She's been doing that all her life. Bringing home hurt strays. Though I must say you're her biggest find to date."

"How long . . . ?"

"Three days."

It seemed impossible. McAllister pushed the covers aside and tried to get up, but the doctor gently held him down.

"You're not going anywhere for a while yet, Mr. McAllister. Even if you could get out of this bed, which I doubt, you wouldn't get ten feet with your injuries. In fact by rights you should be dead. Most men don't take well to bullets in the skull."

"The Agency . . . the Bureau . . ."

"You're safe here," Albright said. "Get some rest now, Stephanie should be home soon."

It was still dark when McAllister awoke again. He had a feeling that it was very late at night, though why he felt that he didn't know. He turned his head. Stephanie Albright was asleep, curled up in a big easy chair in the corner by the door. She was dressed in blue jeans and a sweatshirt, her features softened by the tiny night light on the bureau.

The house was very quiet. Outside in the distance he thought he could hear a siren. But then he remembered that he was in Baltimore, and like any big city, Baltimore was never completely quiet.

Pushing back the covers he sat up. The dizziness was gone, as was the double vision. He felt much better than he had earlier, though he was still terribly weak, and there was a deep, hollow feeling in the pit of his stomach.

He glanced back over at Stephanie. She had awakened, and she was looking at him, her eyes blinking.

"Your father is quite a man," McAllister said.

"Yes, he is."

"If you'll get me my clothes, I'll leave. It's too dangerous for him and you with me here."

"You're in no shape to be going anywhere yet," she said.

"If I have to do it on my own, I will."

"No," Stephanie said. "No one suspects a thing. They all think you're dead."

McAllister stared at her. "They?"

"Langley. My boss, Dexter Kingman, and your boss, Mr. Highnote."

"How?"

"They found Sikorski's truck, and they found the blood all over Mr. Highnote's sailboat, and the powerboat where you'd evidently tried to pull yourself out of the river, and then fell back in. The search has spread all the way down to Norfolk."

"How did you know I was at the boat?"

"Just a guess. I saw the photograph on your bookshelf."

"Why haven't you turned me in?" McAllister asked. "I don't understand."

"Neither do I," she said after a long hesitation. "But you're not a killer. You should have killed me and Sikorski when you had the chance, but you didn't."

"I'm a traitor."

She shook her head. "You don't believe that, and I don't think I do either."

"What then?"

"I think you stumbled onto something in Moscow that has a lot of people scared silly. Something that no one at Langley is talking about. Something even Sikorski omitted when he gave his report."

"Go ahead," McAllister prompted.

"Everything was fine with Sikorski at first. He was willing to listen to you, I think, until you whispered something. It made him crazy."

"You heard?"

She nodded. "But I had no idea what it meant then, nor do I have any idea now. But before I go poking around records, I thought I'd better talk to you about it."

"About what?" McAllister asked carefully. "What exactly was it you think you heard?"

" '*Look to Washington. Look to Moscow. Zebra One, Zebra Two.*' What's it supposed to mean?"

There it was, the same words again. He could see Voronin's frail, crippled figure seated in his chair. He could hear the words coming from the man's lips; slurred but clearly understandable. Cadence and syntax, not the insane ramblings of a drunken, bitter old man.

"I wish I knew," he said, shaking his head. "I just know that within a half an hour after hearing those words I was arrested by the KGB."

Stephanie got up and came across the room. She sat on the foot of the bed, and looked into his eyes. "I think you'd better tell me everything, Mr. McAllister. From the beginning. Maybe we can figure it out together."

"I've got to ask you again: Why are you doing this?"

"And I've got to tell you again: I don't know."

"It's very dangerous for you and your father."

"I know."

"Maybe I am a traitor. Maybe I was brainwashed, my mind altered. They had me at the Lubyanka for more than a month. It's certainly possible."

"The three Russians you said you killed in Arlington Heights were found," Stephanie said.

"So I'm a double gone bad."

She shook her head. "The two men who tried to kill you on the sailboat were Americans. I heard them speak."

"Everyone is after me," McAllister said bitterly. "Including my wife."

Stephanie's eyes were wide and serious. Her lips compressed. "I think you'd better start at the beginning. Tell me everything, every single thing that you can remember, from the moment you heard those words, until right now."

"And then?"

"Then we'll try to figure out a way of keeping you alive."

Part Two

Chapter 10

The coming days were difficult for McAllister and doubly difficult for Stephanie. He was on the mend, but it was going to take some time before he would be fully mobile. Each day he could feel his strength coming back. Each day he pushed himself to the limit with his exercises, often falling into the narrow bed totally exhausted from the effort, his body bathed in sweat.

Stephanie had to arise each morning before dawn so that she would have enough time to drive down to Washington to go to work. The questions about her kidnapping and escape from McAllister had finally stopped, and she'd been allowed to return to her routine of background checks on prospective Agency employees, but she had to constantly watch herself, lest she make a slip of the tongue.

She'd offered only the vaguest of explanations for her absence to her roommate, but the girl was too busy with her own life to pay any real attention. "Have a good time, Steph, whoever *he* is," she'd said.

In the evenings they talked. Hesitantly at first, feeling each other out, learning about the other's background, their likes and dislikes, their fears, their hopes. McAllister still wasn't sure exactly why she was doing what she was doing, but he was grateful. Without Stephanie and her father he knew that he could not have possibly survived. He owed them his life.

"Let's just say that what I was seeing didn't add up to what I was hearing," she said. "It was the look on your face when your wife called you a traitor. I can't explain it, but it wasn't the look of a spy. And you should have shot me that night. You didn't."

"Not very scientific," he said.

She smiled. "My father said the same thing to me."

"Does he realize the danger he's in?"

Stephanie nodded, her expression serious again. "He's not particularly proud of what I do for a living. He always thought that I'd become a vet and take over his practice some day."

"No brothers or sisters?"

She shook her head. "Just the two of us."

"What about your mother?"

"She died when I was in college." Stephanie looked toward the dark window. "I dropped out of school and came back here to help out. But it didn't last a year before he made me go back." She shook her head. "He was so lost in those days. But he was right, of course."

"What about afterward?" McAllister asked.

"I got my degree in psychology and joined the air force as a second lieutenant, exactly what every veterinarian's daughter does with her life."

She laughed, the sound gentle, almost musical, and McAllister had to smile with her.

She was given a top-secret crypto-access security clearance, and spent her four years' service career running background investigations on young enlistees. She got to travel all over the country, as often as not in civilian clothes, working with local FBI offices and police departments. She got to know a lot of good people. Interesting, if not always exciting work, until she fell in love, and her world was suddenly turned inside out.

"He was a captain, my section chief; very tall, very handsome, and very, very married," she said wistfully. "Sap that I was, I actually believed that he was going to leave his wife for me."

"It didn't work out?" McAllister asked gently.

"No," she said tersely. She looked at McAllister. "I was going to reenlist, we were going to get married as soon as his divorce was final, and we were going to see the world together, courtesy of Uncle Sam." She shook her head again. "Instead I resigned my commission and came back here to my father, and worked in the clinic for a year."

"Until you were hired by the Agency?"

She nodded. "I knew Dexter Kingman from my University of Maryland days. I'd worked with him a couple of times while I was in the Air Force, too. It was he who approached me, asked if I wanted a job."

"No regrets?"

She smiled wanly. "A lot of regrets, but then who doesn't have them?"

The Office of Security were the paper pushers, she said, though she was given the short course out at the Farm shortly after she'd been hired.

"I wasn't very good on the small-arms range, even though I did learn one end of the gun from the other." She smiled. "It came as quite a shock to me when Dexter handed me a pistol and assigned me to the team watching your house."

McAllister's gut tightened. Their conversations had been leading up to this point, and now that they had arrived she seemed nervous, less sure of herself than before, almost hesitant. Gloria had called out her name on the stairs. They'd obviously spoken during that day. "I'm sure it was a shock to you. What about my wife?"

"What about her?"

"Was she surprised when you showed up on her doorstep?"

"No. Mr. Highnote had set up the surveillance."

"She was to be used as bait."

Stephanie nodded glumly. "They figured you'd be showing up at home sooner or later. But I never dreamed that she would pull out a gun . . . that it would turn out the way it did."

"Neither did I," McAllister said looking away, the pain of the memory every bit as hurtful as his wounds, in some respects even more so because he had no idea how he could heal that particular hurt.

They had both spent a great deal of time talking about the distant past, and the very immediate present, but had until now scrupulously avoided any discussion of the future. McAllister was presumed dead. His body would show up sooner or later somewhere downriver. And yet there seemed, to Stephanie, to be an undercurrent running through the Agency.

"A lot of people are walking around on eggshells," she said.

"Such as?"

"Mr. Highnote, for one."

"He's a good man," McAllister said. "He's been caught in the middle."

Stephanie started to say something, but then evidently changed her mind. She got up from where she'd been sitting and went to the window. It was nearly midnight. Traffic below had settled down, but it had begun to snow lightly. Winter had finally arrived.

"What is it?" he asked, watching her back. Her hair was pinned up, her neck long and thin, her ears tiny and delicate.

"I don't know," she said after a long time. "There's something not quite right. Something about . . ."

"He's been my friend for a lot of years."

"Everyone talks *around* that night at his sailboat," she said. "The official word is that the Russians killed you, though how they traced you there is anyone's guess."

"But they weren't Russians."

"No," Stephanie said, turning back. "They definitely were not."

"Then who?"

On the afternoon of the fifth day, McAllister got dressed and went downstairs to the kitchen in the rear of the big house. The surgery was in the front of the house, in what used to be the living room–dining room–library area so he had been assured that there was no risk of being spotted should he come down.

The house was located downtown, just a half a dozen blocks up from the bayfront, in what used to be a terribly run-down neighborhood, but that was now becoming a charming place to live and work. "The Yuppies have discovered Front Street," Nicholas Albright said.

He'd run his small-animal practice out of this house for nearly twenty-five years, and at this stage of his life was disinclined to move out into the countryside. In any event, the suburbs were now starting to move in to him, and his practice was thriving.

McAllister made himself a sandwich and opened a bottle of beer. He was seated at the big table when Nicholas Albright came in, smelling of disinfectant, a little blood on the side of his short white lab coat.

"I see my two-legged patient is up and about. How are you feeling today?"

"Caged."

"I have a few of those out back, that is if you want to change your accommodations."

"No thanks," McAllister said. "But I'm going to have to get out of here pretty soon. Am I fit to travel?"

Albright looked at him critically. "How do you really feel?"

"Tired. A little weak and sore, but better than I did when I first got here, thanks to you."

"If you were a dog, I'd say go out for a short walk in

the sun—on a leash—maybe piss on a few fire hydrants, then come back and sleep in front of the fireplace. But you're not a dog, and I'm not a people doctor, but I do know that five days ago you were damned near dead. Discounting the bullet wounds and the subsequent loss of blood, whoever smacked you on the back of the head meant to do you a great deal of damage . . . and managed, in a manner of speaking, to accomplish just that. You're still suffering, to one degree or another, from a concussion, and I can't guarantee that your vision won't go double on you whenever it feels like it. Nor can I say that you won't simply collapse in the middle of the street somewhere if you push yourself too hard."

"Thanks for the words of encouragement."

"Those are the good parts, Mac," Albright said. "Seriously, you should have a nice long R and R someplace in the sun, for at least six weeks. Have a checkover by a real doctor."

"I don't have the six weeks."

"No."

"I'm putting you and your daughter in danger by being here like this."

Albright nodded. "Yes, you are. But if you haven't learned by now, I'll let you in on a little secret: Stephanie gets what Stephanie wants. And at this moment you are the object of her . . . interests."

"What did she tell you about me . . . about the situation?" McAllister asked.

Albright held him off. "Nothing, and that's more than I want to know. Stay if you will, go if you must, but be honest with my daughter. She's in danger, you say, so tell her everything so that she'll know exactly what she's up against." He smiled wanly. "She's no longer a little girl, you know. She's grown into a very strong, very capable woman."

"I know," McAllister said softly.

* * *

Two days later Stephanie brought him a gun. It was Friday and she had the weekend off. When she came in, she laid the bundle on the table by the window where McAllister had been sitting reading the newspapers.

"Anything?" she asked.

"Nothing," he said, glancing at the package wrapped in brown paper. "What's this?"

"It's for you," she said. "I borrowed it from a friend. Told him I was tired of being kidnapped off the streets."

The instant McAllister picked up the package he knew what was inside. He opened it. The gun was a German P38, 9 mm with two loaded clips of ammunition. The weapon was old, but seemed to be in very good condition. He worked the well-oiled slide back and forth a couple of times, then looked up.

"A discreet friend?"

"Very," she said. "We were lovers for nearly a year. He still has a thing for me."

"He's in the Agency?"

She nodded.

"Would I know him?"

"His name is Doug Ballinger. He works in town for Technical Services."

McAllister had never heard the name. "You're sure he won't mention this to anyone? If it got out somebody might put two and two together and come up with your father's name."

"It's a risk I'm willing to take," she said. "Besides, he won't say anything. Not Doug."

"I'm going to have to get out of here."

"I know, Dad said you were starting to make rumbling noises."

"I'll need a car."

"That can be arranged."

"Something that can't be traced here."

"I can do it," Stephanie said. "The question is, where are you going?"

"I have a couple of ideas."

"Such as?"

"You're not included," McAllister said firmly. "Someone is trying to kill me, and Langley thinks I'm a traitor. To this point you're not publically involved. The moment they know that you're helping me, however, you will become their next target."

"I can handle it . . ." Stephanie started to protest, but McAllister held her off.

"Probably. But I don't think I can. If they grabbed you it would make me vulnerable."

"I wouldn't tell them anything," she flared.

"You might not be given that choice," he said softly.

Her eyes went round, but she said nothing for the moment.

Get out . . . traitor! Go back to your Russian friends. Get out before I kill you myself.

What had Gloria been told? God . . . it didn't make any sense.

McAllister got up and went to the nightstand where he'd left his cigarettes. He lit one, drawing the smoke deeply into his lungs.

Look to Washington. Look to Moscow.

He'd been to Moscow, and now it was time to continue looking to Washington. The answers were down there somewhere. At Langley, most likely . . . or at least he found himself hoping that the answers, if they could be found, would be contained to Langley, and that the sickness hadn't contaminated another institution . . . let's say the Pentagon. That thought was too frightening to contemplate.

"Was Voronin to be trusted?" Stephanie asked.

McAllister turned to her—out of his thoughts. "At first he was."

"But not later?"

"I wasn't sure. I was starting to have my doubts about him."

"In fact, you told me that you were finished with him on the night you were arrested."

"I thought he was talking gibberish."

"And the Russians never asked you about it? About what you were doing out so late?"

"No."

"Didn't that strike you as odd?"

Odd? he thought. At first it had, but then later his body had been so filled with drugs that he'd begun to distrust his own thoughts, his own sanity even. The only reality for him then was the present; whether he was being beaten or being questioned, there had been no past or future, only the present.

"Maybe they didn't consider it important," he heard himself saying.

"Or so important that they didn't want to give it validity by questioning you, therefore putting it in the record."

"That doesn't make any sense."

"Maybe they already had the answers."

"Then why was I released?"

"Maybe to do exactly what you've done; come back to Washington and look for answers."

McAllister ran a hand over his eyes. "Answers, hell, I don't even know the questions. They were Russians in Arlington Heights."

"And Americans in Dumfries. Perhaps it's a fight between two factions. And perhaps you *do* know the questions."

"Look to Washington. Look to Moscow," he repeated the words softly.

"A man in Moscow and one in Washington? An agent and his controller? It's possible, isn't it?"

"Which would mean that I was released to come back here and dig them out."

"They'd try to stop you, of course, 'Zebra One and Two.' They'd have to protect themselves. The Russian controller sent his people after you, and his American agent has done the same thing."

"Yet whoever signed the order releasing me had to have a certain amount of power himself. A position within the KGB."

"Maybe the man trying to stop you is even more powerful," Stephanie said, her eyes alight. "Maybe your release was a mistake on his part. A lapse of concentration. Maybe you just fell through the cracks, and by the time he realized what was happening, he arranged for the two hit men to meet your plane in New York."

"They would have shot me first."

"You're not thinking logically, Mac. You were unarmed. Their first job would have been to eliminate the firepower. They hadn't counted on you reacting so quickly. And when it began to fall apart they got out of there. If they had been captured it would have blown everything."

"For someone who can't shoot straight, you have a devious mind."

She shook her head. "Not deviousness, just logic. Which leads us back to Langley, and who is the most likely candidate."

"Bob Highnote," McAllister said it before she could.

She nodded. "The three Russians were waiting for you outside his house. And the two Americans came to you at Highnote's boat."

"It's too pat."

"Highnote ordered the surveillance on your house. He must have told your wife something to make her react the way she did."

"Still too pat. I've known Bob for years. He wanted me to come to Langley with him that night. He said that we could have straightened everything out."

"Do you think you would have made it that far?"

"Not Highnote," McAllister said with finality, though he had begun to harbor the same thought at the back of his mind. Impossible, wasn't it, to know someone for so long and yet not really know them? Kim Philby had been everyone's best friend for years, the perfect spy, and yet in the end he'd turned out to be a Russian agent.

"I think you're going to need some help, Mac," Stephanie said. "Someone on the inside. A sympathetic ear."

"You?"

She inclined her head. "For a start."

"The answers are at Langley," he said.

"Yes. We just have to keep you alive long enough to find them."

One of the answers came that night a few minutes after eleven. McAllister was alone in his own room, trying to sleep, but his mind was seething. Over the years Highnote had been more than a friend; he had been a mentor, a confidant, a never-ending source of information and support. To believe that he was a traitor was impossible.

In the morning he would take the car that Stephanie had promised to get for him down to Washington where he would set up in a small, out-of-the-way hotel. From there he would again approach his old friend and lay everything out for him. If Highnote was a mole, it would show up in his eyes.

Zebra One, Zebra Two. Was it possible that Highnote was Zebra One? All these years?

The bedroom door crashed open, and in the light spilling in from the hallway Stephanie's figure was outlined through the thin nightgown she wore. Her face was animated.

"It's happening now. On the news," she said excitedly.

McAllister sat up. "What?"

"Hurry, or you'll miss it."

He got out of bed and hurried after her to her room at the end of the corridor. She stood in front of the television set, a stern-faced newscaster reading a story.

"What is it?" McAllister asked.

"Listen," Stephanie shot back, motioning for him to keep silent.

". . . sentenced today in U.S. District Court in Washington to life imprisonment," the newsman was saying.

A photograph of a husky man with graying dark hair and a neatly trimmed beard appeared on the screen.

"O'Haire, along with his younger brother, U.S. Air Force Captain Liam O'Haire, and seven others pled guilty last month to charges that they operated a spy ring for the Soviet government. Calling themselves the Zebra Network, the O'Haires stole Star Wars data which they passed over to an as-yet-unnamed Soviet contact in Washington. . . ."

"There," Stephanie said softly.

McAllister was staring at the television set, the newscaster's words flowing around him. *Look to Washington. Look to Moscow. Zebra One, Zebra Two.* Was this what Voronin had meant to tell him? The Zebra Network passing its secrets to a contact here in Washington who in turn was pumping it to Moscow?

But the network had been smashed. It was over.

Or, was it?

"I should have known," Stephanie was saying. "When I heard the words, there was something at the back of my head. It was as if I had a memory that I couldn't quite put my finger on. Until just now."

"The answers are still in Washington," McAllister said.

"You bet. Their 'as-yet-unnamed Soviet contact,' and I'll bet anything that it's Robert Highnote, our deputy director of operations."

"No," McAllister said. "That I can't believe. Not yet."

Stephanie turned down the television sound and looked at him. "I'm telling you that you'd better go easy with him until you know for sure. Whoever is Zebra One—whether or not it's Highnote—is going to do everything in his power to protect himself. Friend or not, if it is him he won't hesitate a second to kill you."

McAllister's thoughts were ranging far ahead. "If I surface, whoever he is, he'll have to come after me."

"That's right," Stephanie agreed, her eyes narrowing.

"For the moment everyone thinks I'm dead."

She nodded.

"It's time then, to show them otherwise."

"Don't be stupid. . . ."

"When I surface, all hell is going to break loose. And while that's going on, I'll be getting the information we need to expose him. Whoever he is."

"Robert Highnote or not?"

"Right," McAllister said.

Stephanie had stepped a little closer, and McAllister suddenly became aware of the fact that they were alone together in her bedroom, and that she was dressed in nothing more than a thin, almost translucent nightgown and he in a pair of her father's pajama bottoms. She reached out for him, but he stepped back.

"No," he said softly.

She started to protest, but then backed down, letting her hand fall to her side. "I understand," she said. "I do."

It was morning and the snow that had begun in the night was still falling, lightly blanketing the city of Washington. The husky man in the charcoal-gray overcoat and dove-gray fedora stood just within the main hall of the Lincoln Memorial, his hands folded behind him, staring up at the inscription on the wall behind the statue.

In this temple, as in the hearts of the people for whom he saved the Union, the memory of Abraham Lincoln is enshrined forever.

This was his favorite place in all of the city. It reminded

him, in many respects, of Lenin's Tomb in Moscow's Red Square. Both men had been revolutionaries, in a manner of speaking. Each had saved his nation, and was rightly venerated now.

"It's pleasant here in the summer," someone said behind him.

The man didn't turn, he didn't have to because he recognized the voice from years of association. "Not so bad now," he said, his English very good with hardly a trace of accent.

"McAllister is still alive."

"You have heard something?" the man said, his heart quickening.

"His body hasn't been found, and he's a very resourceful man. Until we can be absolutely certain, we must go on the assumption that he survived, somehow."

"Is he God then, this one?"

"No," the voice behind him said. "Just very good, very dedicated. We must be sure."

"What do you suggest?"

"We must go back over his track, beginning in Moscow. No stone must be left unturned. No possibility must be ignored, no matter how fanciful. Do I make myself clear?"

"Perfectly," the Russian said. "And here in Washington?"

"His wife is being questioned and so is Sikorski."

"What about the girl?"

"Albright?"

"Yes, her."

"Her too. No stone will be unturned, as I was saying. The instant he is spotted he must be killed. There can be no question of it this time. None whatsoever."

"I agree," the Russian said, his eyes lingering on the words above Lincoln's statue. "There is simply too much at stake here. Far too much."

Chapter 11

Washington was a weekday city. Saturday traffic was light on Interstate 95 as McAllister drove the thirty-seven miles down from Baltimore in the Buick Regal Stephanie had rented for him. He'd wanted to keep her at arm's length so far as that was possible, but, as she had explained to him last night, she was already involved and nothing he could do or say would change that fact. It was a risk, she said, that she and her father had been willing to take from the moment she'd brought his wounded, bleeding body home.

She'd driven back to her apartment in Alexandria earlier this morning so that if the Agency did try to contact her there, she would be home to take the call. Short of that her roommate would be able to say with honesty that Stephanie was here in the city.

He was going to get a room at the Best Western Center City, a few blocks up from the White House. She was going to come over at noon to meet him there. If something came up, their fallback would be the bar at the Marriott Twin Bridges Hotel, across the river.

It was nearly eleven by the time he entered the city and headed over to Georgetown. He had not been honest with her this morning. Nor, he realized, could he ever be completely honest with anyone until this insanity was resolved.

There were still large areas of his memory that were gray, incomplete, as if he had lived most of his weeks in captivity in a surrealistic dream. It was frightening.

"The longer you are out and around the more likely it will be that someone will spot you," she'd said.

"They think I'm dead, remember?"

"You have friends, acquaintances, people who would recognize you. Are you so sure you won't bump into one of them?"

Over the past days Stephanie had bought him some clothes, a toiletries kit and a nylon overnight bag, shopping at different stores in Baltimore and in the suburbs so as not to attract attention. She'd also trimmed his hair and picked up a pair of clear-lensed glasses. His appearance was altered only slightly, but enough, they'd both hoped, to throw off at least a casual observer. The changes would not fool anyone who knew him well, but the cop on the beat who might have his photograph wouldn't look twice.

There were acceptable risks and unacceptable risks. What separates the two is the desired goal. The more important the object, the larger the acceptable risk.

"The answers are in Washington," he'd told her. "I can't avoid that fact. Nor am I going to run away."

"I didn't expect you would."

"We'll meet at the hotel at noon."

She'd looked at him, wanting to say more, but she finally nodded, grim-lipped, and left.

He parked the car on Q and 30th streets and walked back the long block, turning right on 31st toward Tudor Place around the corner from his house. It was odd being back like this in his old neighborhood, made doubly odd by an almost detached feeling that had gradually settled on him over the past days.

Walking along the nearly deserted streets, snow still lightly falling, he was reminded of a similar weekend years ago when he and Gloria were trying to decide if they wanted to buy in this area. It had been early winter like now, and they had taken a walk around the neighborhood to get a feel for the place. They'd liked what they'd seen, and on Monday had signed the papers.

They'd not been back here together for more than a few months at a time since then . . . between foreign postings . . . so that this place had not really become home for him. He'd always looked upon the house as a vacation spot—or, rather the place they would come to when he finally got out of the business; something Gloria had been pressing him about for the past four or five years.

She, on the other hand, loved this place, and despite their frequent long-term absences had made it into a home. Whenever they were back she would hold cocktail parties or dinners for people they knew from the Agency. She was a good hostess, and he looked back on those times with warm thoughts.

But now he was returning a fugitive, and he had no real idea why he was taking this risk, except for the notion at the back of his head that the surveillance team would have been pulled away, and that Gloria would be home and that he could see her, find out what she had been told, convince her that she was wrong, that he hadn't become a traitor.

His father had fallen in love with Gloria. "Now there's a decent woman for you, boyo," he'd said when McAllister had told him they were engaged. "A man in this business needs his Rock of Gibraltar to keep the home fires burning and the cannons loaded."

Someone to give you a reason to come back. Someone to tend your wounds, soothe your hurts.

His mother had died when he was very young, and his father had never remarried. "No one to replace her," the old man had said. "And I'm too busy now to go looking for another one."

He reached Avon Place and started around the corner, but pulled up short and stepped back. A black Cadillac was parked in front of his house, its engine running, the exhaust swirling white in the cold wind.

From where he stood, McAllister had only to lean forward slightly and he could see around the edge of the brownstone on the corner. He closed his eyes for a moment, the pain rising up through his body. He knew who would be coming out of the house. He knew whose car it was. But he didn't want to think why. Too many things that Stephanie had told him seemed to fall into place now, and he knew that this was the very reason he had come here.

The front door of his house opened. Gloria emerged on Robert Highnote's arm. At the foot of the stairs they stopped a moment and said something to each other, Gloria looking up into his face. Highnote was carrying one of her suitcases.

They crossed the sidewalk and Gloria got in on the passenger side.

She was to be used as bait. They knew you would be coming home. She was your refuge. She and Robert Highnote.

So far as anybody knows you're dead. They're looking for your body, expecting it to turn up sooner or later. Your body, not you.

But Gloria was not grieving. He had been near enough to see that she had been smiling up at Highnote. No black veil over her face, no body slouched over in the pain of loss. Only a man and a woman together. Going where . . . to do what . . . to speak what words together?

Highnote walked around to the driver's side of the Cadillac and got in behind the wheel. Suddenly McAllister realized that within seconds they would be driving past him. His slight disguise might fool a stranger, but it would not fool his wife and best friend.

He turned and hurried down the street, ducking through an iron gate that led down to a basement entrance to one of the brownstone houses just as Highnote's car came around the corner and sped past.

When they were gone, McAllister came back up to the street level, hesitated a moment and then trudged back to where he had parked his car. He had the distinct feeling now that he was a man who had just witnessed his own funeral. The problem was, no one had been grieving.

They almost missed each other. Stephanie had been waiting for nearly fifteen minutes, and thinking that something had gone wrong, was about ready to drive over to their fallback when he showed up.

The relief on her face when she spotted him was clear, but then her expression darkened when she understood that something had happened to him.

She got out of the van when he pulled up and hurried over to him. "I've been going out of my mind. I thought they'd grabbed you. Is everything all right?"

"No," McAllister said climbing out of the car.

"What happened?"

He looked into her eyes. "I didn't want to do this, Stephanie, but I'm afraid I'm going to need your help."

"You have it, I told you that before. Now, what happened to you this morning?"

"I saw something that I didn't want to see. Something I never thought I'd see."

Sudden understanding dawned on her face. "You've been to Georgetown," she said softly. "To your wife."

"She and Bob Highnote were there at the house. Together."

"They didn't see you, did they?"

McAllister shook his head.

"Are they still there?"

"They left."

Stephanie thought about it a moment. "Doesn't prove anything. You said you've been friends for years."

"Merrilee wasn't with them. She should have been the one to be there."

"Have they got a thing for each other, is that what you're suggesting?"

"No," McAllister blurted, surprised with the intensity of his denial.

"Your best friend and your wife both think that you're a traitor. There isn't much left for you, is there?"

"Christ . . . I don't know any longer."

"But you're innocent. You're not a traitor."

"Maybe I am . . . maybe . . ."

Stephanie reached out and touched his face. "I can understand why the Russians came after you the way they did. And I can understand why you defended yourself. But . . . and listen to me very carefully . . . no matter what the FBI or the Agency thinks about you, we simply don't do things like that in this country. Those were two Americans who came after you on Highnote's sailboat. They flushed you out of hiding and shot you. No arrest, no trial, nothing. They simply shot you and left you for dead. If that had been an Agency operation the entire town would have been crawling with security officers. You would have been given a chance to give yourself up and stand trial. But if there had been a shooting, there would have been three dozen guns opening fire, not two."

McAllister looked at her. Despite her naïveté she was right. Something else was going on here. Something terribly dark and dangerous, and he was at the core of it, but he had no idea why.

They registered as husband and wife under the name G. Arthur. Their room on the third floor was clean but old and tattered. Stephanie left through the back, parked her van in a garage a couple of blocks away just off Vermont Circle, and returned on foot.

Her face was flushed and her eyes bright when she came in and tossed her coat on the bed. "What we need is information. And Dexter Kingman is the man to get it for us."

McAllister had done a lot of thinking in the twenty minutes she was gone, and he had come to a similar conclusion, but along a different line.

"I agree," he said. "But if we get your boss involved, you'll lose your anonymity."

"I don't give a damn. . . ."

"I do," McAllister said. "Up to this point you still have freedom of movement, which means you can get into headquarters without question, something I cannot do."

"What are we supposed to do, sit here all weekend? Sooner or later they'll realize that you're not dead, and then they'll tear Washington apart looking for you."

"For me, not *us*."

Stephanie was frustrated. "What are you going to do?"

"We need information. Voronin's Zebra One and Two might be nothing more than a coincidental use of the word. It may have nothing whatsoever to do with the O'Haire network."

"You don't know that."

"No, and you don't know otherwise. So it's our first step. If there is a connection we have to find it. And there's one man who can give me that information. One man who will agree to meet with me on my terms, without involving you directly."

"You're going to call Highnote and tell him that you're alive and here in Washington?" she asked incredulously.

"Yes."

"Why him?" she asked. "Aside from the fact that you don't want me getting myself openly involved with you, which is what would happen, of course, if I called Dexter. Why not wait until Monday when I'm back at the office? I can poke around and possibly find out something for you."

"Too dangerous."

"Don't make me laugh . . . too dangerous. Your meeting with Highnote wouldn't be? Come off it, there's something else going on here. You're out to prove something to him. But what if he's Zebra One? Have you thought about that?"

"Then I'd have that information."

"You'd have a bullet in the head," she said. "He'd get a medal for killing you, that is if he didn't call out the troops and have them do his work for him."

"Either way I'd have my answer."

"If he is the penetration agent, do you plan on killing him?"

McAllister nodded.

"If he isn't?"

"Then he'll help me."

Stephanie shook her head. "Are the choices that simple for you? Or are you just trying to prove something to him, or to your wife, or to yourself?"

"I don't know," McAllister said. He went to the window and looked down at the street. "My life ended a month and a half ago when I was arrested in Moscow. I want it back, that's all. Is that so difficult to understand? I'll do whatever's necessary to settle this insanity one way or the other. Whatever is necessary."

"Then I'll help you, if you'll let me."

"What if I fail?" he asked, turning back to her.

"Then we'll fail together."

He stared at her for a long time. "Why are you doing this? Why are you helping me? Turn around and go back to your apartment. On Monday report for work and forget about me."

"No," she said.

"Why? Can you tell me that?"

"I don't know," she said, taking time with her answer. "I just know that it started at Sikorski's house when you didn't kill me, and again on Highnote's sailboat when you were left for dead."

"I'm not one of your strays."

"No, you're not. And I'm no longer my father's little girl."

"Then we'll do it my way," McAllister said.

"As long as I'm included."

"I don't think it would be so easy to get rid of you."

"No it wouldn't be."

The early evening was dark, made even more so by the overcast sky, as McAllister entered the cavernous main hall of Union Station on Massachusetts Avenue. He angled left directly toward a bank of telephone booths across from the National Visitors Center. The station closed at midnight, but at this hour on a weekend the concourse was all but deserted.

Entering the third booth from the far right he glanced at his watch. Stephanie would be in place by now fifteen miles to the north at the Guilford Rest Area on I-95. She had left her van at her apartment and had borrowed her roommate's nondescript Chevette for the night. It would avoid the risk that Highnote might spot the van and recognize it. That wasn't very likely, but he didn't want to take any more chances than necessary. As it was there was far too much that could go wrong; far too much over which he had no control.

The telephone rang a minute later and he picked it up immediately. "Yes?"

"I'm in place," Stephanie said.

"Is there any traffic?"

"Not much. It's still snowing up here, how about there?"

"It's stopped, but we'll allow an extra ten minutes. Anything happens, get the hell out of there."

"Good luck."

"Right," McAllister said. He broke the connection, plugged a quarter into the slot and dialed Highnote's home number. He hit the timer function on his wristwatch. If there was automatic tracing equipment on the DDO's telephone it would take two minutes for an exchange to come up, three minutes for the complete number. He was giving himself ninety seconds, maximum.

Merrilee Highnote answered on the third ring. "Hello?"

McAllister deepened his voice. "This is Mr. Highnote's office. Is he at home, ma'am?"

"Yes, just a moment please." She hadn't recognized his voice.

McAllister watched the digital numbers on his watch. A full twenty seconds from the moment he had completed dialing elasped before Highnote came on the line.

"Who is calling this number? You know the SOP. . . ."

"It's me," McAllister interrupted.

For several long seconds the line was silent. McAllister kept an eye on his watch. On incoming traces you stall the caller for as long as possible using any ploy that comes to mind. Highnote was an old pro.

"You *are* alive," Highnote said softly. "I knew it."

"We have to meet, tonight."

"Where have you been, Mac? What happened to you in Dumfries? My God, we've been searching the river for more than a week."

"I want you to come alone and unarmed. Don't call anybody, don't leave any messages."

"Whatever you say. It might be easier for you to come here, but I'll come to you, if that's what you want. Just tell me when and where."

"There is a rest area just south of Guilford, Maryland, on I-95. It's about fifteen miles north of Washington."

"I know where it is," Highnote said. "I can be there in a half hour, maybe forty minutes."

"You'll have to exit at Guilford and come back. I'll be waiting on the southbound side."

"Are you alone, Mac?"

"I'm alone," McAllister said. "And you'd better be too."

"I won't say a word to anyone, I swear it. Just don't do anything foolish this time."

"Like what, defend myself?" McAllister asked. More than seventy seconds had already elapsed.

"They were Russians in that car."

"And Americans at your boat, Bob. I want some answers. A lot of answers."

"I'll do my best. But it would be a lot safer for both of us if we met at the Farm."

"I'll expect you in fifty minutes at the outside," McAllister said. "And from where I'm standing I can see a long way in every direction."

"Can I bring you anything . . . anything at all . . . ?"

The ninety seconds were up. McAllister cut the connection, then left the phone booth and walked rapidly out of the station back to where he had left his car in the Quality Inn parking lot a block away. He had a fifteen-minute head start on Highnote, and he figured he'd need every minute of it.

Stephanie waited in her roommate's car parked in the southbound Guilford rest area, watching the traffic. Her window was down a couple of inches so that she would be able to hear approaching sirens, if any, or the noise of helicopters coming up from the south. It had been a full thirty-five minutes since she had spoken to McAllister, and during that time she had begun to imagine all sorts of things going wrong. Highnote wasn't home, or he had refused the meeting. Someone had spotted Mac and there had been a shootout. His telephone call had been successfully traced and he was cornered now. There were any of a dozen possibilities which plagued her as she sat in the cold car, waiting.

Nothing had happened so far. Most of the traffic were semis. A dozen of the big trucks, their engines running, were parked just now in the rest area. There'd never been more than three or four cars at a time. And no car that had come in since her call to McAllister had remained for more than a few minutes.

From where she sat she could see across the wooded median to the northbound rest area several hundred yards away. Traffic had been about the same over there. Although she wasn't able to pick out individual makes of cars because of the darkness and the distance and the snowfall, she could tell them from the trucks.

As she watched, a car backed into a parking spot, its left blinker went on, then off, its highbeams flashed once, then a second time, and then were extinguished. It was McAllister's signal: He had made it after all. One flash without the directional meant their plan had been aborted for one reason or the other. One flash with the directional meant Highnote was on his way. A second flash was her signal to wait an additional five minutes and then telephone him.

She looked at her wristwatch, then got out of the car and hurried through the darkness past the parked semis back to the rest area's facility building. The men's room was on the left, the women's on the right, with a large map of the interstate system beneath an overhang between the two. A telephone hung on the wall next to the map.

No one had shown up. No sirens. No helicopters. No strange cars with too many antennae.

She went into the women's rest room, entered one of the stalls and sat down on the toilet seat as she nervously watched the minute hand of her watch. Still so many things could go wrong. Highnote was not to be trusted. There'd been too many coincidences around him. The Russians waiting outside his house. The assassins at his sailboat. Mac's wife.

After four minutes, she left the stall and at one of the sinks washed her hands, and then powdered her nose.

At five minutes exactly, she stepped outside and dialed the number for the pay phone at the northbound rest area. McAllister answered it on the first ring at the same moment Robert Highnote drove up in his Cadillac.

"Yes?" McAllister said.

Stephanie turned away. "He just pulled in," she whispered urgently. "Alone."

"All right, get out of there now!"

"I can't. He's parked not more than fifty feet away from me."

"Go into the ladies' room. Whatever you do, don't let him see you. I'll be there in a couple of minutes."

Stephanie hung up, turned, and as she stepped back into the ladies' room, she chanced a look over her shoulder. Highnote, wearing a dark overcoat with a fur collar was just coming up the walk, an angry scowl on his face.

His uninterested gaze flicked past her, and then she was inside, her heart hammering against her ribs. He'd seen her. It was impossible that he could have missed her. But there had been no sign of recognition on his face.

Chapter 12

McAllister reached the wooded median strip separating the northbound and southbound lanes of the interstate, and held up. From where he stood in the darkness, the snow falling all around him, he could just see the southbound rest area facility on a low rise, though it was set back in and among a stand of tall pine trees.

Highnote's familiar figure was outlined in the lights on the building as he paced back and forth. Though he couldn't see it, McAllister figured his old friend's car had to be parked somewhere in front.

No sirens, no helicopters, no chase cars, no backups so far as he was able to tell. Highnote had come alone as he had promised he would. And now he was waiting for McAllister to show up.

A man came out of the restroom, passed Highnote without looking at him, and crossed the parking area to one of the big semis. He hauled himself up into the cab, and a minute later the truck's engine roared and the behemoth started left toward the exit ramp, moving slowly. The instant the truck passed in front of the facility building, McAllister hurried out of the woods, scrambled across the depression beside the pavement, and raced across the dark highway, reaching the safety of the trees on the other side as the truck accelerated down the exit ramp.

Highnote had disappeared! From where he stood now McAllister could see the Cadillac parked just in front of the building. The car was empty. Highnote must have gone into the men's room.

McAllister raced up from the woods, crossed the parking area, and climbed into Highnote's car on the passenger side just as the DDO emerged from the men's room. He pulled out the gun Stephanie had supplied him, and sat well back, away from the light spilling from the stanchions.

Highnote looked at his watch, then turned and went to the telephone where he hesitated for a half minute before turning around. Shaking his head he walked down the sidewalk to his car. When he was ten feet away he spotted McAllister and stopped in his tracks for just a moment, before continuing.

"I thought you weren't coming," Highnote said getting in behind the wheel. He glanced at the gun in McAllister's lap.

"Are you armed?" McAllister asked.

"No."

"I'll accept that for the moment because I'm going to have to trust you completely. Do you understand?" McAllister had watched the DDO's eyes. They were clear and steady.

"If you're asking for my help, I'll do everything I can for you, Mac, starting with a piece of advice: Come with me right now. I'll take you back to headquarters and we can start to get this all straightened out. I'll guarantee your safety and a fair hearing."

"That's not within your power, Bob."

"What are you talking about?" Highnote said, his eyes narrowing. "I'm going way out on a limb being here like this."

"So am I," McAllister said. "I asked you to check on ballistics for me."

"Are you sure you want to hear this?"

"Yes."

"We found the weapon that was used to kill Carrick and Maas in a trashbin at LaGuardia. It was Carrick's weapon, and it had your fingerprints all over it."

"That's impossible."

"There were no bloody coveralls anywhere in the entire airport, though we did find one set in another trash bin, this one in the men's room near Piedmont Airline's boarding gates."

Given the organization and the manpower, practically anything could be accomplished. Any set of facts could be altered to support any line of logic. It was in the book.

"As I said before, Mac, you are not responsible for your actions. At least you weren't that morning when you stepped off the plane. You'd been pumped so full of drugs you couldn't have known what was happening. You got spooked, somehow got Carrick's gun away from him and shot him and Maas dead. From that point on you were working on instinct alone. You ran. And you've been doing a damned good job of it ever since. Where'd you find the doctor?"

"If I insisted on my original story, what would that tell you?"

Highnote looked at him for a long time. "That you were lying."

"No reason for it at this moment. I'm a fugitive and here and now I have the upper hand. Are there any other possibilities?"

"That you were so heavily drugged you couldn't separate reality from some dreadful fantasy."

"By your own admission I did a pretty good job of getting out of there. Not bad for someone so drugged out of his skull that he didn't know if he killed someone or not."

"Which brings us back to the lie. . . ."

"Goddamnit, Bob, what about a third possibility?"

Highnote's nostrils flared. "That you're telling the truth?"

McAllister nodded. "Try it."

"It would admit that you had been set up for some reason by a fairly sophisticated organization. By someone with a lot of connections."

"Exactly."

"Why?"

"We'll come to that in a minute. Somebody opens fire on me in New York, and when I get to Washington my wife calls me a traitor and tries to kill me."

"That was my doing," Highnote said heavily. "As soon as you skipped we figured you might head home. Gloria was to be your bait. We had to tell her everything. But I swear to you I had no idea that she would react the way she did."

"Outside your house I was set upon by three Russians. I killed them."

Highnote nodded.

"Sikorski was next. He called me a traitor and tried to kill me. It was open season."

"We thought you'd be heading out there sooner or later. He was told the same thing Gloria was told."

"So I ran to your boat."

"We didn't think about that one."

"Someone did. And they weren't Russians. They were Americans. They shot me and left me for dead."

"What happened down there?"

"You tell me, Bob," McAllister said softly. His grip tightened on the gun.

This time Highnote's eyes opened wide in genuine shock and anger. "Is that why you called me up here, to find out the extent of the Agency's evidence against you?"

"How did you know about Dumfries?"

"The dockmaster found the blood all over the bow of my boat and the cockpit of another. I was called as an owner, and put two and two together. It was your blood type."

"Was it an Agency operation?"

"We don't operate that way and you know it," Highnote exploded. "Come on, think about it!"

"The Bureau?"

"They would have had half their Washington staff down there. You know that too."

"Then who were they?"

"I can't answer that, because I simply don't know. But I suspect you do. And I suspect you're going to tell me what you think is going on."

Don't ask a question unless you already know its answer. The cardinal rule of all interrogation. But he had no answers. He barely had the questions.

"Does the name Viktor Voronin mean anything to you?"

Highnote shook his head. "Should it?"

"He was a former KGB officer. I was working him in Moscow and the product was pretty good for a while. The night I was arrested I was coming from his apartment."

"Were you questioned about him, about the operation?"

"No, which I found odd. But even odder was the last thing Voronin said to me that night. He'd been rambling on and on about nuclear war, and peace and he said he had a warning for me."

"Which was?"

"His words exactly . . ." McAllister hesitated a moment. He sat forward a little so that he could better see Highnote's face. "Look to Washington. Look to Moscow. Zebra One, Zebra Two."

Highnote had no reaction, absolutely none, except for a mild impatience when McAllister did not continue. "Is that it?"

McAllister nodded. "Does it mean anything to you?" He couldn't decide if he was disappointed or glad.

"Not a thing. Does it to you?"

"It didn't at first."

"But it does now?"

"Zebra One is an Agency officer, and Zebra Two is KGB. Or at least I think so. One in Washington, one in Moscow. I think they're working together."

"Good God Almighty," Highnote breathed. "You think there is a penetration agent within the Agency."

McAllister nodded.

"And you think it's . . . me?"

"Is it, Bob? Is it you?"

"Don't be a fool," Highnote said offhandedly. "How many years have you known me?" Highnote was looking away, his hands tightly gripping the steering wheel, his head shaking. "It explains so much. So much . . ."

"Talk to me," McAllister said. Whatever reaction he had expected it wasn't this. "There have been too many coincidences surrounding you. The Russians outside your house. The hit men showing up at your boat. You and Gloria . . . this morning."

Highnote turned to him, his eyes wide. "You were there?"

"I saw the two of you coming out of the house."

"I took her to my place. She wanted to be with Merrilee. She didn't want to stay in Georgetown any longer. Do you think that she and I . . . ?"

"You said that it explains so much. What did you mean?" The atmosphere in the car suddenly seemed very close.

"More than you can possibly imagine, Mac," Highnote said with some excitement in his voice. "But you're right about one thing, you can't turn yourself in now. If there is a penetration agent working within the Agency, it would be almost impossible for me to guarantee your safety. I mean, who could we trust? You're going to have to keep on the run until I can find out who it is. Good Lord . . ."

"In the meantime the Agency and the Bureau are hunting for me," McAllister said.

"Nothing I can do about that without blowing the whistle."

"Tell Gloria at least."

Highnote started to say something, but then cut himself off. He looked at McAllister with a new shrewdness in his eyes. "If you're telling me the truth."

"If not it would be a pretty elaborate lie, Bob. And for what reason?"

"You say you were never asked about this during your interrogation?"

"No."

"But you were drugged. You could have mentioned it without knowing that you'd said anything."

"It's possible," McAllister said. He could see Miroshnikov's face swimming overhead.

"Have you mentioned these words to anyone else? Here or there?"

McAllister started to tell him about Sikorski, but something made him hold back. "No," he said.

"Don't," Highnote replied. "But they know of course. They'd have to. It explains why you were released the way you were, and why they tried to kill you in New York and again outside my house and on my boat. Russians in at least one instance and Americans in another."

"You've lost me."

"Don't you see, Mac, it's a faction fight. Someone within the KGB wants to expose the connection."

"Why?"

"Power politics? Who knows? But as soon as you were released the word went out: You had to be killed before you could talk." Highnotc was thinking hard, his mind racing. McAllister knew his old friend well enough to read that much from his face. "It might not be someone within the Agency. It could be anyone you know. The Pentagon, National Security Agency . . . anyone."

"Will you help me?"

"Yes," Highnote said, looking at him again. "But you're going to have to keep yourself hidden . . . even from me.

Keep your ass down, Mac, because the bullets are going to start flying, I think."

"You can't possibly trust him," Stephanie said. It was nearly midnight. They were back in their hotel room downtown. She sat on the edge of the bed while McAllister paced back and forth.

"He was convincing. And he did come alone."

"Don't you see that he had nothing to lose and everything to gain by complying with your wishes? You're old friends. He knew that you wouldn't shoot him in cold blood, whatever he thinks about you. But he had to know what you were doing, what information you had."

"If he is the penetration agent he wouldn't have been so sure of that. He would have been taking a very large risk by meeting with me."

"You still don't see. You simply are not that type of person."

"The Russians had me for more than a month under drugs. Supposedly I killed Carrick and Maas in New York. And there's no denying I killed the three Russians in Arlington Heights."

"One is an assumption, the other you've freely admitted. But when you had the chance—in fact the need, to protect your own safety, you did not kill me, nor did you kill Sikorski. Your true colors were showing."

"He was still taking a big chance."

"Then why didn't you tell him about Sikorski's reaction to the words?"

"I don't know," McAllister said.

"I do. You were simply protecting yourself again. Something at the back of your head, some instinct, told you to hold back. And from where I'm sitting, I think your instincts are about the only thing that have saved your life so far. Trust them."

The fact was, McAllister thought, he no longer could. His life *had* truly ended a month and a half ago in Moscow, and he felt at times as if he were struggling now to get out of the womb, to be reborn; only he had no idea who he would become. The thought was frightening. "I didn't tell him about the possible connection between Voronin's warning and the O'Haire network either."

"No matter what he is, he's certainly not a stupid man," Stephanie said. "We have to assume that he's at least considered the possibility that you've made the connection."

"If there is one."

"The O'Haires' control officer has never been named."

"Highnote?"

"Possibly."

"If that's the case, he'll be pulling out all the stops to find me now," McAllister said, pausing by the window. "We're going to need more information about the Zebra Network. Somewhere there has to be a track backward."

"The library has all the back issues of *The New York Times* and *Washington Post,* there might be something. . . ."

"No, I meant details that haven't been published. Something in the Agency's files. Perhaps in the FBI's records."

"I can telephone Doug, ask him to make a few discreet checks for me."

"The one who gave you the gun?"

"Yes," Stephanie said. "He knows a lot of people. And he's good."

"No questions asked?"

Stephanie smiled sadly. "He's still in love with me. He'll do it."

McAllister turned back and looked at her. "Why are you doing this?"

"We've already gone through that, Mac," she said getting up and going around the bed to the telephone.

"But you never gave me a proper answer."

She shook her head. "Nor do I think I can. At least not at this moment. Give it a little time, I'll come up with something for you." She picked up the phone, got an outside line and dialed Doug Ballinger's home number. He'd just come in and he sounded tired.

"Sorry to bother you, Douglas," Stephanie said. "But I need your help again."

"Come on over, darling, we'll talk about it."

"I can't tonight. But I need you to make some quiet inquiries for me. I need some information, and fast. Like yesterday."

Ballinger's voice cleared. "Are you in some sort of trouble, Steph?"

"What makes you ask that?"

"Well, first you borrow my gun, and then you call me in the middle of the night asking for information. What's up?"

Stephanie sighed. "I could be in some trouble, Douglas, so I'm counting on you to keep it cool."

"What do you need?"

"Are you familiar with the O'Haire case?"

"Everybody is," Ballinger said cautiously. "They were sentenced the other day. What's your connection?"

"Their Soviet control officer has never been named. Any ideas on that score?"

The line was quiet for a long time. "What have you got yourself involved with, Stephanie? This is big business."

"I know. I just need that information, Douglas. Quietly."

"I don't know if I can do that for you—or should. At least not until you tell me why. My ass could be hanging out on a very thin limb."

"I can't. You're just going to have to trust me. Can you help?"

"Goddamnit, Stephanie, talk to me! I'm not kidding now!

Those people were big-time traitors. They sold us down the river. Now you're asking me about their control officer? What the hell is going on?"

"I'm not involved with them, Douglas, I swear it to you. I just need the information."

"Then go to your office and punch it up on the computer. You've got the clearance."

"I can't do that."

"Why?"

"Look, you either trust me or you don't!" Stephanie snapped. "If you do, all I can promise is that you'll get an explanation sooner or later, and then you'll see why I had to do it this way."

Again there was a longish silence on the line. When Ballinger came back on he sounded cold. "Call me here in the morning. About ten."

"Thanks, Douglas," Stephanie said, but the line was dead. Ballinger had hung up on her. She slowly put down the telephone.

"He wasn't very happy with you," McAllister said.

"No," she said. "But he'll do it. I'm supposed to call him back at ten."

"Will he tell someone about this?"

"I don't think so. Like I said, he's in love with me."

"Are you in love with him?"

She shook her head. "I was, a long time ago, but not now. We were friends."

McAllister caught her use of the past tense. "I'm sorry, Stephanie."

"Yeah, me too."

It was very late. Without turning his head to look at the clock, McAllister figured it had to be at least four in the morning. He stared at the window, the curtains partially drawn, waiting for the dawn to come. Stephanie was on the other bed.

Their next moves depended in a very large measure on what Ballinger would come up with, because at this point he might be their only viable hope for any sort of a lead. *If* there was a connection between Voronin's cryptic warning and the O'Haire spy network, and *if* Ballinger could provide them with a clue as to their control officer, they might be able to act.

The answers are in Washington.

What if Zebra One turned out to be Highnote? What if he had been the O'Haires' control officer? How long had it been going on?

Can you ever know anyone, really know them?

In this business you can trust no one, boyo.

The words should have been chiseled in granite on some monument somewhere, dedicated to man's inhumanity to man; dedicated to his perfidy. MICE was an old CIA acronym for why men became traitors: Money, Ideology, Compromise, and Ego. Which one? Where in God's name was it leading, and did he want to know?

"You asked why I'm helping you," Stephanie said in the darkness.

He turned to look at her. She was staring up at the ceiling. "You should get some sleep."

"I think you were set up."

"By Highnote?"

"Him or someone else. It doesn't matter. Someone powerful. Someone who wanted to protect himself."

"But the O'Haire network has been smashed. It's over."

"If that's all there was to it," she said. She turned and looked at him, her eyes wide and bright. "They might have been nothing more than the tip of the iceberg. There could be more, a lot more."

"Then we'll find it out," McAllister said. "In the meantime go to sleep."

"I'm frightened," Stephanie said. She pushed back her covers and got out of bed, her movements soft and liquid.

She was nude. In the dim light coming from outside he could see her small breasts, narrow hips, and swatch of dark pubic hair. She'd recently been in the sun, or under a tanning lamp, because he could clearly see her bikini line of white flesh against the darker tan.

He didn't know what to say.

"Hold me," she said, coming to his bed. "Please?"

He held the covers open for her, and she slipped in beside him, her body pressed against his as he took her into his arms. He felt terribly guilty, as if he were the betrayer, the great destroyer, and yet for the moment at least, this felt somehow right.

In the morning they both carefully avoided talking about what had happened. Around eight-thirty they went downstairs to the hotel's coffee shop and had breakfast while they looked through the Washington and New York Sunday newspapers. Still there was nothing about the search for his body, or about the investigations into the shooting deaths of two Agency officers in New York, or the three Russians in a car in Arlington Heights.

They were back in their room just at ten, and Stephanie dialed Ballinger's home. His phone was answered on the first ring by Dexter Kingman.

"This is the Ballinger residence. Who's calling?" He sounded harried. Stephanie could hear that there were other people there. A lot of them.

"Dexter? This is Stephanie. Is Doug there? Can I speak to him?"

"I was just about to telephone you. Are you at home?"

"No, I spent the night with a friend. What's the matter?"

"Ballinger is dead."

"Oh, my God . . ."

"He was shot to death sometime last night, or early this morning. The FBI is looking for you right now."

"What's going on . . . why are they looking for me?"

"Your name was written on a pad of paper beside his telephone, along with the notation ten A.M Were you supposed to meet him or something this morning?"

"We were going to spend the day together," Stephanie said, trying to control her voice.

"Get yourself back to my office. I'll set up your interview there."

"Dexter . . . who killed him, do you know? Have you any idea yet?"

"It looks as if the Russians did it," Kingman said heavily.

"Russians?"

"It's not very pretty, Stephanie."

"Tell me," she said, steeling herself.

"It looked like a standard Center assassination. A *mokrie dela*. He was shot three times in the face at very close range."

"They killed him," Stephanie said hanging up the phone. "My God, they killed him. . . ."

Chapter 13

"I'm sorry, Stephanie," McAllister said. "You can't know how sorry I am, but this has got to end right now."

She was sitting on the edge of the bed looking up at him, her eyes filling, her face pale and drawn. "He asked somebody the wrong questions and they killed him for it. My God, it doesn't seem possible."

"How did Kingman know it was done by the Russians? Were there witnesses?"

"He called it a standard Center assassination. . . ."

"A *mokrie dela*?"

She nodded. "Yes, those are the words he used. What does it mean?"

"Literally it means 'wet affairs,' the spilling of blood. Was he shot in the face?"

"Yes," she said softly. "And now the FBI wants to talk to me. Doug wrote my name on a pad of paper by the telephone."

"You're going to that meeting," McAllister said. "And you're going to tell them that you don't know a thing. You and Ballinger were supposed to make a day of it, just like you told Kingman."

"I can't."

"You must," McAllister insisted. "If you don't show up, they'll come looking for you. And when they discover that you're with me, you'll be a marked woman."

"Don't you see, Mac, I already am a marked woman. My name was lying in plain sight beside Doug's telephone. Whoever killed him had to have seen it. If I show up for that interview they'll kill me."

"One doesn't necessarily lead to the other," McAllister said. "Unless you don't show up for the interview."

"No," she said firmly. "Whatever happens, I'm with you until this thing is settled. One way or the other."

"Why? Can you tell me that now?"

Her lips compressed. "Because I don't like being pushed around."

"It's just starting."

"Let's finish it!"

They used the rental car that Stephanie had picked up in Baltimore. McAllister figured this would be the last time it would be safe to use the Buick, however, because when she failed to show up at Langley they would come looking for her and it wouldn't take long before they found out about this car.

Outside the city they stopped so that she could telephone her father and warn him that someone would probably be by to ask him some questions about her.

"What they'll tell you won't be true, Father," she said.

"Are you in any danger?"

"Yes, I am."

"Are you with him?"

"Yes."

"Take care of yourself, I'll be all right."

"I know you will, Father," she said.

The day was cold and overcast. There was very little

traffic on the highways so they were able to make good time along the Capital Beltway. They turned west on the Dulles Airport Access Road.

"There'd be no reason for them to go after your father," McAllister said. Stephanie's mood had deepened since she'd spoken with him, and McAllister was worried about her.

"It's a chance I'm willing to take," she said.

"There's still time to back out."

She looked at him. "Don't say that again, Mac. It doesn't make this any easier for me. I'm along for the ride. Let's just hurry."

Since this morning a plan had begun to formulate in McAllister's mind. It was obvious that Voronin's warning did have a concrete meaning, and that somehow it was tied to the O'Haire spy network, or more specifically to the network's control officer. But it was just as obvious that without more information there wasn't a thing he could do about it. It came down to the old question: Whom do you trust when it's impossible to separate the liars from the innocents?

He slowed down as they approached the Reston turnoff. What little traffic they'd passed was heading to the airport. He'd not seen a police car or an identifiable Agency or Bureau unit since they'd left the hotel. Of course no one would be expecting him to return to Sikorski. Not after what had happened out there that night. He glanced in his rear-view mirror just before he hit the ramp in time to see a chocolate-brown Ford Thunderbird coming up behind him at a high rate of speed. He veered a little to the right to get out of its way, and the car passed them, the driver and lone passenger both intent-looking men.

"It's them!" Stephanie cried, sitting forward.

"Who? What are you talking about?"

"That car! The brown Thunderbird! It's the same one from Dumfries!"

The car had already passed through the stop sign at the top of the hill and was racing toward the north, toward Reston, toward Sikorski. McAllister jammed the accelerator to the floor and they shot up the ramp, fishtailing a little as they hit an icy spot on the roadway. There was no other traffic so McAllister didn't even bother slowing down for the stop sign, swinging wide through the intersection, almost losing the back end again. He had to force himself to slow down. To go off the road now would eliminate any possibility of catching up with the two assassins ahead of them.

"Are you certain it's the same two men?" McAllister asked. The Ford had already topped the next rise and had disappeared beyond. The side road up to Sikorski's cabin was barely a half a mile beyond.

"No, I didn't get that good a look at them as they passed us. But it's the same car. New Jersey license plates."

He glanced at her. She had taken out a small gun from her purse. It was another .32 automatic.

"They're on their way to Sikorski's."

"To kill him," Stephanie said. "Just like they killed Doug."

"These two are Americans. We both heard them that night on the sailboat."

Stephanie looked at him. "If you wanted to kill someone, and make it appear as if the Russians had done it, what would you do?"

McAllister nodded. "The question is, where the hell are they getting their information?"

"From inside Langley. From Highnote."

"We'll see," McAllister said grimly. They came over the rise and raced down the long hill, the town of Reston in the distance. The Thunderbird was nowhere in sight. The road led straight into the distance. The only place the car could have turned off that quickly was the road back up through Sunset Hills. What few lingering doubts McAllister had had, evaporated with the certainty. One by one someone was eliminating everyone he'd had contact with since his release from the Lubyanka.

Everyone, that is, except for Robert Highnote.

They reached the secondary road and turned off. Sikorski's driveway was a couple of miles farther into the hills. The snow that had fallen last night blanketed the trees and brush. The small community of Sunset Hills was to their right; he turned left and drove another mile, finally slowing and stopping at the dirt road.

One set of tire tracks led up the road, none came back. No one had been in or out since the last snowfall. Only the Thunderbird had come this way.

McAllister started up the dirt track, the trees closing in around them. A few hundred yards up, he stopped again and shut off the engine. The road was very narrow just here, the embankments on either side very high, impossible to drive up over. Whatever happened now, the Thunderbird would not be able to get back to the main road this way.

"Hide yourself in the woods," McAllister said. "If they come back this way open fire on them, and then get the hell out."

"I'm coming with you," Stephanie said.

"You'll do as I say, goddamnit," McAllister snapped. "If something happens to me I want you to get to Kingman and tell him everything. . . . I mean *everything*. At least you'd have a chance."

Stephanie's eyes were wide, but she nodded in agreement.

They got out of the car. For a second she hesitated, but then she climbed up over the dirt embankment where the road had been cut through the side of the hill, and disappeared into the thick woods.

McAllister started toward the cabin. The snow was soft and slushy, and within ten yards his feet were soaked. He took out the P38, switching the safety off.

The Thunderbird was parked just at the edge of the clearing that led down to the cabin. Crouching low he hurried up behind it, keeping it between himself and the house. No one was around. The cabin seemed deserted. There were no sounds or movements.

From where he hid behind the big car he could see two sets of footprints leading down the clearing where they split up, one set going left, the other right. They'd circled the cabin, coming up on it from both sides. Sikorski's pickup truck was back in its carport, but no tracks other than the footprints led across the clearing. Nothing had moved in or out since the snow. It was that one fact that was bothersome to McAllister just now.

He moved around to the driver's side of the car. The window was open, the keys dangled from the ignition. He reached inside, took the keys and pocketed them.

Now, he thought grimly, the odds had been evened up somewhat. Whatever happened, they wouldn't be getting out of here so easily. They would have to stay and fight.

A man in a dark bombardier jacket came around from behind the cabin. McAllister ducked farther back behind the car, certain that he hadn't been spotted yet. The man's attention was toward the cabin itself.

The front door opened and the second man, dressed in a dark overcoat, unbuttoned, came out. He was stuffing his gun inside his coat. The man in the bombardier jacket said something to him, and he shook his head. McAllister could hear the voices, but not the words.

They had expected to find Sikorski at home, but evidently the old man had left with someone before the snow had finished falling. Now they would be coming back up to their car.

McAllister eased back behind the Thunderbird and then scrambled up into the woods, moving from tree to tree until he was well hidden yet barely fifteen feet from the car. He could hear the two of them talking now, their voices much closer as they came up the hill. He still couldn't quite make out the words, but it sounded like English.

The one in the bombardier jacket came into view first on the driver's side of the car. McAllister steadied his pistol with both hands against the bole of the tree, waiting for the second one to appear.

"Sonofabitch," bombardier jacket swore, spinning away from the open window, his hand reaching for his gun. The second man had just come into view on the other side of the car. He looked up in alarm.

"Somebody's got the fuckin' keys," bombardier jacket swore.

"Hold it right there," McAllister shouted.

Bombardier jacket had his gun out and was diving to the left. The other man was dropping down behind the car.

McAllister squeezed off a shot, the gun bucking in his hand, the bullet smacking into the driver's side door a half a foot behind the man in the bombardier jacket, who snapped off a shot as he fell, the bullet hitting the tree inches from McAllister's face.

McAllister fired again, this time catching the man in the throat, his head snapping back against the car's front fender, a horrible gurgling scream coming from him as he tore at the jagged wound, blood pumping out all over the snow.

These were Americans, not Russians! He had not wanted this! Not this kind of a confrontation!

It took the man nearly a full minute to die, and then the woods were silent again, only a very slight breeze rustling the tree branches.

McAllister stood sideways to the tree, his heart hammering, his stomach heaving. The other man had not moved from behind the big car. For the moment it was an impasse.

"We didn't kill him," the man said, his accent New York or New Jersey. "We found him that way, I swear to God. I don't know what happened. I don't know who did it. . . .'' The words were almost hysterical, but the tone was too measured.

Janos dead? If these two hadn't killed him, who had?

''I gotta have a guarantee. I'm not going to get myself shot like Nick.'' The voice had moved to the rear of the car.

McAllister leaned forward slightly so that he could just see around the tree. The man in the bombardier jacket lay in the snow in a big puddle of his own blood.

''Throw out your gun, no one will hurt you,'' McAllister called.

''He's a mess in there,'' the man said. ''In the back.''

''I said throw out your gun.''

The man popped up over the back of the trunk lid and fired twice, both shots coming within inches of McAllister, who ducked back behind the tree. Whoever they were, they were both good shots, professionals.

He remained hidden until he heard someone crashing through the trees and brush on the other side of the road. He looked back around the tree in time to see the man disappearing into the woods and he snapped off a shot knowing even as he fired that there was no chance of hitting him.

McAllister ran through the woods back toward the Buick where Stephanie was waiting. The only way out of here was in that direction, and sooner or later the man would have to show up on the road. He was slipping and sliding all over the place in the snow. He stopped and listened. In the distance, across the driveway, he could hear someone crashing through the forest, and then the sounds were lost.

If Stephanie had hidden herself well, the man might run past her, never seeing her. If she was out in the open, she would be in trouble. McAllister redoubled his efforts, angling back toward the dirt road where he would be exposed but where he knew he would make better time.

He was in the field again; in the Rhodope Mountains just inside the Bulgarian border with Greece. He'd been running all night and now with the sun coming up he had less than a kilometer to safety across the border, but the Bulgarian Secret Police patrol was gaining. He could hear them coming, he could hear the dogs and the helicopters, still he kept running because he had no other option.

There was the distant crack of a single pistol shot, and then nothing. McAllister pulled up short just at the edge of the road and held his breath to listen. The Buick was parked twenty-five or thirty yards farther up the dirt road. Nothing moved. Again the woods were silent. His side ached, and he thought he could feel something oozing down from his left arm. He figured he had probably opened one of the stitches.

He slid carefully down to the road, and crouching to keep below the level of the embankment, hurried up the road to the car. He stopped again to listen, but the woods were still silent.

"Stephanie?" he called out.

"Here," she shouted from the woods a moment later.

McAllister stepped around the front of the Buick and looked up over the embankment in the direction her footprints in the snow led. He couldn't see a thing except for the trees. He climbed up into the forest.

"Stephanie?" he called again, this time her answer seemed fainter, and to the right.

"Here," she called. "I'm over here."

The hair at the back of his neck prickled. Something was definitely wrong. She was in trouble. He could hear it in the few words she had spoken.

"Coming," McAllister shouted, and he started noisily along the path of her footprints. After ten feet he stopped to listen, then stepped off the path and taking great pains to make absolutely no noise, circled widely to the left, moving from tree to tree as fast as he dared.

He came to a narrow clearing about twenty-five yards up the hill. A set of footprints led from left to right, disappearing into the woods above. She had to be close, though he could not see a thing as he moved across the clearing and once again held up just within the forest.

"Where are you?" Stephanie called, her voice shockingly close. Just to the right now. "Mac?"

He searched the trees and brush out ahead of him, moving his eyes slowly, searching each square foot of dark against white. They were there. Behind a large tree. The man in the dark overcoat held an arm around Stephanie's chest, while with his right hand he held a pistol to her head. They were barely ten yards away and slightly above, their backs to him.

McAllister got down on his stomach and crawled up the hill, keeping the trees and brush between him and them as much as possible. They were concentrating in the opposite direction, back toward the road.

When he was barely ten feet away he got slowly to his feet and raised the pistol in both hands. "Stephanie," he called out loudly.

The man in the dark overcoat, startled, looked over his shoulder and started to bring his gun around. It was all the opening McAllister needed. He fired, the shot catching the man in the forehead, taking off a big piece of his skull in the back, splattering Stephanie with blood. The man slumped down against the tree, his legs giving way beneath him and then fell face forward into the snow.

Stephanie, a horrified expression on her face, stepped back away from the man, and suddenly she leaped forward, raced down the hill and fell into McAllister's arms.

"I heard the shots and then all of a sudden he was there behind me," she cried in a rush. "He made me fire my gun into the ground, and call for you. We could hear you coming. I wanted to warn you. But then there was nothing. Oh, God, Mac . . ."

"It's all right," he said, looking over her shoulder at the dead man.

"What about the other one?" she said, suddenly stiffening in his arms, and pulling away.

"He's down by their car. I killed him."

She looked into his eyes. "They were here to kill Sikorski," she said.

"He's already dead. But this one said they found him that way," McAllister said tiredly. His head was spinning. "Are you all right?"

She nodded. "You?"

"I think so," he said. He went up the hill and turned the dead man over. Stephanie helped him. They went through his pockets, coming up with five or six hundred dollars cash, which McAllister took, and his wallet. He was Treffano Miglione, from Jersey City; a member of the Sons of Italy and the Teamsters Local 1451. Apparently he was married. There were several snapshots of three young children and a fairly good-looking young woman.

McAllister sat back on his heels and looked up at Stephanie. "This one wasn't with the Agency or the Bureau."

"No," she said. "Mafia?"

"Yeah," McAllister replied. "They were independent contractors. Someone hired them to get rid of me, Ballinger, and Sikorski. So, who hired them?"

The dead man's weapon was a 9 mm SigSauer. McAllister removed the clip from the gun, ejected the shells from it, and pocketed them. He needed them for his own weapon.

He stood up. They were isolated here in the woods so that it was unlikely that anyone had heard the gunshots. But he didn't want to take any more chances. It was time to get out.

"Where do we go now?" Stephanie asked.

It was almost axiomatic, he thought, that the further you got into an operation, the more restricted your options became. He could feel the so-called "funnel-effect" pulling him inexorably downward. But toward what?

"You're going to arrange a meeting between your boss, Dexter Kingman, and me," he said. "For tonight."

Janos Sikorski's shoeless, shirtless body lay over a pile of fireplace logs in the woodshed behind the carport. He had been dead for at least two days, his body frozen stiff in the cold. He had been beaten to death, his arms and legs broken by repeated blows from a large piece of wood.

McAllister stood just within the doorway, the dim light spilling across the floor on the old man's half-naked body. His ribs had been broken, his teeth knocked out, and finally the side of his skull crushed.

"What did you tell them, Janos?" McAllister mumbled half to himself. Because of the cold there was no smell in the shed and yet he could imagine the odors of death, and his stomach heaved.

Stephanie was right behind him. She gasped when she saw the body, and she turned away and threw up in the yard.

The two up in the woods had probably killed Ballinger, so who had done this to Sikorski? More important: Why? Was it a faction fight after all?

An organization will of necessity protect itself from any and all invasions. A basic tenet. But which organization had done this, and how far was it willing to go in its effort at self-protection?

McAllister stepped the rest of the way into the woodshed and tried to close Sikorski's eyes, but the lids were frozen open.

"Ah, Janos, what did you know about Zebra One and Zebra Two?" McAllister murmured.

Traitor, Sikorski had screamed. *They'll give me a medal for your body.*

Who would have given you a medal, Janos? Goddamnit, who?

* * *

They parked the Buick in the clearing in front of Sikorski's house and drove the Thunderbird over to Dulles Airport, where McAllister, using one of the assassin's driving licenses and credit cards, rented a Chevrolet Celebrity from the Hertz counter for Stephanie. She followed him back into the city, and they stashed both cars in the same parking garage a couple of blocks from their downtown hotel.

It was three in the afternoon by the time they were back in their room, and Stephanie rebandaged the wound in McAllister's side which had opened and was leaking.

She was clearly shook up. This morning she'd still had a choice: stay or go. Now it was too late for her. She had crossed over. Now it would be impossible for her life ever to return to normal.

"We're back to square one," she said. They were having a much-needed drink together. "If I set up a meeting between you and Kingman he'll have half the Agency waiting to grab you."

"Just what I want," McAllister said. He was staring out the window across the city. It looked as if it were going to snow again soon.

"Actually we're worse off than before," she said. "They'll suspect that you killed Sikorski. And sooner or later the Mafia is going to come looking for their people. That Thunderbird is going to stick out like a sore thumb."

McAllister turned back to her. "The only reason I took their car is because of what I found in the trunk. I need it."

"Such as?"

"Burglar tools."

She looked at him, her lips pursed. "For what, Mac? What are you going to do?"

"First things first," he said. "Let's say that you call Kingman this afternoon, right now and tell him that I want a meeting. Just the two of us, tonight at ten o'clock in front of the Naval Observatory. What will he do? Exactly?"

"If you're going to have any chance of getting in and out, without being taken, we'll have to provide ourselves with a couple of blinds. Wouldn't be difficult to set up. A call to a telephone booth, for example. But he would be followed. He won't come alone."

"No fallbacks," McAllister said. "What if we tell him up front when and where I want the meeting?"

"Within an hour of my call he'd have his people stationed all over the place, you know that. There wouldn't be a chance of your getting in without being spotted."

"He'd agree to the meeting if you called him?" McAllister insisted.

"Certainly. He'd try to talk some sense into me. He would be disappointed. But he'd come. I suspect you've become a very big prize."

"Kingman would come in person, but so would a lot of his people."

"Half the Agency," Stephanie said. "And I'm sure he'd get the FBI involved. Probably even the district cops."

"Our little meeting would draw a lot of people over to the observatory. A lot of sensation."

"Naturally . . ." she started to say, but then what he had been trying to tell her began to penetrate, and her eyes opened wide. "While they're all looking for you to show up at the meeting, you would be someplace else. A diversion."

"Exactly," McAllister said. "But I'll want you nearby so that you can see who shows up and exactly what they do. Close, but out of sight."

"The Holiday Inn," she said. "It's on Wisconsin Avenue just a couple of blocks from the observatory. Doug and I stayed there once."

"You'd have a clear line of sight to the observatory grounds?"

"From the upper floors," she said. "But what about you? Where will you be?"

"Getting us the information we're going to need if we want to stay alive," he said.

She started to reply, but then backed off, a wry smile on her lips. She nodded. "I understand," she said softly.

"Call him now."

It was snowing again by the time McAllister pulled off Georgetown Pike and parked the Thunderbird on a dark street below Langley Hill. The CIA's grounds were just on the other side. He sat in the darkened car for several long minutes, watching for traffic, but nothing came. It was a little past nine-thirty. By now Kingman's people would be in place around the observatory north of Dumbarton Oaks Park, and no one would be getting suspicious for at least a half hour yet. Security would still be tight, but Kingman and Highnote and the other brass who might be involved in this business would certainly be gone. He needed access to a computer terminal in one of their offices.

He got out of the car and from the trunk took out the long-handled bolt cutters and the small tool kit he had found earlier. The two assassins had come down from Jersey City well prepared for their assignment. In addition to the tools, he'd also discovered a high-powered rifle and night spotting scope in an aluminum case, a MAC 10 compact submachine gun with three hundred rounds of ammunition, and a short-handled sawed-off shotgun for close work, leaving absolutely no doubt as to exactly what line of work they'd been in.

Careful to lock the trunk, he stepped off the road, down into a ditch and then up the other side toward a line of trees at the edge of a clearing at the top of a shallow hill, scrambling on his hands and knees at times because of the slippery going.

At the top he ducked into the protection of the woods and looked back the way he had come. The snow was falling in earnest now, so it wouldn't be too long before the marks he had made coming up the hill would be partially covered, masking his trail.

Luck, he thought, turning toward the northeast. So much of his life had depended upon it.

Within a hundred yards he came to a tall chain-link fence topped with barbed wire. A big metal sign warned that this was government property, and that entry was prohibited.

Putting down the tool kit, McAllister quickly cut a large square opening at the base of the fence with the bolt cutters, peeled it back and crawled through. On the other side he crouched in the darkness, waiting, listening for the sound of an alarm. But the night was still, even the occasional traffic sounds from the Georgetown Pike were muffled by the trees and falling snow.

Leaving the bolt cutters behind, he hurried down into the shallow valley, and then up the other side, stopping every hundred yards or so to listen for the sound of one of the patrols that operated back here twenty-four hours per day.

But there was nothing. He could have been alone in another universe, surrounded by dark trees, slanting snow and except for the noise of his own movements and breathing, total silence.

Look to Washington. Look to Moscow. Zebra One, Zebra Two. Voronin's words.

The O'Haires' organization had been called the Zebra Network. The soldiers were all safely in prison. What about the generals? Zebra One and Two?

Their control officer or officers had never been named. Why? Lack of information, or were they being protected for some reason?

Three-quarters of a mile from the fence he came to the first paved road. There were no tire marks in the fresh snow. He stood by the side of the road. If he crossed here the next patrol to come along would spot his footprints.

He turned and followed the road directly north for a few hundred yards, coming at length to an intersection which had been recently traveled. It was exactly what he had been looking for. Fresh tire marks led off toward the northeast, and in the distance he thought he might be able to make out the soft glow of lights.

Stepping out onto the paved roadway, he walked in the tire tracks, his footfalls crunching in the snow. He could definitely see the glow of lights ahead now, almost pink in the falling snow. It would be the rear parking lot behind the construction site. A big earth mover parked beside the road loomed up ahead of him, and beyond it two cement trucks and a crane, its boom lying down on the bed of a long trailer, waiting for the Monday morning shift. McAllister followed the road as it curved toward the right, finally opening onto a vast parking lot, mostly empty at this hour. In the distance was the seven-story CIA headquarters complex, with its addition under construction outlined, as if by deck lights, like a hulking ship at sea in a storm. He pulled up behind a dump truck.

The questions had been posed in Moscow; were the answers to be found here, he wondered.

He was suddenly very cold.

Headlights flashed at the far end of the parking lot, and McAllister crouched down behind the big dump truck as a light-gray pickup truck raced across the parking lot and passed him, heading down the road he'd just come up. He caught a glimpse of the driver and his passenger, who was talking into a microphone. Had the hole in the fence been discovered already? The truck's taillights disappeared into the night, and McAllister quickly crossed the road and hurried along the edge of the parking lot.

Construction on the new addition had been started nearly a year ago. The last bulletin he'd read indicated that it would be spring before the new offices would become available, because of numerous, as yet unexplained, delays. Scaffolding rose on all three sides of the U-shaped building that butted up against the original headquarters. Construction equipment and piles of material lay everywhere.

He crouched again in the darkness for a full minute, studying the building, but nothing moved, no lights shone from any of the windows. Around front the main building was brightly lit from the outside, for security's sake, but most of the office windows were dark. Operations would be fully staffed, as would communications and a few of the other vital functions, but for the most part the building would be quiet.

McAllister worked his way around to the north side of the new building. Reaching the scaffolding he stuffed the small tool kit in his coat and started up. The windows on the fourth floor and above had not yet been installed. The canvas that covered the openings billowed and moved slowly in the light breeze.

When he reached the fourth story he was sweating lightly, and he had to stop for just a moment to catch his breath before he ducked beneath the lower edge of the canvas and stepped inside the building.

He was not alone. He stood stock-still in the nearly absolute darkness waiting for a sound, a movement, anything to accompany the cigarette smoke that he could smell. Someone was here. Very close.

Gradually his eyes became accustomed to the darkness and he was able to distinguish shapes and outlines of walls, hanging wires, and pipes and piles of construction materials. He remained standing by the canvas-covered window opening listening and watching. He was in a large, unfinished room. Directly across from him was an open doorway into a broad corridor. A man in the corridor, somewhere to the left, coughed. McAllister pulled out his gun and crept forward, feeling ahead with his free hand so that he would not trip over something.

At the doorway he stopped again to listen. The smell of

cigarette smoke was much stronger here and he could feel the warmth of a portable heater wafting back to him. It would be a guard on duty. The new building was attached to the old just here. There would be a door. Some access from the new into the old. Someone would have to guard it. One guard or two? How much further would his luck hold?

Gripping his gun a little tighter, McAllister stepped around the corner. A lone guard sat at a small table in front of a plywood bulkhead into which a padlocked door was set. A portable heater was set up at his feet. He was reading a magazine, smoke curling up from a cigarette in an ashtray in front of him. A single light bulb dangled from the ceiling.

McAllister was halfway down the corridor before the guard realized that someone was coming, and looked up, his eyes growing wide in alarm, his mouth opening. He reached for his walkie-talkie lying on the desk.

"Don't," McAllister said raising his pistol.

The guard hesitated just long enough for McAllister to reach him and snatch the walkie-talkie, his initial surprise turning to anger.

"Here, who the hell do you think you are?" the man sputtered jumping to his feet.

"I don't want to have to kill you, but I will if you force me to it," McAllister said, keeping his voice low and menacing. He hadn't wanted this at all. There was no way he was going to kill this man, no matter what happened.

Getting what he had come here to get had suddenly become more than difficult.

In the next moment McAllister's luck completely ran out.

"Raise your hands very carefully, if you please, Mr. McAllister," someone said behind him.

McAllister stood absolutely still. He knew the voice, remembered it from somewhere years ago. He wracked his brain trying to come up with a face and name. Someone from the last time he had done desk duty here at Langley.

"I asked you to raise you hands, sir, and I'm not kidding now."

"Who is that?" McAllister said, turning very slowly. The man was very short and well-built with thick graying hair and dark eyebrows over wide eyes. The face was vaguely familiar, still he couldn't put a name to it.

"Tom Watson, sir. We were told that you might be showing up here. Now if you please, raise your hands."

McAllister remembered. Watson had been one of the front-door guards. They'd often bantered back and forth when McAllister had come to work. He was holding a .38-caliber Smith & Wesson in his right hand. He wasn't carrying a walkie-talkie. McAllister raised both of his hands; in one he held the walkie-talkie, in the other his gun. "Now what, Tom?"

"Disarm you, then call for help," Watson said warily. "Get his gun, Frank."

The other guard came up behind McAllister and reached for the gun. It was a mistake on his part. McAllister turned as if he were going to hand his gun to the guard, but then continued to swivel around until he was completely behind the man, his left arm clamped over the man's throat, his pistol at the man's temple.

Tom Watson moved forward, raising his gun, a frightened, uncertain look of surprise on his face.

"I don't want to shoot him, Tom, but I will if I must," McAllister said.

Tom Watson stopped in his tracks. "Damn you," he said.

"Do as I say for the next five or ten minutes and I promise you that no one will get hurt."

Chapter 14

Something had gone wrong. Stephanie watched from the seventh-floor room she'd taken in the Georgetown Holiday Inn as two men got out of a car parked on Observatory Place and rushed back into the woods. Moments later they returned in a hurry with two other men, got back into the car and raced out of sight around the main building.

She had checked in here around six o'clock after calling Kingman, who had been deeply upset, and had watched from her darkened room as the first of the surveillance units had begun to show up shortly before seven. It was ten after ten now.

Kingman had given his word that McAllister would not be taken by force. "I'll talk with him, Stephanie, if that's what you want," he'd said coldly. "But I can't guarantee anything else."

"That's all he wants. But if you come in there in force, he won't show up."

"If I come alone, he'll shoot me in cold blood just like he's done the others."

"The only people he has killed were three Russians outside Mr. Highnote's house, and then only in self-defense."

She assumed the trouble at Sikorski's had not yet been discovered.

"I'm not going to argue that point with you. I'll meet with him, and I promise no force."

"If it doesn't work out, you'll let him turn around and leave?"

"If he's innocent, as you say he is, he won't have to leave. We'll work it out together. But Stephanie . . ."

She'd hung up on him then, and driven directly over to the Holiday Inn, where she'd been waiting and watching ever since. She had counted at least eleven different units in and around the Naval Observatory grounds, and she figured there were twice as many she had been unable to see from her vantage point.

A District of Columbia police car, its red lights flashing, raced up from Whitehaven Street, turned at Circle Drive and entered the observatory grounds from the southeast.

They'd all hidden themselves. But now they were out in the open. Stephanie turned away from the window and looked at the telephone on the nightstand between the twin beds.

McAllister had not told her where he was going tonight, but she'd known just the same. There was only one place where he could get the information he sought. As crazy as it seemed, she had to admit the logic of what he was trying to do. Zebra One, Zebra Two, his contact in Moscow had told him. And the O'Haire organization had been known as the Zebra Network. If there was a connection between the two—and judging from Sikorski's reaction that first night she strongly suspected there was—then any further information would be buried in the CIA's archives. More specifically in the Soviet Russian Division's computerized records. Fourth floor at headquarters. She knew the territory well because she'd been assigned temporary security duty on more than one occasion—watching suspected Soviet spies operating out of their embassy here in Washington when division chief Adam French didn't want to involve the FBI.

She tried to envision just how he would have gotten himself into the building and then up to the fourth floor. He would have to find an office with a computer terminal. He would have to know the correct access codes. So much could have gone wrong.

Outside, two more District of Columbia squad cars, their lights flashing, their sirens blaring, emerged from the observatory grounds and raced south on Thirty-fourth Street. Moments later Dexter Kingman's car came around the corner and sped off into the night.

The meeting had been aborted. But at this point, McAllister was barely ten minutes late. Too soon for Kingman to have shut down the operation. The prize was simply too great for him to have quit this early.

Four other cars and a windowless van came out of the observatory and hurried down Thirty-fourth Street toward the Key Bridge—across which was the parkway, CIA headquarters a scant eight miles to the northwest.

McAllister had pocketed the walkie-talkie, relieved both men of their handguns, and watched them as Tom Watson unlocked the bulkhead door into the old building. The corridor was long and broad, only dimly lit, deserted at this hour of a Sunday evening.

"What's the night guard's schedule for this floor?" McAllister asked, keeping his voice low.

"I don't know," Tom Watson said, and the other guard looked up sharply at him.

"You've got to believe me, Tom, when I tell you that I don't want to hurt anybody. If you know the schedule, it would be best if you told me now. I don't want a confrontation."

"On the half hour," Tom Watson said after a hesitation.

McAllister glanced at his watch; it was a few minutes

after ten, which gave them twenty minutes at the outside to get in and get out—and only that long if his entry onto the grounds hadn't already been discovered. "Let's go," he said.

"I don't know what sort of trouble you're in, sir, but don't do this. You'll just be compounding . . ."

"And you don't want to know," McAllister said, prodding him in the back with the gun. "Down the hall. Now."

Adam French's office was at the end of the corridor, which branched left and right. Since he was head of the Soviet Russian Division, immediate access could be obtained to records through his terminal. That is, McAllister thought, if they hadn't changed the access code on him over the past three years. A lot of ifs here; too many.

He made both guards lie facedown on the corridor floor while he selected a slender, case-hardened steel pin from the tool kit he'd taken out of the Thunderbird's trunk, and had the door lock picked in under twenty seconds.

"Inside," he told the two men.

They got to their feet, a deep scowl on Watson's face, a look of terror on the other's, and they entered the office, where McAllister made them lie face down on the carpeting as he closed and relocked the door.

"I'll only be a couple of minutes," McAllister said. "If you cause no troubles I promise you won't be harmed."

"You won't get away with this," Watson snarled.

"You'd better hope I do," McAllister said, sitting down at French's desk, and flipping on his computer terminal. The screen came to life, with the single word: READY.

This terminal, like hundreds of others in the building, was connected to the computer's mainframe in the basement. Records were compartmentalized, access given only on a section-by-section and need-to-know basis. Three years ago the Soviet Russian Division's access code was S/R DIV METTLESOME. It had been someone's abstruse comment on our Soviet policy.

He typed in the words, and hit the ENTER key.

FILE? the word in amber letters popped up on the screen.

McAllister glanced at the guards who hadn't moved, then turned back to the keyboard and typed the most obvious choice. O'HAIRE NETWORK, then hit the ENTER key again.

ACCESS RESTRICTED—PASSWORD?

He stared at the screen, suddenly conscious of just how little time he had left. He'd been afraid that the file might be restricted, and now it was anyone's guess what the correct password might be. The major problem was that he only had three chances to get it right. After three incorrect tries an alarm was set off on the mainframe, indicating that someone was attempting to gain access to a restricted file.

Where to begin? He had come this far, he wasn't going to back out. Not yet.

He typed the first thing that came to mind. ZEBRA, and touched the ENTER key.

INCORRECT PASSWORD.

It was like looking for a needle in a haystack. The O'Haires had operated what was widely considered to be the most damaging spy network against the United States since the Second World War. There was a certain logic to these passwords.

He typed: SPIES, and hesitated a moment before touching the ENTER key.

INCORRECT PASSWORD.

Again McAllister glanced over at the two guards on the floor. Tom Watson had raised his head and was glaring up at him. "You don't want to see this, Tom. Believe me, it's for your own good."

"Give it up, sir."

"Put your head down."

Watson complied after a moment, and McAllister turned back to the terminal, another thought striking him. This would be his last chance. He typed: ARBEZ, and hit ENTER.

INCORRECT PASSWORD.

He stared at the screen for a long moment or two, conscious of his heart hammering in his chest. He had begun to sweat again. The clock was running now. Someone would be coming to see what the trouble was up here. If they had already guessed he was somewhere on the grounds this now would bring them on the run.

He had lost. Yet he had come so close. So tantalizingly close. The O'Haire files were somewhere in the computer. One word. One key and he would know. . . .

In desperation he typed the only other thing he could think of. HIGHNOTE, and the ENTER key.

This time the screen was suddenly filled with a long list of file choices, labeled alphabetically under the heading: ZEBRA NETWORK DIRECTORY.

"Bingo," he murmured, running his finger down the individual file choices, among them: History and Background, Investigating Authorities, Budget Line Summaries, Damage Assessments, Transcripts—Telephone, Transcripts—Nonsubject Interviews, Transcripts—Subject Interviews, and under the label Code M, the file, SUSPECTS.

He typed M and the ENTER key.

Instantly the directory was replaced by a list of four names, a brief bit of information on each, and instructions for bringing up other files that contained more detailed information.

Four names.

Reaching over he turned on the printer and touched the PRINT key; immediately the machine started to whine as the computer spit out a hard copy of what had come up on the screen.

"Gun or no gun, I won't stand for this," Tom Watson shouted, jumping up and lunging over the desk.

McAllister had barely enough time to rear backward out of Watson's grasp, and grab for his gun lying on the desk, when the telephone rang. Watson lashed out at him, then reached the telephone and snatched it off its hook.

"It's McAllister!" Watson cried.

The other guard had jumped up. McAllister had no choice. He smashed the butt of his heavy pistol down onto the base of Watson's skull, and the man cried out and crashed off the desk to the floor. The second guard reached the door when McAllister aimed the pistol at him.

"Stop," he shouted.

The man, his hands fumbling with the door lock, looked over his shoulder, his eyes wide with fear, and he froze.

The printer stopped and in the sudden silence McAllister could hear a thin, shrill voice calling his name as from a great distance. It took him a moment to realize it was Stephanie on the telephone. He jumped up and came around the desk. Watson, out cold, had dragged the receiver off the desk with him. McAllister picked up the phone.

"It's me," he said, keeping his eye on the guard at the door.

"Kingman and the others just left in a big hurry," she shouted in a rush.

"When?" McAllister demanded. There was no time to wonder how she had known he was here.

"No more than two minutes ago. Get out of there, Mac."

"On my way," McAllister said, and he yanked the telephone cord out of the wall.

He bent down over Watson and felt for a pulse in the man's neck. It was strong and regular. The man was out, but not dead, and McAllister gave silent thanks for that much at least.

Back behind the desk, he tore the computer readout from the printer and shut down the terminal.

"All right, Frank, we're getting out of here now."

"What about Tom?" the guard asked fearfully.

"He'll be all right, and so will you if you do as I say," McAllister said. "Where is your pickup truck parked?"

"In the back, by the elevator."

"Let's go," McAllister said.

The guard unlocked the door. The corridor was still deserted. No one had come up from the computer mainframe yet to check on the restricted access-code violation, but someone would be showing up at any minute. They hurried down the corridor and back through the bulkhead door into the new building.

McAllister was just relocking the padlock when the walkie-talkie in his pocket came to life.

"Security Four, Control."

The guard stiffened.

"Is it you?" McAllister asked.

The man hesitated, but then nodded.

McAllister pulled out the walkie-talkie and handed it to him with one hand, while raising his pistol to the man's head with his other. "Everything is fine here," he said.

The guard keyed the walkie-talkie. "Security four," he said. His hands shook.

"What's your situation up there?"

"Normal," the guard said.

"Keep on your toes, you might have some trouble coming your way. We've got an intruder alert."

"Ask them who it is and how they knew about it," McAllister said.

The guard keyed the walkie-talkie. "Who is it, Control, and how did we find out?"

"It's McAllister, somebody apparently phoned it in a couple of minutes ago. He's armed, so watch yourself."

McAllister nodded, his gut tight. Who had phoned? How in God's name had they known?

"Roger," the guard said, and McAllister grabbed the walkie-talkie from his hand and pocketed it.

"Who else is guarding this building?"

"No one else in this wing except for Tom and me."

"Earlier I saw a pickup truck outside in the parking lot."

"Unit five. One of the outside patrols."

"I hope for your sake that you're not lying," McAllister said.

"I'm not, sir."

The elevator was located at the end of the corridor. They took it down to the ground floor where they hurried across the mostly completed entry hall and then outside. It was still snowing. In the distance they heard the sounds of a lot of sirens. McAllister ordered the guard behind the wheel of the light-gray pickup truck, then he got in on the passenger side.

"Drive," he said.

"Where?"

"West."

"But there's no exit. . . ."

"Do it," McAllister ordered, and the guard hastily complied, heading across the parking lot toward the back road that McAllister had used.

He had to have time to think. Stephanie was an intelligent woman. She knew what he had gone looking for, and she could have guessed where he would have to go to get the information. It explained her telephone call to Adam French's office warning him that Kingman and his people had deserted the rendezvous. But she was the only one who knew that he would not be at that meeting. If she had tipped off Kingman, why had she called French's office? None of it made any sense. It was madness.

Four names he had gotten from the computer. It was the information he had been seeking, if only he could keep alive long enough to find out what they knew.

McAllister cranked down his window. They had left the sirens far behind, back toward the headquarters building. He figured they had come nearly a mile.

"Stop here," he said to the guard.

"Jesus, Mr. McAllister, I'll do whatever you want," the man said in alarm.

"I'm not going to hurt you. Just stop here and I'll let you out. You can walk back."

The guard wanted to believe him, but it was obvious he

thought he was about to be shot to death. He pulled up to a halt.

"I've got a family. . . ."

"Get out of here, and don't look back," McAllister said.

The guard hesitated a second or two longer, then shoved open the door, jumped out and started running down the snow-covered road, disappearing into the darkness.

McAllister slid over behind the wheel, slammed the truck into gear and drove another quarter mile before pulling up, dousing the lights and shutting off the engine.

He jumped out of the truck, stepped off the road, and plunged into the forest, heading in the general direction of the place where he had come through the fence.

Twice he heard sirens in the distance, and somewhere to the north, he thought he could hear a horn honking, but for the most part the woods were silent as before.

He came to the fence five minutes later, and followed it back to the northwest for another hundred yards before he found the hole he had cut. His were the only footprints in the snow, already partially filled in. No one had discovered how he had gained entrance. Once again his luck seemed to be holding.

In another five minutes he had reached the crest of the hill overlooking the street. The Thunderbird was still parked where he had left it, no one around, though once again he could hear sirens in the distance.

He scrambled down the hill, climbed into the car, and drove off.

McAllister parked the car in front of the J. Edgar Hoover Building which houses the FBI's headquarters on Pennsylvania at Tenth Street, leaving the walkie-talkie and the guards' weapons under the front seat.

Sow confusion where you can; it will help mask your movements in a difficult situation.

The car would create a lot of interest when it was discovered what it contained.

But whom to trust?

If Stephanie had been able to guess where he had gone, others could have done the same. It wasn't much of a hope, but it was something.

It took him almost a half hour to reach their hotel on foot. He figured she would be back from the Holiday Inn by now. There was almost no traffic, and absolutely no activity around the hotel. He waited in the darkness across the intersection for a full ten minutes to see if anyone showed themselves. If the hotel was staked out, there would have been a movement; a slowly passing car or van, a head popping up, a cigarette lit, something. But there was nothing.

He crossed the street, entered the hotel, the sleepy clerk glancing away only momentarily from the television show he was watching, and took the elevator to the third floor.

She opened the door for him.

"Oh, God, am I glad to see you," she cried, falling into his arms once he was inside.

The relief in her eyes, in her voice, and in the way she held him, her entire body trembling, was genuine, pushing back his doubts about her.

"They knew I was coming," he said.

"Impossible."

"How did you know where to reach me?"

Her eyes widened. "What are you saying, Mac?"

"I repeat, how did you know where I would be?"

"You wanted information about the O'Haires. About the Zebra Network. There was only one place where you could possibly get it."

"What did you tell Kingman?"

"You were standing right behind me when I talked to him," Stephanie flared.

"I couldn't hear both sides of the conversation."

"What are you trying to say?" she snapped. "Spit it out!"

"Someone telephoned them. Told them that I was coming and that I was armed and dangerous."

"And you think I did it?"

"What did you tell Kingman? What did he ask you?"

"Nothing," she said, tears coming to her eyes. "What did you tell your friend Highnote?"

Zebra One, Zebra Two. Highnote knew nearly everything.

"If I wanted you dead I could have left you in the river," she cried. "I could have put a bullet in your head at my father's house, or here at this hotel, or out at Sikorski's, any of a dozen times and places."

"Why didn't you?" McAllister asked miserably, his voice catching in his throat.

"I don't know . . ." she started to say, and she tried to pull away.

He took her by the shoulders and looked into her eyes. "Why, Stephanie? What are you doing here with me? Why are you risking your life to help me? It doesn't make sense."

"Because I love you," she blurted.

He didn't know what to say. It was as if the floor had opened up beneath his feet.

"There," she said pulling away from him. "Are you satisfied, you bastard?"

The TWA flight out of St. Louis was already forty-five minutes late, putting them into Washington after eleven-thirty at night. Louis Jaffe, assistant general counsel for the CIA, sat back in his first-class seat and closed his eyes for a moment. John Norris, who'd flown out with him for the interview at Marion Federal Penitentiary in Southern Illinois, was sound asleep in the next seat.

Highnote insisted that someone from Operations be included, and in fact it had been Norris who'd asked most of the questions.

It was terribly odd, Jaffe thought, this particular piece of information surfacing now. But as Norris had said in his sardonic way, they were looking for a deal . . . when no deals were possible. "So we send them a life jacket. We don't have to tell them it's full of holes."

Jaffe opened his eyes and switched on his pocket tape recorder, the voices in the earpiece distorted but understandable.

". . . the name McAllister mean to you?" Norris's voice.

There was a scraping sound and a sudden loud hiss as James O'Haire lit a match and put it to his cigarette. "As in David Stewart?" he asked, his Irish accent pronounced.

"You tell me," Norris said.

"The bastard. He was playing both ends against the middle there at the end. Last I heard he was still playing it close in Moscow. Probably skipped by now, though, if I know my man."

"David McAllister was part of your network?" Jaffe heard himself ask.

"From the beginning."

Jaffe ran the tape forward. ". . . had his network people over there who'd pump him the questions that needed answering. You know, hardware, technical data, that sort of sport."

"And here in this country, who was your control officer?" Norris asked.

O'Haire laughed, the noise roaring in Jaffe's ear. "You've been watching too many spy movies."

Jaffe ran the tape forward again. ". . . telling you all this now because my brother and I want a deal. Not so hard to understand, is it?"

"Do you want to go live with your pals in Moscow?" Norris asked.

"Hell no," O'Haire exploded, laughing again. "We'd

be willing to tough it out here, say for a year maybe two. Until the dust settles. Then you could quietly let us out. Might go to Spain, perhaps France. Somewhere in Europe. We're not greedy."

"Would you be willing to testify in court about McAllister's involvement . . . ?" Jaffe had asked, but O'Haire cut him off.

"You play ball with us, Mr. Jaffe, and we'll play ball with you. I'll tell you this much, though, watch out for McAllister. He's one tough sonofabitch. I always admired that one, I did."

Chapter 15

"They're lying," Robert Highnote said, looking across the conference table at the other three men gathered for the early morning meeting at CIA headquarters. "Besides, as I understand the laws of evidentiary procedure, the word of a conspirator would not be valid in a court of law."

Dennis Foster, the agency's general counsel, nodded. "We're not talking about a court of law here, Bob. But considering everything that McAllister has allegedly done over the past week or so, it gives one pause, wouldn't you agree?" He was a slightly built but patrician-looking man with white hair and wire-rimmed glasses that gave his face a pinched expression. His voice was soft, cultured.

"Hell, at the very least the man is a killer," Dexter Kingman said. He was just the opposite of Foster; rawboned, large, at times loud. More than one person had underestimated his intelligence, however, because of his outward appearance. Oftentimes to their regret. He was angry just now.

"And he was here last night," Adam French, the director of the Soviet Russian Division added. "You can't deny that."

"No," Highnote said. "But so far, all the evidence that we've gathered has been contradictory. You can't deny *that*."

"The man is trying to save his own ass," Kingman said. There was a deep scowl on his face. "Now he's snatched one of my people."

Highnote glanced at the written report in front of him. "From what I've read here, she could have been a willing victim."

"Probably had a gun to her head," Kingman growled.

"She's still alive. And so are those two guards last night. He could have pulled the trigger. He didn't."

"What are you trying to do, defend the bastard?" Kingman said, his voice rising. "You were friends, but let's not carry this so far we become blinded."

"What the O'Haires told our people does fit," Dennis Foster interjected. "If you think about it, it does make some sense."

"Not from where I sit," Highnote said heavily. "None of this makes any sense. I saw him, remember? I spoke with him face-to-face the night he came out to my house. He's confused, he's running for his life, I'll grant you that, but we trained him to do that. And he's doing it well."

"At the Russians' behest," Foster said.

"Is that what you think, Dennis?" Highnote asked seriously. He looked at the others. "Is that the consensus here this morning? Because if it is, I'm telling you that I just can't go along with you."

Kingman threw up his hands in frustration. "Then what the hell are we doing here, Bob? What do you want from us? Do we let the bastard go, let him do whatever he wants? Offer him amnesty? Forget everything that's happened?"

"On the contrary. He has to be stopped."

"Fine . . ." Kingman started to say, but Highnote held him off.

"Hear me out, Dexter. All of you. We're dealing with

a highly trained operative who is obviously motivated. Simply put, McAllister is looking for something. And looking hard. I think it would be wise to find out what that might be. He didn't have to return here to Washington. He could have taken off, hidden himself, and it would have taken us years to dig him out, if we ever did. Why has he come back? What does he want?''

''Revenge,'' Kingman said simply.

''For what?''

''The failure of his network.''

''We've not agreed that he actually worked with the O'Haires.''

''It fits,'' Kingman said. ''The Russians arrested him to throw off suspicion, and then they released him on the hope that he would be allowed back into the fold. When we obviously wouldn't buy that, he ran amok. You saw the ballistics report from New York. Carrick was killed with his own gun. So was Maas. McAllister's fingerprints were all over it.''

''What about the three Russians outside my front door?'' Highnote asked.

''I don't know. A deal gone bad, perhaps?''

''And the blood all over my sailboat? McAllister was there. We found the Walther he took from my study. Who tried to kill him?''

''Again I don't have the answers, Bob. But my guess would be the Russians themselves. Maybe they'd realized they had made a big mistake releasing him. Maybe they're trying to stop him.''

''Now you're trying to say that McAllister is an independent?'' Highnote asked. ''Trained by us and molded by the Russians? With drugs, perhaps torture? He's a tool?''

''Gone bad,'' Kingman said. ''I think the man has gone over the edge. I think he is insane.''

''If that's the case,'' Highnote said sitting back in his seat, ''we're all in trouble, gentlemen. Very big trouble.''

"We trained him, it's up to us to stop him," Kingman replied, only the smallest look of satisfaction on his face. "The question is, how? The bastard is smart."

"If we knew what he was looking for, it might give us a clue as to his next moves," Dennis Foster said. "If we assume that what the O'Haires told us is true, we could start there. . . ."

"No assumptions, Dennis," Kingman said. "I don't think we can afford the luxury. Besides, if McAllister's brain was altered by drugs, he wouldn't be the same person as before. No, we've got to start from the beginning. From his beginning. If he has come back here for revenge . . . we've got to find the object of his revenge." He turned to Adam French. "He broke into your office and used your computer terminal. Was there any record of what he was looking for?"

"It could have been almost anything," French said. "All that we do know for sure was that once he got into the division archives, he evidently called for a restricted-access file, and failed three times with the password."

"Did he get it right on the fourth try?"

"Possibly," French said. "Tom Watson said he printed out a hard copy of something."

"No way of retrieving that either?" Kingman asked.

"No."

"He came here at great risk to himself to find out something. He needed a piece of information which he evidently managed to get. What information?"

"I have a guess," French said. He reached down to his briefcase on the floor beside his chair and brought out a buff-colored file folder with the orange diagonal stripes signifying it contained top-secret information. "Dennis and I spoke briefly this morning before this meeting, so I knew what had transpired at Marion with the O'Haires. As you may know we maintain the O'Haire Zebra Network file in our archives. I figured that if McAllister was connected with them he might have been seeking more information . . . perhaps he was looking to discover just how much we knew."

He withdrew a half a dozen computer printout sheets and passed them down the table to Highnote. "No telling if that was the file he was looking for, but the connection is there, and the password is yours, Bob."

While French was talking, Highnote quickly scanned the pages which included the coded listing of the various O'Haire files. Files that he knew only too well because it was his department that had been most deeply involved in the investigation. The connection was there. It was definitely there!

Everyone was looking at Highnote. The decision was his, and they all knew it. They also respected the fact that he and McAllister had been friends for many years. It was Highnote, in fact, who had recruited the man.

Highnote laid the computer printouts down on the table. "His father was the best in the business. Practically a legend."

"Nobody is pointing a finger," Kingman said gently. "Nobody is holding you accountable."

"What I mean to say is that up to the point that McAllister was arrested by the Soviets there was nothing wrong with him. I sincerely believe that he was a good, loyal American. One of the best field men I've ever seen."

"I agree with you," Kingman said. "We all do, so far as it concerns his abilities. But the O'Haires have named him."

"Someone told them to do it, Dexter. There has to be a conduit to them. I'd be willing to bet anything that Mac was not involved with them."

"Then something happened to him in the Lubyanka," Kingman said.

"Yes," Highnote agreed softly. "They did something to him, warped his mind, altered him somehow, and then sent him back here hoping we'd accept him. But they were too crude about it."

"They've been cruder," Adam French said. "Now they're just as afraid of him as we are."

"He must be stopped," Highnote said with obvious difficulty. "Brought in, if humanly possible, but stopped."

"He's fighting for his life . . . or at least he thinks he is," Kingman said. "He won't be so easy to . . . capture."

Dennis Foster bridled. "I don't know if I should be hearing this." He started to rise, but Highnote waved him back.

"We've haven't crossed that line yet, Dennis. What we're doing here is well within our charter. We're not contemplating anything illegal. The optimum scenario is that we bring him in, and find out what happened to him."

"I repeat, that won't be so easy," Kingman said. "He obviously knows what he's doing, and just as obviously he has some plan in mind."

"What about this woman he snatched?"

"Stephanie Albright is young, idealistic, and good," Kingman said, his jaw suddenly tight. "You might not know, but her name was written on Ballinger's phone pad. They were supposed to have met that morning."

"Are you saying that she killed him?" Highnote asked aghast.

"No. I'm saying that McAllister had her set up the meeting and then he killed Ballinger."

"Why?"

French interrupted. "I know why," he said, his complexion suddenly very pale. They all turned to him. "Ballinger telephoned me, wanted to know something about the O'Haire network. Said it was something he was working on . . . that he might have something new for us."

"What'd you tell him?" Highnote demanded.

"Nothing. I told him that he would have to clear it with you, or at the very least go through Dexter's office. He said he'd do just that."

"He didn't call me," Kingman said.

"Nor me," Highnote said.

"He's definitely after the O'Haires," French said. "If only I had known . . ."

"Or someone connected with them," Dennis Foster said. "They're all safely in prison. But there could be others. Their control officer, for one."

"Which means McAllister wouldn't have murdered Ballinger," Highnote said. "He went through the woman to get information, and when that didn't work he went directly to the source. The Russians killed Ballinger because they wanted to stop McAllister from learning something. They must know what he's up to. It was probably they who called security warning them that McAllister was on his way out here."

"That's a weak guess, Bob," Kingman said.

Highnote slammed the palm of his hand on the tabletop. "We don't have anything else to go on, goddamnit. I'm trying to save lives, don't fight me."

"If he's after something or someone connected with the O'Haire network, let's give it to him," Kingman said.

"Bait?"

"Exactly. If he responds we'll know for sure what he's up to."

"What have you got in mind? Any ideas?"

"We'll get a message to him."

"How?"

"There is only one way to make sure that we get his attention," Kingman said. "We let it leak to the press that we're on the verge of arresting the O'Haires' control officer. We'll even go so far as to name him as a former Agency officer: David McAllister."

"You're nuts," Foster said. "Every cop in the country would be gunning for him."

Kingman shook his head. "We give a bogus description.

Something not even close. Different age, height, hair. McAllister will know that we're trying to reach him, and why."

"So will the Russians."

"And they'll go gunning for him, because they know what he really looks like. In the meantime we'll be watching them. Sooner or later they'll lead us to him."

"If they get to him first they'll kill him," Foster said.

"It's the chance we all agreed to take when we raised our right hands, Dennis."

"You must have taken a different oath than I took," Foster said. "I for one want no further part of these proceedings, and I suggest that this entire case be turned over to the Bureau. It's in their bailiwick. Let them handle it."

The telephone at the head of the table burred softly. Everyone stopped as Highnote picked it up. They'd all heard him instruct his secretary that there were to be no interruptions of this meeting, except in an emergency.

"I see," Highnote said softly, the expression on his face impossible to read.

Foster had gotten to his feet and was halfway to the door. Even he hesitated.

"This morning?" Highnote asked. "Yes, I see, thank you." He hung up. For a long time he sat stock-still, staring at the telephone.

"What is it, Bob?" Kingman asked, the first to break the suddenly ominous silence.

Highnote looked up. "It was Janos Sikorski," he said. "He was found tortured to death at his home outside of Reston this morning."

"Good Lord," Foster said.

"Any witnesses?" Kingman asked, his eyes bright.

Highnote shook his head. "It's not all straightened out yet, but the killers evidently came in two cars. They left one behind. There was a lot of blood. . . ."

"Any idea who the car belongs to?"

"It was a rental unit. Out of Baltimore."

"A name?"

"Stephanie Albright."

"Oh, Christ," Kingman said. "Oh, Jesus Christ."

Chapter 16

Live a hundred years, learn a hundred years, still you die a fool. Better to turn back than lose your way. A bad compromise is better than a good battle.

The proverbs were a Russian litany; the response, survival.

The man in the charcoal-gray overcoat and dove-gray fedora crushed out his cigarette in the Mercedes's ashtray and attempted to settle back in his seat and relax. But he was tense. So much had gone wrong that it was becoming increasingly difficult to see how the situation could possibly turn out for the best.

He looked up as a car came around the corner and slowly passed him, his heart quickening until he realized it was not for him.

So much history here, he thought, far and near. Since coming to Washington he had steeped himself in the city's heritage. So goes Washington, so goes the nation. The irony of meeting in the parking ramp of the Watergate Hotel was not lost on him. A president had been toppled by events that had happened here. An entire government had very nearly fallen. Was it possible again? He shuddered to think of it.

McAllister was still alive, and now he had help. They

had learned nothing from Sikorski, and what's more his carefully nurtured contacts among the underworld in New Jersey were threatening to pull out unless their fee was substantially increased.

"We're talking about my country here," the heavily accented Italian voice had screamed at him over the telephone. "It's gonna cost you, and cost you plenty."

Coming up with the extra money, though not impossible would be difficult. "I have accountability too," he'd said.

"Breaks of the game. But the price of poker has just gone up, gumba. Twenty-four hours."

McAllister was the key. He had been released from the Lubyanka by whom? Someone had to have signed the release order. Someone high up within the Komitet. But who? And why? It simply made no sense from where he sat.

The door at the far side of the ramp opened and the Russian turned his head in time to see his American counterpart emerge from the stairwell. He watched how the man walked, holding himself close as if he were in pain, as well indeed he might be considering the circumstances. Stem the tide. They had to not only stop McAllister, but they had to learn who was directing him and why.

The American reached the Mercedes and got in on the passenger side. He was visibly distressed, his complexion pale, his hand shaking as he lit a cigarette.

"It's time we thought about pulling out, unless you can tell me what the hell is going on here," the nature of his words stronger than the tone of his voice.

"What are you talking about?"

"McAllister is getting help."

"Yes, this woman . . ."

"No, I'm talking about outside help. Somebody is feeding him information. They must be, he can't be that good."

The Russian studied the American for a long moment or two. How much did he know that he wasn't telling? How many secrets had they kept from each other over the years? There was so much at stake here. They could not pull out, of course. Besides, there was nowhere on this earth for them to run and be safe. Nowhere.

"Then it is up to us to stop him before he goes too far."

The American shook his head. "You don't understand, Gennadi, how far he has taken it already."

"Then you will tell me, and together we will see what must be done." The Russian forced a calmness into his voice that he did not feel. He had worked with this one for enough years to understand that when he was upset it was for good cause.

"Someone must be feeding him information."

"From where?"

"Moscow."

"How? Where is his pipeline? Who does he see? Where do they meet?" With care, he thought.

"You're in a better position to find that out than I."

"There has been nothing, trust me when I tell you this," the Russian said. "I have made . . . inquiries. If McAllister is getting information it is coming from somewhere here in Washington, or very nearby. And by the way, that was an inspired guess on your part that he would actually break into CIA headquarters."

"He was after the O'Haire files."

"Did he get them?"

"I don't know. But we're going to have to assume that he did. And you know what that could mean."

"They've received their instructions. I think we can assume that they are safely out of harm's way for the moment."

"He broke into headquarters, for God's sake, Gennadi," the American shouted. "Do you think Marion is going to be any more difficult for him?"

The Russian shook his head. "I asked you once if

McAllister was a god, and you told me he was not. He was just an ordinary man with extraordinary abilities. What has changed your mind?"

"We've failed four times to stop him."

"Yes," the Russian said turning away. "Either he is very good and very lucky, or he is getting help."

"Then you agree with me," the American said excitedly.

"Only insofar as it may . . . and I stress the word *may* . . . be coming from someone local. The wire and satellite links have contained nothing. I guarantee it."

"Any ideas?"

"One name comes to mind," the Russian said.

"Who?"

"Someone you don't know about."

"What sort of a game are you playing at now?" the American said, raising his voice again.

"It won't do you any good to shout. Life goes on, as it must. We have nurtured this one for a good number of years, even before my time. He was just beginning to produce when this came up, and for the past couple of weeks it is my understanding that he has been silent. If you knew who he was you would understand just how strange his silence is just now."

"You're talking in circles, Gennadi. Who is this man?"

"Nicholas Albright," the Russian said, watching the American's face very closely.

"My God!"

"It was thought that his daughter's entry into the Agency would provide us with an ongoing source of information about new Agency recruits."

"Is she working with you as well?"

"No, of course not. But from what I understand she is very close to her father. She tells him things."

"Then he knows where McAllister is hiding?"

"I don't know."

The American's eyes narrowed. "What are you saying to me?"

"Albright is not my project, never has been. But if there is some maniac in Moscow who is trying to stop us, Albright could very well be his contact here. Now it seems more than logical. But I can't directly make an approach for fear of tipping my hand. You can see the delicacy?"

"What can I do?" the American asked.

"For the moment, nothing other than what you have already been doing. I'll attend to Albright personally."

"That would be very dangerous. . . ."

"I don't mean myself physically, I meant I'll have Albright taken care of. That section of Baltimore is very dangerous. Break-ins are not unheard of. If we can get the information from him, we will at least know who our enemies are."

"McAllister."

"He's only the tool, my friend. We must learn the identity of the craftsmen now."

The American looked away. "Do they realize what is at risk?"

The Russian did not answer. Fear, as a powerful, dark force, threatened to engulf him.

"McAllister cannot be allowed to continue."

"No."

"God help us all if he succeeds," the American said.

"Or even convinces someone else that he's not crazy."

After a successful strike you must wait and watch for the enemy's reaction before you make your next move. It is essential that this order of battle be strictly adhered to, especially when the odds are so heavily stacked against the operative in the field.

McAllister looked up from the last of the newspapers he had been reading. Stephanie was already finished.

"Anything?" she asked.

He shook his head. "Nothing yet," he said wearily.

He was tired of being cooped up in their hotel room, and he could see that she was too. Yet it was far too dangerous for either of them to wander far from the hotel now. After last night the Agency, the FBI, and the District police would be searching for them both. But until something happened they could do nothing but wait.

They'd both managed to get some sleep, and in the morning neither of them had mentioned her outburst of the night before. But her confession hung in the air between them like a thick veil that neither of them was ready to part.

For his part, McAllister didn't know what to say or do, because in fact he didn't know how he felt about her or his wife; except that he found Stephanie very attractive and sincere, and that his marriage had been failing for a long time before his wife had called him a traitor and had tried to kill him. He was confused, and hurting. Everything had been turned upside down for him in Moscow. No matter what happened or didn't happen, though, he knew for a fact that his life would never be the same, could never be the same. The circumstances had changed, but so had he.

"What makes you so sure that they'll say anything to the news media?" she asked. "They haven't so far."

"The Bureau is involved now, and so are the District police. It's bound to attract some attention. They'll have to make some kind of a statement."

"It could be anything. It might mean nothing."

"Even their silence could tell us something," McAllister said, though he wasn't at all sure what that might be. Something inside of him, however, some instinct told him that it was not time yet to move. They needed more information.

"We have four names," Stephanie was saying. "It's what you were looking for. Let's follow up those leads at least."

"Not yet," McAllister said. He glanced at his watch. It

was nearing noon, time for the television news broadcasts. He got up, crossed the room and turned on the television to the local ABC affiliate. A commercial was playing.

"What are you waiting for?" Stephanie asked, her voice rising.

"A message."

"What?"

"I did the unthinkable as far as they are concerned," he said, turning back to her. "I broke into headquarters and outsmarted their restricted-access codes. They're going to have to strike back. They're going to have to react, publicly. It's the only way they can let me know one of two things. *A*—that they want to make a deal with me, in which case it'll mean that someone is running scared, that I'm getting too close."

"*We're* getting too close," Stephanie corrected.

He nodded. "Or, *B*—that they're going to pull out all the stops and come after me as if I were public enemy number one."

"And what will that tell you?"

"It'll tell us who is conducting the investigation—someone legitimate, who honestly believes I'm a traitor. Or, the penetration agent who knows that I'm onto him and must be stopped."

"How can you be sure?" Stephanie asked, her frustration mounting.

"I can't," McAllister said. "Anymore than you can be sure of me, especially after last night."

She had picked up one of the newspapers, then slammed it down on the table. "Do you think I wanted this? Do you think I planned it? I ought to have my head examined!"

"Me too."

"There's something you're not telling me. Something else you found out last night besides those four names."

He said nothing.

"Don't you think I deserve at least that much? The truth

at least? My life is on the line too. If there is an APB on you, then there certainly is one on me. I made it clear to Dexter that I was not being coerced."

"Even the strongest would have cooperated if there had been a gun pointed at her head."

"I'm not getting out of this! You're not going to push me away. Goddamnit, talk to me! Let me help you. Trust me."

Trust me.

It came down to that. It always did in the end.

"There," she said pointing at the television, sudden fear in her voice.

McAllister turned around, and for a moment he was totally confused. What appeared to be a police composite drawing of a thick-necked, heavily jowled man with thick gray hair, long mustache, and square glasses filled the screen behind a news announcer. Beneath the picture was his name. But it wasn't him. He turned up the sound.

". . . considered armed and extremely dangerous. In a tersely worded announcement, the Federal Bureau of Investigation named McAllister as one of the top control officers of the O'Haire spy network. The O'Haires, as you remember, were recently sentenced to life imprisonment for their part in a spy ring that stole SDI secrets and turned them over to the Russians.

"Allegedly, McAllister worked with Soviets in Moscow to learn which areas of SDI technology the Russians most needed. It was his job, the Bureau spokesman said, to relay these questions back to the O'Haires. When the information had been gathered here in the U.S., it was transmitted to McAllister who had been stationed with the Central Intelligence Agency at the American Embassy in Moscow.

"The CIA refused to comment this morning, except to say that it was their understanding an arrest was imminent.

"McAllister was recently recalled to Washington for questioning, but disappeared two weeks ago from New York

City. It is believed, however, that now he is in the Washington area. In other news . . ."

"It's not your picture," Stephanie said.

McAllister had been staring at the television screen. "No," he said absently.

"It's your message, though," she said breathlessly. "But what are they trying to tell you?"

"I don't know," he said. His head was spinning. He had expected anything but this. They'd obviously insulated the public from any involvement. There would be no chance of a passerby spotting him and turning his description over to the police. But what else was going on here? Was it possible they were trying to lull him into a false sense of security? Not likely, he thought. The drawing was so obviously wrong, and had been supplied by someone who obviously should know what he looked like, that there had to be some meaning to it.

"The Russians know your face, and so does the Mafia," Stephanie was saying. "They'll see this, and they'll know that it's open season on you."

Was that it? Was that the message? Perhaps it wasn't meant for him. Perhaps it was meant for those trying to stop him. Go ahead and catch McAllister, we won't interfere. Was that what it meant?

"Let's get out, Mac. Before it's too late for both of us." Stephanie looked up at him, her eyes wide.

It was tempting, considering everything that had happened in the past couple of weeks. Yet he wondered if there was anyplace they could run that would be very safe for long. If the CIA or KGB wanted you badly enough, they would find you. Their networks were simply too extensive worldwide for anyone to hide from them. Sooner or later someone would come. For the rest of their lives they would be constantly looking over their shoulders, constantly tensing their muscles waiting for the bullet from a sniper's rifle.

"I've spent my life working for the Company. I can't give it up now."

"What has it gotten you?" she cried.

"I won't turn my back on it, Stephanie."

"Then they'll kill you," she said. "You'll make a mistake. You'll be in the wrong place at the wrong time. You'll trust someone you shouldn't. They won't keep missing. Sooner or later they *will* succeed."

"Then you go," he said gently. What did he feel toward her? His sense of responsibility and obligation clouded his inner thoughts.

"I'm not leaving, David," she said, using his given name for the first time. "I meant what I said last night. I love you. I won't abandon you. Let's get out of here. Far away. Now. Together. Please!"

"I . . . I can't," McAllister said, the words choking in his throat, a heavy feeling in his chest. "I can't just leave it."

"You must! You can't win, not against all of them!"

"I have to try."

"Why?" she shrieked. "What are you trying to prove?"

"Someone set me up, someone is trying to kill me." He was seeing Miroshnikov's face swimming in a mist in front of his eyes. The Russian interrogator was smiling.

We have made great progress together, you and I. I am so very proud of you, Mac, so very pleased.

How could he ever forget the pain and the humiliation he had suffered at the hands of the Russians? Of one Russian in particular.

"They'll keep trying, don't you see that?" Stephanie cried.

"It means I'm on the right track," he said. Sweat popped out on his forehead.

Stephanie came across the room to him and hesitantly reached up and touched his face, his cheeks, his lips as if she were a blind person trying to learn what he looked like.

"I had to try," she said softly. "For you. For us. But I think I finally understand why you can't turn your back on everything and run away. I could do it, but not you. It's the Company. Your father. Your friends. Your obligations . . . your wife."

McAllister closed his eyes. He could see Gloria's face now, contorted into a mask of fury and hate, the gun in her hand. *Traitor,* she had screamed at him, and she had sincerely meant to kill him. The pain was almost beyond endurance. He had to know why. At least that much.

"I understand, darling, believe me I do," Stephanie was saying.

McAllister opened his eyes and reached for her, drawing her close. "Do you?" he asked.

"Yes," she said, her heart beating against his chest. "Whatever you do I'll stay with you. I won't desert you, I promise."

"And afterward?" he asked. "If there is an afterward?"

She looked up at him. "That will be up to you," she said. "But for now we have four names to follow up, four leads from the computer. It's something."

"Five," McAllister said.

A look of confusion crossed her features. She glanced over at the computer printout on the table. "Four . . ." she started.

"There *was* something I didn't tell you about last night," McAllister said.

She looked up into his eyes, waiting for him to continue. She was shivering.

"The O'Haire file was restricted. Entry required a password. I tried *zebra,* spelled forward and backward, and I tried the word *spies*. Nothing worked. Finally, in desperation I used the only other word I could think of: *Highnote*."

"That was the correct password?"

McAllister nodded.

"Oh, God."

"Before I go after the other four, I've got to see him again."

"No, David, I won't allow that. Anything but that."

"I must."

"I can't stand by and watch you commit suicide," she said, pulling away. "Don't you see that? It's been Highnote all along. It has to be!"

"Then I'll find that out."

"No," she cried.

"Yes. It's the only way. Everything else would be meaningless. I must know."

Chapter 17

It was only a few minutes after six, yet it was already dark. Traffic on Langley's Washington Parkway was heavy. The day shift at CIA headquarters had just let out. McAllister watched from where he was parked at the side of the highway three-quarters of a mile south of the Agency.

He was taking an enormous risk by being here like this. Stephanie had wanted to help, but in the end he convinced her that it would be much safer if he approached Highnote on his own. If anything went wrong, she would still be free. She could get to Dexter Kingman with the entire story. It was something at least.

Earlier when he had walked over to the parking ramp where they'd left the Chevrolet Celebrity they'd rented at Dulles in the name of Treffano Miglione, it had struck him that the city was decorated. Colored lights were strung across the streets, noel candles and brightly lit wreaths were hung on lightposts, and many of the store windows held elaborate displays. It was less than two weeks before Christmas. He'd forgotten completely about it, and with the realization came a sudden ache for something he'd never really had as an adult: a family, someone for whom Christmas would mean something.

At first he'd thought about telephoning Highnote, setting up another meeting like the one they'd had at the rest stop off the Interstate north of the city, but he suspected there would be monitors on all incoming calls now. Nor would it be safe to approach his old friend at home again. There was sure to be a surveillance team on duty out there.

Do the unexpected. His investigation had taken on a life of its own, sweeping him and Stephanie along, at times in an uncontrollable headlong rush; as if they were trapped in a small boat racing downstream toward a deadly waterfall.

He'd been watching in the rearview mirror as traffic from the north passed beneath a tall sodium-vapor light a hundred yards back. A black Cadillac approached. McAllister looked up as it passed, recognizing Robert Highnote behind the wheel. He flipped on his headlights and pulled out into traffic, speeding up to get directly behind the Cadillac.

Highnote was alone. McAllister had counted on that, as he had counted on the fact that his old friend was a creature of habit who almost always took off work at six sharp and drove directly home. Despite the pressure the man had to be under because of recent events, he apparently was maintaining his schedule.

A couple of miles south, Highnote got off the Parkway at Arlingwood. McAllister held his position behind him for a half a mile until there was a break in traffic, then pulled out to pass.

As McAllister got alongside, he matched speed, glancing from the oncoming traffic over to Highnote, who after a moment, realizing that something was happening, looked over. His reaction, when it finally came, was one of incredulity.

McAllister smiled wanly, motioned for Highnote to follow him, then sped up, pulling in front of the Cadillac. His old friend had two choices now. He could either follow, or he could pull off at the nearest telephone and sound the alert. He knew the car now, and the license number.

The road split a mile later; south toward Arlington Heights, and east toward Falls Church. McAllister hung far enough back so that there was not enough gap between his and Highnote's car for someone to pull between them. He turned east, Highnote remaining directly behind him, and he breathed his first sigh of relief. For now, at least, there was going to be no trouble. Highnote was apparently at least willing to listen.

The countryside here was hilly and very dark. Twenty minutes later it had begun to snow lightly as McAllister pulled into the parking lot of a small but elegant dinner club a couple of miles beyond Falls Church. The parking lot was half filled at this hour. It was just the sort of place he had been looking for, and had expected to find here. He parked in the back and got out of his car as Highnote pulled up and parked beside him.

"I got your message," McAllister said, as Highnote climbed out of his car. They stood facing each other.

"Where is Stephanie Albright?"

"Safe."

"Then she is working with you?"

"You wanted to talk to me," McAllister said. "I'm here. Let's go inside."

"Send her back. It's not her fight."

"Nor was it mine, Bob. At least it wasn't until people started shooting at me. A lot of them, Russians and Americans. I think it's time that we talk about the Zebra Network."

"Then you did break the access code," Highnote said, his complexion suddenly pale in the outside lights.

"An inspired guess," McAllister said. "Let's go inside."

The supper club had once been a large house. To the right of the entry hall were the separate dining rooms, large windows looking down into a steep valley garden. To the left was the barroom. They took a leather booth at the back. Forties music was playing from the jukebox.

After the waiter brought them drinks, McAllister sat back with a cigarette and looked across at his old friend. *Whom to trust.* Always, always it came down to that in the end. The older he got the harder that question became to answer.

"How's Gloria?" McAllister asked.

"Confused," Highnote said, sipping his martini.

"We don't have much time here tonight, I suspect, so let's not bullshit each other. How is Gloria holding up?"

"She's written you off," Highnote said coldly. "If that's what you really wanted to hear."

Something clutched at McAllister's heart, though the response had not come as a total surprise. Their marriage had been over years ago, he supposed. This now was merely a last excuse. Yet it hurt. "And you? Have you written me off as well?"

"I'm here, aren't I?" Highnote said. "I must say that you've done a lot better than I thought you would."

"What's going on?"

Highnote's right eyebrow rose. "Exactly the question I want to put to you. We found poor Janos. Was that necessary?"

"I didn't kill him," McAllister said. "That should have been obvious. If you want an ID on those two bodies, I can give it to you."

"What two bodies?" Highnote asked with a straight face.

"One in the driveway, the other back up in the woods, about a hundred yards off the road."

Highnote shook his head. "There was some blood beside the driveway; O-Positive, your blood type I believe, and some tire marks. No bodies other than Janos's."

McAllister closed his eyes. The Mafia had sent two hired guns out to question Sikorski. When they didn't return someone else would have gone out to check on them. That was logical. But it still didn't answer the question of who had tortured Sikorski if they hadn't.

"Someone has set me up for the kill," he said, opening his eyes.

"The Russians."

"Why?"

"Our best guess is that you are a project gone bad for them."

"You know damned well that I did not work for the O'Haires," McAllister said.

"They named you."

"Then somebody got to them!"

"The whole world is wrong and you're right, is that it?" Highnote asked, leaning forward. "I don't know what happened to you in the Lubyanka, and I don't think you do either, but I believe that you were set up—brainwashed, if you will—to come back here and wreak havoc."

"Then why are the Russians trying to kill me?"

"Because I think they lost control of you. And if you were brought in, and the secrets that are locked inside your brain were released, you would prove to be a very large embarrassment."

"Then I'm an innocent victim . . . ?"

"No," Highnote snapped. "I think you worked with the O'Haires all along, and when the network fell the Russians arrested you, hoping to throw off any suspicions about you. While they had you, they decided to play their little game. Nice friends."

"You believe that, Bob?" McAllister asked.

"I don't know what else to believe."

"Why? Where are my motives?"

Highnote lowered his eyes and shook his head. "That's the damndest part of it all, Mac. I just don't know." He looked up. "Burn-out? Gloria told us that you'd been acting strangely ever since you'd been assigned to Moscow. Maybe you saw what you took to be the futility of the business. Maybe you thought your father had wasted his life. He did kill himself, after all. I don't know, but it happens sometimes to the best of them."

McAllister fought back the one memory of his father that he had never allowed into his consciousness. Shame? Fear? Whatever, he had avoided thinking about it for a very long time.

"Why was the message sent to me? That's what the business with my name and false description was all about, wasn't it?"

"It was Dexter Kingman's idea. He thought it might flush you out. And it did."

"Yes," McAllister said. "It did. So here we are, talk to me."

"Do you want it straight?"

McAllister nodded.

"Let Stephanie Albright come in. Nothing will happen to her, I promise you."

"Then you'll help me?"

"There is nothing I can do for you, Mac," Highnote said, his voice low. "Put a bullet in your head. End it now. It would be for the best."

McAllister shivered. "Is that your advice?"

"James O'Haire was Zebra One here in Washington, and you were Zebra Two in Moscow. It's my guess Voronin was warning you that your identity had been discovered. I looked up his track. He had been in a position to know such things."

"That's how you see it?"

"Yes," Highnote said. "You got into the computer to find out if we suspected you. Well, you know by now that we did not, although sooner or later we would have caught on to you."

McAllister's head was spinning. Nothing made any sense.

Nothing was real. Yet there was an internal logic to what Highnote was telling him. Except that the Russians had arrested him and then inexplicably released him after the trial to make the CIA believe that he indeed was the O'Haires' control officer in an effort to protect the identity of the real man or men. Still there was one man in Moscow and one here in the United States.

"The last time we talked I asked you to consider the possibility that I was telling the truth, and that I had been set up."

"I considered it, Mac, believe me. And I came to the conclusion that you *are* telling the truth so far as you know it. But can you tell me exactly what happened to you every moment you were being held in the Lubyanka?"

Miroshnikov's face swam into view. The barroom suddenly seemed very warm and close.

"I can see that you cannot. They are sophisticated, Mac. You know the drill. They had you for more than a month. They could have done anything to you. Anything at all. Turn you into anything they wanted. Turn you into their creature, even."

"But what if that's not the case?" McAllister insisted. "Give me that much at least. Give me that consideration, just for the sake of argument."

"Go on," Highnote said after a moment.

McAllister ran a hand across his eyes. "I was a thorn in their side in Moscow so they arrested me and subjected me to a month of interrogation. And believe me, Bob, it is an experience that you would never forget."

"Why were you released?"

"I think there are two possibilities. The first is that they had made their point. They'd caught an American spy, they'd tried him and found him guilty, and at that point he was of no further real value to them, so they simply released him."

"They had your confession," Highnote said. "You named all of your old network people. Times, places, operations. Everything."

"The second is that it was a mistake. Whoever was in charge of my case hadn't been given all the facts. Zebra One and Two meant nothing to my interrogator. But someone else could have listened to the tapes, read the manuscripts. Perhaps too late they realized that I was being released."

"So, thinking that you knew more than you really did, this unknown Russian ordered your assassination in New York before you could cause any damage. Is that what you're saying to me?"

"Either that or he told his American counterpart about me, and my assassination was ordered locally. And it didn't stop there. They were Russians waiting for me outside your house, but they were Americans at your sailboat and there were two men out at Sikorski's. Possibly Mafia."

"We found no bodies."

"Someone came out and cleaned up the mess before you got there."

"Zebra One and Two are still in place, if I'm to believe you. One man here in Washington and one man in Moscow. Probably someone within the Agency. Someone we both know, and trust."

"That's right," McAllister said. "But there's even more to it than that."

Highnote's eyebrows knitted. "I'm still listening, Mac."

"I didn't kill Janos, but neither did the two I had the shoot-out with."

"Who then?"

"I don't know. Janos had been dead for at least a day and a half. Before the snowfall. There were no tire marks in or out of his place."

This news more than anything else seemed to affect Highnote the most. He sat back in the booth a deep, pensive look on his face. "If I believe you, Mac, and I'm not saying I do, it would mean that there is a third party at work here. Someone not connected with your penetration agent." He shook his head. "Doesn't make a whole lot of sense. I mean, can you explain the logic to me?"

"No," McAllister said heavily. "But if I'm not telling the truth, for whatever reason, then my lies are very elaborate. Too elaborate. And for what reason?"

We have made great progress together, you and I. I am so very proud of you, Mac, so very pleased.

Can you tell me exactly what happened to you every moment you were being held in the Lubyanka?

Look to Washington. Look to Moscow. Zebra One, Zebra Two.

"I don't know if there is anything I can do for you, or should. Too much has happened. If you had turned yourself in at the beginning it might have been different. But now, I just don't know."

"I would have been dead by now."

Highnote shook his head sadly, and he glanced toward the door. McAllister followed his gaze.

"Is someone coming?" he asked.

Highnote looked away guiltily.

"You said Dexter Kingman had the idea to flush me out. Are his people on the way out here now? Did you call them from your car?"

"Something is going on, Mac. I don't know what it is. . . ."

"You *did* call someone," McAllister said, and he got up abruptly.

Highnote's eyes were round. "Run," he whispered. "I'll do what I can for you."

McAllister reached into his coat pocket for his gun as he went to the entry hall. In the short space of time he and Highnote had been here the place had filled up considerably. A number of people were waiting to be seated. He came around the corner at the same moment the front door opened and two men walked in. One of them was Dexter Kingman.

"McAllister," Kingman shouted.

McAllister pulled out his gun and fired a shot over everyone's head, the bullet smacking into the wall above the door. Kingman and the other man fell back out the door. A woman screamed as McAllister turned on his heel and raced into the dining room, threading his way through the tables, pandemonium spreading in his wake.

A waitress, balancing a large tray of food in her right hand, was just coming through the swinging doors from the kitchen. McAllister slammed into her, sending her flying, plates crashing everywhere.

"Some maniac is out there with a gun," he shouted, racing through the kitchen, concealing his own weapon.

"What's going on?" one of the chefs screamed.

Someone was shouting into a telephone.

McAllister reached the rear door and outside, leaped down off the delivery platform, as a panel van was pulling up. He yanked open the passenger door and jumped in even before the van had come to a complete halt. He pointed the gun at the young man's head.

"Drive away from here! Now!"

"Is this a stickup?" the frightened kid stammered.

"Get us out of here, goddamnit! Move it!"

The driver slammed the van into reverse, pulled away from the loading dock, then spun around in the slippery driveway and headed out to the highway.

McAllister cranked down the window and turned the big wing mirror so that he could see the rear door of the restaurant. No one had appeared by the time they turned the corner and reached the highway, accelerating back toward Washington, sirens finally sounding in the distance.

James Franklin O'Haire had not slept well from the moment he and his brother Liam had been transferred to the federal penitentiary at Marion, Illinois. The judge, out of some perverse sense of patriotism, had specified the general-population prison, knowing that the O'Haires would not be well received by their fellow prisoners. "No country club incarceration for these two," he'd said at the sentencing. Rape, murder, and bank robbery were acceptable crimes, not spying. Even criminals should feel a sense of national loyalty.

Jim O'Haire raised his left arm and looked at his watch. It was a few minutes before midnight. Something had awakened him; a noise, a metallic click. He didn't know what it was.

He sat up in his cot, shoved the covers back and swung his legs over the edge. He was a husky man with graying hair and violently blue eyes. His roommate was sound asleep in the upper bunk. The lights from the main tier hall cast shadows in the narrow cell. From somewhere he could hear music. He figured one of the guards was listening to a radio.

A large black figure, dressed in prison dungarees, appeared at the cell door. "O'Haire," the man called softly.

Jim O'Haire recognized him as George Hanks, one of the trustees from downstairs. He got up, but remained uncertainly by his bunk. Something was wrong here, drastically wrong. All the inmates were supposed to be locked down at this hour.

"Let's go," Hanks said. He glanced over his shoulder, then eased the cell door open, taking care to make as little noise as possible.

"What is it?" O'Haire asked. "What do you want?"

"You're gettin' out of here, that's what it is," Hanks said. "Now move your honky ass and fix up your bunk, we're runnin' out of time."

The sound he had heard was the electronic door lock. Somehow Hanks had gotten to the control board, or one of the guards was in on this. O'Haire didn't want to get his hopes up, not this soon after talking with the two Agency pricks who had come out here the other day. Besides, this simply didn't feel right to him. Hanks and the other prisoners had given him a lot of shit over the past week.

"What are you talking about?" he asked.

"Shit, I'm not going to stand here all fuckin' night waitin' on you. We got word from the man that you're gettin' out of here. Tonight."

Christ, was it possible? "What about my brother?"

"He's on his way. Now move your ass!" Hanks whispered urgently.

O'Haire hesitated only a moment longer before he turned and stuffed his pillow beneath his blanket so that from the cell door a passing guard might be fooled at first glance into believing that someone was in the bunk. There was no way he was going to sit rotting in this place when there was a chance of immediate escape. No way in hell.

At the barred door, O'Haire slipped out onto the walkway three tiers up from the main floor. Hanks, his powerful muscles rippling beneath his thin prison shirt, eased the door shut, the lock snapping home, then turned and nodded silently for O'Haire to follow him.

At the end of the walkway they took the stairs down to the main floor where Hanks produced a key and opened the steel door, admitting them to a holding vestibule. On the far side was another steel door, a small square window at eye level. Hanks unlocked this door, and O'Haire followed him out into the access corridor which ran the length of the main building.

A guard should have been stationed here, but his desk was empty, the corridor completely deserted. Hanks had a plan, and the organization and contacts to carry it out. They were attributes that O'Haire admired, and he allowed a faint smile as he followed the big man down the corridor and outside into the bitter-cold night.

They held up in the shadows as a light-gray station wagon crossed the prison yard from the laundry plant.

"What's the plan?" O'Haire whispered.

Hanks looked back at him, the expression on his face unreadable. "You and your brother are getting out in the morning garbage run."

"What about outside?"

"Somebody will be waitin' on you. It's all set up."

"How about clothes?"

"Man, quit raggin' my ass. You'll be taken care of."

"I want to know," O'Haire demanded, grabbing the man's arm and pulling him around.

Hanks shoved him up against the brick wall, his eyes suddenly wild, his muscles bunched up. "Don't mess with me, motherfucker! I said you were going to be taken care of, and I meant it!"

O'Haire spread his hands. "Sorry. My ass is hanging out here."

"Yeah, so is mine," Hanks said, backing off.

The car was gone, and they hurried to the far end of the building, passed through a tunnel, crossed a broad courtyard and driveway, then entered the garbage-collection facility through a side door, the sudden odor of rotting food and an open grease trap assailing their nostrils.

The prison garbage was separated here into recyclable items such as cans and glass bottles which were crushed and shipped out, and paper and plastic products that were dried, shredded, and sent over to the electrical generating plant for burning. Everything else was loaded aboard trucks each morning and taken out to the country dump off prison grounds.

Four big garbage trucks were parked in the main garage. Hanks led the way behind the trucks and through another steel door into the big separation room adjacent to the prison kitchen.

Jim O'Haire's younger brother, Liam, stood leaning up against a table, his arms folded over his chest. He straightened up when he spotted his brother.

"We're getting out of here," he said.

"Right . . ." Jim O'Haire started to reply when Hanks suddenly swiveled on him, grabbed a handful of his shirt and bodily threw him up against the table.

"Motherfucker," Hanks swore.

"What the hell," Jim O'Haire shouted, regaining his balance and spinning around.

Six black men had appeared out of the shadows, each of them armed with a knife. Hanks pulled out a switchblade and thumbed it open with a soft click.

"Mother of God, what's going on here?" Jim O'Haire shouted.

"Go ahead and scream, boy, nobody's going to hear you," Hanks said, he and the others advancing.

"We did our part," Jim O'Haire shouted. "Goddamnit, we did as we were told."

Chapter 18

The number at her father's house in Baltimore rang ten times before Stephanie finally hung up. She'd used the pay phone in the corridor between the cocktail lounge and the lobby.

Calls from their room could be too easily monitored by the hotel operator. Mac had told her that. She believed in him. God in heaven, she'd done everything he'd told her.

She glanced down the darkly paneled corridor toward the cocktail lounge. A couple of men sat at the bar talking with the woman bartender. Other than that the hotel was quiet at this hour.

Where is my father? she asked herself. It was a Monday night. He should have been home asleep in his bed unless there had been an emergency call to the practice. But he never got emergency calls.

And where was Mac? He had been gone nearly seven hours now. Where was he? What was happening? She had a vision of his bullet-riddled body lying beside a dark road somewhere in the country.

She didn't think she could take much more of this. Sitting alone, waiting. She'd never been very good at that. Highnote was somehow at the center of this business. In at least that much she and Mac were now in total agreement. But where he was blinded by past friendships, previous loyalties, she was able to see with an unprejudiced eye. Mac had been set up from the moment he'd been arrested in Moscow. Highnote was the logical man behind it all. He was Zebra One. He was the man in Washington who had controlled the O'Haire network . . . and probably still controlled whatever was left of the organization. Mac, by going to see him, had been walking into a trap.

So write him off. Turn around and get out. Run. But to where? Mac had not returned and her father did not answer her call. She was alone, and she was frightened.

She walked back to the elevator and took it up to their third-floor room where she went to the window. It was snowing quite hard now.

I can't stand by and watch you commit suicide. . . . It's been Highnote all along. It has to be!

Then I'll find that out. It's the only way. Everything else would be meaningless. I must know.

"Must know what?" she cried to herself, laying her forehead against the cool glass. "What is driving you, my darling? What are you seeking? Who are you looking for?"

She closed her eyes and grabbed a handful of the thick drapes. Her stomach felt hollow and her legs were suddenly so weak they were barely able to support her. She'd known that she was being told lies from the moment she'd been assigned to McAllister's house and had talked with his wife. The woman had seemed frightened . . . but not for her husband, rather for herself. Stephanie had not understood it at the time. It wasn't until Mac had shown up and had confronted his wife on the steps that Stephanie had been able to give voice in her own mind to what she had instinctively felt. Gloria McAllister wanted her husband dead not because she thought he was a traitor, but because she herself was hiding something, or she no longer cared for him. She'd gone off with Highnote. Were the two of them somehow working together?

"Oh, father," she cried softly. "I need you now. I don't know what to do."

McAllister parked the delivery van in front of the FBI headquarters building in the same place he had left the Thunderbird and walked back to the Best Western. It was going to drive them crazy finding the van this way. Before long they would begin searching all the hotels in an ever-expanding radius downtown. Sooner or later they would get lucky. It was time to move.

He had let the young driver off in the country between Highview Park and Cherrydale hours ago, but instead of driving directly back into the city and ditching the van, he had driven over to Arlington Cemetery where he had lingered alone with his thoughts. It was a dangerous game he'd been playing. It couldn't have taken the driver very long to get to a telephone and report what had happened. They'd be looking for the van by now. He'd increased his risk of being taken by his delay, yet he found that he wasn't ready to face Stephanie.

For a while, sitting in the darkness smoking a cigarette, he thought about leaving her. Simply turning around and running away. But in the end he knew that was impossible. She was a part of this thing now, no matter what he did or didn't do. Whoever wanted him dead would also be gunning for her.

As he had done the night before, he was careful with his tradecraft, making absolutely certain that he wasn't being followed. Across the street from the hotel he held up in the darkness for a full five minutes, making sure that the place had not been staked out.

Highnote had done exactly what any good and loyal government servant should have done. The moment he had spotted McAllister he had telephoned Security. Mac had forgotten about his car phone. It had been a mistake on his part that had very nearly cost him his life.

But in the end Highnote had listened. He had admitted the possibility that something more than met the eye was going on. And in the end he had told Mac to run. He had warned him.

Run where? To whom? To what? Where else could he turn?

He went around the corner and entered the hotel through the parking garage, taking the stairs up to the third floor where again he held up, studying the empty corridor before continuing. There weren't too many options left open to them. But Highnote, he was fully convinced now, was on his side; reluctantly perhaps, and understandably so, but on his side. Stephanie would have to be made to understand that it was time for her to get clear. Not back to the Agency, of course, but she would have to go into hiding now. Somewhere out of harm's way.

She opened the door for him, slipping the security chain and then stepping back. Her eyes were wide and shining, she'd obviously been crying. Her hand shook badly when she reached up and touched his cheek.

"I didn't think you were coming back," she said, her voice tremulous.

"Are you all right?" he asked, taking her into his arms, and realizing that somehow over the past few days he had begun to care for her. "Did something happen here?"

"No," she said. "Not really . . ."

"What do you mean by that? Stephanie, what happened?"

She shook her head. "Did you see Highnote? Did you actually get to talk to him?"

"Tell me what's going on."

"Goddamnit, David, talk to me!" she snapped. "You've been gone seven hours, leaving me to sit here imagining all sorts of things."

Tears had come to her eyes again, and her entire body was trembling.

"Easy," McAllister said soothingly, holding her close. "I saw him and we talked. There's not much he can do for us, but he is on our side."

Stephanie pulled away and looked up into his eyes. "Oh, David, how can you believe that after everything that's happened?"

"He listened to me. At first he was skeptical, but in the end he believed me. He warned me. Told me to run in the end. It saved my life."

"Run from what?"

"He called Dexter Kingman from his car phone. It was something I hadn't counted on. They were just showing up when I got out."

"It would have been convenient if you'd been shot and killed trying to escape," Stephanie said. "My darling, can't you see what's happening? How he's maneuvered you? He's given you the same advice each time you've talked to him. He can't help you and he tells you to run. David, only guilty men run. How else could Dexter have seen it?"

"He could have said nothing. Kept me busy. I would have been trapped."

"There would have been a shoot-out. You would have been killed."

"That might have been the plan in the beginning, but he changed his mind."

"What did he say?"

"They think I was working for the Russians all along, running the O'Haire network. He said they named me as their control officer."

"Why were you arrested in Moscow? Did he have an explanation for that?"

"To throw suspicion off me, at first. But then I was brainwashed in the Lubyanka. I supposedly became one of them. But something went wrong, and they lost control of me. They decided in the end I would be better off dead."

"All wrapped up in a neat little package," she said disdainfully. "Too neat." She shook her head in irritation. "That explains only why the Russians want you dead. What about the Mafia? What have they got to do with it?"

"There were no bodies at Sikorski's," McAllister said. "Someone cleaned up the mess out there before the FBI showed up."

"Then they think that you killed Sikorski?"

"Yes."

"Highnote told you that?" Stephanie asked, watching his eyes.

"I convinced him otherwise. At least I got him thinking that there was another possibility."

"Which is?"

"That there is a penetration agent in the CIA. Someone at high levels who is working with a counterpart in the KGB."

"Zebra One and Two."

"That's right."

"Your release from the Lubyanka, then, was nothing more than an administrative mistake. Crossed signals."

McAllister nodded.

"And Highnote accepted that?"

"Only after I told him the one thing that doesn't fit anywhere. The one thing that makes absolutely no sense. The two men I stopped at Sikorski's hadn't killed Janos. They found him like that. He'd been dead for at least a day and a half. So who killed him and why?"

"If not the Mafia, then the Russians," Stephanie answered. "Can't you see it? Zebra Two is the Russian. He has his own people working for him, probably out of their embassy right here in Washington. But Zebra One, the American, can't use CIA people for his dirty work, so he hires professional hit men. It all still points back to Highnote."

"You had to be there, face-to-face with him. I know the man. He genuinely wants to help, but his hands are tied."

"Then what's left for you, my darling?" Stephanie asked softly. "What's left for us?"

"The list."

She looked at him questioningly. "What?"

"The four names from the computer. I'm going after them. They're our only leads. If there are still connections between the O'Haire network and whoever was running it, they might know."

"Highnote knows that. He'll have his people waiting for you."

McAllister pulled away. "Goddamnit, you haven't listened to a word I've said. Highnote is not Zebra One."

"I'm sorry," Stephanie said. "But even if you're right, he'll have to follow up with those four names. It's his duty. He'll have to go to them for the same reasons you want to go to them."

McAllister was shaking his head, and sudden understanding dawned in Stephanie's eyes.

"You didn't tell him, did you?" she said.

"No."

She smiled. "You held back that one piece of information. Why? Can you answer that?"

"It never came up," he said weakly.

"Because you didn't bring it up," she said triumphantly. "Whatever you say you believe, there is something at the back of your head, some instinct for survival that told you to keep it from him. Just in case."

"There's nothing he could have done. . . ."

"No," Stephanie interrupted. "Do you know what I think? I think that something did happen to you in the Lubyanka. Something that changed you, something that made you unsure of your own abilities. But deep in your gut you know what moves to make, you know how to protect yourself. What happened in New York, and what's been happening ever since proves that. Let yourself go, David. Let your old habits, your old instincts take over. Do what you know is the right thing. You have the tradecraft, use it."

"We'll have to get out of here first thing in the morning," he said, going over to the window and looking down at the empty street.

Tradecraft was what you used against the enemy, not against friends. Put a bullet in your head. . . . End it now. . . . It would be for the best. Gloria has written you off.

"Where are we going?"

"Out of Washington," he said.

"Where? To do what?"

He focused on her pale reflection in the dark window glass. He'd lived with pain for so long he was surprised now that he wasn't used to it. She didn't look real to him; her hair was in disarray, and she was dressed simply in a loose sweatshirt and blue jeans, yet he knew that he wanted her. It astonished him, this sudden feeling. He'd either come a long way in the past weeks, or he had fallen—he couldn't decide which, or if at this moment it really mattered.

"He told me to send you back." McAllister said. "In a way he was right."

"What are you talking about?"

"I can't afford you any longer. You'll slow me down to such a degree that they'll catch up with us, and we'll both be dead." His words sounded hollow in his ears. "Sooner or later they'll get to your father and use him to pry you loose. I'm not going to wait for that to happen."

He turned to her. Tears were slipping down her cheeks. "I don't have anyplace to go," she said.

"Dexter Kingman would make sure nothing happened to you."

She was shaking her head again. "I'm not going to leave you, David. Not now, not after everything that has happened."

"You're not listening to me," McAllister said, his voice rising. "They're probably going to win. There are too many of them, they're too well organized. Sooner or later I'll simply wear down, my luck will run out, and it'll be over."

"They'd hunt me as well."

"Not if they were convinced that you knew nothing. That I'd held you against your will."

"I'm not leaving you, David," she said. "Whatever it is I have to do to convince you, I will."

"Why?"

"Because I love you," she cried. "I told you once, didn't you hear me? Didn't you believe me? I love you. There is no life for me without you."

He turned back to the window again, unable to face her. He knew what he wanted to say, but he simply could not speak the words. Not now. The insanity was everywhere. With him there was death, away from him there was at least the possibility of life. Something was driving him, something had always driven him for as long as he could remember. But even now he could not give voice to the demons inside of him.

"It's the game that gets to all of us sooner or later," Wallace Mahoney had said at the Farm. He'd lost his wife and both sons to the business, yet he'd gone on because there were no other possibilities for him.

The only reality is in continuing with your life for better or for worse. The Russians have a proverb: Life is unbearable, but death is not so pleasant either.

"You have to believe me," Stephanie said.

"You cannot stay with me."

"There is only one thing that would make me go," she said. "Turn around and look at me!"

McAllister turned.

"Tell me that you don't care for me. Tell me that it doesn't matter that I love you. Tell me that you will never care for me. Then I'll leave you."

"I can't."

"You must."

"I can't tell you that, because I do love you. It's why I wanted to send you away, to keep you in hiding, to keep you safe, to protect you. I don't care what happens to anyone else, only you. If you want to stay I won't send you away."

She took off her sweatshirt. Her shoulders were tiny and rounded, the nipples of her small breasts were erect. "I want to stay," she said. "I'll never leave."

McAllister came across the room to her, and took her in his arms, his lips finding hers. She shuddered as she pressed against him, the heat of her body penetrating his shirt. He ran his hands down her back, her flanks, the mounts of her bottom, small and tight in her blue jeans. She shuddered again.

"Please, David," she said looking into his face. "Make love to me now."

He picked her up and carried her across the room where he laid her on the bed. Undoing the waistband of her jeans, he pulled them down around her boyish hips, and peeled them off her long, straight legs. He kissed her breasts, his tongue lingering at her nipples, and then brushed his lips across her belly, the tops of her legs, her inner thighs as she spread her legs, her pelvis rising to meet his touch.

When he stepped back to get undressed, she watched him, her lips parted, a faint flush coming to her complexion. He laid his gun on the table beside the bed, and let his clothes fall where they would.

"Hurry," she said. "Hurry."

He came to her on the bed, her legs parting for him, and he entered her without preliminaries. She opened her lips as they kissed, her fingers pulling at his back, her legs wrapped around his body, her hips rising to meet his thrusts.

"I'll never leave you, David," she cried softly. "I'll never leave you."

Later, lying beside each other, McAllister watched her breasts rise and fall with her breathing. Her odor was slightly musky and very sensuous.

"I don't know how this is going to turn out," he said. "But I'm not going to give it up. I don't think I have that choice."

She looked at him through heavy-lidded eyes, a faint smile on her lips. "Do you love me?"

The snow was falling very hard outside now. He touched her lips with his fingertips. "Yes."

"Say it," she said.

"I love you."

"Then nothing else matters. We'll do it together, David." She smiled. "Now make love to me again. I need you."

It was very late. McAllister woke with a start, suddenly realizing that he was alone in the big bed. He sat up, shoving the covers back. The television set was still on, but the screen was blank and the sound had been turned down. The only other light came from the partially open bathroom door.

"Stephanie?" he called, getting out of bed.

There was no answer. She was not in the bathroom, and her clothes and purse were gone. The clock on the nightstand read a few minutes before five. Where the hell had she gone?

He was pulling on his trousers when a key grated in the door lock. Crossing the room in two strides he snatched up his gun, slipped off the safety and spun around as the door opened.

Stephanie's figure, backlit by the corridor lights, appeared in the doorway and she slipped inside, stopping in her tracks when she saw that McAllister was out of bed, standing in the middle of the room, the gun in his hand pointed at her.

"Oh," she said.

McAllister's heart had jumped into his throat. He lowered the gun with a shaking hand and stepped back. "Christ," he said. "Where did you go?"

"It's my father," she said breathlessly. "I went downstairs to call from the pay phone. But there was no answer."

"What?"

"David, he should be home. Something has happened to him. Something terrible. I just know it!"

Chapter 19

Robert Highnote was careful with his driving. With all the snow that had fallen in the night the roads at this hour of the morning were extremely slippery. The dawn had brought an uncertain gray light. Traffic was very heavy on the Capital Beltway around the city, and cars still drove with headlights on.

The telephone call he had received a scant hour ago had come as a complete surprise, as had the peremptory tone Paul Innes, the U.S. associate deputy attorney general had used.

"A few of us are getting together for breakfast at my place this morning, Bob. We want to talk to you."

Highnote hadn't slept well. He glanced at his bedside clock. It was barely six. "A hell of a time to be calling. What's this all about?"

"I won't discuss this on an open line. But I want you here as soon as possible. We've all got extremely tight schedules this morning."

"I'll just give Van a quick call. . . ."

"Already been done. We'll be expecting you within the hour."

Van was Howard Van Skike, director of central intelligence. Whatever was going on at Innes's house this morning had to be very important. "I'll be there."

Highnote got off the highway at the U.S. Department of Agriculture Research Center and took Baltimore Avenue south into College Park adjacent to the University of Maryland. A good deal of Washington's workaday business was conducted at such breakfast meetings. A lot of interservice liaison was accomplished without the red tape attendant to normal office hours meetings. Innes had been the prosecutor on the O'Haire case, and on reflection Highnote had a feeling what this morning's meeting would be about. He turned off the main road and headed up a long, sloping driveway through the trees. His only question was how much Innes knew and who else would be present this morning.

The snow had eased up, but several inches lay on the ground and as Highnote got out of his car in front of the huge three-story colonial house, he heard the crunch of footsteps behind him. He turned around as a very large man, dressed in boots and a white parka came around from the side of the house.

"Good morning, sir," the man called out as he approached.

Highnote's heart skipped a beat. He stood beside the car waiting until the man reached him. FBI was written all over his face and bearing.

"Are you armed, Mr. Highnote?"

The question was extraordinary. "No, of course not."

"Very good, sir," the man said glancing into Highnote's car. "Just go right in, they're expecting you."

There were no other cars here, though there were tire tracks leading around to the back of the house. Crossing the driveway and mounting the stairs to the front door Highnote had the impression that he was being watched. He rang the doorbell. When he turned around, there was no one behind him.

* * *

They were waiting for him in the breakfast room at the rear of the house. Large bow windows looked out over what in summer was a lovely rose garden, sprinkled here and there with a collection of ornately carved marble fountains.

Three men were seated around a glass-topped wrought-iron table. On the left was Paul Innes, who got to his feet when Highnote entered.

"Thanks for coming this morning on such short notice," Innes said shaking hands. He was a thick-waisted man with pitch-black hair and heavy eyebrows. His grip was firm. Like Highnote he had come out of Harvard, serving with a prestigious New York law firm before becoming assistant district attorney for New York State. He'd served on the bench as a federal judge in the Seventh Circuit before being called to the Justice Department during Reagan's first year in office. The man was a survivor. He'd been one of the few who had somehow managed the juggling act of appearing to support his boss Edwin Meese while maintaining a very low profile with the news media.

Introductions were unnecessary. Highnote knew the other two men very well. Across from Innes was Alvan Reisberg, deputy associate director of the FBI, and during the past six months also acting assistant director of the Bureau's Special Investigative Division—two hats which he wore exceedingly well. With his nearly obese figure and bottle-thick glasses, which gave him a permanently bemused air, he was often mistaken for an academic, when in reality he was the nation's top investigative officer. He looked up and nodded.

To Innes's left, opposite the empty chair, was Melvin Quarmby, general counsel for the National Security Agency, and former assistant dean of the Massachusetts Institute of Technology. Quarmby was almost Spanish in his aristocratic bearing and manner. In addition to his law degree he held

Ph.D.'s in physics and chemistry and was said to be a competent electronics engineer and computer expert. He half stood up, holding his napkin in his lap with his left hand, while reaching across the table with his right to shake Highnote's hand.

"Have you eaten?" Innes asked as they sat down.

"Just coffee," Highnote said, and Quarmby passed the sterling server.

"I'll be brief, as I expect you gentlemen will be," Innes began. "I spoke with the President at five o'clock this morning. It was he who suggested this initial meeting."

"What exactly are we talking about here?" Highnote asked.

Innes looked at him cooly. "Before we get started, I want it stated for the record that this meeting is being taped. I want no doubt of that afterward in anyone's mind." He turned to Reisberg. "Alvan?"

"Alvan Reisberg, FBI, I understand."

"Melvin Quarmby, National Security Agency, so advised."

Innes turned again to Highnote.

"Robert Highnote, CIA. I understand these proceedings are being recorded, but I have not yet been advised of the nature of this meeting."

"Thank you," Innes said. "This morning the President appointed me as special prosecutor in the matter of David McAllister, a man whom in a manner of speaking you are all familiar with . . . in Bob's case, intimately."

Highnote was stunned. "This has been an internal matter, and it's a damned sight premature to be talking about prosecution."

"I can't agree," Innes said. "Especially in light of what happened last night."

"You've obviously seen my report. We damned near had him. But I think he showed remarkable restraint under the cirumstances in avoiding any civilian casualties."

"We'll certainly get back to that, Bob. But for now I'm speaking about another incident." Innes glanced at the NSA man, Quarmby. "This will probably not come as a surprise to you."

"Like the others, I'm here and I'm listening," Quarmby said.

"Last night James and Liam O'Haire were murdered at the federal penitentiary at Marion, Illinois. Their bodies were found in a trash container ready for shipment off prison grounds. They'd been stabbed at least one hundred times."

Quarmby's eyebrows rose. "If you understand the significance that act has for the NSA, then I commend you on your range of information."

"The President handed me everything this morning. There will be no secrets among us in this room. I can't stress the importance of this business too strongly."

"None of us expected the O'Haires to last very long in a general-population prison," Highnote said. "But evidently I'm missing something of significance."

"Yesterday afternoon a National Security Agency communications intercept unit at Fort Meade recorded a high-speed burst transmission emanating from Moscow and directed to an as yet unknown location here in the Washington area," Innes said.

"Our guess, of course, would be the Soviet Embassy," Quarmby added.

"A portion of that message was decoded last night. Unfortunately it came too late to be of any use. Two names showed up in the message: McAllister and O'Haire."

"McAllister couldn't have killed them, if that's what you're driving at," Highnote said.

"That's right," Innes said. "But the message does prove, or at least strongly suggest, a connection."

"You've no doubt read all my reports. You must know our assessment."

"You're talking about his arrest and incarceration at the KGB's Lubyanka center?"

"They had him for more than a month, Paul. God only knows what they did to him there, how they . . . altered him."

Innes nodded thoughtfully. "You've spoken with him twice. Face-to-face. You tell me how he appeared to you. Was he deranged?"

"He's driven, I can tell you that much. And yes, he is changed. At the very least they gave him massive doses of drugs, and possibly some torture. He admitted just about everything to them. William Lacey, our chargé d'affaires in Moscow, was given a copy of his confession. There was a lot of fallout."

"Fallout?" Innes asked. "What exactly is meant by that?"

"McAllister named a lot of names. Many of them were still active behind the Iron Curtain. There wasn't much we could do to help them, because of the timing. The Russians had the information, at least some of it, for weeks before we were given a chance to see his confession."

"There were arrests?"

Highnote nodded. "Arrests, trials, and in some cases executions. In other instances there were . . . accidents."

Innes's eyes narrowed. "Our people were simply assassinated?"

"Yes," Highnote said.

"And what are we doing about this?"

Highnote sat back in his chair and looked at the others. "There hasn't been much we could do about it. As I said, by the time we got this information, it was already too late."

"But surely once McAllister had been arrested by the KGB, you must have suspected that they would get that information from him. Certainly you are aware of their methods, of that technology. You must have known that McAllister could not have held anything back. Why weren't your networks rescued, or at the very least warned off?"

Again Highnote hesitated for a moment, his thoughts ranging far afield. "I think we're getting into an area here that I don't have the authorization to speak about. There are certain sensitive ongoing projects."

"I appreciate that," Innes said. "But as I've told you, I have the President's complete confidence in this matter. Nothing is to be held back. Nothing."

"I'm sorry, but some of what you are asking this morning has no bearing on McAllister."

"The President is waiting for your call," Innes said without blinking. "Any of you may speak with him before we proceed."

"I don't think that's necessary."

"I do," Innes said. "I will not be lied to, nor will I be sidestepped. If need be you will be subpoenaed to appear in camera before the Senate Intelligence Committee."

"Perhaps that would be for the best," Highnote said, starting to rise.

"I think you wouldn't find it so."

"What exactly do you mean by that?" Highnote asked coldly.

"From what I understand, McAllister is your close personal friend. Has been for some years now. I would hate to think that you would seriously consider obstructing justice here."

"I won't stand for this," Highnote roared. "My service record is there for anyone to see."

"Then cooperate with this investigation."

"To what end? This continues to be an internal matter."

"I can't agree, and neither does the President," Innes said. "The President wants to offer McAllister amnesty if he will come in and tell us what happened to him in Moscow, and what has been happening to him since his return."

Highnote was stunned. He sank back in his chair and looked dumbfounded across the table at the Justice Department prosecutor.

"It's going to be up to us this morning to figure out exactly how to accomplish that."

"He doesn't know anything," Highnote said. "His time at Lubyanka is blank in his memory. He told me that."

"He knows something," Innes said. "There are enough inconsistencies here for us to at least consider the possibility. Too many people have already lost their lives—we want to stop it."

"You're talking about a trap here," Highnote said.

"No."

"Yes, he'd be shot to death coming in."

"You have my word that wouldn't happen."

"You'd be out there in the field? You'd lead him in by the hand, is that what you're telling me?" Highnote looked to the others for support. None was forthcoming. "I've spoken with him. I've seen him . . . twice. You can't imagine how desperate he is, how driven. At the least sign of trouble he'll run and when he does someone is bound to get hurt."

"We want to avoid that at all costs, Bob. Believe me when I tell you that we want nothing more than to sit down and talk to him."

"He won't trust you."

Innes leaned forward earnestly. "That's why you're here. You're his friend. He trusts you. He's come to you before, and he'll come to you again. But we need your cooperation."

"He knows that I called Security last night. I doubt if he'll trust me again."

"He could have shot you, but he didn't," Alvan Reisberg said softly. "Another inconsistency."

Highnote focused on the FBI cop. "What are you talking about?"

"McAllister is, as you say, a driven man," Innes broke in. "But who is driving him? And why?"

"We know that someone is trying to kill him," Reisberg said.

"How do you know that?" Highnote asked apprehensively.

"Because he told us."

The dark-blue Jeep Wagoneer pulled up and parked at the corner of 31st Street and Avon Lane in Georgetown. A lone, well-dressed, good-looking man sat behind the wheel, his heart pounding. No time. There was no time left and yet it was up to him to put this ultimate insanity into motion. God in heaven, how could anyone be expected to do such a thing?

Once in you will be along for the duration, he'd been told. Some of it will not be pretty and certainly not pleasant. But all of it will be terribly necessary.

Expediency is the watchword. His orders had been crystal clear. The source, unimpeachable. But Jesus Christ, if something went wrong; anything, even the slightest hitch, everything would blow up in their faces.

He thought about Dallas and Los Angeles and Beirut and a dozen other places around the globe over the past twenty-five years or so. Such a terrible waste. Such risks. Was it worth it? Had it been worth the price paid?

Considering the consequences, he thought, his eye on the brownstone house halfway down the narrow side street, there were no other alternatives. He'd known that too, when he'd signed on.

He reached inside his coat pocket, feeling for his gun, then shut off the car's ignition and got out as a bus rumbled by. He went around the corner and hurried down the street, crossing to the other side in midblock. There was very little traffic about, for which he was grateful (God only knew what explanation he could give for being here like this, if someone recognized him) and what passed paid him absolutely no attention as he mounted the steps to McAllister's house and unlocked the door.

He was just another man coming home. He looked as if he belonged in the neighborhood. No eyebrows would be raised. No one would question him, unless he was recognized.

Just inside the stairhall he closed and relocked the door then stood and listened, conscious of his heart hammering in his chest. Time. There was precious little of it. And even now they might already be too late.

The house was silent. He looked toward the head of the stairs. They were here. He knew that for a fact. This was the last place anyone would think to check. McAllister wasn't coming back, and his wife was safely ensconced at Robert Highnote's home in Arlington Heights. Nothing could possibly go wrong at this end, and yet everything could go wrong.

"It's me," he called out, starting up the stairs, his right hand trailing on the banister.

Halfway up he stopped again to listen. A car horn tooted outside, but the house remained absolutely still. The hall smelled faintly musty, unused, as if the house had been closed up, unlived in for a long time. Which in fact it had. The McAllisters had been in Moscow for nearly three years. They would never be returning here.

At the top he turned right and went into the living room. A thin, attractive woman stood to one side of the window, a faint smile on her lips, as if she had just heard an amusing, slightly off-color story.

"Hello, Don," she said.

He pulled up short, startled that she knew his real name. "Where's Royce?" he started to ask, when he detected a movement out of the side of his eye, just to his left and behind him. He started to turn when the barrel of a silenced pistol was pressed against his temple. His insides immediately tightened.

"Did you come alone?" the man whispered harshly.

"Yes."

"You were not followed?"

"No."

The woman turned to the window and barely parted the drapes enough so that she could see down into the street. "Where'd you park your car?" she asked.

"Around the block, on Thirty-first."

"The blue Jeep?" she asked.

"Yes."

"How does it look?" the man with the gun asked, his voice soft, his accent flat, perhaps midwestern.

The woman turned away from the window, letting the curtain ease back into place. She wore a dark-gray sweater and blue jeans. "It's clean."

"Very well," the man behind Donald Harman said, withdrawing his gun and stepping aside. "We're here. What have you got for us this time?"

Harman turned and looked at the man. It was the first time he had ever seen Royce Todd's face. Very few people had, and lived to describe it. Harman was struck by his eyes. They were empty. There was no bottom to them, and he shivered. Todd and the woman, whom he knew as Carol Stenhouse, had come highly recommended. They were simply the best in the business, professional in every sense of the word.

"We have a very large job for you," Harman said finding his voice. "But it must be done immediately, this morning. In fact within the next hour."

Royce glanced at the woman. She nodded slightly, her lips still parted in a half smile.

"There won't be time for the usual confirmation from Geneva that our funds are in place," Todd said.

"You'll have to trust us on this one. It's the reason I came in person." Harman glanced at the woman. He thought she looked like a wild, nocturnal animal. Someone you would never willingly turn your back on. "We're paying five hundred thousand. Each."

The woman's left eyebrow rose slightly. It was the only reaction either of them displayed at the mention of a fee that was five times more than they'd received for Sikorski.

"You have our undivided attention," Todd said. "And since time is apparently of the essence, I suggest you get on with it. Whom do you want us to kill, how do you want it done, and what provision have you made for our escape afterward?"

"I have it all here," Harman said pulling a thick envelope from his pocket.

Chapter 20

For the first time since they'd gotten word that McAllister had been arrested in Moscow, Robert Highnote was at a loss for understanding. He'd always prided himself on his ability to see the big picture; to keep track of all the variables in any situation. Real life was fluid. There were no blacks and whites, only delicate shades of gray. Misunderstandings, coincidences, changes of plan or heart, made the complex business grist only for the man of intuitive genius. Highnote felt for the very first time in his career, that he might be in over his head.

He shoved his coffee cup away. "You've been in contact with him, then? He's approached you?"

"No, nothing so dramatic as all that," Alvan Reisberg said. He'd taken off his glasses and was polishing the lenses with his handkerchief. His eyes seemed naked.

"Then what in heaven's name are you talking about? You say he told you that someone is trying to kill him?"

"I mean in addition to the three Russians we found in that car near your home," Reisberg said, "the Mafia is now involved for some reason."

"If you're talking about the incident in New York, ballistics showed us that the murder weapon was Carrick's own gun. We also have the testimony of the New York City cop. He saw McAllister with Carrick's gun in his hand."

"I'll grant you that," Reisberg said, putting his glasses back on. "But as I say, there is a Mafia connection here as well. A Ford Thunderbird was found parked outside our headquarters building two nights ago."

"I don't see what this has to do with anything," Highnote protested, but Innes held him off.

"Let him continue, Bob."

Reisberg nodded. "We traced the car to a Jersey City Cosa Nostra family. Very big. One of our informants told us that two family members, contractors, hit men in other words, were missing after coming down to the Washington area on some assignment. He wasn't very clear on that point. He's frightened out of his mind that he'll be discovered and will be murdered. But he was certain that he'd never heard the name McAllister before."

"So what's the point?" Highnote asked.

"McAllister's prints were all over the car. He left it there for us to find."

"Why?" Highnote asked.

"Exactly my question," Innes said.

"There is no doubt that he used the car on two separate occasions. We matched the tire prints in Janos Sikorski's driveway, as well as in Langley Hill just below where he made entry onto CIA grounds."

"Maybe he is working with them," Highnote said. "It would explain how he's been able to drop out of sight."

"There were bullet holes in the side of the car," Reisberg said. "The calibers match the casings we found on Sikorski's property. We think McAllister went back out to Sikorski's to talk to his old friend, and came upon the Mafia already there. Either that or the Mafia followed McAllister to Sikorski's, though we're betting on the former because of the arrangement of the tire tracks. The Thunderbird came first, and then another vehicle came after it. The one that was registered in Stephanie Albright's name.''

''And you're saying that there was a shoot-out there between McAllister and these Mafia people?''

''We found traces of blood—not all of them McAllister's type—and evidence that someone else had come out to clean up the mess.''

Highnote once again sat back in his chair. ''Why wasn't I told about this?'' he asked. ''We agreed to liaise on all aspects of this investigation.''

''The reports have been sent over to Dexter Kingman in your Office of Security,'' Reisberg said. ''We're holding nothing back. His reports come to us as well, including the complete dossier on Ms. Albright.''

''We appreciate that you and McAllister are friends,'' Innes said, his tone conciliatory. ''We honestly do. But you must understand, Bob, what we're dealing with here.''

''I don't,'' Highnote said angrily. ''And I'm still waiting for someone in this room to explain it to me.''

''How do you see it?'' Reisberg asked.

Highnote turned on him. ''McAllister is a good man, one of the best.''

''I think we all agree with that statement,'' the FBI cop said, his voice very soft.

''I think he was brainwashed in Moscow. I think they altered him and then sent him back here to do as much damage as he possibly could. And he's done just that. But it's not his fault, none of it is.''

''What is your recommendation?''

''We bring him in, of course, there's no question of that. We must.''

''To help him?''

''Yes.''

Reisberg glanced at Innes and Quarmby, then spoke. ''We've come to much the same conclusion, in that he must be brought in and helped, which is why the President has offered him amnesty. But we think the evidence shows something else may be occurring here. Something that has us . . . disturbed."

"Go on," Highnote said.

"First let's go back to the beginning, if we may. To Moscow. What exactly was McAllister working on for you?"

"There were a number of ongoing projects," Highnote said. "There always are. McAllister was a network man. His specialty has been setting up lines of stringers from scratch and then working them."

"He is a people person," Reisberg pressed.

"If you want to call it that, yes. He deals with personalities. With motivations."

"What specifically was he doing the night of his arrest? What I mean to ask is, who was he seeing that night?"

"I don't know," Highnote said. "There was nothing on his day sheets, and of course he was never given a chance to tell us afterward."

"Anything in his confession to the Russians that would indicate to you whom he had seen that night?"

"No," Highnote said.

"Didn't it strike you as odd that the Russians made no mention of why he was arrested on that particular night?"

"Yes, Alvan, it struck me as odd. It struck all of us as odd, but again, as I've said, Mac never had the chance afterward to tell us."

"It never came up in the two conversations you had with him?"

Highnote bridled. "I resent the implication. You've seen my reports."

"Nobody is implying anything here, Bob," Innes broke in gently. "We're trying to get at the truth, that's all."

"He's a driven man."

"Yes, we all agree with that. But the fact of the matter is, someone is trying to kill him. Not only the Russians, but the Mafia as well. The question is: If the Russians wanted him dead, why did they release him in the first place? And who has hired the Mafia to go after him, and why?"

"More to the point," Reisberg interrupted, "what were the Mafia doing at Sikorski's place . . . assuming we're correct in our guess that they got there first?"

"If they were after McAllister, it would be logical that they would go after his old friends. People they might think he would try to contact."

"Exactly," Reisberg said. "Where are they getting their information?"

Highnote's breath caught in his throat. "I see," he said.

"They also made the connection between you and McAllister," Reisberg continued. "The Russians were at your house, waiting for him. And then when he ran to your boat in Dumfries they went after him there . . . someone did . . . and shot him and left him for dead. The blood we found *was* his type. And there was a lot of it."

"You're saying that whoever is after Mac is getting inside information?"

"It would appear so," Reisberg said.

"We're getting ahead of ourselves now," Innes said, filling the sudden silence.

"Yes?" Highnote said, holding his temper in check.

"When we first began to put this together, we came up with four areas of concern."

"Who is *we*?"

"I approached Paul with this just yesterday," Alvan Reisberg said.

"Because you had questions for which there were no answers?"

"Yes."

"The first, of course, was McAllister's arrest and subsequent release by the Russians," Innes said. "Naturally we weren't involved in that business until the incident in New York."

"Naturally," Highnote said.

Innes ignored the sarcasm. "The second was the disturbing possibility that not only were the Russians trying to kill him, but that someone had hired the Mafia to stop him as well. In each case it appeared that someone was feeding them inside information about McAllister. The third was the apparent connection between McAllister and the O'Haires. In the first place your own people were told that McAllister had worked with them as their Russian pipeline. And in the second place, NSA intercepted the burst transmission within hours of which the O'Haires were murdered."

"We can go two ways with this," Reisberg interjected. "Whoever is trying to silence McAllister set up the O'Haires to implicate him on the hope that we would do their job for them. In other words, if we believed that McAllister had been the O'Haires' control officer all along, we might not hesitate to shoot to kill when the opportunity arose. The O'Haires, of course, were then silenced so that they would have no chance to recant. Either that, or we can believe that McAllister indeed was their control officer, and still is very much in charge of the network, and had to silence them himself . . . or at least arrange for them to be killed."

"Not the act of a desperate, driven man," Highnote said.

Innes shook his head. "Which brings us to Stephanie Albright, who apparently has agreed to help him."

"I don't think that has been established with any degree of certainty," Highnote said.

"Forgive my skepticism," Reisberg countered, "but I think there can be no question that she is willingly helping him. In fact it would be my guess that it was she who helped him in Dumfries."

"What?"

"She apparently visited McAllister's home in Georgetown on the night she managed to escape from him at Sikorski's. It's possible that she saw a photograph in the living room which showed McAllister and his wife aboard your sailboat. The Dumfries Yacht Haven sign is clearly visible in the background."

"That's quite a leap," Highnote said. "But assuming that was the case, why would she have done such a thing? I've looked at her file. She is totally above suspicion."

"Yes," Reisberg said. "My thought exactly. She is a woman totally beyond reproach. We went up to Baltimore to interview her father, who told us that she is a headstrong girl, but that she is an idealist; very much in love with her country, which is why she sought employment with the CIA."

"What did you tell him?"

"Just that we were doing a routine, prepromotion background check."

"Had he heard from her?"

"Not for months," Reisberg said. "But it strikes me as curious that such a patriot as Stephanie Albright should be so actively helping McAllister, that she was willing to lie to her own boss about setting up a meeting between him and McAllister, which of course gave McAllister the opportunity to break into CIA headquarters."

"What's your point?"

"Our point, Bob, is that Stephanie Albright wouldn't be helping McAllister unless she believed in him," Innes said.

"Come off it. . . ."

"In itself, the notion is a weak one. We all agree with you. But taken with everything else . . . well, it's given us pause for some serious thought."

Highnote looked from Innes to Reisberg to Quarmby and back again. "Which brings us to the actual purpose for this meeting."

"The President is offering McAllister amnesty, and I think it's up to us in this room to figure out how to get to him as soon as possible with the message, and without any more casualties," Innes said.

"Because he knows something?" Highnote said. "Because he evidently learned something in Moscow that has the Russians concerned . . . and possibly someone else . . . so concerned that they are willing to risk exposure in order to make sure he doesn't talk?"

"Yes."

"Which is?"

"We believe that there is more than a fair possibility that a Soviet penetration agent is working within the CIA at fairly high levels. We think that somehow McAllister stumbled onto this information while in the Soviet Union."

"Good Lord," Highnote said. "Then why did they release him in the first place?"

"An error, we suspect," Innes said. "Once it was realized however, they tried to kill him. And they will keep trying. The Russians with their own people, and the mole using Mafia contract killers."

David McAllister's white Peugeot 505 sedan got off the Capital Beltway at Baltimore Avenue and proceeded south just within the speed limit. Traffic had been quite heavy from Georgetown, but Royce Todd was an excellent driver, and the directions Donald Harman had provided them were complete.

This was the big score they'd both been waiting for. After this they would be able to retire for at least a few years until the furor died down. Which it would eventually, Harman had assured them. With his help.

"Another half a mile," Carol Stenhouse said, looking up from the sketched map.

It is essential that you not fail. It is the reason we are offering so much money. I need your assurances.

We're here. It's a job and we will do it.

No need for confirmations in this case. I'm sure I'll be reading about it in the afternoon papers.

The whole world would be reading about it, Royce Todd

thought. And the beauty of it, is that the police would be searching for the wrong couple, giving them more than sufficient time to get out of the country.

"Are you ready?" he asked, glancing over at Carol.

She looked into his eyes and smiled. "Of course," she said softly, competently.

They turned off the main road and started up the long driveway through the heavily wooded piece of property adjacent to the University of Maryland. It was quiet back here, and dark. Todd could see where other cars had already come this way this morning. He counted at least three sets of tire tracks in the snow.

Carol took out her suppressed .22 magnum automatic, levered a round into the firing chamber and switched off the safety. Todd took his out of his pocket and laid it on the seat beside his right leg.

They'd met five years ago in Honduras, where they had both been doing contract work for the CIA. He had been a graduate of the Delta Force out of Ft. Bragg, and was working with a Nicaraguan contra assassination team, and she, a former United States Army noncombat helicopter pilot, had been running arms across the border.

She had literally saved his life during a night raid in which he had gotten cut off across the border. She had spotted the intense gunfire in the hills a half mile inside Nicaragua, had choppered down to investigate, and when she had spotted him alone, had picked him up and flew him back into Honduras.

They'd gotten out of Central America when the Sandinistas began shooting down contract pilots with regularity, and the CIA, with as monotonous a regularity, began denying their own people.

Carol had changed into a short khaki skirt and blouse before they'd left McAllister's house. As they came up over a rise that opened the last fifty yards to the large three-story Colonial, she shifted in her seat so that her skirt hiked up, exposing her thighs all the way to her lace panties. She spread her legs, the dark swatch of her pubic hair clearly visible.

The driveway circled around to the right of a big cement goldfish pond and marble fountain. A black Cadillac was parked beneath the overhang in front. As they pulled up beside it, a large man dressed in boots and a white parka came around from the side of the house. A second man appeared right behind him. They separated as they approached.

Carol powered her window down, as Todd opened the door and got out of the car. He held his gun beside his leg so that the two men could not see it. He stood just behind the open car door.

"Good morning," the guard nearest said pleasantly. The other one angled toward the passenger side of the car.

"We're here to see Mr. Innes," Todd said. He switched off his weapon's safety with his thumb.

"Yes, sir," the guard said. "If you would just step away from your car. Ask the lady to get out as well."

"My damned seatbelt is stuck," Carol called out her open window.

Todd smiled and looked back in at her. The second guard had reached the passenger side.

"I feel like such a fool," Carol said.

The guard bent down so that he could see into the car, his eyes automatically going to Carol's spread legs. "What seems to be the problem? . . ."

She raised her pistol and shot him in the forehead at point-blank range.

Todd turned back, bringing up his pistol, and fired one shot a split second later, catching the first guard in the left eye, his head snapping back, and his arms flying outward as he crumpled in the driveway. The entire time elapsed from the moment the two guards had first appeared until they lay dead, was less than ten seconds, the two silenced shots inaudible more than twenty feet away.

Carol was out of the car and across the driveway by the time Todd had reached the front door. He stood to one side as she came up onto the porch. He nodded.

Holding the gun at her side, she tried the doorknob. It wasn't locked. She opened the door and Todd slipped past her inside the main stair hall.

A woman in a pretty print dress was just coming down the stairs. Without hesitation Todd shot her, the bullet smacking into her chest just below her left breast, piercing her heart, killing her instantly. Her legs collapsed beneath her, and she tumbled halfway down the stairs, her eyes open, and her lips parted for a scream she hadn't been able to utter.

The meeting was to be held either in Innes's study or in the breakfast room. Both were at the back of the house, making it unlikely that anyone witnessed what had happened out front in the driveway.

Todd started down the corridor to the left of the staircase, Carol directly behind him. She did not close the door, nor had they closed the Peugeot's doors or shut off its ignition—all steps to save them precious seconds if need be.

The corridor was one step up from the stair hall. To the right was the living room, to the left a drawing room, its French doors slightly ajar. Todd hesitated as Carol stepped around him and ducked inside, sweeping her gun from left to right.

She shook her head and rejoined him just as the door at the far end of the corridor opened and they could hear voices.

"It's simply a matter of procedures now, but you must understand the importance," someone said from within the room.

A fat, academic-looking man with thick glasses stepped

out, clutching a bulging file folder. He started to say something to the others in the room when he realized that someone was in the corridor. He brought up his right arm as if to fend off a blow, as Todd fired two shots, the first catching Reisberg in the face, destroying the bridge of his nose, the second hitting his chest, driving him back against the door frame.

Pandemonium broke out in the breakfast room.

Todd raced the rest of the way down the corridor without a word, confident that Carol was right behind him as backup.

Turning the corner he stepped over Reisberg's body, his eyes automatically scanning the small room, right to left.

Paul Innes, his tie loose, was shouting into a telephone. Todd shot him in the side of the head, the telephone flying out of his hand as he crashed sideways into the long glass buffet table.

A glass door leading out to the rose garden crashed open and Todd switched his aim left, firing one shot that went wide and to the right, just as Robert Highnote disappeared across the narrow veranda.

"Get him," Todd whispered, and Carol stepped behind him, and rushed across the room.

Melvin Quarmby had snatched up the sterling silver coffee server and he threw it at Todd in a final desperate act. Todd easily sidestepped it, and fired one shot, this one catching the NSA counsel in the throat, destroying his windpipe and severing a carotid artery. The man fell backward as he clawed at the fatal wound.

There was an unsilenced shot outside. Todd reached the glass door in time to see Carol sitting down hard in the snow, clutching her left shoulder with her right hand.

Highnote was racing across the rose garden with surprising speed and agility for a man of his age. Todd crouched in the classic shooter's stance, followed Highnote's retreating figure and squeezed off a single shot, the bullet catching

Highnote high in the back, his body falling forward and lying still.

Carol was just getting to her feet when Todd reached her.

"Are you all right?" he asked.

She nodded, grim-lipped. "Are we finished here?"

"Yes," Todd nodded. "It's time to go."

Chapter 21

Stephanie had wanted to leave the hotel immediately, but McAllister convinced her that they would run less of a risk of being spotted if they waited a couple of hours until normal workday traffic began. They wouldn't stand out as the only ones on the street.

They checked out a few minutes after seven-thirty, paying their bill and walking three blocks down to New York Avenue directly across from the sprawling Washington Convention Center.

The dawn was gray and overcast. Traffic was extremely heavy and still ran with headlights. The gaily lit Christmas decorations seemed somehow out of place, especially considering Stephanie's dark mood. She had convinced herself that something terrible had happened to her father, and McAllister had no real idea what he could or should say to her, because he thought there was a better than fair possibility she was correct.

They found a cab almost immediately, the driver a young black man with Walkman headphones half over his ears, beating a rhythm on the steering wheel.

"Can you take us to the Baltimore-Washington Airport?" McAllister asked when he and Stephanie got in the backseat.

The driver looked at their images in his rearview mirror. "Man, in this shit?" he asked, indicating the thick traffic.

"A hundred dollars," McAllister said. "We've got a plane to catch, and we can't afford to screw around."

The driver grinned, hitting the button on his trip meter as he pulled out into traffic. He reached down with his right hand and turned up the volume on his Walkman, his head bobbing with the music that was suddenly so loud McAllister and Stephanie could hear it in the backseat.

McAllister looked over his shoulder a couple of blocks later to see if they had picked up a tail. He decided after a few moments of watching traffic, that they had not, and he sat back. They'd done the impossible, so far, he thought. But from this moment on it was going to start getting difficult.

Stephanie was holding his hand, her palms cold and wet, her entire body shivering. She looked into his eyes. "If something has happened to him, I don't know what I'll do," she said, her voice cracking.

"Someone from the Agency and probably the FBI was sent up to interview him," McAllister said. "But I don't think they'd do anything more than ask a few questions."

"He wouldn't have told them anything."

"Of course not."

"It's not them I'm worried about, David. It's the Russians, or the Mafia."

"There is no reason for them to go to him," McAllister said, not really believing it himself. "It's me they're after."

"And me, because I'm helping you."

"But they're not after my wife. There's no reason to suspect they'd go after your father."

"God, I wish I could believe you," Stephanie whispered, sitting back. "I wish it was that easy."

He let it rest for the moment. Trust your instincts, she had told him.

I think that something did happen to you in the Lubyanka. Something that changed you, something that made you unsure of your own abilities. But deep in your gut you know what moves to make, you know how to protect yourself. . . . Let yourself go, David. Let your old habits, your old instincts take over. . . . You have the tradecraft, use it.

"He doesn't know anything," she said softly. "I didn't tell him what we were doing, just that we were together."

He squeezed her hand. "It may be that we won't be able to get to him."

"What do you mean?" she asked, her eyes wild.

"You're on the run. Dexter Kingman might figure that you'd try to contact your father. They could be watching the place, waiting for you to show up."

"Then why didn't they put a tap on his phone?" she asked. "There was no answer last night and again this morning."

"Because they knew that even if you did call him, you wouldn't reveal your location."

She suddenly saw what he was driving at. "They could have shunted his incoming calls to a dead number, making me believe that something had happened to my father. Bait. It could be a trap."

McAllister nodded, thinking that in a way it would be much easier on her if that were the case, and yet doubting it.

They reached the parkway just past the National Arboretum, and the driver sped up across the Anacostia River, merging smoothly with the traffic that had thinned out. Most people were coming into the city at this hour, not leaving it.

They were in Maryland now, and a couple of minutes later as they passed over Landover Road, three highway patrol cars, their lights flashing, their sirens blaring, raced beneath the parkway heading northwest toward Hyattsville and College Park.

Stephanie stiffened, but when the police cars did not take the entrance ramp onto the parkway, but instead continued northwest, she relaxed slightly.

McAllister watched out the rear window as the squad cars were lost in the distance, then he cranked down his window a couple of inches. At first he could hear nothing but the roar of the wind. The driver, feeling the sudden cold air, looked up. Then in the far distance, McAllister thought he could hear sirens. A lot of sirens.

An accident, he wondered. Or was it?

It was nearly nine by the time the cabbie dropped them off at the Eastern Airlines passenger departures entrance of the Baltimore-Washington International Airport in Ferndale just south of downtown Baltimore. After McAllister paid the driver, he and Stephanie hurried into the terminal, took the escalator downstairs to the baggage pickup area, and stowed their two overnight bags in a coin-operated locker.

Their driver had taken the down ramp around and was waiting in front for a fare back to Washington. It had begun to snow lightly again. Christmas music was playing on the overhead speakers. It was faintly depressing. A young couple climbed into the cab a few minutes later, and when it was gone, McAllister and Stephanie went outside and got a cab into Baltimore, Stephanie giving the driver an address a couple of blocks from her father's house.

Once again McAllister got the odd feeling that he was coming back on his life. That he was retracing old steps. That he was making no progress. Stephanie sat on the edge of the seat, her hands together in her lap, holding herself rigidly erect as if she were afraid she would break something if she moved.

If anything, downtown Baltimore was even more decorated for the holidays than was Washington. A tall Christmas tree stood in front of the Civic Center, and a few blocks south in the harbor, the USS Constellation on permanent display, was decked out with all her flags. At night she would be lit.

The cabbie dropped them off in front of Union Station on Exeter Street. They waited just within the main entrance until the taxi had disappeared around the corner. McAllister took Stephanie's arm. "Come on," he said.

"Where are we going now?"

"To phone your father."

They crossed the cavernous departure hall, angling to the left when McAllister spotted the bank of telephones along the far wall. Stephanie plugged a quarter in the phone and dialed her father's number. When the connection was made she held the phone away from her ear so that McAllister could hear as well. After ten rings she looked at him and shook her head.

"Same as last night and early this morning," she said, hanging up. "He should be there."

"Has he got an assistant, maybe a secretary working with him?"

"Only in the summers when he sometimes takes a couple of interns from the college. The rest of the time he prefers to work alone. David, it's never been a very large practice."

"Is there anyplace else he might have gone last night? An emergency call, or something like that? Friends? Maybe a woman friend?"

"It's Tuesday. He might go away for a weekend, he sometimes does that, but never on a weekday. Something has happened."

McAllister glanced across the large hall. The station was fairly busy at this hour. Across from the telephones were a few shops and a small snack bar. He felt for the gun at the small of his back.

"Have you still got your gun?"

"Yes."

He took her shoulders and looked into her eyes, wanting to impress her with the seriousness of what he was about to say. "This part is very important, Stephanie," he said. "If we're confronted or cornered, or anything like that, and they clearly identify themselves as FBI or the police or even the Agency, you won't resist. You'll put down your gun and surrender immediately."

"They'll kill us."

"Maybe," McAllister said grimly. "But we're not going to start shooting innocent people. Not now, not ever. Clear?"

She nodded.

"Let's go," he said. "Keep your eyes open."

Albright's house was on Front Street about three blocks from Union Station in a neighborhood of similarly large houses that had at one time probably belonged to ship captains. For years the neighborhood had deteriorated, but over the past few years Baltimore had revitalized its harbor area and had gone on an inner-city cleanup and rebuilding campaign. Stephanie's father, she'd told him, had weathered all the changes in the more than twenty years he had lived and worked in the neighborhood.

There was a fair amount of traffic this morning, all moving slowly because of the continuing snowfall that made the streets very slippery. A few BMWs, a Mercedes, and several American-made cars were parked along the curb, but none of them sported any extra antennae, nor were any of them occupied. There were no lingering taxis, windowless vans, or suspicious-looking trucks parked anywhere in the vicinity, and so far as McAllister could see there were no people on foot in the near vicinity of Albright's house; no meter-readers or telephone repairmen, no newspaper delivery boys, no bakery or delivery people. Nothing or nobody who could be a cover for a surveillance team.

They passed a corner grocery store and crossed the street after a big Allied moving van rumbled by. McAllister watched it turn the corner at Union Station and when it was gone he and Stephanie waited across the street for a full five minutes, half expecting the truck to come back around the block. When it did not reappear, they continued.

Coming up on the house, McAllister could see nothing out of the ordinary, nothing out of place at first, but Stephanie let out a little gasp and pulled up short.

"What is it?" he asked.

"It's my father's car," she said.

McAllister could just see the rear deck of a dark-brown station wagon parked in the back. "He doesn't have another?"

"No," she said softly.

They came up the walk and mounted the steps. McAllister turned and looked back to the street. No one was there. No one was watching this place. The neighborhood felt empty, somehow deserted to him.

A cardboard clock with the message WILL BE BACK AT was hung in the front-door window, the hands pointing to nine o'clock. It was well past that time now. But nine o'clock last night or this morning?

The door was locked, but Stephanie produced a key from her purse and opened it. She started inside, but McAllister held her back. He took out his pistol, switched off the safety and stepped just inside the vestibule.

A tall oak door with an etched-glass window leading into the main stairhall was half open. Today's mail lay in a pile on the vestibule floor behind the outside door. McAllister moved on the balls of his feet to the partially open inner door and looked inside. Straight ahead, the stairs rose to the second floor. A corridor led back to the kitchen. On the left was Albright's office, on the right, in what originally had been the living room and dining room were a small waiting room, a surgery, and a laboratory. The house smelled faintly of disinfectant and an odd, animal odor. From somewhere at the back of the house he thought he could hear a cat, or perhaps a small dog, whining softly.

Stephanie came the rest of the way into the vestibule.

She closed and locked the door. She heard the whining. "It's coming from the animal cages on the back porch," she whispered. She was very pale, and her nostrils were flared, her lips half parted, as if she were starting to hyperventilate.

McAllister went the rest of the way into the house and looked into the waiting room. A half a dozen chairs were grouped around a low plastic coffee table on which several magazines lay in a disarrayed pile. The sound of the animal's pitiful whining was a little louder now, and it set his teeth on edge.

Stephanie came up behind him.

"You take the upstairs," he whispered to her. She had taken out her .32 automatic.

"Is someone still here?" she asked.

"I don't think so, but be careful."

She hesitated a moment, but then nodded and turned away. McAllister watched her go up the stairs, the gun at her side, then he went across the waiting room to the swinging door that led into the surgery, careful to avoid stepping in the narrow puddle of blood that had seeped under the door and had dried to a hard black crust. She had not come far enough into the waiting room to see it. But he had. And he knew exactly what it meant, and what he would find inside.

Steeling himself, McAllister pushed open the surgery door and went inside. The room wasn't very large, perhaps ten feet by fifteen feet overall. On two sides were glass-fronted cabinets that had contained medical supplies. On a third side was a long Formica-topped counter which ran the length of the room. On the fourth were shelves containing medicines, and a doorway that led into the laboratory. Nicholas Albright's nude body was trussed on the stainless steel examining table in the middle of the room. He had lost a lot of blood before he died, some of it pooling up beside him on the tabletop, more of it running down onto the floor where it had gathered and trickled along the white tile floor to the waiting room door.

McAllister looked away from the corpse, his stomach rising up into his throat. The room had been thoroughly searched. The glass on the cabinet fronts had been smashed, and most of the instruments and medicines had been pulled down and scattered all over the room.

Outwardly it appeared as if someone had come here looking for drugs. When they hadn't found any they had tied Albright to the examining table and had tortured him for the information. But McAllister saw beyond that. The overhead light fixtures had been taken apart, the cabinets had been moved away from the walls, and even the heating vents had been uncovered. Whoever had done this were professionals. They had come here to find something; something hidden in this room. He could see through into the laboratory. Nothing had been disturbed in there, nor had anything been touched in the waiting room. It was here in Albright's surgery that the search had been concentrated.

Still careful not to step in any of the blood, McAllister crossed around behind the examining table to the long counter on the opposite wall. A small cabinet had been left partially open. Using his thumbnail, he eased the door open all the way. The cabinet was empty except for several electrical wires leading from inside the wall. McAllister stared at them for a long time. One of the wires carried power, another was a ground connection, and the third obviously led to an antenna, the barrel of the coaxial plug dangling. A transmitter. Why?

He turned again to look at Albright's body. The scalpel they had used to cut him with was jutting from his left eye socket. His arms were tied behind him beneath the table, as were his legs. They had cut long strips of flesh from his abdomen, from his arms, and from the sensitive areas around his nipples and his inner thighs. His mouth was filled with gauze pads to stop him from screaming while they tortured him.

His penis had been slit lengthwise, his scrotum had been opened and he had been castrated, and in the end they had cut the main arteries high on his legs near his groin so that he had bled to death.

The scalpel thrust into his eye had probably been done out of frustration. It was possible that they had got nothing from him.

He had to look away from the body again, his stomach rolling, the disinfectant smell of the surgery suddenly cloying at the back of his tongue. Stephanie could not be allowed to see this.

They had come looking for something. A transmitter, perhaps. Still, he was missing something. He knew that much, but for the life of him he could not think it out. They'd come for more than a clue as to Stephanie's whereabouts. In the first few minutes it would have become evident that the man didn't know anything.

Unless he had been working for them. The thought was chilling.

They had stuffed his mouth full of gauze so that he couldn't make enough noise to rouse the neighbors. But he could not talk either. This was a warning. The brutality of it struck him. The Russianness of it. He had seen things like this before. A *mokrie dela*. A wet affair. Blood will be spilled as a warning to all other spies.

The animal at the back of the house had stopped whining, and Stephanie's sudden scream at the surgery door shattered the eerie silence.

Chapter 22

The limousine of Howard Van Skike, director of central intelligence, was admitted without ceremony at the west gate past the executive offices onto the grounds of the White House. His car drew up beneath the overhang and a uniformed guard came down and opened the door for him. He got out and sniffed the air; tall, imperious in his immaculately tailored suit and top coat. He was a presence on the American political scene, and even more of a presence in the intelligence community.

This noon hour he was preoccupied, even angry. He strode up the steps and into the west wing, taking the elevator to the President's second-floor office, a thin alligator briefcase under his left arm.

Up to this moment he had remained relatively aloof from the business of David McAllister. He had known the man's father, and in fact had modeled much of his intelligence career after the grandfather, Stewart Alvin, who by the time Van Skike had known him was already one of the holy cows of Whitehall who'd been to Moscow in the early days and who knew the Soviet mentality inside and out.

"Speak softly and carry a big stick," the elder McAllister maintained was the only decent quote ever to have come out of the Americas. But good Lord he had known the business inside and out. They were still writing books about him.

McAllister's father had been a power in the OSS and the early days of the CIA as well, and the son, by all accounts had been the natural extension, continuing the long family tradition that had stretched back to the First World War.

Now, as hard as it was to believe, the tradition had fallen apart somehow, giving Van Skike pause to consider in the deepest recesses of his mind just what sort of a star he had hitched his wagon to.

Van Skike entered the President's study, the door closing softly behind him, and crossed the room to the massive desk. John Sanderson, director of the FBI, had been speaking with the President. They both looked up.

"You've heard?" the President asked, his voice as always, no matter the circumstances, soft. Some years ago he had been DCI, so he well understood what Van Skike was faced with at this moment.

"Yes, Mr. President, I have, though I've not yet seen any of the details."

"Well look at these," Sanderson said, stepping away from the President's desk, and indicating a half a dozen photographs spread out there.

Van Skike laid his briefcase on a chair and bent over the black-and-white photos.

"Two of my people were killed in the driveway," Sanderson said. "They used twenty-two-caliber silenced automatics. Highly accurate. One at point-blank range, the other at ten to fifteen feet; whoever was doing the shooting knew what they were doing."

The first photographs showed the FBI agents lying in the driveway, blood staining the snow.

"They got Paul Innes's wife on the stairs, Reisberg at the study door, Paul at the telephone . . . he was talking to our desk-duty operator . . . Quarmby at the end of the table in the breakfast room . . . and Highnote outside in the backyard."

The other photographs showed a woman in a print dress sprawled on a stairway, Reisberg's body crumpled in a doorway, and Innes half sitting up against a glass buffet.

"Quarmby is in critical condition," Sanderson was saying. "And Bob Highnote is in serious condition, but he'll probably make it. The bullet hit half an inch from his spinal column."

"The others?" Van Skike asked, looking up.

"Dead," Sanderson replied. He pulled out his pipe and tobacco, and turned away. "He was your boy, Van."

Van Skike looked to the President. "Was it McAllister?" he asked. "Has that been established?"

The President nodded. "The Albright woman was with him. His car was spotted leaving Paul Innes's place. From what I understand, the tire prints match."

Sanderson turned back. "We interviewed McAllister's neighbors. He and the Albright woman were spotted at the house. Around seven they definitely saw his Peugeot leaving his garage. They saw him and a small dark-haired woman leaving together."

"Why?" Van Skike asked. "Bob Highnote was his friend. And how could he have known that Paul had called such a meeting?"

Sanderson and the President exchanged glances, which secretly infuriated Van Skike.

"There's more," Sanderson said. "McAllister and Albright were at the house. We're definite about that. But someone else was there too. Someone came to visit them early this morning."

"Who?"

"We don't know yet," Sanderson said. "A man, well dressed. Came on foot, let himself in as if he belonged there."

"Yes, and what does this prove?"

"I think you'd better listen to this, Van," the President said.

Sanderson came back to the desk and switched on a tape recorder.

". . . is offering McAllister amnesty, and I think it's up to us in this room to figure out how to get to him as soon as possible with the message and without any more casualties."

"That's Paul Innes's voice," Sanderson said. "He recorded the meeting."

"Because he knows something?" another man asked. Van Skike recognized the voice as Highnote's. *"Because he evidently learned something in Moscow that has the Russians concerned . . . and possibly someone else . . . so concerned that they are willing to risk exposure in order to make sure he doesn't talk?"*

"Yes."

"Which is?"

"We believe that there is more than a fair possibility that a Soviet penetration agent is working within the CIA at fairly high levels. . . ."

Sanderson switched off the tape recorder. "You will be provided with a copy of this tape, of course."

"It sounds as if they thought McAllister was innocent. That the KGB was after him," Van Skike said.

Sanderson advanced the recording.

"Then why did they release him in the first place?" Highnote asked.

"An error, we suspect," Paul Innes said.

Sanderson switched off the tape recorder. "Not an error," he said. "McAllister is trying to protect whomever he is working for, whoever showed up at his house this morning with the orders to kill Innes and the others."

Again Sanderson advanced the tape recording.

". . . a matter of procedure now, but you must understand the importance," Innes said.

A moment later two soft noises came from the speaker, almost as if someone had closed a book, softly, and then closed it again. The hair prickled at the nape of Van Skike's neck. He recognized the sounds as silenced pistol shots. The murders had been taped. He was listening to them now.

There was a sudden cacophony of noises. Innes was shouting something, wildly; more silenced shots were fired; there were crashing sounds, the sounds of breaking glass and then a man whispering as if from a very great distance, said: *"Get him."*

Sanderson shut off the tape recorder. "McAllister and Albright," he said.

"Are you certain, John?" Van Skike asked again. "Absolutely certain?"

"Yes," the President interjected. "I'm convinced. David McAllister and Stephanie Albright have stepped over the edge. No matter what happens or does not happen, they must be stopped. Immediately. At all costs."

"Am I understanding you correctly, Mr. President? . . ." Van Skike started.

"No screwing around now," Sanderson said. "I've given my people explicit orders. McAllister and Albright are to be shot on sight. They can never be allowed to go to trial."

Van Skike looked aghast at the President who looked away. He understood the logic of it, the necessity. But God in heaven, weren't we a nation of laws; presumed innocent until proven guilty?

"Gentlemen," the President said, "they must be stopped."

Part Three

Chapter 23

McAllister sat on the edge of the bed stroking the back of Stephanie's head with a gentle touch. They were in a nightmare that neither of them seemed able to wake up from. Yet in this dream world real people were dying. She was still shaking, her breath coming in great sobbing gasps.

"Why?" she kept crying. "There was no reason for them to have killed him . . . especially not like that. He didn't know anything."

He didn't answer her.

It had been very difficult to pull her away from the surgery door and calm her sufficiently so that they could go upstairs to her old room, where he threw a few of the things she kept there into a small suitcase and then walked with her arm-in-arm back to Union Station, where they caught a cab to a dumpy little hotel near the State Historical Society.

"She's not feeling well," McAllister explained to the indifferent clerk. "She's pregnant. It's morning sickness."

Upstairs in their shabby room he took off her coat and shoes and made her lie down on the bed.

"Why, David?" she sobbed. "It can't be possible."

"Russians," McAllister said, staring across the room.

But it hadn't been a simple torture and killing in an effort to find Stephanie.

"What?" Stephanie asked, looking up at him.

McAllister focused on her. "The Russians did it to your father."

"How do you know that?"

Like I know a thousand other things, he thought. It's tradecraft, part of the game, part of the knowledge that a field man needs in order to keep alive. "It's the way they do things," he said. "I've seen it before."

"Because of you? Us? Because I'm helping you?"

"Yes," he said. The truth was crueler than she could imagine.

We are making great progress together, you and I, Mac. And I am so very pleased.

It was Miroshnikov speaking to him. His face loomed in McAllister's head. It was always there. It had always been there, and always would be. There was no escape.

"What is it?" Stephanie asked, sensing something of his pain.

There was a continuing symmetry, of course, to the Zebra Network in the four names he had taken from the Agency's computer archives. Suspects, evidently, that the investigators had no evidence to prosecute. They'd still be in place so that they could be watched.

The first, Ray Ellis, was a civilian communications expert working out of the American Embassy in Moscow. McAllister thought he might recognize the name, but he couldn't fit a face to it. He'd be the Russian conduit. The link from Moscow through which information was passed.

The second link would be Air Force Technical Sergeant Barry Gregory, who worked as a cryptographic-equipment maintenance man in the Pentagon's vast communications center. He would be the stateside relay point.

Some information could have come from Charles Denby, the third name on the list. He worked as an engineer with

Technical Systems Industries in California's Silicon Valley outside of San Francisco. TS Industries was one of the major contractors on the Star Wars research program.

And finally Kathleen O'Haire's name appeared on the list of suspects by simple virtue of the fact she was the wife of James O'Haire, the head of the Zebra Network. The weak link?

"David?"

"We've got to get out of Baltimore," he heard himself saying. But he was still drifting. Free associating. Thinking out the possibilities, the pitfalls, the moves they would have to make, the ramifications.

"Not back to Washington?" Stephanie was asking.

"California."

She was staring intently at him. "The list," she said. "How will we get out there? When?"

"I'll get our bags. We'll take a flight out of New York. This afternoon. Tonight."

"What about our guns?"

"They'll get through with the checked-in baggage in the hold. It can be done."

"Denby and Kathleen O'Haire will be watched in California."

"Then we'll have to be careful," McAllister said, finally looking up out of his thoughts. "We don't have any other choice now."

Stephanie left their room ten minutes after McAllister had gone to take a cab back to the Baltimore-Washington Airport to fetch their bags. She had splashed some water on her face, and had paced back and forth until she could not take it anymore. It wasn't the inactivity that bothered her, it was the fact that she knew she was never coming back here to Baltimore. Her old life was gone forever, and she couldn't stand leaving it this way.

The clerk at the front desk didn't bother looking up as

she emerged from the hotel, turned left and walked rapidly two blocks up toward the Maryland General Hospital on Madison Street, where she caught a cab back to Union Station.

Early afternoon traffic was in full swing and the snow had not let up. If anything it had increased again. The cabbie was playing Christmas music on the radio, and despite her resolve she felt tears slipping down her cheeks for all the years that were now lost. Her father had never told her in so many words that he would like to have grandchildren, but she could tell he had thought about it.

On weekends she would often come to visit, helping out in the surgery during the day, and talking until all hours of the night over dinner and a bottle or two of wine. Her father was her best friend. She told him about her work, about her day-to-day life, and about her loves . . . or lack of them. Always he had listened with keen interest, but never with criticism, though when she'd asked for his advice he would never hesitate to give it. Always thoughtful, always kind. She was going to miss him very badly.

She wasn't going to leave him this way.

Take care of yourself. I'll be all right.

I know you will be, father.

They were among the last words they had spoken to each other. There would be no more.

After the cabbie dropped her off she lingered inside Union Station for another ten minutes, watching the passengers coming and going, listening to the occasional rumble below as a train arrived or departed, studying the train schedules, looking at the people in the coffee shop.

Mac had ordered her to remain in the hotel. "It's too dangerous for you to be out on the streets now."

Can't you see, my darling, that this is something I must do? she cried inside.

The big clock on the back wall of the main departures hall read one-thirty as she finally left the station and hurried on foot up Front Street. It was very dangerous coming here like this, but nothing seemed to have changed in the few hours since she and Mac had been here. There were no police cars out front, no crowds of curious onlookers wondering what was going on, nobody waiting at the front door with a dog or a cat needing the doctor.

Her father's station wagon was still parked in the back when she mounted the steps. The newspaper boy had brought the early afternoon edition of the paper already. It was lying on the porch in the snow. She picked it up and let herself into the house, passing through the vestibule into the stairhall where she laid the paper on the table.

The house was quiet. Mac had let the two dogs out of their cages and had opened the back door for them. Outside they'd at least have a chance for survival. Here was . . . only death.

She went to the waiting room door and stopped. For the moment her legs would carry her no farther. She could see the blood that had seeped under the surgery door and lay now in a black, crusty patch on the tile. Her stomach turned over, and she thought she was going to be sick.

Insanity. All of it was insane, including her coming back here.

She forced herself across the waiting room to the surgery door, took a deep breath and opened it, her legs instantly turning to rubber.

"Oh, Father," she whispered.

She'd not really seen him the first time. A haze had filled her eyes, as it threatened to do now. But she made herself look at him, study his body, study the destruction that had been wreaked on him.

Russians, Mac had said. Animals.

Even now she had the crazy thought that her father was going to sit up at any moment and laugh. "It's a joke, Stephanie," he would say. But she pushed that macabre thought aside and went the rest of the way into the surgery where she got a pair of shears from one of the drawers and concentrating only on what her hands were doing, cut the tape that held her father's arms and legs together beneath the table.

His body was cold but surprisingly loose. Bile rose up at the back of her throat as she lifted his legs up onto the steel table, and then his arms, folding his hands together over his chest.

She hurried upstairs, tears blinding her eyes, where she got a clean bedsheet from the linen closet and brought it back to the surgery. She draped it over her father's body.

"I'm sorry, father," she said staring at the bulge in the sheet where the scalpel handle stuck out of his eye. All the rest she had been able to do. That one thing was impossible.

She backed to the surgery door then hurried across the waiting room to the stairhall where she raced to the downstairs bathroom and was violently ill in the toilet.

The body in the surgery was her father's, but it wasn't him, she kept telling herself. The thing was flesh and bone, and fluids. Her father had been a bright, alive human being; a personality, someone who gave sage advice and warm comfort. The body in the surgery was not capable of such things.

"Father!" she screamed rising up suddenly and swiveling on her heel.

At the door she had to hold onto the wall for support lest she collapse. She was going to have to go on. There was no other possibility. Mac was everything now. There was nothing . . . absolutely nothing else in her life.

She staggered out into the stairhall. She could see through the front windows that the snow had intensified and that the wind had begun to rise. They were in for a full-fledged storm. She shook her head. Would it ever end? Could it ever end?

At the vestibule door she turned and looked back toward the waiting room, a sudden panic rising up in her breast.

Her father was alone. He would lie there until someone came to investigate. Strangers would come, handle his body, and take him away.

How could she stand it?

She took a step back when her eye fell on the newspaper lying on the table. It was folded into a plastic bag, Mac's photograph staring up at her.

With shaking hands she picked up the newspaper, pulled the plastic wrapping off and opened it to the front page. Hers and Mac's photographs stared up at her beneath the headlines:

MASSACRE AT COLLEGE PARK
SUSPECTS SOUGHT IN MULTIPLE SLAYINGS

Chapter 24

McAllister waited outside the baggage pickup area at the Baltimore-Washington Airport for the next available taxi. The airport was much busier now than it had been earlier this morning. Some flights had already been canceled or delayed because of the deteriorating weather, and the disappointed passengers were irritable, pushing and jostling for transportation back into the city.

If this kept up, he and Stephanie would have to take the train to New York. With luck they still would be able to get a flight out to the West Coast first thing in the morning.

He glanced over at a man dressed in a business suit, an overnight bag and attaché case at his feet as he got a newspaper from one of the machines lined up by the doors. For just a split second McAllister caught a glimpse of the front page and he stepped back, stunned.

The businessman folded the newspaper without looking at it, picked up his bags and came over to where McAllister was standing.

"They canceled my flight, what about yours?" the man asked.

"I'm waiting for someone," McAllister mumbled, and

he turned and went back into the terminal, the man staring after him.

He took the escalators back up to the main departures hall, his heart racing. His and Stephanie's photographs had been plastered all over the front page of the newspaper. He hadn't caught the headlines, but they were big.

The message had been sent two days ago with a false description of him. What had happened in the meantime to change all of that?

He approached one of the magazine and smoke shops where he could see several newspapers. All of them carried the same photographs beneath similar headlines: MASSACRE IN COLLEGE PARK. The clerk behind the counter was reading a newspaper. McAllister backed away without going in, turned and hurried across the terminal to the front doors where cabs and buses were drawing up dropping off anxious people still hoping to catch a flight out.

Massacre—the word kept running through his head. Massacre of whom, and when? On the way up they'd heard a lot of sirens: Had that something to do with this?

He dug some coins out of his pocket, and before he caught one of the departing cabs, bought a newspaper from one of the machines. "The Historical Society," he told the driver, avoiding any eye-to-eye contact.

"You got it," the cabbie said, and pulled away from the curb. "Some weather, huh?"

"Right," McAllister said absently, his eyes riveted on the front page of the newspaper.

The photographs looked like standard Agency head shots out of their files, Stephanie's more recent than his, but both of them very recognizable except for the fact that his hair was much shorter now, and he still wore the clear-lensed glasses Stephanie had bought for him.

He quickly scanned the lengthy article with a growing disbelief. Innes and Reisberg had been killed outright.

Quarmby was in critical condition at Bethesda Naval Hospital where he was not expected to live, and Highnote was in guarded condition, but was expected to recover.

Highnote was not Zebra One. He was not a part of the network after all.

Look to Washington. Look to Moscow.

The penetration agent was not Highnote. Whoever he was, the mole was still in place. Highnote had tried to help and he had nearly lost his life for his effort. Carrick and Maas had been killed in New York, then Sikorski in Reston, Ballinger in Washington, and Stephanie's father here in Baltimore. Now Innes, Reisberg, and probably Quarmby. It was nearly beyond belief.

The story had been released just a few hours ago by a spokesman for the FBI, who reported that the meeting had been called at the home of Paul Innes, associate deputy attorney general, because of the overnight slaying of James and Liam O'Haire at the federal penitentiary outside of Marion, Illinois. "See related story on page 2A."

McAllister turned the page. The O'Haires had been found very early this morning stabbed to death. There were no clues as to the identity of the murderers, but prison officials said they believed that there had been trouble between the two brothers and some of the other prisoners.

Back on page one, McAllister continued with the main article. "Neighbors of the McAllisters, in their posh Georgetown neighborhood, reported seeing McAllister and a woman matching the description of Stephanie Albright, leaving in a white Peugeot sedan registered to McAllister. Tire tracks at the scene of the multiple slayings matched those of the Peugeot.

"In addition to the four government officials, also killed were two FBI officers, as well as Caroline Innes, wife of the associate deputy attorney general."

McAllister, the article went on, had been named in connection with four other recent murders; two in New York, one in Washington, and the fourth near Reston.

According to an "unnamed source within the CIA," McAllister, who had recently returned from assignment in Moscow, had worked with the Russians as a source for the O'Haire's spy network. It was believed that McAllister and Stephanie Albright were still at large in the Washington area, and were to be considered armed and extremely dangerous.

McAllister let the paper drop to his lap. There was no going back for either of them now. Whatever faint hope he had held for using Stephanie as a backup should he fail—having her approach Dexter Kingman with the entire story—was completely shattered now. According to the article, two weapons had been used in the massacre. The implication was that both McAllister and the woman had participated in the killings.

Stephanie, he thought, *what in God's name have I done to you?*

The lobby of their hotel was mostly deserted, and no one paid the slightest attention to McAllister as he crossed to the elevator. He could not hide this from her, of course, but he had no idea how she was going to take the news that she was wanted for murder. If she folded on him it would make things impossible. Coming so soon on the heels of the shock of seeing her father's mutilated body, however, he was worried about her.

Stephanie opened the door for him, her eyes going from his face to the overnight bags he was carrying, and then to the newspaper folded under his arm.

"You've seen it, then," she said. She was pale and obviously frightened.

"Was it on the television?" he asked coming in and putting down the bags. But then he spotted the newspaper spread out on the bed and he turned on her. "Christ, I told you to stay in the room. I told you not to leave the hotel under any circumstances."

"I'm sorry," she cried. "But it was something I had to do."

"What was so important?" he asked, raising his voice.

"My father," she replied, turning away. Her breathing was erratic, and she was holding her hands together to stop them from shaking.

"What about him?" McAllister snapped, realizing the moment the words escaped his lips how callous and insensitive he must sound to her. "Listen, Stephanie, I'm sorry. . . ."

"Don't be, you were right. I shouldn't have left the hotel. But I didn't know about this." She turned to face McAllister. "I couldn't just leave him like that, David. I don't know if you can understand, but he was alone, and when someone shows up at the house, I didn't want them to see him like . . . that."

McAllister fought to control his sudden fear. "Did you call someone?"

She shook her head. "I was going to, but then I saw the paper . . ."

"What did you do?"

She told him in a halting voice, and his heart broke for her. But there was simply nothing he could do to make it any easier.

"I understand," he said when she was finished. "I really do."

She looked at him, searching his eyes to make sure that he wasn't patronizing her. He managed a slight wan smile and she came across the room to him. He took her in his arms and held her close, her entire body shaking.

"Where does it end, David?" she asked softly. "There were witnesses who say they saw us."

"Either they were lying, or they were mistaken. Whoever

did the killings may have dressed up to look like us. They went to my house, took my car and went out to College Park."

She looked up at him. "Highnote isn't a part of it, then," she said, her eyes wide and moist.

"No," McAllister said.

"They'll try again to kill him, won't they?"

"Probably. But I'm sure he's being closely guarded now. It won't be so easy for them the next time. But now we've got an ally. Someone to trust."

"If he recovers."

"Yes," McAllister said, his mind drawn for just a moment back to the years and years he and Highnote had been friends. To the good times and the bad. They'd accomplished so much together, had confided so often in each other; Highnote the mentor, Mac his brightest pupil. It hurt that he had ever doubted his friend.

"I'm sorry," Stephanie said. "I was wrong about him from the beginning."

"You were going on what you knew. On the apparent facts," he said, trying to think it out.

"Did you know any of those people?"

McAllister focused on her. "Just Quarmby over at NSA. He was a good man."

"I knew Alvan Reisberg from the old days. The question is, David, what were those four doing meeting together?"

"What are you getting at?"

"Think about it. The O'Haires were killed last night, and this morning those particular four men held a meeting. Whatever it was they were talking about had to involve us. And it had to be important enough for Zebra One to want to stop them and blame their deaths on us."

"Now there's an all-out manhunt for us."

"But why kill Innes and the others unless Highnote was there to convince them that we were innocent?"

Suddenly McAllister did see it. "You're right. Christ, it

was staring me right in the face. Whoever arranged the killings has just proved Highnote wrong.''

''It's another message.''

''It's more than that,'' McAllister said, suddenly seeing everything. ''There is a common thread. Zebra One is someone highly enough placed so that he knows not only Highnote's movements, but he also knew about Innes at the Justice Department, Reisberg at the FBI, and Quarmby at NSA.''

''My God, who?''

''I don't know, but the list has got to be small,'' McAllister said, his thoughts still racing. ''From the deputy director of the CIA all the way up . . . as far up as you want to go.''

Stephanie was shaking her head in disbelief. ''You may have been right when you said we couldn't fight them,'' she said. ''What are we going to do?''

''Pray to God that Highnote recovers so that I can talk to him, warn him. He's our only hope now.''

''That's going to take some time.''

''Time we don't have. For the next forty-eight hours every cop on the Eastern Seaboard is going to be looking for us. At least as long as they think we're still on the move. We've got to go to ground for a few days.''

''We still have to get to California. Besides Highnote, the list is our only lead.''

''Not now,'' McAllister said, thinking. ''We'd be too visible on an airplane, too confined. If we were recognized the pilot would only have to radio ahead and we'd be taken the moment we landed.''

''If we took a plane,'' Stephanie said.

''What are you talking about?''

''The train, David,'' she said excitedly. She looked at her watch, it was a few minutes past three. ''We have a little more than an hour.''

''What train?''

"Amtrak from Union Station. I saw the schedule when I was there this afternoon. It leaves at twenty after four to Chicago, and from there to Los Angeles. It's got to take at least three or four days to get to the coast, time enough with luck for Highnote to recover, and time to let things die down here."

They've trained me well. I know all the moves for staying alive behind enemy lines; the subterfuges, the little ploys; when to run, when to freeze like a rabbit in the woods whose only two defenses are his speed and his ability to remain absolutely still, blending perfectly with the environment.

She was looking at him. "David? Are you all right?"

McAllister nodded. "We've no other choice." He managed another slight smile.

She returned his smile though he could see the deep pain in her eyes. "Then let's stop the bastards once and for all," she said.

Stephanie left the hotel the back way and waited outside while McAllister paid their bill to a harried clerk. Because of the mounting storm, which already was making travel nearly impossible, a lot of people were booking rooms against the likelihood they would be stuck in the city.

The wind had risen and whipped snow in eddies around buildings, and in long, ragged plumes down the streets on which traffic had thinned dramatically in the past hour or so.

They had to walk nearly three blocks before they found a cab on Cathedral Street. McAllister's appearance was different enough from the photograph in the newspapers so that he didn't think he'd be so easily recognized. And Stephanie had pinned her hair back in a severe bun, had removed all of her makeup and had tied a scarf over her head, giving her a spinsterish look. The slight alteration in their appearances wouldn't fool a trained observer, but it would be enough, he hoped, to get them onto the train unnoticed.

"Are the trains still moving?" McAllister asked the driver.

"You got me, buddy," the cabbie said, glancing at their reflection in the rearview mirror. "If they are, they're the only things going anyplace. Where are you folks headed?"

"New York," McAllister said, glancing at Stephanie. "We've got to catch a flight to Paris first thing in the morning."

"Yeah, well good luck."

Sooner or later they would be traced to Baltimore. It was possible that the cabbie would remember the couple he'd taken to the train station who were on their way to Paris. It wasn't much, but the ruse might buy them a little extra time if it came to that.

It was nearly four by the time they made it to Union Station. The trains were indeed moving, and the station was crammed. Just inside Stephanie stopped him.

"Get our tickets and wait for me downstairs on the boarding platform," she said.

"What?"

"Do as I say, David," she snapped. She looked up at his hair. "I'll be right back."

"Where are you going?"

"There's a drugstore around the corner, I've got to pick up a few things." She handed him her bags. "I know what I'm doing, it's okay," she said. She turned on her heel and went back out into the storm.

McAllister waited for only a moment then he headed across the departures hall to the ticket windows, walking with an exaggerated limp, his eyes downcast.

The line moved very slowly and it took nearly ten minutes before it was his turn, and another five minutes before the irritated clerk had booked him a double compartment first class to Chicago, returning next Tuesday.

"Why didn't you wait until the last minute?" the clerk said sarcastically. "Baggage?"

"Three, all carryon."

"You'd better hurry, pal, or you'll miss your train," the clerk said handing him his tickets. "We're running on time."

McAllister looked at his watch as he crossed the big hall; it was ten past four. He looked for Stephanie at the escalators but she was nowhere to be seen. She should have been back by now unless she had run into some trouble. Anything was possible.

He debated with himself for a moment whether he should go outside to try to find her. She said she was going to a drug store around the corner. For what? But there was no time now. She was either waiting for him down on the platform or she wasn't.

At the bottom he saw her standing just beyond a knot of people. She was clutching a paper bag in her left hand, her right stuffed in her coat pocket where she had her gun.

When she saw him she hurried over, pulling a wool knit cap out of the bag. "Put this on," she whispered urgently.

He pulled the cap on without question, and together they hurried down the platform along the line of their train.

"I think our cabbie recognized us," she said.

"Are you sure?"

"He was out front when I came back, talking to a couple of cops."

"Did they spot you?"

"No," she said. "At least I don't think so."

"Well, we'll find out soon enough," McAllister said, as they reached their porter and he handed over the tickets.

Chapter 25

Snow streaked diagonally past the window as they slid south through the outskirts of Baltimore, the train swaying and lurching gently as they picked up speed. Several last-minute passengers had boarded, but there had been no police, no delays, no suspicious people.

Their options were fast running out. It was as if they were being directed by unseen hands toward something. But what?

McAllister stood at the window and he could see Stephanie's reflection in the glass. She stood with her back to the door, her right hand still in her coat pocket. She was shivering. They'd not spoken a word to each other since they'd boarded. He lifted his left arm and looked at his watch; it was four-thirty. The train had departed on time, and it would take them at least overnight to get to Chicago and another two days to reach Los Angeles.

Go to ground, that was the drill. Get out of the line of fire when it becomes so intense, so well directed that there is no defense.

The train was the Cardinal. Their accommodations were on the upper level, with a large window looking trackside and an even larger, curtained window looking out on the corridor. A sofa and armchair faced each other on the opposite side on which was a small door that opened onto a tiny bathroom complete with a toilet, sink, and shower.

Someone knocked on the door. McAllister spun around. Stephanie stepped away from the door as if she had been shot out of a cannon, the gun in her hand.

He motioned for her to keep silent. "Yes?" he called.

"It's the porter, sir. Will you and the missus be needing anything this evening? May I turn down your beds later?"

"No thanks," McAllister called. "We're just fine. I think we'll turn in now."

"Yes, sir," the porter said after a hesitation.

"What time will we reach Chicago?"

"Eight-fifteen, sir. In the morning."

"Will we be on time?"

"I expect so, sir."

"Thanks," McAllister said.

"The dining car will be serving until ten, and the club car until two. Are you folks sure you won't be needing anything tonight?"

"We're tired, we'll be going to sleep now. Thanks again."

"Yes, sir," the porter said, and he sounded disappointed. Moments later they heard him knocking on the door of the next cabin, and Stephanie let out the breath she had been holding.

"We're all right," McAllister said softly.

Stephanie glanced at him, but she cocked an ear to listen to the exchange between the porter and the passengers in the next cabin. After awhile they heard him knock on the next door down the line and she finally relaxed, tossing her gun down on the couch. She looked as if she were on the verge of collapsing.

"They would have stopped the train if I'd been spotted, wouldn't they?" she asked.

"Probably," McAllister said, but again he was thinking ahead. They'd be in Washington within the hour where they would meet their first big test. If Stephanie had been spotted entering the station, and if the ticket clerk had remembered him, they might be putting it together now. Someone would be coming aboard when they pulled into the station and there would be no escape for them.

He looked out the window again. They had continued to pick up speed. If they were going to jump, it would have to be now. But then what? Where would they go? It was possible that one of them would be injured in the fall. If that happened they would have lost.

There were four names on the list he had taken from the Agency computer. Only one of them, Kathleen O'Haire would be easily accessible. The others, by virtue of their jobs and their locations, would be difficult if not impossible to approach.

Was she the weak link? Or would they have someone watching her around the clock, expecting him to show up sooner or later. It was very possible, he thought, that they could be walking into another trap.

"They must have thought my father had some answers for them," Stephanie said.

He turned back to her. "They were sending us another message."

"What message, David?"

"Just how important they think we've become."

"By killing him? By torturing him?" Her voice was rising. She was working herself up.

"Let it go," McAllister said gently. "There's nothing we can do about it."

"Oh yes there is," she said, her nostrils flared, color coming to her cheeks. "Oh yes there is, David. Only now they're going to have to kill me, and it's not going to be so easy."

He went across to her and tried to take her in his arms, but she pushed him aside.

"Do you remember when we went to my father's house this morning and you told me that if the FBI or the Agency or anyone in authority showed up, I was to lay down my gun and give myself up?'' Her lips compressed. She shook her head. ''I'm not going to do it. I'm not. Anyone who gets in my way—anyone, David—I'm going to kill without hesitation.''

''Stephanie . . .''

''Kill or be killed, that's the routine isn't it? Well, I'm waiting for the opportunity. I'm waiting!'' She turned away raising her hands to her face.

He took her shoulders. For a moment she resisted, but then she allowed herself to be drawn back against him, her body still tense. He thought he understood why she had gone back to see her father's body, but it had not done her any good. She had turned her own morality corner, as a result. It was the first major crisis that any field operative had to face sooner or later. The point came when the agent suddenly saw that what he was doing, the actions he was taking fighting the enemy were no different from the actions his enemy was taking.

There came the time when the good operative began to have difficulty seeing any difference between his country and the enemy's. For a lot of operatives it was their first and last crisis; many of them quit at that moment. Others got past it somehow. While still others became tainted. Their hands were dirty and they could never get them clean. They were the ones who ended up being fired in disgrace, committing suicide, or being shot down in some alley somewhere.

''I'm sorry,'' he said softly into her ear.

She pulled away and looked at him, her eyes filled with anger. ''So am I,'' she said. ''For you, for me, for everybody.''

''But it doesn't change anything.''

''No,'' she said. She glanced toward the window. It was already very dark outside. ''We'll be in Washington soon.''

''Yes.''

"Go wash your hair," she said, pulling off her coat and dropping it over the chair.

"What?"

"I said wash your hair, we don't have much time." She opened the bag she'd brought with her and pulled out a pair of scissors, a small hair dryer, and a frosting kit.

"Now," she said looking up at him. "Unless you want to spend all night at this."

At that moment McAllister didn't think he knew her.

Stephanie was in the tiny bathroom when they pulled into the station in Washington to pick up passengers. McAllister sat in the dark compartment, his gun beside him, the window shade open a crack so that he could see the platform.

"Are we there?" Stephanie asked, opening the door.

"Turn out the light," McAllister said without looking up.

She did it, and he felt her come across to him. She perched on the edge of the couch. "How does it look?"

"Busy, but there are no cops," he said. "At least not yet."

"If they had spotted us in Baltimore they would already be here."

"You'd think so," he said absently. There was a lot of activity on the platform, people coming and going, most of them carrying suitcases, some of them with little children, several of them military men in uniform toting duffel bags.

He let the window shade fall back, picked up his gun, and moved silently to the corridor window, where he parted the curtain slightly.

The porter stood with his back to the window, talking to a man and a woman. McAllister could hear the voices but not the words. They seemed to be arguing about something.

He let the curtain fall back. Everything was normal. No alarms had been raised, no men rushed across the platform, guns drawn. Nor had the platform been emptied of passengers. Was it too normal out there, or was he imagining things? Something whispered at the back of his head. Some undefined danger signal was ringing. He could see Stephanie's silhouette outlined by the light filtering through the window shade. She was looking at him.

"What is it?" she asked softly.

"I don't know," he said. "Nothing."

"No one got a good look at us as we boarded," she said. "Not even the porter. He won't notice the change."

The gun still in his hand, he went back to the outside window and looked out on the platform. Stephanie stood beside him. He could smell the lingering odor of the strong chemical solution she had used to streak her hair. She looked different. Aged by twenty years. She stood with a stoop and tottered a little as she walked. The change was startling in her. There'd not been enough time to dye his hair, but she had cut it very short, and with a little pancake makeup and the glasses he looked different enough from the photographs being published in the newspapers that no one would be likely to give him a second glance.

Already the crowds had begun to thin out. The train would be pulling out very soon. What was it? he thought glumly. What was he missing? What if they had been spotted in Baltimore? What if it had taken this long to question the ticket clerks to find out what train they had boarded? Someone would be meeting the train farther west. As far as Chicago.

Self-doubt will come to all of us at one time or another, boyo. He could almost see his father, hear the old man's voice. But there was no reason to think they had been seen, other than the cabbie talking to the cops outside the station. He could have been talking to them about the weather, about traffic, about football scores, anything.

And what about his feeling that they were being followed now, that they were being watched? Where were the clues? Where was the out-of-place man or men on the platform, the look in the porter's eye when they'd come aboard, the note in his voice when he had called through the door? There was nothing. It was paranoia. Just like the old days. Sofia, East Berlin, Prague, Warsaw; a dozen places, two dozen incidents ranging back over fourteen years until his tradecraft had slipped that night in Moscow. *Fallbacks, don't ever forget your back door, kiddo.*

Christ, he'd known the routine. He'd known how to cover himself, yet he had become sloppy. And his lapse had caused the deaths of a lot of innocent people.

The train lurched and Stephanie bumped against him. He held her with his free hand while he continued watching out of the window as the station began to slip away. No one came running at the last minute. No one. Moments later they were in the darkness again, and he let the window shade fall back, dropped his gun on the couch, and took Stephanie in his arms.

When they kissed she shuddered deeply, as if someone had just walked over her grave.

Gennadi Potemkin hunched up the collar of his charcoal-gray overcoat and adjusted the angle of his fedora as he hurried out of the lobby of the Hyatt Regency two blocks from the train station and approached the waiting Lincoln Continental.

A squat, very dangerous-looking man dressed in a sharply tailored tuxedo, a white scarf around his neck, looked out from the back seat as the driver opened the door for Potemkin, who climbed in without a word.

The events of the past twenty-four hours were nearly beyond belief. Potemkin hoped against hope that this one would have good news for him now. But his hopes faded as he looked into the Italian's eyes.

Their driver got in behind the wheel and they headed away from the hotel, plunging into the storm that made driving extremely difficult. Washington seemed, at that hour, like a city under seige.

"This weather's a bitch, ain't it?" the thick-waisted Italian said, his Sicilian accent heavy.

"I've paid you a lot of money," Potemkin said harshly. "I didn't come here to listen to your bullshit about the weather."

The Mafia boss turned to look at Potemkin, his eyes hooded. "You'd better listen, because we missed them."

A sudden cold wind blew through Potemkin's soul. "What?" he shouted.

"We weren't sure about the train, but we didn't miss them by much more than a half hour."

"Where are they headed? They didn't get off here in Washington? You're sure?"

"Chicago."

"West," Potemkin mumbled, his insides like water. "Go after them."

"Impossible in this weather, that's what I meant. Nothing's moving out there, and I mean nothing except for the trains."

"Take another train."

"Isn't one."

The heavy car fishtailed around the corner, but then straightened out. Potemkin tried to reason out the possibilities. He felt as if he were losing control of the situation. It was dangerous. So dangerous it was hard to keep his head on an even keel.

"You're sure it was them? No doubts?"

"Our guy drove them to the station. We had the word out. There was no doubt of it. He told the cops, just like you said to do, then he called us. They're on that train all right. Just took us a while to find out which train."

"No way of catching them?" Potemkin asked, struggling to maintain his control.

"Not a chance in hell," the Sicilian said. He grinned. "But there is another possibility."

"Yes?"

"It'll cost you."

Potemkin looked at the man with disgust. "Up to this point you haven't done a thing for what you've already been paid."

The Sicilian leaned forward suddenly and grabbed a handful of Potemkin's coat. "It was my son out there in Reston. That sonofabitch wasted him. You understand, gumba? I got a stake in this now. But it'll still cost you."

The man's immense greed was beyond belief. But Potemkin had worked with this type before. Often. "You'll get your money," he said, changing tack.

The Sicilian let go of his coat. "You haven't heard how much. . . ."

"I don't care what the figure is, you'll get it," Potemkin said, interrupting. "On one condition."

The Sicilian nodded warily.

"You'll get paid for success; there'll be nothing for failure."

"Half now . . ."

"No," Potemkin interrupted sharply again. "Only for success."

"Don't fuck with me. One phone call to the Feds and you'd be through here."

"Do you know what we do with traitors?" Potemkin asked conversationally, sure now for the first time that he had regained some control. "We have a thing called *mokrie dela*. Your people shoot kneecaps as a warning, we shoot faces. Your mother wouldn't recognize you."

The Sicilian laughed. "This is my backyard now, gumba. My country."

"Don't be so sure of that," Potemkin said softly, and something in the tone of his voice backed the Mafia boss off.

They drove for a few minutes in silence, passing the Capitol building that against the backdrop of black skies and falling snow looked more like a Hollywood set than the real thing. Something was happening that Potemkin couldn't understand. He was fighting back blindly, but fighting the only way he knew how; directly and with force.

"There is a family in Chicago," the Sicilian said. "They owe me a favor."

"There can be no mistakes now," Potemkin said. "McAllister and the girl must not be allowed to get beyond Chicago. Under no circumstances."

They swung back toward the Hyatt, again lapsing into silence, Potemkin sinking into his own morose thoughts. Control, that was everything. But his was slipping and he knew it. What he couldn't understand, what he could not fathom, was the incident at College Park this morning. Had he underestimated McAllister that badly?

"Is this asshole one of yours?" the Sicilian asked.

"No," Potemkin replied, shaking his head. "He is definitely not one of ours." He turned. "Kill him. This time, make sure."

They'd come out of the storm sometime in the early morning hours. Stephanie stood at the window looking out at the passing countryside, lit now by a full moon that was so bright it obliterated the stars. She wore nothing but a long sweatshirt, her shoulders hunched forward, her forehead against the cool glass.

"You should get some sleep," McAllister said from where he lay in the lower bunk.

"You too," she replied, tiredly, mechanically.

"I'm sorry about your father."

"You've already said that. But what happens if there are no answers for us in California?"

"I'll talk to Highnote."

"What if he dies, or if he decides there's nothing he can do?"

"Then we'll go to the others."

"One of them in the Pentagon, the other in Moscow," she said, contempt in her voice. "Let's stop kidding ourselves."

Her skin looked pale as a ghost's in the moonlight, but he could almost feel the heat radiating off her, as if she were an engine at idle ready to spring into motion at any moment. At one point he could have saved her life by turning around and walking away from her. That was no longer possible. He was sorry for it, and yet he wasn't.

He could see her breath fogging the window. The train swayed rhythmically, the motion nearly hypnotic at this time of the night.

As the dawn began to break over the Indiana countryside they made love, slowly, gently, tenderly as if they were afraid of hurting each other—which in a measure they were—and as if it were their last time—which possibly it was.

Afterward, they lay in each other's arms, and she began to talk about her father; how it had been when she was a young girl and her mother was still alive, and afterward when she would come back from college to be with him. He had been her Rock of Gibraltar, her mentor, her best friend, her confidant; the one person in the world for whom she had to put on no false face, the one person on this earth who knew and loved her for exactly what she was.

As she talked, McAllister thought about his own father, and the fact that although he had had a deep love and respect for the old man, he had felt cheated because of when and how his father had died.

It had been listed as an accident. The fact of the matter was he had simply worn out and had taken his own life.

There had been no note, no explanation, no last words. He couldn't remember the funeral, but he could remember in vivid details the nightmares afterward in which he thought about his father lying in a dark, cold grave alone on a windswept hill.

Chapter 26

They entered the city from the south a few minutes past eight, the tracks angling away from Lake Michigan, morning traffic in full swing on the Dan Ryan Expressway. In the distance the Sears Tower rose up into the cobalt-blue sky. Chicago hadn't got much snow, what there was lay in dirty piles. It looked extremely cold outside.

Stephanie had worked on their makeup again this morning, giving them a sallow, used-up look. The transformation was complete. Looking at himself in the mirror, McAllister could believe that he wasn't himself. He looked almost military.

The train had slowed down in the city. They entered the tunnel that would bring them into Union Station downtown. Stephanie got up as McAllister flipped on the compartment lights, and she took her gun out of her coat pocket. She took the clip out of the butt of the gun, cycled the round out of the firing chamber, reloaded the bullet into the clip, snapped the clip back into the gun, and cycled a round back into the firing chamber, checking to make sure the safety catch was on before she stuffed the gun back into her coat.

She looked up, catching McAllister watching her.

"I meant it, what I told you last night," she said, the tenderness that had been in her eyes while they made love gone.

"Don't become one of them," he said.

"I don't want to hear it," she snapped, a catch in her voice. She was frightened but she was also angry.

"We can't fight them all, not this way."

"No?"

"No," McAllister said. "You're going to do it my way, and you're going to follow my instructions."

"Up to the point that someone tries to arrest me. I won't let it happen."

"You'd shoot an innocent cop trying to do his job?"

"If need be," she said evenly.

McAllister held out his hand. "Give me your gun," he said.

She backed up a step and shook her head, her left eyebrow rising. "No."

"Not that way," McAllister said. "I want your gun."

"Goddamnit, David . . ." she started to protest when someone knocked at their door, and he held up his hand for her to keep silent.

"Yes?" he called out.

"Five minutes until the station, folks," a man's voice called back. It wasn't their porter from last night.

"All right, thank you," McAllister said.

"If you'll just let me in, sir, I'll give you a hand with your bags," the man said, and there was something about his accent that was suddenly bothersome. There was a connection somewhere. McAllister had heard that voice before, or one similar to it. Where?

The door handle turned slowly. "I'll get you a redcap in the terminal, sir."

The accent was Italian. A snow-covered road, a dark-brown Thunderbird. A man in a bombardier jacket. It was the same accent. New Jersey. Mafia. The Mafia controlled a segment of the Teamsters union. Cabbies, train porters?

Stephanie's eyes had grown wide. She had made the same connection. She grabbed her gun out of her coat pocket.

McAllister motioned for her to move aside as he pulled out his gun and flipped off the compartment lights, plunging them into darkness.

"All right," he called out. "Just a moment please." He moved to the door and silently slipped the lock. He glanced at Stephanie, then yanked the door open.

A short, heavyset man with thick features, a blue watch cap perched on the back of his head, stood there, his right hand inside his sheepskin jacket. His mouth dropped open when he caught sight of McAllister. "What?" he stammered.

McAllister grabbed a handful of his jacket and pulled him into the compartment, spinning him around, and slamming him up against the bathroom door, his pistol against the man's neck, his left hand holding the man's gun hand in place.

Behind him, Stephanie closed and locked the door, then turned on the compartment lights. The man's eyes were bugging half out of their sockets, and he kept swallowing over and over, though he did not resist.

"The window shade," McAllister said.

Stephanie lowered it.

"It's a mistake," the man croaked, talking difficult because of the gun jammed into his throat.

"No it's not," McAllister said. "Who sent you?"

"I don't know what you're talking about," the man said, but it was obvious he was lying.

Stephanie reached around and pulled his hand out of his coat, and then reached inside and pulled out his gun, a big .357 Magnum with a thick silencer tube screwed onto the end of the shortened barrel. A devastating weapon, especially at close range.

"Who sent you?" McAllister demanded, pressing the barrel of his gun even harder into the man's throat. "Now, or I'll blow your neck apart!"

"I don't know," the man croaked. "We got orders from out East that you and the broad were coming in on this train. I got on at Dyer."

"Orders from whom?"

"I don't know, I swear to God I don't know. We just got a call, that's all."

"Is someone waiting in the station for us?"

"No," the man said. Stephanie brought the barrel of the silenced Magnum up against his temple. "Yes . . . yes," he cried.

"How many of them?"

"Four. A redcap, two by the stairs, and a cabbie outside."

"How will we recognize them?"

"They're all dressed like me, except for the redcap."

"Then what?" McAllister asked. "What were your orders? Specifically."

"Just to take you, that's all." The train was slowing down, coming to a stop.

Stephanie cocked the Magnum's hammer.

"Oh, Jesus and Mary, mother of God," the man stammered. "I was supposed to kill you. If that didn't work, you'd get it on the platform or out on the street. Somewhere. We weren't supposed to fail. This was a big job."

"Who sent you? You've got to have a name."

"I don't know, I swear it."

"This was a big job?" Stephanie asked.

"Yeah, yeah, important, like I said . . ."

"Like Baltimore?" Stephanie asked.

"Yeah, like Baltimore . . ." the man said.

At the last instant McAllister realized what was about to happen, but he was powerless to stop it. He managed to step back as Stephanie moaned, the sound animallike, coming from the back of her throat, and she pulled the trigger.

The man's head was slammed violently against the bathroom door, a large piece of the back of his skull blown away, his eyes and nose and mouth filling with blood as he crumpled on the floor dead.

Stephanie stood, violently shaking, the big gun in her hand pointed at the inert figure on the floor. "Oh, my God," she cried softly, tears streaming down her cheeks.

The train had come to a complete stop. Outside in the corridor they could hear the sounds of departing passengers. The others would be waiting on the platform for this one to show up or for a young couple to get off. They were going to have to get out of here now, while they still had the advantage of time, and of their disguises.

"I killed him," Stephanie was blubbering. "My, God, his . . . head . . ."

McAllister stuffed his gun in his belt and took Stephanie by the shoulders, pulling her around. "Stop it," he snapped.

She looked up into his eyes. She was on the verge of collapsing.

"Listen to me, Stephanie. It was either him or us. He was sent here to kill us both. There was nothing else you could have done."

"I shot him," she said.

"Yes, and now we have to leave. Immediately." He took the big Magnum from her hand, laid it on the couch, then helped her on with her coat, stuffing her gun in his pocket, and pulling on his coat. He picked up their three bags.

"No," she said, suddenly coming out of her daze. "David, they're out there waiting for us."

"They don't know what we look like yet. Nor do they

know that this one has failed. But we don't have much time. You've got to pull yourself together. Now!"

She was shaking her head and she started to back away. McAllister dropped their bags, grabbed her arm with one hand and slapped her in the face, her head snapping back and a cry catching in her throat.

"We have to get out of here, Stephanie! Now!" McAllister said.

She took a deep breath, nodded and straightened up. "Yes," she said. "I'll be all right. We have to leave."

She averted her eyes from the body on the floor as McAllister again picked up their bags, listened at the door for a moment then opened it and stepped out. A young couple coming up the corridor stopped respectfully to let them get out of their compartment and close the door. McAllister nodded at them, and smiled, then headed for the end of the car with a limp, Stephanie shuffling along directly behind him.

They would have to get away from the train station as quickly as possible. It wouldn't take long for someone to discover what had happened. Going to ground and lying low for a few days was no longer one of their options. Speed was their only defense.

Do the unexpected. Strike back. Hit them until it hurts and they begin to bleed. Keep them off balance. Frighten them into making a mistake.

The porter helped McAllister down from the tall step, and then took Stephanie's arm and helped her.

"Hope you folks had a nice trip with us," he said pleasantly.

McAllister nodded absently as his eyes scanned the busy platform. A large man in a redcap's uniform stood about twenty feet away, watching them, but then his gaze was diverted as the next passengers were helped down from the train.

Stephanie took McAllister's arm and together they walked slowly down the platform to the gates, then past a big knot of people, among them two men dressed in sheepskin coats intently watching the departing passengers, and then they were on the escalator going up to the main ticket hall.

The cavernous, ornately decorated station was decked out for the holidays. Christmas music played from the public address system, interrupted only when train announcements were made. There were a lot of people hurrying back and forth. Two police officers stood by the main doors.

"Easy," McAllister said under his breath, Stephanie's grip tightening on his arm as they headed directly across the hall.

The two cops barely glanced at them as they reached the doors and stepped outside into the very cold morning. A stiff wind was blowing off the lake. Taxis were coming and going. The driver of one of them near the head of the line, was dressed in a sheepskin jacket, just like the others below on the platform and the one who had come aboard the train for them. And like the others, he looked their way for just a moment, registering the fact they were not his targets, before his concentration went back to the doors.

McAllister tossed their bags in the backseat of the lead taxi and he and Stephanie got in. "Is there a hospital nearby?"

The cabbie looked at them. "You sick or something?"

"My wife is going to have a baby," McAllister said with a straight face.

For a moment a startled expression crossed the driver's face, but then he grinned and laughed. "Yeah, sure, a baby," he said. "Mercy Hospital is just a few blocks from here, that be okay?"

"Just fine," McAllister said. "Actually it's my ticker."

"You going to be okay, mister? I mean is this an emergency?"

"Slow and easy," McAllister said, his accent broad, southern. "That's the ticket."

* * *

They got off in front of the emergency room entrance, and as soon as the taxi was gone, they walked through the hospital to the front where from a pay phone McAllister called for another cab, this one out to O'Hare Airport.

While they waited for the cab to arrive, McAllister went into the men's room where in one of the toilet stalls he quickly broke down both of their guns, unloading the clips and distributing the parts and the bullets in all three suitcases. They would check their bags through, rather than try to carry them aboard. He didn't expect any trouble.

"Where are we going?" Stephanie asked, her manner lethargic for the moment now that they were out of immediate danger, and the realization of what she had done suddenly hitting home.

"Los Angeles," McAllister said. "It's time to strike back."

Chapter 27

It was just one-thirty in the afternoon when their plane landed at Los Angeles International Airport. McAllister got their bags while Stephanie waited for him by the walkway to the parking ramp. They'd had no trouble getting a flight out of Chicago, nor had they encountered any questions because of what their baggage contained. Nevertheless the flight had been a difficult one; for him because he had no idea what they would find when they got out here, and for Stephanie because of what she had done.

I have killed in the name of revenge. It wasn't a pretty sight, and I am not proud of myself. The act did not fulfill me as I had led myself to believe it would.

Help me, David. I believe in you. Please hold me, and for God's sake, never let me go.

But he could not help her, not now, not until this insanity had been resolved. Somehow they had been traced to Chicago. The message would already have reached Washington: They're heading west! Stop them, at all costs, stop them!

"Are you all right?" he asked, reaching for her. She was pale, and there was a light sheen of sweat on her forehead.

Los Angeles was considerably warmer than Baltimore or Chicago, and she was extremely nervous.

"Somebody is going to come looking for us once they realize we've left Chicago," she said.

"Probably," McAllister said. "We're going to have to move fast now."

"How? We can't rent a car, not now, not in our own names."

"You're right," he said. "We're going to steal one."

They took the moving walkway to the long-term parking ramp at the outer perimeter of the terminal building. An elevator brought them up to the sixth level where he made her wait as he hurried down the rows of cars looking for just the right one.

He found it five minutes later. The car was a newer model Mercedes 300D, with the long-term parking ticket lying in clear view on the dash. There was quite a lot of traffic in the ramp, but no one paid him any attention as he took out his lock-pick set and started to work on the driver's door lock.

The date and time stamped on the ticket had been early this morning. The car's owner would not have left it here if he hadn't planned on being gone at least overnight. Which meant they'd have at least eighteen hours to use the car before any alarm was raised.

The car was equipped with electric locks, and within twenty seconds all four door locks popped open, and he got in behind the wheel, found the trunk release button and hit it, the trunk lid clicking open.

Around back he opened the trunk, found the tool kit which he knew all new Mercedeses were equipped with, and took the largest flat-bladed screwdriver out of it. Closing the trunk lid, he got back in behind the wheel.

A blue Chevrolet station wagon came slowly past him, and then turned the corner at the end of the row and headed down the ramp to the exit.

McAllister inserted the screwdriver blade beneath the lip of the ignition lock on the steering column and pryed it outward with a sharp twist, putting his muscle into it.

The lock popped neatly out of its hole, automatically releasing the pin that held the steering wheel in position, and exposing a bundle of wires.

Again checking to make sure that he wasn't being observed, McAllister bared three of the color-coded wires, twisted two of them together, then used the screwdriver to short across that pair and the third wire. The Mercedes's engine roared to life.

The countdown had begun, and although he had no idea what they would find, if anything, there was no turning back for either of them.

Los Angeles was a huge, sprawling city. Traffic on the freeways was heavy even at two-thirty in the afternoon. In a few hours it would be bumper-to-bumper. Kathleen O'Haire lived in Canoga Park, a pleasant suburb in the Valley about twenty miles north of the airport. McAllister had only been to Los Angeles twice in his life, but Stephanie had spent time here when she was in the air force and she knew the city fairly well so was able to direct him.

The Zebra Network had been a fabulously successful operation for a number of years. James O'Haire, who had been a U.S. Army Delta Force graduate, had drifted into the world of the so-called soldier of fortune, fighting for a time in Central America and then Africa where presumably he had made his Soviet contacts in Libya.

How much had his wife known about his activities? Her name had appeared in the Agency file, yet she'd never been arrested. It was possible she knew nothing.

"What if she's a dead end?" Stephanie asked.

They'd reached Sherman Oaks and turned west on the Ventura Freeway. McAllister glanced at her. "Then we'll try Denby up in San Francisco."

"And him? What if he's a dead end too?"

"I don't know. We'll just have to see."

"We'll just have to see," she repeated, and then fell silent, looking out the window at the foothills in the hazy distance.

On the way out from the airport she had dug out the parts of their weapons from their luggage and had assembled them; her lightweight .32 automatic with a fair degree of proficiency, and his P38 with a little bit of coaching from him.

"They didn't teach us that one at school," she'd explained. It was Doug Ballinger's gun, and before she handed it to McAllister she turned it over in her hands, shaking her head.

"What is it?" he asked.

She looked up. "I keep thinking that none of this should ever have happened," she said. "And yet another part of me realizes that it couldn't have been any other way."

"If we don't win, they will."

"This time," she said earnestly. "There'll always be another time, and another. It'll never end."

There was no answer, so McAllister had concentrated on his driving, the big car handling smoothly in traffic, and she had turned to stare out the window.

The broad, treeless street in Canoga Park was typical of southern California. The houses were all long, low ranch style, with two-car garages, paved driveways, and cars, vans, campers, and bicycles parked everywhere. Some backyards had aboveground swimming pools, others had redwood patios. The sameness of the houses was faintly depressing. This was the great American threat that the O'Haires and their spy network had tried so hard to bring down.

It was three-thirty in the afternoon when they drove slowly past Kathleen O'Haire's house, a white Camaro parked in front of the open garage door. So far as McAllister could tell there was no movement from within the house, but it was a safe bet that the woman was at home.

At the corner he drove back a couple of blocks to a 7-Eleven store on Sherman Way, the main highway through the town, where Stephanie called Kathleen O'Haire's number from a pay phone. It rang only once before a woman with a pleasant southern accent answered. Stephanie immediately hung up.

"She's home."

"Then we wait," McAllister said, pulling out of the parking lot and heading back around the block again.

"For what?"

"For her to leave so that I can get into the house and have a look around."

"Or until someone shows up looking for us," Stephanie said.

"Or that," McAllister replied.

They parked at the corner a half a block from Kathleen O'Haire's house. McAllister left the engine running, his eyes automatically scanning the street, the houses, the parked vehicles. There was nothing out of the ordinary here. No watchers. No one waiting for someone to show up, unless they were in the house with the woman. That was possible, though for some reason he doubted it. If Kathleen O'Haire had been an active part of the network, their control officer would be leaving her alone now. And if she knew nothing, there'd be no reason to go after her, unless someone had figured that he and Stephanie would be showing up.

He lit a cigarette, pulling the smoke deeply into his lungs, his fingers drumming on the steering wheel. He had never been much good at waiting, though he had done a fair amount of it in his career.

Patience has got to be a part of your tradecraft, boyo, his father had told him in the early days. *Good things come to those who wait . . . and watch.*

Stephanie had withdrawn into her own world, her eyes directed down the street to the neighborhood, but he didn't think she was seeing anything other than blood and death and senseless destruction.

He looked in the same direction she was staring and he wondered if they were seeing the same things. A normal, middle-class neighborhood, nothing more. Relatively quiet on weekdays—meter readers, garbage collectors, repairmen, newspaper delivery boys, mailmen. In the evenings the houses would be lit, kids would be coming home from school. And on weekends lawnmowers would be buzzing, barbecue grills would be smoking, pool parties would be noisily in progress. What had James O'Haire and his brother and the others wanted? What claims did their brand of socialism have over this domestic scene?

Careful the man who becomes maudlin in this business, boyo. There's no room for that claptrap sentiment. It could cost you your life. No rose-colored glasses here. This is the real world.

At a few minutes before five, Kathleen O'Haire came out of her house. She was a large woman, tall and red-haired. She climbed into her car and backed out of the driveway.

McAllister got out of the car and Stephanie slid over behind the wheel.

"When she starts back, call the house. Let it ring twice, then hang up."

"What makes you think she's coming right back?"

"She would have closed her garage door," McAllister said.

Stephanie nodded.

"Give us five minutes, then come in," McAllister said. "But watch yourself. And make damned sure that no one is following her and picks you up as well."

"Good luck."

"You too," McAllister said. There was so much he wanted

to say to her, but now wasn't the time. He crossed the street as she drove around the corner and accelerated after Kathleen O'Haire's Camaro.

A young girl, her long hair streaming from beneath a baseball cap, canvas newspaper sacks attached like saddlebags to the back of her bicycle, rode past him, tossing newspapers up on the lawns with practiced ease. Four doors down from the O'Haire house several boys were playing basketball in the driveway. Music came from one of the houses across the street. Normal sounds and sights, he thought.

McAllister picked up Kathleen O'Haire's newspaper and walked up the driveway. The garage was a mess, junk piled everywhere; a small freezer sat in a corner near the kitchen door, a washer and dryer next to it. But there were no toys. The O'Haires, he'd read, had had no children. For a moment he wondered if they'd missed not having a family as much as he did at times.

The kitchen door was unlocked and McAllister went in. Straight ahead were the sink, stove, refrigerator, and dishwasher, a window overlooking the big aboveground pool in a pleasant backyard. To the left was the dining room, a tall glass-fronted hutch facing an oak table and chairs, a basket of fruit in the middle of the table. He laid the newspaper down.

Standing just within the kitchen he was struck again by the ordinariness of the neighborhood and of this house in particular. From here one of the most successful spy rings ever to be operated in this country was directed. He had to wonder if the conspirators had sat around the dining room table in the evening talking out their strategies, sharing the product, planning goals.

Had Kathleen O'Haire participated? Had she been here making coffee perhaps, serving sandwiches to her husband and brother-in-law and the others in the ring? Or had they sent her away at such times to visit friends or neighbors while the boys played poker?

An almost overpowering sense of dread came over him as he wondered if he were making a terrible mistake by being here. Kathleen O'Haire could be an innocent victim. By coming here like this he could be putting her into extreme danger.

But her name had been in the Agency's files. Why, unless there was at least the possibility she knew something of value to the investigation?

Straight through the dining room a small alcove led to a bathroom beyond which was a bedroom. To the left, a broad archway opened into a small, but pleasantly furnished living room, shelves along one wall filled with a few books, a stereo system, some knickknacks, and several photographs. A big framed poster over the couch depicted a scene, which might have been in Ireland, of a castle perched on a hill across a lush green valley. A small Christmas tree, its decorations sparkling, was set in front of the window. There were no presents beneath it. A corridor led to the right past another bathroom to the three bedrooms. The lowering sun sent shafts of light through the windows at the rear of the house.

McAllister had to rouse himself to do what he had come here to do. Starting at the back of the house, he quickly and efficiently went through all the rooms, searching the closets, the chests of drawers, the cabinets, behind pictures on the walls, in the medicine cabinets and behind the toilet tanks, beneath the beds and behind the curtains and even in the refrigerator, stove, and dishwasher. But there was nothing here that would in any way tie Kathleen O'Haire with her husband's spying activities. One closet was completely filled with his clothes, as was one of the chests of drawers, but there was nothing among those things that provided any clues either.

It was well past six and getting dark when the telephone in the living room rang twice, Stephanie's warning call. McAllister stepped out of the kitchen his gun in hand as Kathleen O'Haire began to speak.

"Hello, you have reached the O'Haire residence. I'm sorry that I can't be here to take your call. But if you'll leave your name, number, and a brief message after the tone, I'll be happy to get back to you as soon as possible."

It was an answering machine.

A long beep sounded, followed immediately by the dial tone, which cut out after a couple of seconds.

McAllister stared at the machine. He had seen it but had dismissed it on his first go around. He rewound the message tape, and hit the play button.

The unit beeped, a dial tone sounded for a second or two, cut off, and the unit beeped again, another dial tone coming on. These were callers who had not wanted to talk to the machine, and had immediately hung up once Kathleen O'Haire's message had started.

The machine beeped again, this time a woman's voice came from the speaker. *"I hate that damned machine, Katy. This is Chris, give me a call as soon as. Bye."*

Two more series of beeps and dial tones cycled through the machine until the sixth caller who did not hang up.

At first McAllister could hear little or nothing from the speaker and he turned up the volume. There was a soft, hollow hiss on the line. Long distance. Then a man spoke.

"Mrs. O'Haire, I would like very much to talk to you as soon as possible. You don't know me, but I assure you this is of the utmost importance to your safety . . . especially in view of what has recently happened in Washington and of course in Illinois."

The voice was vaguely familiar to McAllister. But from where? He couldn't place it.

"Please call me anytime day or night, but very soon. It's

extremely important that we talk. My extension is 273, and the number is 202-456-1414."

McAllister stared at the answering machine, his mouth half open. Suddenly he could not breathe. This was impossible to believe. Completely. He hadn't been able to put a name to the voice, but he had recognized the number immediately. The area code was for Washington, D.C. The number belonged to the White House!

The connection was broken, the dial tone buzzed for a second or two and then was cut off. The rest of the tape was blank. It had been the last call. But when had it come? And had Kathleen O'Haire listened to it? Had she gone out in response to telephone the number away from the house?

How could it be possible that someone from the White House was calling the wife of a convicted spy so openly, and then leave his number for her to return the call? What was he missing?

Look to the anomalies, Wallace Mahoney, the old sage of the Company had taught them at the Farm. Look for the bits and pieces that don't seem to fit in the natural order. There you will likely find the truth, or at least a clue to the correct direction.

Kathleen O'Haire's Camaro pulled up in the driveway. She got out with a bag of groceries and walked into the garage.

McAllister waited out of sight in the living room until he heard the kitchen door from the garage open and then close a moment later.

He stepped around the corner. Kathleen O'Haire, the bag of groceries still in her arms, stood at the counter. Her eyes widened when she saw him and she dropped the bag with a loud crash, something breaking inside of it.

"Oh," she said in a small voice, her eyes going to the gun in McAllister's hand.

Chapter 28

"I've come to talk to you about the Zebra Network," McAllister said.

"My husband's dead," she cried, holding out her hand as if to ward him off. "It's over."

McAllister put away his gun and spread his hands to show her he meant her no harm. She glanced toward the door. She wanted to run; only her immediate fear and uncertainty kept her in place. Her eyes were red. It looked as if she hadn't gotten any sleep in days.

"Too many people have lost their lives besides your husband and his brother. I want to end it."

"Who in God's name are you?" she asked. "I don't know you. What are you doing here in my house? I'll call the police. Leave!"

"My name is David McAllister, and I'm afraid I can't leave. Not yet. I need your help."

"Oh, my God," she cried. "Jim's not even in the ground yet. Go!"

"Please."

She bolted suddenly, but McAllister reached her before she got the door open, and he pulled her back into the kitchen, shoving her up against the refrigerator, holding her hands behind her back, pressing against her body with his.

She was a big, athletically built woman; still she was no match for his superior strength. After a few moments her struggles ceased, and she looked into his face, her eyes blinking, her lips parted.

"I mean you no harm, Mrs. O'Haire, I swear to you. But I need answers. And I can't afford to be delicate."

"I don't know anything, I swear to God. I wasn't involved."

"With what?"

"They're dead! Leave me alone!"

"They were spies for a long time, you must have suspected something."

"No," she cried, again trying to push him away, but he overpowered her, shoving her back against the refrigerator. Her breathing became erratic, and he could feel her heart hammering against his chest.

"I just want to talk."

"I'll scream. The neighbors will hear me, they'll call the police."

"Long before the police came you'd be dead," McAllister said harshly. "My life depends upon your cooperation, Mrs. O'Haire, and now so does yours."

"I don't know anything," she wailed.

"I think you do, starting with the message on your answering machine." Slowly he released her arms and eased his weight off her body, finally stepping back away from her. "Did you return his call?"

She rubbed her wrists where his fingers had caused red marks, as she studied him. For a half a minute she didn't speak. He could feel the heat radiating off her.

"What message?" she asked finally.

"On your answering machine."

She looked toward the living room. "From Chris?"

"No, the other one. From the man, the one who left his telephone number."

She shook her head. "I don't know what you're talking about."

It was obvious she was not lying, at least not about this. "After the call from your friend, Chris, did you go out?"

"Yes, I went over to see her. She lives . . . nearby."

The call had evidently come while she was out, and she had not bothered to check her answering machine afterward. "Then I think you'd better listen to the message."

"I want you to get out of my house."

"I can't, not until I get my answers."

"What answers?"

"Who is trying to kill me and why. It has something to do with your husband's spying."

"He's dead, leave it alone," she cried.

"There is a very good possibility that you'll be next," McAllister said.

"You're insane."

"No. But I think we can help each other. You can save my life, and I can protect yours."

"From whom? Protect me from whom?"

"Whoever ran the network. Whoever it was gave your husband and the others their orders."

"It was you."

"No," McAllister said. "Those are lies. Do you think if I were involved I would have come here like this? What would be the point? I'm just as much in the dark as you say you are. But if I'm right, they won't stop until I'm dead, and now you're involved more deeply than you can imagine."

"Only because you came here."

"Because of the call on your answering machine."

"What call?" she shouted wildly. "For all I know you put the message there. Or one of your friends did it."

"Listen to it, and you tell me."

A car pulled into the driveway and the O'Haire woman stiffened, her mouth opening to cry out. McAllister pulled out his gun and motioned for her to keep silent. It could be Stephanie, but it also could be someone else.

"Were you expecting someone this evening?" he asked.

She was staring at the door. "Yes," she said woodenly. "Friends. My friends are coming over." This time she was lying. She turned to him. "Leave right now and I won't say anything. You can get away. I promise."

They heard a car door open and close and someone came into the garage.

The O'Haire woman wanted to cry out, but she was watching the gun in McAllister's hand.

"David?" Stephanie called out.

"In here," McAllister answered.

Kathleen O'Haire stepped back toward the stove, her hands going to her mouth, her entire body shaking.

The kitchen door opened and Stephanie came in, her gun in her hand. She looked from Kathleen O'Haire to McAllister then closed the door. "Are you all right?"

McAllister relaxed and stuffed his gun in his belt. "So far," he said. "Was there anybody out there?"

Stephanie pocketed her gun. "No, she's clean. She went to a supermarket a half a dozen blocks from here and came directly back."

"Could she have called someone from inside?"

"I followed her," Stephanie said. She picked up the grocery bag Kathleen O'Haire had dropped and put it in the sink. Orange juice was leaking out of the bottom. The O'Haire woman was watching her warily, as she might watch a wild animal.

"We mean you no harm, Mrs. O'Haire," Stephanie said gently.

"Then get out of my house now. Both of you. Leave me alone."

"Someone called this afternoon and left a message for her on the answering machine," McAllister said. "She hasn't heard it yet."

"About us?" Stephanie asked, her eyes bright.

"Probably," McAllister said. "Will you listen to it?" he asked the woman.

She had shrunk back against the stove. "Please leave me now."

"I'll set it up," McAllister said. He went into the living room and advanced the message tape to the end of the fifth call. When he looked up Kathleen O'Haire was perched on the edge of the easy chair, Stephanie right behind her. She was very pale, and she clenched her hands together in her lap. Either she was a very good actress, or she was innocent.

McAllister hit the play button. *"Mrs. O'Haire, I would like very much to talk to you as soon as possible. You don't know me, but I assure you this is of the utmost importance to your safety . . . especially in view of what has recently happened in Washington and of course in Illinois. Please call me anytime day or night, but very soon. It's extremely important that we talk. My extension is 273, and the number is 202-456-1414."*

The connection was broken and McAllister shut off the machine.

"That's the area code for Washington," Stephanie said.

McAllister nodded. "Who was the man?" he asked the O'Haire woman, but she was shaking her head.

"I don't know," she said.

"One of your husband's friends? Someone who might have called here before?"

"I've never heard that voice. I swear to God, I haven't. You must believe me."

"I have," Stephanie said softly. "Or at least I think I have."

"From where?" McAllister asked.

She shook her head, trying to think it out. "I don't know, for sure. Somewhere." She looked up. "How about you?"

"The same. It's familiar and yet I can't put my finger on it. But I do know the telephone number."

"What is it?"

"The White House," he said, watching for Kathleen O'Haire's reaction.

But she was merely puzzled. "I don't understand," she said. "Why would someone from the White House be calling me . . . like that?"

"David," Stephanie said urgently. "I do know that voice. I remember now."

"Who is it?"

"I saw him at the Iran-contra hearings last year. He wasn't a part of that, I don't think, but he was speaking for the White House. His name is Donald Harman. He's a special assistant to the President, for God's sake."

"Zebra One?" McAllister asked half under his breath. It would explain a lot of things. A man such as Harman would naturally be in a position to know what was going on in the intelligence community. He would be privy to reports from all the agencies; the CIA, the National Security Agency, the FBI, the military intelligence services, the Defense Intelligence Agency . . . all of them. He would have the confidence of key senators and congressmen on the Hill, the National Security Council, the President's cabinet and the President himself. His power would be enormous; he would be even more important than the DCI himself.

Stephanie and Kathleen O'Haire were watching him.

Everytime Highnote had done something, had made a move on behalf of McAllister and Albright, his report went to the DCI, who in turn included it in his twice-daily intelligence summaries to the President. Harman had evidently been privy to all those reports as well.

How to fight a man so powerfully entrenched as that? This was Philby, only ten thousand times worse.

"What are we going to do?" Stephanie asked.

McAllister looked at her. "The only thing we can do," he said. "She's going to call him, find out what he wants."

"No," Kathleen O'Haire cried, the single word strangled in her throat.

"But why did he call her on an open line, and then hand out his telephone number, David?" Stephanie asked. "It doesn't make sense."

"Because he thinks he's above suspicion. Because he thinks, like we do, that she knows something. That she might have overheard something her husband said, something that might lead back to the network's control officer."

"Harman?"

"Either him, or someone he's protecting."

"I won't do it," the O'Haire woman said. "You can't make me do it."

"Is it true?" McAllister asked softly. "Did you hear something? Do you know who your husband's control officer was?"

"I told you I don't know anything," Kathleen O'Haire screeched. "Leave me alone! Get out of here!"

McAllister went across the room to her and looked into her eyes. "Don't you understand what's happening here, Mrs. O'Haire? Hasn't it penetrated yet? Your husband and brother-in-law ran a very successful spy ring for years. Whoever they worked for takes his orders from the Russians. From the KGB. What do you think our chances are if that man is Donald Harman, someone in the White House, right next to the President? Or don't you give a damn?"

"It's not my fault," she cried. "They're dead. It's done. I don't know . . ."

"I believe you," McAllister said. "But you're going to telephone Harman and pretend that you do know something. You're going to set up a meeting with him in Washington."

She was shaking her head.

"Tomorrow. At noon. It'll be broad daylight and you'll meet him somewhere in public where you'll be safe, where he won't dare do anything to you."

"And then what?" she asked defiantly.

"You'll talk with him, nothing more. We'll be nearby listening to everything that's said."

She looked to Stephanie, her eyes wild.

"Your husband hurt this country very badly, Mrs. O'Haire," Stephanie said. "But what he did was nothing compared to what a man such as Harman could do if he isn't stopped. It's time now to put an end to it, but we need your help."

"I don't know how to do this," the O'Haire woman cried in anguish. "I don't know what to say."

"I'll be listening with you, I'll help you," McAllister said gently.

"What if he doesn't want to meet with me?"

"He will," McAllister said. "He's going to ask you if we've been here, and I want you to tell him that we were, this afternoon, and that we were making a lot of wild accusations."

"He's going to ask me what you said, I mean exactly. . . ."

"Yes, he will, and that's why you're going to have to meet with him in Washington, you can't discuss this on the telephone."

"What if he still refuses?"

McAllister glanced at Stephanie. "Tell him that we know about someone in the White House, and that we have the proof."

"No," Kathleen O'Haire said, shaking her head again. "I can't do this."

"You must," Stephanie said.

"No, damnit . . ."

McAllister grabbed her arms and pulled her to her feet. "Listen to me, goddamnit. What do you think will happen to you if we turn around and walk out of here now? You don't have to answer, I'll tell you. Donald Harman telephoned you this afternoon, he wants to talk to you. He won't let you off the hook. If he thinks that you know something, if he even suspects you might be lying to him, he'll send someone here to kill you."

"I'll call the police," she cried, hiccuping.

"And tell them what?" McAllister said savagely. "That you think one of the President's advisers is going to kill you?"

She was trying to pull away from McAllister's grasp, but he wouldn't let her go.

"I'm sorry that you're involved in this," he said. "I wish it were different, but it's not."

"I don't want to get hurt," she said.

"Neither do we," Stephanie replied. "We'll do our best, it's all we can offer you."

Kathleen O'Haire sagged, and McAllister let her go. She looked at them both. "When do you want me to call him?" she asked in a small voice.

"Now," McAllister said, hiding the triumph from his voice. "He'll probably suggest a meeting place, but no matter what it is, you'll refuse."

"Where then?"

McAllister glanced at Stephanie, she knew Washington better than he did.

"McMillan Park," she said. "It's on the south side of the reservoir, over by Howard University. There are places we can hide there, and yet it's fairly open. Doug and I used to go there in the summer."

"Will there be people around at this time of the year?"

"Not many, but there'll be some."

"McMillan Park it is," McAllister said. He went to the telephone and dialed the White House number. As soon as it began to ring he held out the phone to the O'Haire woman. "Ask for extension 273," he said.

She hesitated for just a moment longer, but then took the phone and held it close enough to her ear so that she could hear, and yet far enough away so that McAllister could also listen in, their heads close together.

"The White House," a woman operator answered pleasantly.

Kathleen O'Haire looked up at McAllister. "Extension 273."

"One moment, please."

It was nearly seven o'clock here, which made it nearly ten on the East Coast. The extension rang once, there was a slight click on the line, and then it began ringing again in a different tone. The call was probably being automatically forwarded to wherever Harman happened to be at that moment. Most likely at home.

"Hello," Donald Harman answered.

Kathleen O'Haire froze for just a moment, and McAllister had to prod her to get her to speak.

"Hello," she said. "This is Kathleen O'Haire. I was asked to call this number."

"Just a minute," Harman said, and the line went dead for a second, before he came back on. "Thanks for calling, Mrs. O'Haire, are you all right?"

"No," she said. "I'm not all right."

"What is it?" Harman asked, and McAllister could hear the instant caution in the man's voice. "Has something happened out there? Are you calling from California?"

"Yes," she said. "But I had some visitors this afternoon. I don't know what to do. You said I was in danger. . . ."

"Take it easy, Mrs. O'Haire, everything will be fine. You say you had visitors this afternoon. Who were they?"

"McAllister and some woman."

Harman hesitated for a beat. "I see," he said. "Where are they now?"

"Gone."

"They didn't hurt you?"

"No, but . . . you and I . . . we have to meet," Kathleen O'Haire said, and she paused. McAllister motioned for her to continue. "They know about you . . . or about someone in the White House," she said.

"They know what, Mrs. O'Haire?" Harman asked smoothly.

"I don't know," she said convincingly. "They asked about Jim, and then your call came. . . ."

"Were they in the house when I telephoned you?" Harman asked.

McAllister shook his head.

"No, but they said they knew about the White House connection."

"They don't know that I telephoned you?"

Again McAllister shook his head.

"No, they were already gone."

"Did they say where they were going?"

"No, but I'm frightened. Jim told me to be . . . careful."

"And he was correct, Mrs. O'Haire. You are in danger now. I want you to stay where you are, I'll send someone out to pick you up."

"No," Kathleen O'Haire blurted. "I'm coming to Washington."

"All right. I'll arrange a hotel for you. What flight will you be coming in on?"

McAllister put his hand over the mouthpiece. "You're flying to New York tonight, and you'll be taking the train down to Washington in the morning," he whispered. He took his hand away and she repeated what he'd told her.

"I can have someone meet you then."

"No," Kathleen O'Haire said. "I'm frightened. I don't know what's going to happen. I'll meet you at McMillan Park. Do you know where it is?"

Harman hesitated for a long second or two. "Are you alone now, Mrs. O'Haire?"

"Yes," she said. "At noon tomorrow. Do you know where it is?"

"Yes, I do."

"They said they've got proof. I just can't say any more on this line."

"I understand," Harman said. "Are you certain I can't send someone out there for you? You would certainly be much safer. . . ."

"No," Kathleen O'Haire said. "I'll see you at noon."

McAllister broke the connection, then took the phone from her hand and replaced it on the cradle. He let out a sigh of relief.

"How'd he sound?" Stephanie asked.

"Frightened," McAllister said. He squeezed Kathleen O'Haire's arm. "You did very well. Now you'd better pack a bag, we're leaving immediately."

"For New York?"

"Washington direct. They won't be expecting us so soon."

The neighborhood had quieted down for the evening as two men got out of a gunmetal-gray Cadillac convertible parked in front of Kathleen O'Haire's house. It was well past ten and they had raced up from Los Angeles as soon as they had gotten word that McAllister and the woman had probably slipped out of Chicago and might be headed this way. Their instructions were simple: Kill all three of them, then confirm.

They separated, Nick Balliterri going up to the front door, and Frank Pearce hurrying around to the back. The house was dark, and Balliterri had a feeling that they were on a wild goose chase here. The woman wasn't home, she had already skipped.

He waited for a few seconds to give Pearce a chance to get into place, then rang the doorbell. He held his silenced .357 Magnum out of sight at his side.

From the back he heard the very slight noise of breaking glass, and he rang the doorbell again.

Sixty seconds later Pearce opened the door for him, and Balliterri stepped inside.

"Car's in the garage, but the bedrooms are empty," Pearce said.

"Closets?" Balliterri asked softly.

"One of them is open in the big bedroom. Looks like maybe some clothes are missing."

"She skipped," Balliterri said, holstering his big gun, his eyes scanning the room. "Search the place."

"Right," Pearce said, holstering his weapon and heading down the corridor to the bedrooms.

Balliterri crossed the room to the answering machine, rewound the message tape and hit the play button.

Chapter 29

Stephanie went to retrieve their baggage while McAllister went with Kathleen O'Haire across to the Dulles Airport Avis counter where she rented a car in her own name. It would be safe enough, he figured, at least for a little while. No one would expect her to be here like this, so openly.

He hung back as she completed the forms and was given a key. No one was watching her, but the clerk had given her an odd look when she had signed. Had he recognized the name from the newspaper and television stories?

"They're bringing the car around front," she said coming back to McAllister.

She was tired, her eyes red-rimmed and puffy. None of them had gotten any sleep on the overnight flight from Los Angeles, nor had they talked very much. She had sat between Stephanie and McAllister with her eyes closed and her hands clenched in her lap. He'd felt genuinely sorry for her, but there was nothing he could do or say to alleviate her fears.

It was nearly ten, which left them two hours before her meeting with Harman. The man would be expecting her to show up alone, and no one knew that he and Stephanie had changed their appearances, yet being back in Washington made him extremely wary.

"I'll meet Stephanie downstairs at the baggage area," he said. "As soon as you get the car, drive around to the pickup area."

Kathleen O'Haire nodded nervously.

McAllister stepped a little closer to her. "Don't leave without us. You wouldn't last very long alone in this city. Not now. Not with Harman and his people expecting you."

Her eyes were wide. She was convinced. She nodded again.

"And for God's sake, try to act normal."

She looked at him. "You've got to be kidding," she said, and she turned on her heel and headed for the doors.

McAllister watched her leave, then turned and went back down to where Stephanie was just collecting their bags. She looked beyond him for the woman.

"Where is she?"

"Bringing the car around," McAllister said, taking two of the bags.

"Do you trust her?"

"We don't have much of a choice at this point, do we?"

She looked sharply at him. "What's to prevent her from running?"

"Nothing," McAllister said curtly, heading for the doors. "She'd probably be better off if she did."

It was fairly warm outside. The storm had finally abated, the roads had been cleared and the temperature had risen so that the snow was melting. The air smelled of exhaust fumes and burnt jet fuel. The flight had been full, and quite a few passengers, bags in hand, were scrambling for the available taxis and shuttle buses.

McAllister and Stephanie held back out of the traffic pattern as they waited for Kathleen O'Haire to show up.

Look to Washington. Look to Moscow. Zebra One, Zebra Two.

If Harman was Zebra One, the Washington man, then who was the Russian? Someone in the KGB or someone high in the Soviet government who had somehow made contact with Harman and had turned him? It made him sick to think what harm the White House man had been able to do in the years he had been so close to the President.

The O'Haires' Zebra Network, he suspected, was only the tip of the iceberg. For a man such as Harman, there would have to be other ongoing operations. Possibly he had contacts within the CIA, or perhaps the Pentagon as well. Kim Philby, after all, had very nearly become the head of the British Secret Intelligence Service. How much higher would Harman rise within the government?

"Here she comes," Stephanie said softly at his side.

He looked up out of his thoughts as Kathleen O'Haire, driving a dark-blue Taurus, pulled up to the curb. They got in; Stephanie in the front seat and McAllister in the back with the bags.

"Where do you want me to drive?" the O'Haire woman asked looking at his reflection in the rearview mirror.

"Out to the park. Stephanie will direct you."

"Do you want me to drive?" Stephanie asked.

"I'll be all right."

They pulled away from the curb and headed down the long ramp toward the airport exit. McAllister opened their bags, pulled out the disassembled guns and quickly put them together. When he was finished he handed Stephanie hers.

She'd been watching him. "Do you think he'll show up alone?"

"As long as he thinks she's alone, he will," McAllister said. "He's going to want to talk to her."

"What are you saying now?" Kathleen O'Haire asked, alarmed. "What if he sends someone else?"

"Then you'll get the hell out of there, and we'll take care of the situation."

"He could be sending someone to kill me."

"No," McAllister said. "If he wants you dead, he'll do

it himself, but after he finds out what you know, and what we supposedly told you."

"Oh, damn . . . oh, damn," she said, gripping the steering wheel so tightly her knuckles turned white.

As before, on the airplane, there was nothing he or Stephanie could say or do to make it any easier for her. The die had been cast the moment she'd returned Harman's call.

The property around McMillan Reservoir formed a rough triangle; Howard University to the west across Fourth Street; the Washington Hospital Center to the east across Michigan Avenue; and a pretty park along the base leg. The park entrance, off First Street, led to a road that wound around the water's edge. The trees at this time of the year were bare and it looked as if cross-country skiers had used the rolling parklands over the last few days, leaving behind their narrow tracks criss-crossing the snow-covered expanses.

They parked the car a half a mile from the entrance after first passing once completely through the park and coming around past the university, along Bryant Street and back up First.

The water looked cold and dark-gray beneath the still-overcast sky. A few whitecaps were raised by the wind and a piece of newspaper tumbled and slid up the road. Very few people were around.

It had taken them better than an hour to drive across town from the airport, still they were early. Benches and picnic tables were set here and there along the water, trash barrels chained to the trees. A small cement-block building that housed public restrooms was just ahead of them. It was probably closed at this time of year.

A car entered the park and passed, McAllister holding his gun at the ready until he could see that they were no threat; they'd probably used the park road as a shortcut over to the university. He relaxed slightly.

"Stephanie and I are going to get out of the car now," he told the O'Haire woman.

She turned in her seat, her face screwed up in a grimace of fear. "I don't want to go through with this," she said.

"It'll be all right," Stephanie said. "We'll be just down the road a little ways. At the first sign of any trouble we'll come running. He's not going to try anything out here in the open, not with witnesses."

McAllister looked at his watch; it was quarter after eleven. "He's got another forty-five minutes before he's due to show up, but I'm betting he's going to be early. He'll want to do the same thing we're doing, look the place over. He's counting on the likelihood that you'll be coming alone and won't know what you're doing."

Kathleen O'Haire looked down the road as a couple in jogging outfits came around the sweeping curve. "What do I say to him?"

"Let him do most of the talking," McAllister said. "He's going to give you assurances that he's here to help you, but he's going to want to know what we told you, what proof we supposedly have that someone in the White House is a penetration agent."

"What do I say?"

"Stall him for as long as you can."

"Why?"

"I want you to make him mad."

"What are you talking about?" Kathleen O'Haire shouted. "He's meeting me here possibly with the intent to kill me, and you want me to make him mad?"

"He won't try anything until he finds out just how much you know."

"I don't know anything."

"He won't know that," McAllister said. "We'll be nearby, and as soon as it becomes obvious that he's getting agitated, we'll start toward you."

"So what?" Kathleen O'Haire said. "What will that prove? Nothing."

"You'll see us heading toward you. At that moment I want you to say this to him: 'McAllister knows about Zebra One and Zebra Two here in Washington and in Moscow. He has the proof.' "

"What's that supposed to mean?"

"He'll know," McAllister said. "And if he's going to try anything, it'll come right then, but we'll be right there. He won't have any choice but to try to fire on us, if he gets that desperate. But I think he'll run."

"No thanks," Kathleen O'Haire said, shaking her head. "I'm just not going to do this. It's insanity."

"Listen to me, Mrs. O'Haire, Harman can't afford to let you go. If you're not here for this meeting today, he'll send someone after you, and it's a fair assumption that he won't bother talking to you in a public place. It'll be somewhere he'll have the upper hand, where he'll be able to say and do whatever he wants."

"I'll run."

"Believe me, there's no place to run from a man in Harman's position, with his power and connections."

She looked from him to Stephanie. "Why did you do this to me?" she wailed. "Now, of all times."

"To stop the killing," McAllister said softly. "As soon as he shows up, I want you to get out of the car and walk over to him."

"How will I know who he is?"

"You won't have to, he'll know you," McAllister said.

She turned away. "He killed Jim?"

"Him or someone like him."

It took her a moment, and when she spoke her voice was small. "Zebra One, Zebra Two?"

"Here in Washington and in Moscow. I have the proof," McAllister said. "Have you got it?"

"Yes," Kathleen O'Haire said distantly.

McAllister motioned for Stephanie and they got out of the car. Kathleen O'Haire didn't look up. The joggers passed them as they headed toward the restroom building. It wasn't as warm out here as it had been in the city. The wind off the reservoir was sharp. They walked for a little while in silence, McAllister maintaining his limp, Stephanie shuffling like a much older woman.

"It's her, isn't it," Stephanie finally said.

McAllister looked at her. "What do you mean?"

"Ever since we got to California and talked to her, you've been strange; distant, sharp. At first I thought it was me, because of what happened . . . on the train."

He stopped. "What happened, had to happen," he said. "He knew what we looked like, we could not have left him alive."

She looked away. "When he said that about Baltimore . . . being a big job . . . I couldn't help myself." She turned back. "David, I've never killed anyone before. I've never even shot a gun in anger. It wasn't . . ."

"How you thought it would be?"

She shook her head. "No."

"It never is," he said gently. "But you're right, I am worried about her."

They glanced back at Kathleen O'Haire sitting behind the wheel. She was staring at them.

"There is no way of changing this either," Stephanie said.

"No. Harman made the first move. It's up to us now to see how far he's willing to carry it."

They started walking again.

"He might be innocent, you know," Stephanie said.

"I thought about it. But the timing of his call is just too coincidental. And he agreed to meet her here, alone."

"What then?" Stephanie asked. "I mean what happens if he makes a move and we stop him. Then what do we do?"

"Ask him some questions."

"Which he won't answer."

"He will," McAllister said. "He'll answer." He shivered.

It is too bad your father isn't alive now to see this. He was a good man. A brave man. A straightforward man. A soldier. He knew who his enemies were, and he met them head on.

We're finally making progress, and I feel very good about it. And so should you.

They sat on a park bench next to the cement-block building. At ten minutes before twelve, a dark-blue Jeep Wagoneer, one man behind the wheel, entered the park from the east, passed Kathleen O'Haire in the Taurus, and pulled up.

"It's him," Stephanie said urgently. "Donald Harman."

McAllister's hand went into his coat pocket where he had transferred his gun, his fingers curling around the grip, his thumb on the safety catch.

Stephanie started to get up, but he held her back.

"Not yet," he said, looking across the park but keeping track of what was happening out of the corner of his eye. "Give them a chance."

Harman sat in his car for several minutes, but then the door opened and he got out. He was tall, and even from here McAllister could see that he was well dressed. He wore a dark overcoat, a scarf at his neck, his head bare.

He stood beside his car for a moment until Kathleen O'Haire got out of the Taurus and they started toward each other.

"Easy," McAllister said softly, looking directly at them now that Harman's back was turned this way.

They said something to each other and shook hands. Harman gestured back to his car, but the O'Haire woman shook her head and said something else.

There had been neither the time nor the equipment to

provide her with a wire. Under normal circumstances he would have done that. It would be invaluable to know what Harman was saying, exactly how he was reacting to Kathleen O'Haire.

She gestured back toward the park entrance, then vaguely in the direction of the city. Harman said something, and he started to turn away, but then stopped dead in his tracks. The woman said something to him, and he turned slowly back to her.

It had come already. It was obvious from the way the man was holding himself stiffly erect that he was angry, but he had good control.

"Now," McAllister said getting to his feet.

Stephanie jumped up, and together they started down the road, McAllister's grip tightening on his pistol.

Zebra One, Zebra Two. Kathleen O'Haire would be saying those words now.

A white Mercedes entered the park from the same direction Harman had arrived. One man was driving, another sat in the passenger seat. The car was moving fast, much too fast for the narrow park road.

Suddenly McAllister understood that the situation was about to explode! But how had they known?

"Down," he shouted, shoving Stephanie aside.

The Mercedes began to accelerate as it reached Harman and Kathleen O'Haire who both looked up in surprise. The man on the passenger side leaned out the open window and began firing a big, silenced pistol. Harman was shoved off his feet, something flying out of his right hand, blood erupting from at least three wounds, and a split instant later, Kathleen O'Haire's head exploded in a mass of blood, bone, and white matter.

McAllister was tearing at his pocket, trying to get his pistol out as the car raced past them, neither the assassin nor the driver paying him the slightest attention, and then it was gone around the curve.

Chapter 30

McAllister raced up the road knowing that he was already too late. Harman had received three hits to his chest and one that had taken off part of his right cheek. Kathleen O'Haire's face and the back of her head were destroyed.

But Harman had had a gun in his hand. It lay in the snow a few feet from his body; a .38 caliber Smith & Wesson Police Special, the hammer cocked. He had been ready to kill the woman.

McAllister's breath was coming like a steam engine. What had happened? How had it happened? If Harman had been Zebra One, who were his killers?

He reached the Taurus as Stephanie hurried up past the Wagoneer, the side of her coat soaking wet from where she'd fallen when he shoved her aside.

"Move it," he shouted. "We've got to get out of here."

"Potemkin . . . David, it was Gennadi Potemkin driving that car. I recognized him. He's head of KGB operations out of the Soviet Embassy here in Washington."

"Are you sure?"

"Yes!"

He yanked open the driver's door and climbed in behind

the wheel. He had the car started when Stephanie jumped in beside him, and he pulled out around Harman's car and raced out of the park.

Traffic was normal on Fourth Street even though Howard University was all but closed down for the Christmas break. McAllister forced himself to slow down, to act and drive normally. It had been his fault. He had promised the woman he would protect her. But it had been impossible.

Zebra One was for Harman here in Washington.

Zebra Two was for someone in Moscow.

Who was their common enemy? Someone had signed the order releasing McAllister from a Soviet prison, and someone in Washington had ordered the assassination of Harman. Why? What was he missing?

"Where are we going?" Stephanie asked breathlessly.

"I don't know. I've got to have time to think."

Images and snatches of conversation were flashing through his head. He could feel blinding pain stabbing at his groin and across his chest. He could hear his heart hammering raggedly in his ears . . . but then it stopped!

"Are you all right, David?" Stephanie asked softly.

He glanced at her. She was pale and shaking. The insanities they had both endured over the past days had taken its toll.

Wherever he showed up death followed on his heels. One by one every person he had come in contact with since his release from the Lubyanka had been killed. Everyone except for Highnote and Stephanie. How much longer could they possibly hold out? Where were the answers?

Run. Was that the answer after all? Could they go away and manage to hide for the rest of their lives? Christ, was such a thing possible? If not that, then what were their alternatives?

He'd been driving aimlessly. They reached Rhode Island Avenue and he turned right toward Logan Circle, traffic very heavy. A police car, its siren blaring, raced past them, but it was going in the same direction, not back toward the park.

Very soon the bodies would be discovered and reported. Another massacre in Washington. The press would go wild. If someone had seen the Taurus the police would be looking for it.

The only advantage they had now was their altered appearances. No one knew yet what they looked like. Potemkin and the assassin had not paid them the slightest attention, their concentration locked on their targets and then getting away.

He glanced at Stephanie again. She was watching him, deep concern in her eyes.

"Harman was going to kill her," he said.

Stephanie nodded. "I know, I saw the gun fly out of his hand when he went down."

"Which means he was probably Zebra One."

Again she nodded. "Working for the Russians, then why did they kill him?"

"A coverup," McAllister said. "But how did he know that Harman would be meeting with Kathleen O'Haire in that park at that moment, unless Harman told him?"

"I don't know."

"There's one man who does."

"Who?" Stephanie asked, her eyes narrowing.

"Gennadi Potemkin," McAllister said. "And I'm going to ask him. Tonight."

Stephanie walked across the lobby to the pay phones at the back. McAllister had dropped her off at the Marriott Twin Bridges Hotel, where she had checked in and had waited in their room for a full four hours to give him time enough to make his preparations. They were the longest hours of her life. She kept seeing the image of her father's destroyed body in her mind's eye; kept feeling his cold, lifeless flesh, barely able to look at his face for the last time as she covered him with the sheet. *Zebra One, Zebra Two,* obviously code names for two men who had worked at the highest levels of the Soviet and American governments for a long time. Long enough to create the O'Haires' Zebra Network. Long enough to do what else?

When she'd told McAllister's story to her father he had not been happy that she wanted to help, but he had understood, as he'd always understood.

"He may not have known himself what is driving him," her father had said. "And already there has been a lot of killing around him."

"What else can I do?" she'd asked. "I'm already involved. I was from the moment I pulled him half dead out of the river."

"I know. Just take care, Stephanie. Please. For me."

Reaching the telephones, she put her purse on the shelf and placed the call to the Soviet Embassy across the river in D.C. While she waited for the connection to be made, she turned and looked across the busy lobby. Nobody was watching her, no one seemed interested. She was merely a woman making a telephone call. Nothing more.

The number rang and she turned back.

"Good afternoon, you have reached the Embassy of the Union of Soviet Socialist Republics, how may we help you?" a pleasant man's voice answered, his English nearly accentless.

"I would like to speak with Gennadi Potemkin."

"I'm sorry, madam, but we have no person by that name here," the embassy operator replied smoothly.

"I happen to know that you do," Stephanie said, forcing a reasonable tone to her voice. "If you will just pass him the message that McAllister was in McMillan Park this noon, I think he'll speak with me."

"I am so sorry, madam, but . . ."

"It will be the biggest mistake of your life, comrade, if you don't pass that message."

"One moment, please," the operator said, unperturbed, and the line went dead.

It was possible, she thought, that she had been disconnected. The Soviet Embassy received dozens of crank calls every day from disgruntled American citizens and Soviet emigrés. But she waited on the line.

A full five minutes later, another man came on, his voice much older, his accent strong. "Is this Miss Albright?"

"Yes, are you Potemkin?" Stephanie asked, startled by is use of her name, and yet not really surprised he knew it.

"Indeed it is," Potemkin said. "I assume you are telephoning from a reasonably secure location, somewhere within the city?"

"Close," Stephanie said. "We were in McMillan Park this morning."

"Yes?" Potemkin said.

"McAllister would like to meet with you."

"To what purpose, Miss Albright? What could we possibly have to say to each other?"

"Listen to me, you sonofabitch. We know about Zebra One and Zebra Two. We know about the network, and we know a lot more."

Potemkin laughed. "My dear girl, I haven't the faintest idea what you're talking about."

"I think you do, and I think you'd better agree to meet with him. Alone. Both of you alone."

"Impossible."

"You're not listening."

"Neither are you. I don't know what you think you know, but it is meaningless."

"As meaningless as McAllister's release from the Lubyanka within hours of his trial and conviction? No explanations. No prisoner exchanges. No publicity. Nothing."

Potemkin did not reply.

"He's at Janos Sikorski's house right now, waiting for you. It's out near Reston, but I'm sure you know where it is. He wants to make a deal."

"What sort of a deal?" Potemkin asked, his voice guarded.

"His life for yours," Stephanie said, and she hung up as Mac had instructed her to do. Gathering up her purse she turned and walked back across the lobby, her legs weak, her breath catching in her chest. She had done everything she could and now it was up to him.

McAllister sat in the Taurus parked diagonally across Sixteenth Street from the Soviet Embassy a few blocks up from the White House. He had made it down from Reston fifteen minutes ago, about the same time Stephanie had placed her call to Potemkin. He had done what little he could to even the odds after first making sure Sikorski's place wasn't still staked out. Now it was up to the Russian, who, if he was smart, would simply ignore the message.

Do nothing, McAllister said to himself, and you'll be safe this time.

From Kathleen O'Haire, the wife of a convicted spy, to Donald Harman, a presidential adviser. And from Harman to Gennadi Potemkin, head of all KGB operations in the United States. Where would it lead from there? How many more dark corridors would he have to travel before he made his way through the labyrinth?

"Even if he does agree to meet with you, David, he certainly won't go out there alone," Stephanie had objected when he'd laid out his plan.

"He'd be a fool if he did," McAllister agreed. "Which is why I'm going to wait for him outside the embassy and see who goes with him."

"Let me go with you."

"No."

"Damnit, David . . ."

"No," McAllister said again. "You'll stay here and do exactly as I say. No games now. I don't want you out there. I don't want to have to worry about you. I know what I'm doing."

She looked at him for a long time. "If you're spotted it will blow the entire thing."

"Yes," he said.

It's tradecraft, pure and simple, and it won't be very pleasant. It was in his family heritage, in his blood, in the training he had received and the experiences he had survived over the past fourteen years.

Once a spy always a spy, that was the old adage. But after this, if by some miracle he survived, he was through. The business no longer held any fascination for him, if it ever had.

The roof of the embassy bristled with antennae and microwave dishes that bounced signals off a Soviet communications satellite for transmission direct to Moscow. He stared at the complex electronic arrays, his brain making automatic connections, skipping like a computer down long lines of facts and figures, each one leading inexorably to the next.

Anomalies, Wallace Mahoney had called the bits and pieces that didn't seem to add up. Stephanie's father had been tortured and killed . . . because of a transmitter? In his mind's eye he could see the open cabinet door, the wires emerging from the wall. He focused again on the antennae on the embassy roof. Had Albright been communicating with the Russians? Was his murder a part of some coverup as well?

The same white Mercedes 450SEL sedan from the park emerged from behind the embassy, and as it passed, McAllister got a brief glance at its passengers. Potemkin was driving, the assassin from this morning beside him in the front, and three other men in the backseat.

McAllister put the car in gear, drove to the end of the

block, turned the corner, and caught up with the Mercedes on H Street in front of Lafayette Park. He held back, keeping several car lengths behind the big German car, which turned south on Seventeenth Street, the White House to the left, the huge Christmas tree on the front lawn lit up already in the diminishing light as evening approached.

Potemkin was driving at a sedate speed. This would be no time for him to be stopped and issued a speeding warning. He would be careful now; so much depended upon his not being delayed. He would remain scrupulously within the speed limit.

Reaching Constitution Avenue, the Mercedes turned right toward the Roosevelt Bridge, merging smoothly with traffic as it picked up speed.

The question was, which route would the Russians take to get out to Reston? South through the edge of Alexandria then up I-495 through Annandale; north to the Capital Beltway which crossed the Dulles Airport access road; or the shortest route through Arlington on the partially completed I-66 that branched off north of Falls Church?

He got his answer about three miles later when the Mercedes, heading north, passed the I-66 exit and continued toward the Capital Beltway. His luck was holding.

Swinging west on I-66 he speeded up, the sun only a vague brightness low in the overcast sky ahead, traffic picking up, all of it running at a good speed as everyone headed home.

McAllister parked his car about seventy-five yards up from Sikorski's clearing, dousing the lights and shutting off the engine, but leaving the keys. Under the hood he pulled out the main wire from the electronic ignition system, rendering the car inoperative for the moment.

It was nearly dark now. He trotted down the road to the clearing and in the distance to the north he could see the lights of Reston.

The snow was deep up here, the only footprints were his, leading directly across to the front door of the cabin. He hurried down the same path so that it wouldn't appear as if he had come and gone and returned again, entered the dark, silent house and crossed immediately to the kitchen where he let himself out, crossed the backyard well out of sight of the driveway, and scrambled down the steep hill to the path he'd found this afternoon.

Now that the sun had gone down the temperature was dropping rapidly. Still he was sweating and the wound in his side was aching by the time he had circled around to the woods that sloped up from the house parallel to, but above, the driveway.

A few snowflakes began to fall as he stopped about fifty yards from the house, cocking his ear to listen and scanning the dark woods in the direction of the driveway for any sign that Potemkin and his triggermen had shown up. But there was nothing, only the occasional whisper of a light wind in the treetops, and he continued up the hill.

For a while he was back in Bulgaria, racing for the border, the militia hot on his trail. He could hear the helicopters and from time to time the sounds of the dogs. It was winter, like now, and the snow was deep. Then, as now, he had been racing for his life.

He reached a spot directly above where he had parked his car and started down toward the driveway when he saw the flash of a car's headlights below. He pulled up short, leaning against a tree, holding his breath as best he could while he listened.

The light flashed again, and then was gone. Moments later he heard car doors opening and closing, and the muffled sound of someone talking, issuing orders.

Still he held his position. There were five of them, all killers. He needed to even the odds before he confronted Potemkin.

The Taurus's engine turned over, but of course the car

would not start. Whoever was behind the wheel tried again, and then there were more voices, this time it sounded as if at least one of them was angry about something.

Finally the voices began to fade, moving down the driveway toward the clearing. McAllister pushed away from the tree and keeping low hurried through the woods, crawling the last twenty feet on his stomach.

They had left one man with the Mercedes. He was leaning up against the hood of the car, a cigarette dangling out of the corner of his mouth, a big silenced pistol held loosely in his right hand.

McAllister took out his gun and continued crawling the rest of the way down the hill to a spot just a few feet above the driveway and ten yards behind the Mercedes. The lone man was gazing intently down the driveway in the direction the others had gone. He did not turn around as McAllister slipped out of the woods and crept forward to the big German car.

At the last possible moment the man, hearing something or sensing that someone was behind him, started to turn. At that instant, McAllister sprang up, smashing the butt of the heavy P38 into the side of the man's head. He went down heavily, his shoulder glancing off the car's bumper, but still semiconscious he tried to bring up his gun. McAllister grabbed a handful of his coat, pulled him half up and smashed the butt of his gun into the man's face, opening his nose with a gush of blood and knocking him senseless.

Working fast now, with one eye toward the slope of the driveway lest one of Potemkin's people had heard something and was coming back to investigate, McAllister stripped the unconscious man of his belt and tie, trussing his arms and legs together behind his back. He jammed his handkerchief into the man's mouth, holstered his own gun, and snatched the silenced weapon. It was a big, heavy 9-mm automatic. A proper *mokrie dela* weapon for destroying faces.

They'd left the Mercedes open. He popped the hood,

yanked out the ignition wire and careful to make as little noise as possible, closed the hood again, before he scrambled back up into the woods.

Neutralizing the first of the Russians had taken barely three minutes. By now he figured the other four would have reached the clearing where they would be holding up to watch the cabin for signs that this was a trap. Potemkin would probably be dispersing his men left and right so that they could come up from behind the house. They would be moving through the woods, but well within sight of the clearing. No one wanted to get lost in these dark woods. It would take them several cautious minutes to circle the entire clearing and then cross at the back.

It took him precious minutes to find the path he'd made through the woods this afternoon, and then follow it to a spot about ten yards from the clearing and an equal distance up from the driveway.

He thought he might be able to hear someone talking off to his left, and someone else moving through the woods toward his right, but again the sounds faded.

Stuffing the big Russian gun in his belt, he climbed up the tree to the second set of large branches about fifteen feet off the ground where he had left one of Sikorski's hunting rifles with a big light-gathering scope.

From his vantage point he had a open line of fire across the entire clearing.

He spotted the first man to the west, just emerging from the woods. Swinging the scope quickly across the clearing, he spotted a second man on the east side, working his way slowly toward the house. Potemkin and the other one were probably waiting on the driveway.

McAllister swung the gun toward the west again, catching then losing then catching the Russian who had stopped and was looking down toward the house.

Centering the cross hairs on the man's chest, he hesitated for just a moment. Pulling the trigger would make him an assassin . . . no less of a killer than the men he was fighting.

And there it is, boyo, his father had once said. *The time will come when you'll have to make a difficult decision. One of morals. When that happens think out your options, consider the alternatives, work out the consequences not only of your action, but the consequences of your* in-action.

They were killers. He had seen what they'd done to Sikorski, and to Nicholas Albright. He had seen first-hand in Bulgaria and East Germany and a dozen other places what sort of animals they could be. Not all Russians were like that, of course. But the special ones they picked to work the KGB's Department Viktor, the murder squad, they were the worst. They simply had no regard whatsoever for human life.

He squeezed off a shot, finished with his little morality lecture to himself, the heavy deer rifle bucking against his shoulder, the tremendous crack echoing off the hills, and the Russian went down as if he had been struck by a Mack truck.

Quickly he brought the rifle around as he ejected the spent shell, pumping a live round into the firing chamber. The second Russian was racing back to the protection of the woods. McAllister led him and at the last moment squeezed off a shot, the man flopping down into the snow, his arms and legs splayed out.

Hooking the rifle's shoulder strap on a cross branch, he scrambled down out of the tree and headed back the same way he had come, moving from tree to tree, keeping his eye toward the driveway and the spot he had fired from.

After twenty yards he angled toward the driveway, pulling out the Russian's gun, making certain by feel that it was ready to fire.

There was a noise behind him; cloth brushing against a tree trunk, the crunch of a booted foot in the deep snow, and he stopped.

''McAllister,'' Potemkin shouted, his voice coming from farther right than the noise. It sounded as if he were still at the end of the driveway near the clearing.

McAllister moved cautiously down the hill behind the bole of a much larger tree where he again held up, searching the dark woods behind him.

There were two of them; Potemkin in the driveway and the one who had come up into the woods. This one would have followed McAllister's footprints in the snow. Moving slowly just as McAllister had, from tree to tree. Testing each step, scanning the darkness ahead of him.

McAllister remained absolutely still.

''McAllister,'' Potemkin shouted again. ''I've come here to talk. I'll send my people away. It'll be just you and me.''

There was the flash of movement to the left, about fifteen feet away, and then it was gone.

McAllister, his cheek against the rough bark of the tree, didn't move a muscle.

''You're making a big mistake,'' Potemkin called. ''You don't know all the facts. I can help you. As strange as that seems, it's the truth. Just talk. No more killing.''

A big man stepped out from behind a tree and started to move across a narrow open space when McAllister extended the silenced automatic, steadying his aim with his arm propped against the tree trunk.

''Stop and throw your gun down,'' McAllister ordered.

The man snapped off a single shot and dove for the protection of the trees. McAllister fired two shots in quick succession, the first hitting the man in the left leg, and the second in his left side. He collapsed in the snow, thrashed around for a second or two, and then lay still.

McAllister watched him for a full minute before he stepped away from the tree and approached slowly. He was dead, his eyes open, a big patch of blood staining the snow. There was something about the man, perhaps his face, or the cut of his clothes, that was oddly familiar to McAllister, but he couldn't put his finger on it.

Turning, he raced back up through the woods parallel to the driveway, making little or no noise as he ran, finally emerging from the woods at the parked cars, and just ducking out of sight behind the Mercedes as Potemkin, huffing and puffing, came into view, a big pistol in his right hand.

The KGB chief of station was obviously highly agitated. What had promised to be a relatively easy job of eliminating McAllister—the odds had been five to one—had somehow gone terribly wrong, and now he was running for his own life, looking over his shoulder every few yards.

McAllister watched him approach, passing the Taurus and then pulling up short when he saw the man lying trussed up in front of the Mercedes. He looked toward the woods on both sides of the driveway, and then did, to McAllister's way of thinking, the most extraordinary thing possible. He raised his pistol and shot his own man in the head.

McAllister ducked back behind the car, his heart hammering, hardly able to believe what he had just witnessed with his own eyes. Why? It made no sense. Why would he kill his own man?

Potemkin came around to the driver's side and climbed in behind the wheel of the Mercedes. He turned the ignition and the car's engine turned over, but it wouldn't start.

He tried again as McAllister crept around to the side of the car and rose up all of a sudden, yanking the door open and jamming the pistol into Potemkin's temple.

The Russian nearly jumped out of his skin. He started to reach for his own gun which he had lain beside him on the seat.

"I'll blow your head off, comrade," McAllister spat.

Potemkin froze, his eyes nearly bulging out of their sockets.

"Zebra One was Donald Harman. You had him killed this morning. Who is Zebra Two?"

"I don't know what you're talking about," Potemkin stammered.

McAllister jammed the silencer tube of the automatic harder against the man's temple. "I don't have the time to fuck with you. Zebra Two, who is he?"

"I don't know."

McAllister cocked the pistol, the noise very loud. "A name, comrade, and you may live."

"I swear to you, I don't know."

"Why did you have Harman killed?"

"I can't tell you that."

"You are either extremely brave or you are incredibly stupid. Why did you have Harman killed?"

"Because he was going crazy. He was out of control."

"Out of whose control, yours?"

"He didn't work for me."

"Who then?"

"I don't know," Potemkin shouted. "I swear to you, I don't know. But he did work with Albright, I do know that."

"What?" McAllister said, a hot jab of fear stitching across his chest.

"Nicholas Albright was one of Harman's pipelines to the CIA."

McAllister's head was spinning. "A man such as Harman wouldn't need him. Not for that."

"Albright was also his communications link with Moscow," Potemkin said. "But that's something I didn't find out until a few days ago."

"When you had Albright murdered?" McAllister was thinking about the cabinet in Albright's surgery, the wires leading from the wall. He'd been right about the transmitter.

"Yes," Potemkin said.

"Who did Albright take his orders from in Moscow? Who was his communications link?"

"I don't know for sure."

"A name, comrade. A name!"

"It's probably Borodin. General Aleksandr Borodin."

"Is he KGB?"

"Yes, of course. He is director of the First Chief Directorate's Special Counterintelligence Service II. He is a crazy man. This is not beyond him."

Zebra One was for Donald Harman, in Washington. Zebra Two was for General Aleksandr Borodin in Moscow. But there was more.

"What did you mean when you said Harman had gotten out of control?"

"It was he who arranged the killings in College Park."

"Why?"

"To stop you. He wanted to totally discredit you, make everyone believe for certain that you had gone crazy."

"How did you know he would be meeting with the O'Haire woman this morning?"

"I sent someone to her house. They listened to a tape-recorded message on her answering machine. She was already gone, so I figured they'd be meeting somewhere, and I followed him."

Harman and Borodin worked together, Stephanie's father their link. What else?

"Did the O'Haires work for Harman?"

"No," Potemkin said. "They were my network."

The further he went into this nightmare the less sense it made. "Why did you just shoot your own man?"

"He's not mine," Potemkin said disdainfully. "He . . . and the others . . . all of them were Mafia. I hired them. They'll do anything for money. Anything."

Again something tickled insistently at the back of McAllister's head, but he couldn't put a name to it.

"Borodin and Harman worked together. Who is your contact here in the States?"

Potemkin didn't answer.

"It was a faction fight all this time," McAllister said. "Harman wanted me dead, but so did you. Why?"

Potemkin turned his head slowly so that he was able to look up out of the corner of his eyes at McAllister. "Don't you know, haven't you figured it out yet?"

"Who do you work with?" McAllister shouted.

"You're the most dangerous man alive at this moment. Everyone wants you dead."

"Who?" McAllister shouted again.

"Fuck your mother," Potemkin swore and he lunged against McAllister trying to shove him off balance, when the gun went off destroying the side of his head.

Chapter 31

It was beginning to snow again in earnest as McAllister entered the suburb of Arlington a few minutes after eight. He'd fixed the Mercedes and taken it. The diplomatic plates would be less dangerous for at least the next few hours, he figured, than the Taurus, which could have been connected with the McMillan Park shooting by now.

He was tired and sore and wet from crawling around in the snow, and his mind was as badly battered as his body. The spying had gone on at two levels; from the White House through Harman and from the CIA through the penetration agent Potemkin had controlled.

Don't you know, haven't you figured it out yet? You're the most dangerous man alive at this moment. Everyone wants you dead.

But why? Potemkin had been willing to risk his life rather than answer that question. Harman was dead, so his operation was finished. And Potemkin was dead, thus ending the second network. What else was there? What was he missing? What was driving him?

He found a telephone booth in front of a convenience store on Arlington Boulevard and pulled in, parking as far away from the lights as possible and walking back.

He had to ask information for the number and when he dialed it the phone was answered on the second ring.

"National Medical Center."

"You have a patient there, Robert Highnote. May I speak with him?"

"One moment, please," the woman said.

Stephanie would be out of her mind with worry by now, he thought as he waited for the connection to be made. All these years her father had been using their close relationship to gather information from her about CIA operations . . . specifically about who was being considered for employment by the Agency. It had been a sideline for him, however. His major role in the Harman-Borodin connection would have been that of a communications link.

She talked to him. Told him things. It made McAllister sick to think that she'd told her father everything they'd discussed. The man would have relayed the information to Harman who in turn sent his people out with orders to eliminate the threat. Everytime he'd moved, someone was right there behind him.

How was he going to tell her that her father had worked for the Russians? Christ, there was no way he could face her with news like that.

Highnote answered, his voice sounding a little weak. "Hello."

"Are you alone?" McAllister asked.

"Good Lord Almighty . . . yes, for the moment."

"Is this line clean?"

"I think so. Where are you, what's happened?"

"Are you all right, Bob?"

"Reasonably. Now what's happened?"

"You can't imagine how much, but now I'm going to need your help."

"I don't know what I can do from here. I'm not due to be released for another couple of days."

"Donald Harman and Kathleen O'Haire are dead."

"I heard. . . ."

"Gennadi Potemkin killed them."

"How do you know that?" Highnote demanded.

"I was there. I saw it."

"Potemkin . . . head of KGB operations out of their embassy?"

"That's right. He's dead too. I killed him about an hour ago out at Janos Sikorski's place, along with four of his people. Mafia."

"My God," Highnote said softly. "What is going on, Mac, what have you done?"

"It wasn't me and Stephanie at College Park."

"I know that!"

"Then why are the authorities still blaming us?"

"Because they won't believe me. I didn't see who they were. Alvan was just leaving when he was shot down in the corridor. I ran out the back door and almost made it across the yard when . . . I don't remember much after that, except that I knew I'd been hit. Whoever it was took your car from your place."

"Donald Harman arranged the killings, according to Potemkin."

"You spoke with him? Potemkin actually talked to you?"

"He told me that Donald Harman has been working with a KGB general in Moscow by the name of Borodin."

"Aleksandr Ilyich Borodin," Highnote said in wonder. "He's a big man in the Soviet hierarchy, but absolutely off his rocker. Half the Kremlin is afraid of him, and the other half would like to see him dead. But he's got too much power. Potemkin told you that?"

"Just before he died."

"What else?"

"He admitted that he worked with someone here in the States, too."

"Did he give you a name?"

"No. But he said something very odd, something I don't

understand. He said everyone wanted me dead now, and he said that I was the most dangerous man alive."

There was a silence on the line for a long time. McAllister could almost hear his old friend thinking, his thoughts racing to a dozen different connections, a hundred different possibilities.

"You are dangerous to them," Highnote said finally. "There have been two networks working here all along. Harman in the White House, and presumably someone in the Agency. In a matter of weeks, days actually, you've somehow managed to bring both of them down."

"But there's more," McAllister said.

"Of course. The penetration agent is still in place."

"And General Borodin."

"He's out of reach."

"I'm going after him," McAllister said, astonished with himself even as the words came out of his mouth.

"Are you crazy?" Highnote exploded. "We're talking about the Soviet Union now. Moscow. Even if you could get into the country, what could you do against a man like that? You wouldn't even get close. And why go after him in the first place? Harman is dead, his organization is smashed."

McAllister's head was spinning. "I don't know why," he said. "Exactly. But if Borodin was able to get to a man like Harman, turn him and use him, what else is he capable of accomplishing? How much else has he already done? Are you so sure that Harman was his only contact?"

"But this is insanity."

"Listen to me," McAllister said. "Potemkin ran his penetration agent from his embassy. They must have had contact on a regular basis. As soon as possible I want you to get back out to Langley and run it down. There'll be something in the files connecting Potemkin with someone at the Agency. Something."

"But what?"

"I don't know. But whoever Potemkin's agent was, he'll be highly placed. Head of Clandestine Services, the deputy director of intelligence . . . and up from there."

"We'll run him down together," Highnote argued.

"I'm going after Borodin. There's something else happening here, Bob. Something . . . I don't know what. But if anyone will have the answers, Borodin will. In Moscow."

"I'll repeat, you won't even be able to get into the country let alone get to him."

"I think I will," McAllister said. "But I need your help."

"With what?"

"Diplomatic passports."

Highnote's breath caught in his throat. "Plural?"

"I'll take Stephanie as far as Helsinki. If something goes wrong she can start making noises to insure I won't simply disappear into some Gulag somewhere."

Again McAllister could almost hear his friend's mind working, considering possibilities, playing the scenarios out for himself as they both did in the old days together.

"How will you get out of the States?"

"Have our real passports been flagged?"

"No," Highnote said. "At least to the best of my knowledge they haven't been. No one expects you to try to leave the country."

"We'll fly to Montreal in the morning and from there to Europe. How about diplomatic passports?"

"Where are you calling from?"

"A phone booth in Arlington, not far from your house."

"I have a couple of blanks in the wall safe in my study. Do you know where it is?"

"Yes."

Highnote gave him the combination. "There's some cash in there too, but you won't be able to take a gun through customs. Especially not into the Soviet Union."

"I know," McAllister said.

"The passports are blank, what about an artist?"

"Munich."

"And then what, Mac? Say you do get to Borodin by some miracle, do you think he'll talk to you?"

"I won't know that until I try."

"Don't do it," Highnote said earnestly. "Please, think it over."

"I have," McAllister said. "Is your house being watched?"

"No."

"How about Merrilee and . . . Gloria?"

"After the shooting they were taken down to one of our safe houses in Falls Church. I don't think you should go there."

"No," McAllister said, and he was surprised that there wasn't as much pain thinking about his wife as he thought there should be. "But take care of yourself, Bob. Potemkin's penetration agent will have to know that we're on to him once he finds out his control officer is dead."

"Don't do this," Highnote tried one last time.

"No choice. I don't think I ever had a choice," McAllister said, and he hung up.

Stephanie opened the door for him, and the instant their eyes met she knew that he had come to some decision that would change everything. But she was also relieved that he had come back in one piece.

"Did he show up alone?" she asked when he was inside and the door was closed and locked.

"No," McAllister said facing her. "He brought four others with him."

She was holding herself very still. "What happened?"

"They're all dead."

"Including Potemkin?"

McAllister nodded.

"Are you . . . all right?"

"No," he said sighing deeply to relieve the immense pressure in his chest and his gut. "But I'm not hurt."

"Oh, David," she said and she went into his arms. He held her close while he stroked her hair, drinking in her smell, her feel. "I killed them and it was so easy. Easier than you can imagine."

She said nothing.

After a moment he began telling her what had happened from the time he spotted the Mercedes coming from the embassy on Sixteenth Street until he'd driven back to Arlington. He left out nothing, except for the role her father had evidently played, and he did not gloss over any of the details. He felt that in some small measure she needed to hear it all from him because of what had been done to her father. Revenge, perhaps a catharsis; he thought she needed to believe that they were striking back. That they weren't simply sitting still for the terrible events of the past days.

"Was it bad?" she asked when he was finished.

"Yes."

She was searching his face for a sign that it was over now, that they had won. But she wasn't finding it.

"What did you do with the Mercedes?"

"I parked it in a garage downtown and took a cab back here. It'll take them a while to find it. With any luck not until tomorrow or the next day."

Again she looked closely at him. "There's more." She said it as a statement not a question.

He nodded. "I telephoned Bob Highnote at the hospital."

"Is he all right?"

"They'll be releasing him in a day or two. I had to warn him that when Potemkin's body is found the penetration agent will know that we're close."

"He'll run."

"Maybe not. It depends upon how much he's got left to protect here. Perhaps the O'Haires were just the tip of the iceberg. Perhaps someone will take Potemkin's place."

"And what did he say?" Stephanie asked, and McAllister turned away, but she pulled him back. "What else, David?"

There was so much he wanted to tell her, and yet he simply could not. So much she deserved to know, and yet he didn't think she could stand it.

"I'm going after General Borodin."

"In Moscow," she said calmly.

"Yes."

"When? How?"

"Montreal in the morning where we'll change our appearances back to match our real passports. From there to Frankfurt, then by car to Munich where I will get us new passports." He pulled out the diplomatic blanks he'd taken from Highnote's wall safe. "We'll use these."

"After Munich, what?" she asked, barely glancing at the passports. McAllister thought she was on the verge of exploding.

"Helsinki," he said.

"Then Moscow?"

"You're staying in Helsinki."

"To do what?"

"If I'm not out in forty-eight hours, you're going to call Highnote, and if need be our embassy, the Finnish authorities, and even the Associated Press. You're going to put up a very big stink."

She smiled, but it was extremely fragile. "All of this while you're somewhere insidc the Soviet Union. A convicted American spy whom everyone wants dead. With no weapon, up against one of the most powerful generals in the country." She laughed, her eyes suddenly glistening. "David, that is outside the realm of reality. For once I have to agree with Highnote, it's insanity."

McAllister turned away again, this time she didn't stop him. He went across the room and stood by the window.

There are demons in my head, and I cannot control them. There are forces driving me that I cannot understand. He wished that his father were here with him now; he hadn't wished for anything so strongly in his entire life. *I'm frightened and I don't know of what.*

"Stop it, my darling," Stephanie said coming up behind him.

He shook his head. "I can't," he said.

Chapter 32

Howard Van Skike, director of central intelligence, entered the President's study. A lot of worried people were huddled around the desk, talking with the President. One of his advisers was talking urgently on the telephone, and others had gathered in a tight knot across the room, and were deep in conversation.

John Sanderson, the director of the FBI, broke away from the group at the desk and came over. "He's got a news conference scheduled for noon." He looked at his watch. "Gives us a bit more than three hours to come up with something for him."

"What's going on?" Van Skike asked, his gut aching. It was a flare-up of his ulcer. He'd been taking Maalox by the bottleful for the past three days.

"We may have been wrong about McAllister," Sanderson said. "Dead wrong. There are some questions that don't seem to have any logical answers."

"Does this have to do with Don Harman?"

"In a big way, Van. As it looks now, Don was meeting the O'Haire woman with the intent to kill her when they were both gunned down."

"What?" Van Skike breathed, barely able to believe what Sanderson was saying.

"Harman may have been the penetration agent we've been looking for. Or at least one of them. We're not sure, of course, but a lot of the signs are pointing his way. Remember, we had witnesses placing a tall, well-dressed man at McAllister's house the morning of the College Park shooting?"

Van Skike nodded. The President had looked up.

"Hold on for a couple of minutes, would you, Van?" he said.

"Yes, Mr. President."

"It's looking more and more possible now that the man they saw was Don Harman."

"Working with McAllister and the Albright woman?"

"No," Sanderson said. "Innes had taped the proceedings, something McAllister might have guessed, but that the killers missed. One of them said two words: 'Get him.' A man's voice. Our lab people came up with a tape of McAllister's voice from your Technical Services Division. Something recent, from what I understand. They ran it through their voice-spectrum analyzer. Looks like the man who spoke on the tape and McAllister are not one and the same."

Van Skike started to object, but Sanderson held him off.

"It's shaky at best, I know. Impossible to be one hundred percent accurate with two words. But it's an indication."

"Which still leaves us with the question of who was working with Harman, and exactly what McAllister has been doing these past weeks."

"He was fighting back," Sanderson said. "He evidently learned something in Moscow that pointed toward Harman . . . we're just guessing now, of course. When the Russians released him Harman had him set up for the kill. He's been trying to protect himself ever since."

"And doing a damned fine job of it."

Sanderson nodded. "He's the best, there's no doubt of it."

"What now?"

"I'll let the President tell you," Sanderson said, glancing across the room. "Oh, by the way," he added, turning back. "Did you hear that Mel Quarmby died last night?"

"No," Van Skike said. "I'm sorry to hear that. He was a good man."

"How about Bob?"

"He checked himself out of the hospital last night. He feels he has a personal stake in this business. He and McAllister have been friends for a lot of years."

Sanderson gave him an odd look which Van Skike found strangely disturbing at that moment. It was as if the FBI director knew something he wasn't telling.

"Gentlemen, I want you to clear out of here now. Give us a few minutes," the President said. He motioned for Van Skike and Sanderson to remain behind.

The others filed out of the room, the last one to go closing the door softly.

"The shit is about to hit the fan," the President said, coming around from behind his desk when they were alone. "Has John filled you in with the latest developments?"

"Yes, Mr. President," Van Skike replied. "But I'm finding it hard to believe that Don Harman was working with the Russians."

The President smiled wryly. "You're telling me," he said. "In the meantime I've got the media swarming all over the place screaming bloody murder. They want answers, and I can't blame them." He shook his head. "Trouble is, I don't know what I can tell them."

"The truth," Van Skike said. "Or at least a part of it for now."

Again the President smiled. "Which truth, Van? Without McAllister we've got nothing. On top of it all, John thinks Harman might not have been working alone. There might be someone working out of your pasture across the river. Nice thought, isn't it?"

Van Skike shot Sanderson a look, but the FBI director ignored it.

"McAllister may be the only man who has the answers we need. I want him brought in, no screwing around this time. I'm personally guaranteeing his safety. I'll give him a presidential pardon, whatever it takes to convince him that I mean business."

"If you can get a message to him somehow, tell him to call the President," Sanderson put in.

"I'll speak to him," the President said. "Just get to him."

"That may not be so easy," Van Skike said half to himself. He looked up out of his thoughts. "Bob Highnote knows him better than any man alive. I'll put him on it. If anyone can find McAllister it will be him."

John Sanderson met George Mueller, chief of the FBI's Counter-Intelligence Division, at the west exit. Together they went outside and got into Sanderson's car.

"What do you think?" Mueller asked. He was a short, stockily built man with thick dark hair and an intense air about him. He'd been a close personal friend of Alvan Reisberg.

"He'll hand it over to Highnote," Sanderson said.

Their driver pulled away from the portico, and started down the long driveway.

"Did he take the bait?" Mueller asked.

Sanderson looked at him. "I don't know. We'll just have to wait and see."

"In the meantime almost anything can happen. . . ." Mueller growled.

"Easy," Sanderson warned.

Van Skike thought that Bob Highnote looked on the verge of collapse. The man held himself stiffly erect in the chair, and a light sheen of sweat had popped out on his bald head.

"Mac is supposed to be carrying around all the answers in his head, is that it?" Highnote said.

"Sanderson seems to have built a pretty convincing case. Trouble is how do we get to him before anything else happens."

Highnote looked away for a moment. "Could it be another trap? Lure him out of hiding and gun him down when he shows up?"

"No," Van Skike said flatly.

"I've been telling you that he was innocent from the beginning. No one would listen, and now a lot of good men are dead because of it. God only knows what else he'll do if he's pushed."

"Can you find him for us, Bob?" Van Skike asked after a moment.

Highnote turned back. "Yes, I can," he said. "But certainly not in time to do the President any good with his news conference today."

"Do you know where he is?"

"Not exactly, but I have a fair idea."

"Where?"

"He's gone to ground, Van, as I knew he would. But I'll find him for you, only I can't guarantee how he's going to react. He's got to be gun-shy by now."

Van Skike had become more of an administrator and a politician over the past years, than a spy master. The question of whom to trust had always been uppermost in his mind; his technique however had begun to slip with age.

"They don't think Don Harman was working alone," he said.

"Of course not."

"Besides his Russian contact, whoever it is, they think he might have had help right here in the Agency."

Highnote's eyes were wide. He sat forward. "Is that what Sanderson told you?"

Van Skike nodded. His stomach was burning. "Drop

everything else. I want you to give this your undivided attention."

"Who is it, Van?" Highnote asked softly. "Do they have a suspect? Can we nail the bastard ourselves before Sanderson and his head hunters get any further?"

"I don't know. I just don't know. It may be nobody. They might just be guessing. I hope so."

After a beat Highnote got to his feet with some difficulty. "I'll get on it immediately. But I'm telling you one thing, Van."

"Yes," Van Skike asked looking up.

"I'm not turning him over to Sanderson. I just won't. If and when I can get to him, I'll try to bring him in myself. Once we can get the situation stabilized, we can let the Bureau question him."

"And the woman," Van Skike said as Highnote reached the door.

"Her too."

It was a few minutes after seven in the morning when the Air Canada flight touched down at Frankfurt Airport, McAllister and Stephanie traveling under their real names, among the first to get off the plane. He felt naked traveling like this, so openly, but the passport officers barely gave them a second glance, even though they didn't look like their passport photographs.

"The purpose of your visit to Germany, sir?"

"Tourism," McAllister said.

"How long will you be staying in the country?"

"A week, perhaps a little longer."

The passport officer, a young stern-faced man, smiled and handed McAllister's passport back. "Have a pleasant holiday, *mein Herr*."

"Thank you, we will," McAllister said and he moved through the line, waiting on the other side for Stephanie to be cleared.

When she was passed through they took one of the green lines for customs control of hand luggage, which was all they'd taken with them, and five minutes later were downstairs where McAllister changed some money into Deutsche marks, then booked a small Mercedes sedan from the Hertz counter for one week.

They were in Europe. Highnote had been right that their passports had not been flagged. No one had paid them more than a passing interest. But then, this was the easy part.

We have made great progress together, you and I. I am so very proud of you, Mac, so very pleased.

He had made progress, but even now he didn't know toward what, exactly. Stephanie had told him to rely on his instincts, and he had. They had managed to come this far without being taken, but the cost had been insanely high, and he was not proud of what he had done; the killing, spreading death and destruction wherever he went, to whomever he made contact with. There were times, even now, when Highnote's suggestion that it might be better if he put a bullet into his own head, seemed to be a viable option. End the pain, the struggle, finish it once and for all. But he could not do that, any more than he could turn and walk away from it. Something was driving him. It's the business, boyo, his father would say. It gets in the blood ruining a man for a regular life. It's hard to step down with all those secrets running around in your head. For the rest of your life you would be looking over your shoulder for one of the enemies you've made in your career to come up behind you with your nine ounces—A Russian euphemism for a 9mm bullet to the back of the skull.

Look to Washington. Look to Moscow. Zebra One, Zebra Two.

God help him, but he was doing just that.

The weather across Germany was clear but very cold, a

lot of snow was piled up along the autobahns where traffic ran with headlights on at speeds of eighty and ninety miles per hour. He concentrated on his driving. Ever since Montreal Stephanie had fallen strangely silent, and had put a distance between them again as she had after the incident on the train in Chicago. It was fear, he supposed. And disgust with what they had done.

She had killed and so had he. What did that make them? How different from the KGB were they in the last analysis?

By ten they had reached the city of Nürnberg where they turned south on the E6, sometimes passing through vast federal parklands, at other times passing quaint little villages and the matrix of well-laid-out farms, the land beginning to rise up toward the Alps at the foot of which lay the city of Munich, headquarters of the BND—the German Secret Service. He'd been here before, often, liaising with the Germans during his tenure in Berlin. But it wasn't like coming to a familiar place for him this time. Everything had changed. He had changed.

They entered Munich from the north about eleven-thirty in the morning, driving along Schwabing's busy Leopoldstrasse lined with boutiques, restaurants, galleries, bars, and artists' cellars, traffic extremely heavy, the twin towers of Munich's landmark, the Frauenkirche rising up into the clear blue sky. Following the broad, poplar-lined boulevard, he went the rest of the way into the city center, passing a big parking ramp near the ornately designed Hauptbahnhof, one of the largest train stations in Europe.

Coming back around the block, he entered the ramp, got his ticket from the machine and drove down to the lowest level, parking the Mercedes in a dark corner.

"Now what?" Stephanie asked, her voice flat.

McAllister looked at her. "I'm sorry, but I don't know any other way to do this."

"You're going ahead with it then?"

"Yes."

She started to shake, and she grabbed his arm. "It's over, David. Leave it be. Please. For my sake."

"Then they'll have won."

"So what?" she screeched, her face screwed up in a grimace of fear and anger. "You can't go back to the Soviet Union. They'll kill you for sure."

"I must," McAllister said. "Can't you see that, my darling? I have no choice."

"But you do! David, you've broken both networks. Leave it be!"

"No."

They took a cab to a small hotel just around the corner from the parking ramp, registering under their real names and surrendering their passports for the morning's police check. They were both very tired, neither of them had gotten much rest during the transatlantic flight.

When the bellman left them, McAllister placed the chain on the door, then pulled the bed covers back, mussed up the pillows as if they had been slept on, and in the bathroom crumpled up a couple of the towels and threw them on the floor.

Stephanie stood in the middle of the room watching him, her arms across her chest as she hugged herself to keep from shivering.

He unpacked their bags, scattering their clothing throughout the room, hanging some in the closet, laying some over the chairs, leaving others on the floor. Next he placed their toiletries in the bathroom, squeezing a little toothpaste in the sink and dirtying a couple of the glasses.

"Is there anything that you're going to need over the next few days?" he asked when he was finished.

"What do you mean?"

"We're leaving everything behind."

She looked around the room and shrugged. "My purse."

"Get it and let's go."

"Where to?"

"Schwabing," he said.

Schwabing was the artist's quarter of Munich, much like New York's Greenwich Village and London's Soho. After leaving the hotel, they had retrieved the Mercedes and had spent the next few hours shopping at various department stores, purchasing a few articles of clothing, toiletry items, and a pair of cheap nylon suitcases into which they stuffed their things after first removing the price tags and store labels.

Leopoldstrasse, the main boulevard they had used this noon, was coming alive with the early evening when McAllister parked the car along a side street and he and Stephanie walked back up to a small, seedy-looking nightclub in the middle of the block. It was barely six o'clock, yet already the place was more than half filled, the atmosphere dense with smoke, a young long-haired man sitting on a small raised platform playing a Bruce Springsteen hit on his guitar. No one seemed to be listening to him—the hum of conversation was loud.

McAllister found them a small table at the rear, and when their drinks came he got up. "Stay here, I'll be right back," he said.

Stephanie looked up at him but said nothing, and he turned and went to the bar where he sat down with his drink, placing a hundred-dollar bill in front of him.

It took the bartender less than a minute to come over to him, glancing first at the money then at McAllister.

"I need an artist," McAllister said in German.

"The town is filled with them, *mein Herr,*" the barman said. He was a big, rough-hewn man with a beet-red complexion.

"This one would have to be special. Someone very good. Someone most of all discreet."

Again the bartender eyed the money. "You are on the run?"

"Perhaps," McAllister said.

"You need papers, is that it?"

McAllister nodded.

The bartender grinned. "Where're you sitting?"

McAllister motioned toward the back. The barman deftly slipped the hundred-dollar bill off the bar and pocketed it. "I'll send him back."

"What's his name?"

"I never asked," the bartender said, and he moved away.

McAllister went back to Stephanie and sat down. Her eyes were wide, but she was no longer shivering.

"Are you all right?"

She nodded.

"Someone is coming over to talk to us. No matter what happens, don't say anything."

Again she nodded.

McAllister wanted to do something for her, something to make it easier. But there was nothing to be done. Not now.

Five minutes later a very old rat-faced man with bottle-thick glasses that made his eyes seem huge and naked, a liter stein of beer in his hand, came over and sat down. When he grinned they could see that most of his teeth were missing. Everything about him seemed ancient and grubby except for his hands, the fingers of which were long and delicate, the nails well cared for. They were the hands of an artist.

"What sort of trouble are you in, then?" he asked.

"You don't want to know, my friend," McAllister replied easily. "We need a pair of passports."

The old man looked appraisingly at McAllister and then at Stephanie. He nodded. "Do you have the originals?"

"Blanks."

"That'll be easy then. Photographs?"

"No. And we'll need to change our appearances, or at least I will."

"No problem. My studio is just around the corner."

"One more thing," McAllister said. "I'll need some visa stamps in my passport. A lot of them."

"The well-used look," the old man said understanding. "For what countries?"

"I'll leave that up to you, except for one. The most current one."

"Yes, for what country?"

"The Soviet Union."

The old man sat back in his chair, his eyes narrowed. He shook his head. "That's the tough one," he said. "It'll cost you."

"How much?"

"Fifteen hundred for the lady's," he said without hesitation. "Dollars. Two thousand for yours."

It was more than half the amount of money he had taken from Highnote's safe. "We'll need a place to stay tonight."

The old man nodded. "No problem." He sat forward again. "Am I going to have the BND down on my neck?"

"Not if you keep your mouth shut," McAllister said. "Half now, half when they're ready."

The old man hesitated for a moment, but then he sighed. "It's your skin," he said, and he held out his hand.

Chapter 33

A cruel wind blew along the frozen Istra River thirty miles outside of Moscow, whipping the snow into long plumes, whining at the edges of the steep cliffs, and moaning in the treetops of the birch forest. It was early afternoon, but already the sun had sunk low in the western horizon. Darkness came early at this time of the year.

The large, bull-necked man, bundled in a thick parka and fur-lined boots, trudged up from the river, his breath white in the subzero cold. He stopped on the rise and looked across the narrow wooded valley to his dacha, smoke swirling from the chimney.

Someone was coming. He had felt it for several days now, though he had no real idea why. Instinct, perhaps. All he had wanted was containment. Nothing more, at least until the mistakes that had been made over the past months were rectified. But each day brought another new disaster, none of which he could understand. It was as if forces beyond his ken were at work. For the first time in his long, illustrious career, he felt real pangs of fear stabbing at his gut. Explanations would be demanded. But he had none to give.

He looked back the way he had come and clenched his meaty fists in their thick gloves. Lies within lies. He had lived the life for so long that during times such as these he had a hard time recalling the truth.

Everything had somehow tumbled down around him because of one man—David Stewart McAllister. Only he didn't know why, or how. Only that it had happened, was still happening.

Turning, he worked his way down the hill, across the valley and finally up to his dacha which in the old days had belonged to a prince, one of the czar's family at court. Those days were gone, but the new age had its comforts.

Stamping off his boots in the mud room, he hung up his parka and rubbing his hands together entered the main body of the house just as his secretary emerged from the study, an odd look on his face.

"Yes, what is it, Mikhail?"

"It is a telephone call, Comrade General," the younger man, Mikhail Vasilevich Kiselev, said. "From the United States."

Something clutched at General Borodin's heart. "Impossible."

"Nevertheless it is so," Kiselev said respectfully.

Borodin brushed past his secretary and in his small study snatched up the telephone. "Yes, who is this calling?"

At first he could hear nothing on the line except for the hollow hiss of what obviously was a very long-distance connection. Who knew this number? Who could possibly know it?

"General Borodin," a man said in English. "Listen to me."

"Who is this?" Borodin demanded, switching to English. Kiselev stood in the doorway, his left eyebrow rising.

"Harman and Potemkin are both dead, and McAllister is on his way to Moscow. Do you understand me?"

On an open line! General Borodin could hardly believe his ears. He had to hold on to his desk for support. "Who is this? What are you talking about?"

"McAllister knows everything. He even knows your name, and he's coming there for you. He's coming to kill you."

"You're insane," Borodin said. He'd wanted to shout, but he couldn't seem to catch his breath.

"If he's arrested he'll tell everything he knows. Everything will be ruined. You, me, everything, do you understand?"

"No, I don't understand," he said for Kiselev's benefit. The fact of the matter was he did understand now; if not the how or the why, at least the implications. But who was this fool calling him now?

"You must kill him. You are the last hope."

"What are you talking about?"

"McAllister is coming to Moscow to kill you. There's no one else left for me to contact. God in heaven, can't you understand?"

General Borodin said nothing. After a few moments the connection was broken and he slowly hung up the telephone. Kiselev was closely watching him.

"What is it, Comrade General?"

Borodin shook his head and looked up out of his dark thoughts. "I don't know, Mikhail Vasilevich. He was a crazy man shouting something about spies, of all things."

"Spies?" the secretary asked, his eyebrow rising again.

"Yes," General Borodin said, forcing a smile. "He wanted to come to work for us. He is a cowboy, I think. Crazy."

"Do you wish me to make a report?"

"No," General Borodin said, dismissing the man. "I will take care of it myself in the morning."

Robert Highnote stepped off the elevator on the fourth floor of CIA Headquarters in Langley and rushed down to his office. It was Sunday noon, the building was relatively quiet.

Dropping his overnight bag on his secretary's desk, he went inside, snatched up his telephone, and dialed a three-digit number. His eyes were red from lack of sleep, he had a nagging headache, and the wound in his back was on fire. But he could not stop. Not now. McAllister had taken the passports and money from his wall safe and somehow he and the woman had made it out of the country. Highnote had a great deal of respect for his old friend, always had. But since Moscow he hadn't understood a thing that Mac had said or done. Something sinister had happened to him, something totally beyond understanding. Something totally insane.

"Duty desk," the number was answered.

"This is Highnote. Anything on those two diplomatic passport numbers from Helsinki?"

"Yes, sir. We tried to reach you earlier but there was no answer at your home."

"I'm in my office now," Highnote said, his chest tight.

"They showed up in Helsinki all right, just a few hours ago. Both numbers are definitely confirmed."

Highnote was gripping the telephone so hard his knuckles were turning white. "Did you get names?"

"Yes, sir. Last three digits, six-five-nine, was listed as Wilson, Thomas S. The six-six-zero passport was listed to Morgan, Christine M."

"Were you able to come up with the name of the hotel where they're staying?"

"Not yet, sir. But Helsinki station promised they'd give us a shout as soon as they checked with the police. Shouldn't be long now."

"It's early evening over there. I would have thought they'd have that information by now."

"Sorry, sir, that's all they came up with. Do you want us to query them again?"

McAllister had actually made it. By now he'd probably be inside the Soviet Union. Good Lord, was it possible?

"Sir?" the duty officer was asking.

"No, you don't have to carry it any further. Thanks."

"How do you want this logged, Mr. Highnote?"

"Keep it open for the moment, if you would. I'll close it out myself tomorrow."

"Yes, sir," the duty officer said.

Highnote hung up. McAllister was as good as dead. The moment he set foot inside Russia they would arrest him. Short of that, if he actually reached General Borodin by another miracle, he would not survive that encounter. What Highnote knew of Borodin was that the man was incredibly tough. A fighter. Even his own people were in awe of him. No one ever got in his way and escaped unscathed.

Which left Stephanie Albright, who would be toughing it out in a Helsinki hotel room.

Highnote picked up the telephone, got an outside line and called operations at Andrews Air Force Base. "Major Jenkins, please," he said.

The squadron commander came on a second or two later. "Major Jenkins."

"Bob Highnote. Are we ready to go, Mark?"

"It's a green light, sir?"

"Right."

"Anytime you're ready then, sir," Major Jenkins said.

"How's the weather over the North Atlantic?"

"There's a storm cell building over European Russia, but it's heading east, so we're in good shape."

"I'll be there within the hour," Highnote said.

Dexter Kingman, chief of the Office of Security for the CIA, sat across the desk from John Sanderson, in the J. Edgar Hoover Building on Pennsylvania Avenue at Tenth Street. He had come to a slow boil when the FBI director had finally explained what was happening.

"I don't like this one bit, Mr. Sanderson, I don't mind telling you."

"Neither do I," Sanderson replied. "The fact of the matter is, Highnote is on the move."

"Where?"

"At the moment he's in his office."

"It's your opinion that he will lead you to McAllister?"

Sanderson nodded, and leaned forward. "You must understand that the two men have been friends for a lot of years. From what we can gather, Highnote has ostensibly been protecting McAllister ever since the incident in New York."

"From everything else you've told me—not saying I can accept it—it's hard to believe."

"It's no less difficult for us," Sanderson said, sighing deeply. "But it seems likely that Robert Highnote is working for the Soviet government. His control officer was a man named Gennadi Potemkin whom we found dead at Janos Sikorski's home outside of Reston. Between the two of them they ran the O'Haire network, and did a damned good job of it."

"Why would a man like Highnote turn?"

"We don't know that yet, we're still working up a psychological profile on him. . . ."

"What?" Kingman, who was himself a psychologist, asked.

Sanderson spread his hands. "We don't have much to go on. His phones are constantly being swept so there has been no possibility of monitoring his calls. And when he moves, it's often with a great deal of care so he has been difficult to tail. But our best guess at the moment is that sometime over the past five to eight years, he became unbalanced. Pressures of the job, moral dilemmas, we're not sure. But there is enough circumstantial evidence to suppose that he has gone off the deep end. Did you know that he had become fanatical about religion?"

"Doesn't make the man a Russian spy."

"No," Sanderson said.

"What about McAllister? Where does he fit?"

"We think that McAllister learned something in Moscow that might ultimately lead back to Highnote who, under the guise of helping his old friend, has in reality been setting him up for the kill. For a legitimate kill. He's been driving McAllister like a hunter might drive a wild animal toward a dozen other hunters . . . us."

"What about the massacre at College Park? McAllister couldn't have done that."

"No," Sanderson said. "This is a big puzzle. But we believe that a second spy ring was in operation here as well. One in which Donald Harman was working with a so-far-unknown Russian."

Kingman sat back, his head spinning. "Donald Harman, the presidential adviser?"

"Yes."

"Where do I come in?" Kingman asked, trying as best he could to control himself. He was a cop, not a spy. He didn't like skulking around behind the back of a man he had long admired.

The telephone on Sanderson's desk rang, and he picked it up. "Yes," he answered softly. Moments later a startled expression crossed his features. He switched the phone to the speaker so that Kingman could hear too.

"You're there now, at Andrews Operations?"

"I'm watching them roll down the runway right now," George Mueller said. "I can have the flight recalled."

"Where is he going?"

"Helsinki."

"Oh, Christ," Sanderson said, looking at Kingman.

"Shall I stop him?" Mueller was asking.

"Who is on that flight?" Kingman asked.

"Highnote," Sanderson said. "Either McAllister and the Albright woman are in Helsinki, or Highnote is trying to make a run for the Soviet border."

"What?" Mueller shouted. "What'd you say?"

"Don't stop him," Sanderson said. "I'll call the Pentagon and arrange another flight for you and Dexter Kingman. He'll be on his way out there immediately."

"We'll never catch up with him."

"Perhaps not, but we won't be far behind," Sanderson said. "Just stand by out there." He hung up the telephone. "Will you help now?" he asked Kingman.

"If McAllister and Stephanie believe that Highnote is there to help them, he'll be able to kill them with no problem. They won't be expecting it."

"Will you help?" Sanderson repeated.

"Yes," Kingman said numbly. "They could be warned. We could get a message to them somehow."

"I'll call Van Skike, and he can arrange something with the Agency in Helsinki, but they're not to be warned."

Sudden understanding dawned on Kingman. "Mac and Stephanie . . . they're to be used as bait."

Sanderson nodded. "What we have on Highnote is circumstantial. Do you still want to help?"

"I don't have much of a choice, do I?" Kingman said, getting to his feet.

"None of us do," Sanderson said.

Somehow, God help him, the night had passed. Lying fully clothed on his bed in the Berlin Hotel around the corner from the Lubyanka, McAllister tried to put everything into perspective as the sky outside of his window began to lighten with Monday's dawn. He could still feel Stephanie's touch, her body a dark warm secret enfolding him. They'd made love at their hotel in Helsinki before his afternoon flight left for Moscow. They'd been tender with each other until the end when she didn't want to let go. He had been unable to ease her pain or his fear.

"It's crazy," she had cried in anguish.

The last irrational act of an irrational man. But even now when he still had the ability to turn back, to check out of the hotel and take the next flight out to Helsinki, he could not do it. He was driven, there was no denying it. Even in the innermost recesses of his mind he understood that the acts he had set in motion had no basis in reality. At least in any reality that he could put into words so that he could understand.

Look to Washington. Look to Moscow. Zebra One, Zebra Two.

Washington was finished for him. Now it was time for Moscow so that he could complete the circle of insanity that had begun for him one evening late in October.

We have made progress together, you and I. I am so very proud of you, Mac, so very pleased.

His interrogator's name had been Miroshnikov. He was a KGB colonel. That much McAllister knew, but very little else other than a vision of the man's face overhead, his eyes small, narrow, close-set, but with no bottoms. He also could see Miroshnikov seated across from him in the interrogation room. He was a large man, his complexion almost yellow, an Oriental cast to his features.

You thought you could do more for your country with words than bullets, is that it? . . . In the end you will talk to me, they all do. . . . You, my dear McAllister, are definitely a resource. . . . Believe me, we are going to have a splendid time together, you and I. . . .

Bits and pieces of Miroshnikov's words drifted through McAllister's mind, but there was more. There had been much more between the time he had begun to disintegrate and the night his heart had stopped on the table. Wisps of something . . . snatches of conversations that he could not put words to . . . drifted just out of reach at the back of his head.

Zebra One had evidently been Donald Harman, and Zebra Two was General Borodin. But who was Borodin? What was Borodin? How had he managed to get to a man such as Donald Harman and turn him? More important at this point, how was McAllister going to get to the general?

He got up from the bed and walked across to the window where he looked out at Detsky Mir, the children's department store, and beyond it toward Dzerzhinsky Square. It was past seven and traffic was beginning to pick up with the morning. It would be time to go soon, he thought.

They'd had no problem getting out of Munich Sunday morning. The passports were perfect as were the visa stamps in McAllister's. Their first test came in Helsinki, but on the basis of their diplomatic status they had been given preferential treatment and had been passed through customs without any of the usual checks.

Sunday afternoon Stephanie had taken a cab out to the airport with him, and had watched him board the Aeroflot flight for Moscow. As the plane had taxied away from the terminal he had looked for her, but she had already gone.

If he failed, he had thought at that moment, so would she. Their lives had been inextricably intertwined from the moment she had fished him out of the Potomac River in Dumfries.

Thank you for saving my life, darling, but you should have turned your back on me while you still had the chance. Now there was absolutely nothing he could do for her.

At Moscow's Sheremetyevo Airport his passport had received much more scrutiny than in Helsinki, but as with the Finns, the Russian officials treated him with respect, and within twenty minutes of his arrival in customs hall, he had been cleared through passport control and had taken a taxi into the city.

He turned away from the window and tiredly went into the tiny bathroom where he looked at his haggard reflection in the mirror. His hair was extremely short and dyed jet black. His skin all over his body had been made several shades darker than his normal coloring by a dye made from almond shells. His eyebrows had been thickened, he had been given an excellent mustache and once again he wore the clear-lensed glasses Stephanie had purchased for him in Baltimore what seemed like centuries ago.

He ran his fingers across the bristle of his hair, wiped the sweat off his forehead with a towel then walked back into the bedroom. He pulled on his sport coat and then a lined nylon jacket.

Run, he thought.

KGB Headquarters was housed in a complex of unmarked buildings on Dzerzhinsky Square a couple of blocks north of the Kremlin and barely a hundred yards from the Berlin Hotel. The main building of gray stone rose nine stories from street level. Behind it one of the older sections enclosed a courtyard on one side of which was the Lubyanka Prison. It was just eight o'clock and traffic was heavy as the first of the KGB officers and clerks began showing up for work at the six pedestrian gates.

From where he stood, pretending to read *Pravda,* the Communist Party newspaper on display in a glass-enclosed bulletin board, McAllister could see all six of the gates. The entrance to the Lubyanka Prison gate was a dozen steps away. People streamed past him, all of them in a hurry, intent on getting to work. He had been inside. Even now the thought was chillingly unreal to him. They'd held him for more than a month, feeding him drugs, depriving him of proper food and rest, relentlessly questioning him, over and over, and finally the torture. Most of it was gray or even nonexistent in his memory, except that the experience had fostered a deep, smoldering hate in him.

Except for the highest Party and government officials, parking was at a premium downtown. Miroshnikov was just an interrogator, he would not rate a parking space within the complex. The KGB maintained several lots within a block or so of the square, though most lower-grade clerks and officers could not afford to maintain an automobile, so took the subway or buses to work.

Standing shivering in the intense cold, McAllister knew that he was on a fool's mission. Miroshnikov might not be coming to work this morning. Perhaps not until later. Or perhaps he had come early. Or, perhaps there were other entrances, other ways of getting into the complex.

For a while, surreptitiously watching the people, he was afraid that even if Miroshnikov did show up this morning, he wouldn't recognize the Russian. He searched that part of his memory, but the only thing that stood out besides the fact that the interrogator had been a large man, were his eyes. Looking at Miroshnikov, he remembered thinking from the first days of his interrogation, you only saw the eyes and little else.

It was also possible, McAllister worried, that Miroshnikov would not be using the prison gate to enter the complex. He might use any of the other five pedestrian entrances. Perhaps his office was somewhere within the main building that housed most of the KGB directorates.

He stepped away from the newspaper display case and stared intently down the street. He could see the other gates from here, but at this distance he surely wouldn't be able to pick one man out of the crowd; or even if he could, he wouldn't be able to reach him before he entered the building. Once inside he would be untouchable for the remainder of the day.

In despair, McAllister turned back, and Miroshnikov was there! Barely twenty feet away. Towering over most of the people around him, he walked with his head bent, a thick leather briefcase in his left hand, a newspaper rolled up under his right arm.

McAllister was staggered into inaction for several long terrible moments. Miroshnikov's was the one face in all the world he'd never thought he would see again. The interrogator and his subject come face-to-face at last. He suddenly remembered the satisfaction he had gotten that last night when he'd rammed his knee into the man's groin and driven his fist into the interrogator's throat.

Miroshnikov looked up at the last moment, his eyes sweeping past McAllister without recognition. But then he did a double take, his eyes finding and locking into McAllister's, and suddenly he knew. He stopped short.

Two uniformed KGB officers passed, and McAllister stepped around them, reaching Miroshnikov before the man had a chance to move.

"You . . ." Miroshnikov breathed, his eyes wide. "How?"

McAllister smiled, although his gut was churning and his head was spinning. He took Miroshnikov's arm as if they were old friends. "We're going for a walk," McAllister said in Russian, his tone even. "If you refuse, or if you call out, I will kill you here and now."

"Insanity."

"Yes, it is," McAllister agreed. So far they had attracted no undue attention, but it wouldn't last.

"What do you want?"

"Information. Now, let's go or you'll die right here."

"And so will you," Miroshnikov said, starting to pull away.

McAllister tightened his grip. "It doesn't matter. I don't have anything to lose."

The interrogator's expression changed all of a sudden from one of fear, to one of understanding, if not acceptance. "No, I don't suppose you do," he said softly.

"Let's go."

"Where?"

"Your car. Then someplace to talk. Someplace private."

Still Miroshnikov hesitated for a beat. Finally he nodded. "As you wish," he said.

"You are quite a remarkable man," Miroshnikov said.

They sat together in the front seat of his black Moskvich sedan in a parking lot off Puschechnaya Street.

McAllister reached inside Miroshnikov's coat and pulled out his pistol; it was a Makarov automatic. Standard KGB issue.

"Do you mean to kill me now?" the interrogator asked. "For everything that was done to you while you were under my care?"

"That depends on you," McAllister said. There was a constriction across his chest, and he was acutely conscious of his beating heart. He was sweating despite the cold.

"You have come all this way for an explanation?"

"I want to know about a KGB general. Aleksandr Borodin. I want you to tell me how I can find him. Where does he live?"

Surprise spread across the interrogator's face. "What?"

"Borodin. I need an address."

"I don't understand. I thought you had come here for . . ."

McAllister raised the pistol and jammed it into Miroshnikov's side. "I don't have time. I want an address now, or you'll die. Simple."

Miroshnikov shook his head. "He has an apartment here in the city on Kalinina Prospekt, but his wife normally stays there. The general prefers his dacha."

"Where? Exactly," McAllister demanded. Being this close again to Miroshnikov was different than he thought it would be. He felt like a fool, or more accurately like a schoolboy who had done something naughty. Turn the gun over to him, he is your friend. Hadn't that already been established? *We are making such great progress together, you and I, Mac.*

Miroshnikov was watching him closely. "It's on the Istra River. About fifty kilometers from here. Not so difficult to find."

McAllister knew most of the area around Moscow. He'd been to the Istra River region with its Museum of Wooden Architecture on several occasions. An entire replica community of churches, peasant cottages, granaries, and windmills had been brought there from all over Russia.

"Is it near the village?"

"Yes," Miroshnikov said, still puzzled. "Just a few kilometers to the north. There is a covered bridge across the river. He is first on the right."

The parking lot was protected by a tall wire-mesh fence. One of the attendants had come out of his hut and was watching them. McAllister looked up.

"Start the car and drive out of here," he said.

Miroshnikov saw the attendant as well. "To the general's dacha?"

"No. Someplace private. Anyplace. Just get us out of here. Now."

Miroshnikov started the car and pulled out. McAllister lowered the pistol so that it was out of sight as they passed the attendant who watched them leave the parking lot and disappear down the street.

Traffic was heavier than before, and for the next few minutes the interrogator concentrated on his driving. He turned right on Zhdanova Street past the Ministry of Higher and Special Education, and one block later had to stop for a red light. He refused to look at McAllister, his eyes straight ahead on the bumper of the car ahead of them. When the light changed, he pulled forward.

Look to Washington. Look to Moscow. Voronin's words were so clearly etched in McAllister's brain that he might always have known them. But there was something else. Still something that nagged.

"What is this general to you?" Miroshnikov asked, breaking their silence.

"Zebra Two," McAllister said. It no longer mattered who knew.

"What?"

"A spy."

"Of course . . ."

"He was Donald Harman's control officer. He and his people have been trying to kill me ever since I was sent home. Well, they're all dead now, and Borodin is the only one left."

Miroshnikov was looking at him, a very strange expression on his face. "I don't know what you're talking about."

"Zebra One was Donald Harman, an adviser to the President. General Borodin is Zebra Two, his control officer."

"You've come here to kill him?" Miroshnikov asked in wonder.

"Yes."

"Why?"

McAllister started to reply, but no words came. His heart was racing now.

They crossed the Sadovaya Ring with the light, and continued north away from the city center. A banner was stretched above the broad boulevard. LONG LIVE THE SOVIET PEOPLE, BUILDERS OF COMMUNISM. McAllister struggled to maintain his control.

"Why?" Miroshnikov repeated. "You came back here at great risk. Kidnapped an officer of the KGB right in front of headquarters, and I suspect you weren't even armed. And now you are saying that you mean to kill a very important general. I ask you again, why?"

"Because of . . . what he has done."

"To you? To your country?"

"Yes."

"You say this Donald Harman is dead. I read it in the newspapers. And so are some other very important men in Washington. You have done your job, Mac, and done it well. I am proud of you."

"Americans," McAllister whispered.

"And some Russians too, I think. I have seen reports. Gennadi Potemkin is missing. Presumed dead."

"I killed him."

"There, you see? And there have been others."

The traffic thinned out the farther they got from downtown. They passed the Riga Train Station and Dzerzhinsky Park, a big textile plant on the right after they passed beneath a railroad viaduct.

Believe me, we are going to have a splendid time together, you and I.

The interrogator's words flowed around McAllister. The voice then and now, it was hard for him to distinguish which.

They had left the city behind. Birch forests spread away to the undulating horizon, the highway rising and falling like swells on a vast ocean. The sky was overcast, and a wind had begun to blow snow across the road. The countryside seemed alien, as if it belonged on another planet.

"You don't understand, do you, Mac?" Miroshnikov's patient voice came to McAllister. "But of course you couldn't."

A narrow road, barely a track through the snow, led back up into the trees. Miroshnikov downshifted and the little car bumped its way up a shallow hill, then down the other side around a steep curve. When he stopped the car they were completely out of sight of the highway. Only the trees were visible in any direction. Not a single sign of human habitation marred the desolate landscape.

"You won't kill me, I don't think," Miroshnikov said.

McAllister raised the automatic. Little spots of light danced in his eyes, like flickering embers from a campfire.

"I'm going to help you, as I have from the beginning, Mac. Believe me, I will turn out to be a good friend. Your only friend."

The interrogator opened the car door and got out.

"Where are you going?" McAllister shouted, suddenly rousing himself.

"For a smoke, nothing more. We will talk, and in the end you will see that together we can kill this general of yours, and together we will run to the West. We will be heroes, you and I. Believe me, we are going to have a splendid time."

McAllister got out of the car as Miroshnikov was lighting a cigarette. The interrogator offered it across the hood of the car, but McAllister refused. The extremely cold wind bit at his face and ears, and his bare hands began to turn numb, but his head was clearing.

"We'll do it tonight," Miroshnikov said. "He is a difficult man. But with you I think it will be possible. Anything is possible."

"He's one of yours, why would you want to kill him?"

Miroshnikov scowled. "He's Russian, not one of mine."

"And you?"

"Siberian. There is a big and very important difference, Mac. I will explain it to you someday."

With Miroshnikov distanced across the car, and with the cold wind continuing to clear his head, McAllister could begin to think again. He was no longer mesmerized by the interrogator . . . who after all was nothing more than a man.

"What did you do to me in the Lubyanka?"

Miroshnikov had started to raise the cigarette to his lips, but his hand stopped halfway. "I saved your life."

"What are you talking about?"

"You were a spy. You had been caught with a weapon in your possession. You should have gotten the death penalty. I prevented it."

"How?"

"By convincing General Suslev, the head of my division, that you would be of more use to us in the States than in a Gulag, or two meters down."

McAllister could feel his finger tightening on the Makarov's trigger. He had no idea how much pressure it would take before the gun fired.

Miroshnikov saw it.

"What did you do to me?"

"I convinced Suslev that I had turned you into an agent for us. The chances that it would work, that you could convince your people you were legitimate, were slight. But even a small chance is better than none."

"What did you do?" McAllister shouted into the wind. "You sonofabitch, what happened?"

Miroshnikov let the cigarette fall to the ground. "I gave you . . . motivation."

"What else?"

"I gave you my . . . hate. I gave you . . ."

"They were waiting to kill me in New York. Who ordered that?"

"I don't know."

McAllister cocked the Makarov's hammer. "Who told them I would be coming in on that flight?"

"Potemkin," Miroshnikov cried.

"How did he know?"

Miroshnikov said nothing.

"How?"

"I told him that someone ordered your release, and that you knew about the O'Haire network."

"You set me up."

"I knew he would fail. He was a fool, like the others. Not like you! I knew that you would survive. I recognized it in your eyes the first time I saw you."

"Why?" McAllister shouted. "Why did you do this?"

"I knew that if you survived New York you wouldn't stop until you had found out who tried to kill you. I knew that you would discover our CIA agent."

"Harman wasn't CIA."

"I didn't know about him. I'm talking about Robert Highnote. Your friend."

All the air seemed to be gone. McAllister couldn't catch his breath. His hands began to shake.

"You didn't know?" Miroshnikov cried in alarm.

"Highnote?"

"He and Potemkin worked together. Have for years. I wanted to strike back."

Highnote. The years of their friendship, their mutual trust, their assignments together, all of it came as a whole to McAllister. A huge, hurtful, impossibly heavy weight on his shoulders. He was Atlas. Only his burden was overwhelming.

"And you did it," Miroshnikov said. "You struck back. You ruined them."

McAllister was shaking his head. He lowered the pistol and turned away. He remembered an evening in particular; he and Highnote had gone out on Berlin's Ku-Damm and had gotten stinking drunk. They'd been celebrating something. . . . He couldn't quite remember just what. When they got back to the apartment, Merrilee and Gloria were waiting up for them, angry at first, but they'd all ended up laughing so hard that Merrilee had actually wet her pants. Good memories. Fine times.

"Now we'll finish it, Mac. You and I. We've come so far together. . . ."

"It was you all along," McAllister said, amazed.

"Borodin is the last of it. We'll kill him and then get out."

"You," McAllister said, his voice rising as he started to turn, bringing the gun up.

"I saved your life," Miroshnikov screamed.

"But you took my soul," McAllister shouted, and he fired, the shot catching Miroshnikov in the center of his forehead, and he seemed to fall backward into the snow forever.

Chapter 34

Stephanie Albright paid her lunch bill and walked across the crowded restaurant to the elevator. After twenty-four hours alone in her hotel room she had been unable to stand the isolation any longer and had left. For an hour she had wandered around Helsinki's beautiful downtown area, passing the ornately designed opera house and the old church on Lönnrotinkatu, but the weather was so bitterly cold that she had finally ducked into the Hotel Torni with its tower restaurant that afforded a view of the entire city. Alone, as she had often been in her life, she had done a great deal of thinking about David, about the insanity they had somehow lived through over the past weeks. Something was driving him. That had been obvious from the first moment she'd laid eyes on him.

Look to Washington. Look to Moscow. Zebra One, Zebra Two.

Janos Sikorski had known what those words meant. And his reaction when David had spoken them had been immediate and violent.

"Who else have you spoken those words to?" Sikorski had demanded.

Picturing the scene, she remembered that by then she had been out of the kitchen. But just before the shot had been fired, she heard the old man scream: "Traitor! They'll give me a medal for your body!"

It hadn't made sense then, and it made less sense now. Sikorski had been long out of the business, retired to his cabin outside of Reston, and yet he had known and understood the meaning of Zebra One, Zebra Two. Whoever those two were—if they were real—they had evidently been in place for a long time. All the way back to when Sikorski was still active.

But he had called David a traitor. Why? What did it mean?

She'd waited only twenty-four hours. David had asked for forty-eight before she was to begin making noises. But she couldn't stand it any longer. It had gone too far. In fact it had gone too far the moment she'd allowed him to board the plane for Moscow.

Oh, God, David, she cried to herself riding the elevator down, where are you? What is happening to you? It was time now, she decided, for the insanity to finally end. Time to get him out of Russia.

Reaching the lobby she crossed to the line of telephones and placed a call to the American Embassy on Itäinen Puistotie. While she waited for the connection to be made, she tried to calm down. But it was difficult.

It rang, and she tightened her grip on the telephone.

"This is Stephanie Albright, and I need some help."

"Yes, ma'am," a man with a pleasant voice answered. "Are you an American citizen?"

Hadn't he heard that along with McAllister she was wanted for murder? Was it possible? "Yes, I am," she said.

"Are you presently here in Helsinki?"

"Listen to me," Stephanie said. "I want you to tell someone upstairs that I'm here in the city. And I want a message sent to Dexter Kingman. He is chief of the CIA's Office of Security in Langley. Do you have that?"

"Ma'am, I don't know what you're talking about. But if you are here in Helsinki I think it might be easier for you to get help if you came to the embassy. I'm sure that someone here . . ."

"Goddamnit," Stephanie shouted. "You're not listening to me. Take my name upstairs and give them the message."

"Upstairs?"

"He'll be a special assistant to the ambassador."

"Who will?"

"Your CIA bureau chief."

"I don't . . ."

"Just do it," Stephanie snapped. "I'll call back in exactly thirty minutes." She hung up the phone and stood there shaking for a moment or two, until she got hold of herself, then she turned, crossed the lobby to the front doors and outside headed the few blocks to her hotel on Bulevardi.

She and McAllister were registered under the names on their diplomatic passports. It would do the embassy no good to search for Stephanie Albright. Officially she wasn't in Finland.

Time, she thought. It was crucial now. If she could convince someone in the embassy to patch her through to Dexter on a secure line, and if she could convince him of everything that had happened, it was just possible word could be sent to our embassy in Moscow. Someone there would know General Borodin, and would know how to reach David. They had to!

It was just a few minutes past two by the time she reached the Klaus Kurki Hotel, and took the elevator up to her floor. She was thoroughly chilled. Walking outside she had thought again about David in Moscow. He too would be cold and frightened. But he wouldn't be feeling the pain. His concentration would be on one man. For him there would be nothing else.

She unlocked her door and stepped into the room as a smiling Robert Highnote, his overcoat off and tossed casually on the bed, turned away from the window.

"Hello, Stephanie," he said.

Shock mixed with an instant feeling of relief rebounded from her stomach, and her knees were suddenly weak. "Oh, God," she said. "How did you find me?"

"I had your diplomatic passports flagged here in Helsinki. Mac's artist in Munich did a fine job, from what I can gather."

"He's gone to Moscow," Stephanie said, and she suddenly remembered the open door behind her. She turned and closed it.

"After General Borodin?" Highnote asked.

"Yes, and we've got to help him," she said turning back. Her heart skipped a beat.

Highnote held a small, flat automatic in his hand, pointed at her, a wistful expression on his face, almost as if he were sorry for what he was doing.

It all came to her now. The Russians waiting for Mac outside Highnote's house. The killers coming for him at Highnote's sailboat. Even the killers at Sikorski's. Highnote knew Mac's tradecraft well. He knew that Mac would be showing up there sooner or later. And Highnote was the only one who had survived the shooting in College Park. He had taken a terrible risk, but the prize had evidently been worth it to him.

"It wasn't Harman," she said, finding her voice. "It was you all along."

"It was both of us, actually," Highnote said. "Though at first I had no idea that Donald was in on the action as well. We never worked together."

"Then which one of you was Zebra One?"

Highnote shook his head. "I have no idea what that means, Miss Albright. Of course you don't have to believe me, but it's the truth."

"The O'Haire organization was called the Zebra Network."

"That's correct. But there never were any such code words as Zebra One or Zebra Two."

"Who did you work with?"

"Poor Gennadi Potemkin," Highnote said, his jaw tightening. "We had done good things together. And we would have done much more if Mac hadn't come after us."

"Why?"

Highnote managed his wan smile again. "A very large question," he said. "Which I don't have the time or patience to answer at this moment. Suffice it to say that in a world in which fingers are poised over tens of thousands of nuclear triggers, the only guarantee of safety is in knowing each other's true intentions. It is the only way, I can assure you, that we can possibly avoid a nuclear confrontation."

There was an old CIA acronym for why spies defected. She'd heard it during training at the Farm. MICE, which stood for Money, Ideology, Compromise, and Ego. Highnote certainly hadn't become a traitor for money. Ideology? Compromise, as he suggested now? Or had it simply been ego? He was the last bastion of hope for the survival of mankind. Had he become so egocentric that he believed that?

"It wasn't Mac and me at College Park."

"I know that."

"Who then?"

"I'm not one hundred percent sure, but I suspect Don Harman probably arranged it."

"Why?"

"Again the very big question," he said. "Because, my dear, no one believes any longer that you and Mac are traitors or killers. We were meeting to discuss a way in which to convince you of just that. We wanted to bring you in to safety so that we could find out what was going on."

"But we would have been killed the moment we showed our faces."

"Yes."

Stephanie's head was spinning again. "Then what has this entire thing been all about?"

"That is one question I cannot answer, because I don't know. I'm just as much in the dark as everyone else. But it doesn't matter any longer, you see, because Mac certainly won't survive against General Borodin . . . I called him and warned him that Mac was coming . . . and you, unfortunately, won't survive either."

"No," Stephanie screamed, and she dove to the left through the open bathroom door as Highnote fired, the shot plucking at her coat sleeve.

A tremendous crash shook the walls, and the corridor door burst inward, the door lock shattering, the entire frame splintering.

Highnote fired again, someone cried out, and a half a dozen other shots were fired from what sounded like at least three different weapons.

Stephanie was scrambling up and frantically trying to shove the bathroom door closed when Dexter Kingman appeared, blood leaking from his left arm, just below his shoulder.

"Dexter?" she cried.

"It's all right, kid, we heard enough," Kingman said, his southern drawl tinged with pain.

Others were crowding into the room past him. She picked herself up.

"It's not all right, Mac is in Moscow! We've got to help him!"

Kingman was shaking his head. "I don't think that's possible."

General Aleksandr Ilyich Borodin got up from where he'd been kneeling in the snow fifty meters from the end of his driveway, and looked back through the trees toward the main road. It was late afternoon and already getting dark, but he could still make out the silhouette of the covered bridge that crossed the river.

If McAllister came . . . when McAllister came . . . it

would be from that direction. By car or on foot? Either, for the American, would be impossible. Yet McAllister had seemed to have done just that and more already.

Again Borodin struggled with the same questions that had been eating at him all along. Why was McAllister coming? Someone had to have been directing him. No one man was that good. To think otherwise would be to sink into insanity. But who? Suslev, who envisioned himself taking over the directorship one day? Or his own number two in command of the Directorate, Sergei Nemchin, who'd run that fool Harman for these past few years? Or someone on the other side of the Atlantic? Someone who had discovered . . .

He stepped back a pace from the antipersonnel mine he'd just buried in the snow. On foot McAllister would be dead. By car he might survive, though he'd probably be injured.

Picking up his shovel Borodin started back toward his dacha a half a kilometer along the ridge that separated the valley from the cliffs overlooking the river. His footprints from earlier that led left and right off the driveway, had already been covered over by the blowing snow.

He stopped a moment and cocked his ear to listen, but there were no sounds other than the wind in the treetops.

If McAllister survived the land mine, he might suspect the driveway was unsafe, and would take to the woods on either side of the road. Borodin had rigged a pair of Kalashnikov assault rifles, set on full automatic, to trip wires. The American would not survive those . . . possibly.

Borodin hurried the rest of the way back to his house, stopping a moment again as the driveway opened onto a narrow clearing. From here he could just make out a stray reflection from one of the closed-circuit television cameras mounted just beneath the eaves. There was one on each side of the house, covering each of the four possible approaches. They were the latest technology from the Surveillance Directorate's Seventh Department, capable of operating satisfactorily in minimal light.

Inside, he stamped the snow off his boots, laid the shovel aside and hung up his coat. In his study he turned on the television monitors, each showing a different scene just outside the house. Nothing moved.

Taking his pistol out of his pocket, he checked to make sure it was ready to fire, and laid it on the desk. Next, he checked the AK47 assault rifle with its night-spotting scope, leaning it up against the wall near the door, then poured himself a stiff measure of cognac which he drank down before cutting the lights all through the house.

He'd sent his secretary Mikhail away, and his wife Sasha was safely in place in town.

Now there was only him and a lone American. Coming here, of all places.

But who was McAllister? What was McAllister? It was worrisome.

When McAllister reached the Istra River Museum Village, it was already very dark, and the wind had picked up considerably so that at times the little Moskvich was nearly blown off the slippery roads.

It had been very difficult for him to concentrate through the interminably long afternoon. For several hours he had waited off the highway north of the city where Miroshnikov's body lay stiffening in the snow. He'd run the car's engine whenever he got too cold, but the heater did little more than raise the temperature inside the car by a few degrees, though being out of the wind helped.

He'd wanted to get some rest. He desperately needed it. He hadn't slept in more than forty-eight hours, nor had he eaten in nearly as long. But his brain wouldn't shut down.

Zebra One, Zebra Two.

There was still no definitive answer. It was possible Donald Harman had been Zebra One, but it was just as possible, and in some ways more likely, that Robert Highnote had been the prime agent working with General Borodin through Gennadi Potemkin.

McAllister turned that over in his mind for a time, thinking back to the moment he'd said those words to Highnote. He knew the man . . . or at least he thought he had . . . and yet he had been able to detect no reaction, not a trace that Highnote had known what he was talking about.

Which left what?

In the late afternoon, when the light began to fail, he climbed out of the little car and walked around to where Miroshnikov lay on his back. The wind had piled snow up against his body, the flesh on his face tinged blue, his open eyes no more empty in death than they had been in life.

His interrogator, in the end, had become his creator.

"*I gave you motivation. . . . I gave you my hate. . . . I gave you your life. . . .*"

But at what price? McAllister asked the dead man. Stephanie had told him to let go, to trust in his own instincts not only for tradecraft, but for his sense of right versus wrong. Yet all that had been confused by the drugs and the brainwashing he'd been subjected to at Miroshnikov's hands. At this point it was nearly impossible for him to separate his own thoughts and impulses from those that had been implanted.

At one point he had told himself that he could still run. Get out of Moscow before it was truly too late. Break the cycle of events that Miroshnikov had set into motion. Yet even as he'd had that thought, he knew that he could not do it. If Borodin were left alive, then everyone else who had died—and their number was a legion—would have been in vain.

All his life he'd been driven by a sense of completeness. *Never walk away from a job until it is finished. Once it begins, boyo, never turn your back. It's not in our blood. We're not quitters.*

In the end, then, it really didn't matter what was driving him, Miroshnikov's mechanizations, or his own instincts.

Now he had no choice.

There was absolutely no traffic on the highway at this hour, when McAllister found the turnoff a couple miles past the village, and when he reached the covered bridge he shut off the Moskvich's headlights and rolled down the window as he coasted across the narrow river.

A hundred yards farther he came to a narrow, snow-covered track leading to the right, back through the woods, and he stopped the car, shut off the engine and got out, the Makarov automatic in his hand, the safety catch off. There were no noises, no sounds other than his own ragged breathing, the ticking of the cooling engine, and the wind. The driveway was lost in the darkness. Nowhere could he see even the faintest glimmer of light.

He stepped around the front of the car and walked ten yards down the driveway, stopping again to listen, to search the woods ahead for a sign that anyone was here waiting for him. Still there was nothing, and he turned and hurried back up to the car, laying the pistol beside him on the seat and starting the engine.

The Moskvich nearly stalled out when he hit the first snowdrift twenty yards from the road, and he had to gun the engine to get through, the little car lurching forward, accelerating as the driveway cleared.

McAllister had no idea how far General Borodin's dacha was set back into the woods. But he'd seen no tire tracks in the snow so far, which meant no one had come this way for several hours at least.

With the headlights off, his night vision had begun to return, and although the woods were very dark, he could make out the driveway, and the trees crowding in on both sides.

A little more than fifty yards from the road, he was about

to stop the car again and get out so that he could listen for more sounds, when a tremendous yellow flash erupted just beneath him, followed instantly by a huge thunderclap. The Moskvich was shoved violently over on its side, off the road, the explosion destroying the entire front of the car, ripping the front seats from the floorboards. McAllister was slammed into the rear corner of the cabin, his head smashing into the window post, something very hot and sharp slicing through his coat into his left side.

The car was on fire. For a seeming eternity McAllister couldn't make his arms and legs work. His body was tangled in a heap beneath a part of the car's roof and large pieces of one of the seats. His ears were ringing from the effects of the blast, and bright yellow flashes danced in front of his eyes.

Flames. His brain crystallized on that one thought. He had to get out of the wreckage before the car's gas tank in the rear exploded.

It took him several long seconds to scramble out from beneath the debris, and moments longer for him to orient himself, realizing all of a sudden that the front of the car was gone, and he could pull himself through the opening where the windshield had been.

He cut his hands on the broken glass and jagged edges of twisted metal, and then he was tumbling, rolling over and over through the flames, his hair singeing, parts of his nylon jacket melting.

The snow was blessedly cool and soothing to his burns and other injuries, but his legs were numb and the best he could do was crawl down the driveway.

He managed to get thirty feet away when the Moskvich's gas tank blew, destroying what remained of the car, spewing flames and wreckage in all directions.

For a long time, perhaps a full minute or more, McAllister lay facedown in the snow, his head spinning, yellow flashes still dancing in front of his eyes, his ears still ringing.

General Borodin had known he was coming. The road had been booby-trapped. A dozen incidents from Vietnam raced through his head. Car bombings, rocket attacks, land mines.

But how had the Russian known? Who had warned him?

To lie there would be to die. That thought finally came to the forefront of McAllister's mind. He lifted himself up, and with a great deal of difficulty managed to struggle to his feet where he stood weaving back and forth, blood streaming from his hands and from the jagged wound in his side.

General Borodin was here. Waiting for him. The answers were here. All of them.

McAllister lurched forward a few steps, but then stopped dead in his tracks.

The road had been booby-trapped. General Borodin had planted a land mine. Were there others?

He stepped back a pace, searching the trees along both sides of the road, trying to decide, trying to think what to do, trying to think what Borodin might have done.

Finally he stepped off the road and plunged into the woods angling immediately toward the right so that he could still follow the track of the driveway.

Slowly his vision and hearing began to clear, but this time he was unarmed.

He stopped again and looked back the way he had come. Already the flames from the explosion had begun to die down. A few of the trees and some of the brush at the side of the road had caught fire, but it didn't seem as if it would spread. The wind was blowing the flames back toward the driveway. But Miroshnikov's gun had been beside him on the front seat. There was no possibility of finding it now. None.

He turned back. There was no more running. General Borodin wanted him, and the general was going to have him.

McAllister started forward again and twenty feet later he lurched and stumbled, falling forward over a thin wire stretched across the snow.

The Kalashnikov rifle strapped to the bole of a tree ten yards away, erupted on full automatic, one slug tearing into McAllister's side as he went down, and a second smashing into the side of his head, just grazing his skull, but shoving him bodily against a fallen tree, ten billion stars bursting in his brain . . .

When the land mine exploded, General Borodin had jumped up, grabbed his rifle and had run out into the night, staying within the darker shadows at the edge of the house.

Minutes later he'd heard the Kalashnikov on the left side of the driveway fire its full load, and then the night fell silent.

He stood now watching, waiting, his breath white in the intense cold. McAllister was lucky. Somehow he had managed to survive the first explosion and get clear of the car before its gas tank had gone. But he hadn't been thinking straight, and he had left the road, stumbling into the second trap . . . one that he could not possibly have survived.

Nothing moved in the night so far as General Borodin could tell. The flames which had been clearly visible from here, had died down and finally disappeared.

There would be questions, of course. But with McAllister's body as an offering, he could come up with the answers.

After a full five minutes he went back into the house, pulled on his parka stuffing the pistol in his pocket, and with the heavy assault rifle under his arm, once again stepped outside and headed up the driveway.

It was time to get out now. Time to finally step down. After the furor this incident was going to cause died off, he would accept his retirement. He had done his part, after all. He had lived the life of lies, of deceit. The life of fear, of always wondering when a man such as McAllister would be coming after him; or, when he would finally get his nine ounces. He thought of an old Stalinist era proverb: In Moscow they ring the bells often, but not for dinner. But when he died he didn't think the bells would ring. Not for him.

A few hundred meters away from the house, General Borodin stepped off the road and headed directly to where he had set up the trap. He would drag McAllister's body back down to the driveway and lay it out a few meters from the wreckage of the car (where had he gotten a vehicle in the first place?). When he called the militia out here it would look as if McAllister's car exploded, and that the general had shot him down while he was trying to escape. At least the militia wouldn't question the word of a KGB general, no matter how it looked. And whoever had sent McAllister would know enough to keep his mouth shut. He would know that he had lost.

At first General Borodin thought he had gotten confused in the darkness, and had missed the spot where he'd set up the rifle.

But then his gut tightened and a cold chill ran through his body. The strap he'd used to hold the rifle in place lay in the snow. But the Kalashnikov was gone!

Ten yards away he found a depression in the snow, blood all over the place. McAllister had been hurt in the explosion . . . he must have been . . . and he had probably been hit by at least one bullet from the rifle, and yet somehow he had gotten back on his feet, had removed the rifle from the tree and had escaped.

General Borodin stood stock-still, listening. But there was nothing.

McAllister's tracks led from where he had fallen, straight to the tree, and then disappeared.

Where?

General Borodin stepped back all of a sudden and looked

up into the branches of the tree, bringing the rifle up, his heart thumping in his chest. But there was no one there.

Where had he gone?

Back on his own tracks, of course! General Borodin stepped forward again and he could see where McAllister's footprints led back toward the driveway.

The sonofabitch, he thought with the beginnings of fear tinged with a grudging admiration.

But why take an empty rifle? For a moment or two it made no sense, but then he understood that as well. McAllister had stumbled across the first two traps and somehow managed to survive. He had finally gotten smart, realizing that another rifle would have to be set up on the opposite side of the driveway. He'd taken this gun and he was going after the clip of ammunition in the other.

McAllister had had a head start. He was hurt, but he was armed now. Only he didn't know these woods. He'd have no real idea how far away the dacha was located.

General Borodin turned and raced back through the woods, keeping well clear of the driveway. He had to reach the house before McAllister did.

McAllister stood wavering just within the clearing below the driveway, the Russian assault rifle impossibly heavy in his hands. This time he didn't think he was going to make it. His head was pounding, his vision seemed to drift in and out of focus, and for one long terrible moment he had no idea where he was, or even if he was standing or sitting.

"Come on you bastard," he tried to shout, but the words got tangled up on his thick tongue.

He had seen the glint of the television camera over the back door of the house, and he had stepped out of the woods into clear view, willing the general to see him and come out.

Look to Washington. Look to Moscow. Zebra One, Zebra Two.

He had to know for sure who they were. He had to find out now, soon, before he bled to death, or before he simply collapsed and froze.

He took a few steps forward and sank to one knee. It seemed difficult to catch his breath. His feet were an impossibly long distance away, and there was little or no feeling in his hands and arms at times, yet he stood up again by sheer force of will.

"Borodin," he shouted, this time managing to get the words past his lips. He stumbled a few steps farther. "I've come here for you, goddamnit. . . ." Was he speaking English or Russian? He didn't know.

"Who are you?" someone shouted from the left, in the woods above the driveway.

McAllister turned in the direction of the voice, bringing the rifle up, but he couldn't see anybody up there.

"What do you want?" the voice called from the woods.

General Borodin? It had to be. "You," McAllister shouted.

"Why? What are you doing here? Who sent you?"

"Zebra One, Zebra Two. Voronin told me. I know everything."

The woods were ominously silent. McAllister took another couple of steps forward. The rifle had become too heavy to lift. It had become, like so much else in his life, an impossibly heavy burden to carry, and he felt it slipping from his hands.

"Come on, you bastard," he shouted with the last of his strength, and he sat down in the snow, his fingers reaching for the rifle, but not finding it.

All of the insanities that he had endured swirled around him now as if he were a boulder lodged in the middle of a swiftly raging river. He had finally lost his grip on the bottom and he felt himself being propelled downstream.

After a while he looked up into General Borodin's eyes. The man was large, his face not unkind, but very puzzled. He was shaking his head.

"Who sent you?" the general asked, his voice coming as if from down a long, dark tunnel.

"Voronin . . ."

"Yes, my former secretary. A drunk, an idiot," Borodin said impatiently. "What did he tell you?"

"Look to Washington. Look to Moscow. Zebra One, Zebra Two." McAllister's own voice seemed far away.

"Who else knows?" Borodin shouted.

"No one."

"Miroshnikov must have heard you. He must have known. Did he send you?"

"He's dead. I killed him. He didn't know. . . . He didn't have any idea. . . ." McAllister wanted to let go, to lie back in the snow and let the darkness envelop him. Just a little longer.

"Then who sent you?"

"No one," McAllister said with a supreme effort. "Harman's dead. Potemkin is dead. I killed them all. There's only my friend Highnote and you. Zebra One and Zebra Two. Traitors. Killers. No one else is left."

Again Borodin was silent. McAllister managed to raise his head and look up at the man.

"Tell me," he croaked.

"You incredible fool," General Borodin said. "You're telling me now that Robert Highnote is a Russian agent. We'd suspected that for some time. But even I didn't know. He must have worked for Gennadi. I'm not God, I can't know everything. Like you, we are compartmentalized. Terrible waste." Borodin shook his head. "But it is true that my code name is Zebra Two. It has been for a long time. Too long a time."

"Who is Zebra One, you sonofabitch? Who is the traitor in Washington?"

"There is no other traitor in Washington, don't you understand, you poor bastard? I'm the traitor to *my* government. Zebra One is my control officer. I have been working for your government for nearly twenty years."

Like another starburst in McAllister's head, he suddenly could hear Janos Sikorski's last words. *"Traitor,"* he had screamed that night. Janos had known. "Sikorski," he said.

"Yes," Borodin was saying. "He might have known. But no one else. It's the reason we've survived all these years. We've managed to keep it contained. Voronin may have stumbled across the code names but he could have no idea who we were."

"Christ," McAllister said. "Oh, Christ."

Borodin laid his rifle down, and he helped McAllister to his feet. "I don't know what I'm going to do with you, but I can't leave you out here to die. Not like this. . . ."

A rifle shot cracked from the end of the driveway, the bullet smacking into Borodin's right shoulder, sending him stumbling forward, he and McAllister falling down in a heap.

"Traitor," someone shouted in Russian.

Borodin's face was inches from McAllister's. "Kiselev," he said in pain. "My secretary. He's come back." He tried to reach in his coat pocket, but his arm was useless. "My gun," he whispered. "In my pocket! McAllister!"

McAllister managed to get his right arm around, his numb hand fumbling in Borodin's coat pocket, finding the pistol, his fingers curling around the grip.

A short, squat man suddenly appeared overhead, a rifle held loosely in his hands, his right eyebrow rising. "So," he said. "It is a nest of spies."

McAllister pulled the pistol out of Borodin's pocket, thumbed off the safety and raised it over the general's heavy body, his vision going double again, the world starting to spin.

Kiselev started to rear back, bringing the rifle up, when

McAllister fired, the shot catching the man in the right eye, blowing off the back of his head and flinging him backward.

McAllister was drifting then. He laid his head down on the soft, warm snow.

He was vaguely conscious of Borodin's weight being off him, and he wanted to say something, but the general was gone.

Someone else was coming. Lights . . . headlights, perhaps . . . and voices. Drifting, McAllister thought these new people were speaking English, but that wasn't possible. This was Russia, the Istra River . . .

Stephanie's face loomed into view above him, and he managed to smile. There was so much he wanted to tell her, but that opportunity was gone, lost forever, like so many other opportunities.

She was speaking, saying something to him. He could hear the words as they flowed around him, but he could not make out the meaning, nor could he understand when strong hands were lifting him up, carrying him, helping him across the clearing, because the blackness had descended over him and he was safe.

Chapter 35

On the morning that David McAllister awoke from his coma, sat up, and asked the startled nurse for a glass of water in a very clear voice, the sun was streaming in his fourth-floor window.

She immediately rang for the doctor and then eased him back on his pillow. "Take it easy now, Mr. McAllister."

Her voice was soothing, and he found that he was drifting and he really didn't want the water after all. But he was vaguely aware of his body. There wasn't much pain, only a detached feeling. At one point he nearly panicked; this was the Lubyanka all over again, his detachment was from the drugs they were feeding him, and he expected to see Miroshnikov come through the door at any moment. But then the chief interrogator was dead, as were so many others. So many.

Over the next few days, or was it weeks?—he would never be quite sure about this period of his life—the episodes of wakefulness came more and more often, and gradually the feeling of detachment began to leave him.

At times, he was dully aware that there were people around him other than the doctors and nurses; talking, looking at him, but he was never able to put their faces into any semblance of recognizable order, though once or twice he thought Stephanie might have been there, but that too was unlikely unless the KGB had arrested her.

Still at other times he was running through a dark woods, the sounds of his pursuers not very far behind him. The border was just a few hundred meters to the west, but he didn't think he was going to make it. Helicopters were searching for him, and they had sent the dogs to pick up his trail. Once he even cried out in the night, his bed soaked with sweat, and gentle hands were touching his body, a cool cloth on his forehead.

Until one night when he woke from a deep, dreamless sleep and sat up in the bed. The door to the corridor was open. A nurse stood there looking at him.

"Hello," he said.

"Well, hello to you, Mr. McAllister," she said, smiling. "How do you feel?"

"Thirsty," he said. "And damned hungry."

The doctor came before he was fed and asked him a lot of questions about his legs, about his breathing and mostly about his memory which seemed intact. As he was being examined, he thought about everything that had happened to him up to the point of General Borodin's revelation that night at the dacha. After that there was nothing, only the vaguest of feelings and impressions floating just at the back of his brain. General Borodin was Zebra Two, and he had been working for us through a control officer here in Washington. Was it possible? Or had it been another monstrous lie? He didn't know what was going to happen to him now, only that somehow he was back in Washington. Alive.

Dexter Kingman showed up first thing in the morning, shooing the nurse away and closing the door. He drew up a chair next to McAllister's bed.

"They say you'll be playing tennis within two months," the big chief of security said, his southern accent soft.

McAllister grinned. "I'm glad to hear that," he said. "I was never able to play the game before."

Kingman laughed. "Dexter Kingman," he said, holding out his hand.

McAllister shook it. "I figured as much. What's my status here?"

"You're still on the payroll, if that's what you mean."

"Nobody's gunning for me?"

"Not at the moment."

McAllister lay back against his pillow. "It's over?" he asked.

"Except for the questions, and there's going to be a whole lot of those in the coming weeks. Once you're up to it."

McAllister focused on him. "What the hell happened out there?"

Again Kingman smiled. "Stephanie Albright is what happened. She doesn't give up so easily." He hesitated for a moment. "I think some of this is going to come as quite a shock to you."

"I've had quite a few over the past few . . ." McAllister glanced toward the window, but he couldn't see much except for a clear blue sky and some other buildings in the distance. "What day is this?"

"Tuesday," Kingman said. "April fifth."

McAllister's heart skipped a beat. He couldn't say anything.

"Yeah," Kingman said, understanding. "Are you up to this?"

McAllister nodded. "Is Stephanie all right?"

"Just fine," Kingman said. "But she nearly didn't make it. Bob Highnote tried to kill her. He was a penetration agent."

I know, McAllister thought, Kingman's words flowing around him.

Stephanie had put up such a stink in Helsinki that they had no other choice but to arrange a Russian visa in the diplomatic passport she was using, and put her on the first plane to Moscow. She lit another fire under the CIA chief of the Moscow station, and they had driven out to General Borodin's dacha that night, finding one dead Russian lying next to a nearly dead McAllister.

There was no sign of General Borodin, and no one wanted to stick around long enough to find him. They managed to get McAllister back to the embassy, where he was patched up as best as possible and flown out the next morning as an emergency medical evacuation case right under the Russians' noses; first to Rhein-Main Air Force Base in Germany, where he'd been kept for two weeks so that they could stabilize his condition, and then here to Washington where he'd lain in a coma for more than two months.

The Soviet authorities of course put up a huge stink at first, though it finally died down. A crazy American who had somehow forged a diplomatic passport (which was recovered by the KGB from Moscow's Hotel Berlin) had somehow gotten through Russian security into Moscow, where he shot and killed a KGB officer named Miroshnikov and another officer named Kiselev before General Aleksandr Borodin, himself gravely wounded, managed to shoot and kill the intruder. The man's body had not been found, but it was believed that in the spring thaw it would turn up.

"Thomas Wilson," McAllister said.

"That's right. The name you used on your diplomatic passport. A nonperson now."

"And Highnote?"

"Committed suicide. That's the official line. It was the pressures of his job."

McAllister closed his eyes and searched his mind and his gut for any signs of the compulsions that had driven him. But there was none of that, only feelings of tiredness and a sense of terrible waste for all the people who'd died.

"Are you up to this?" Kingman asked.

McAllister opened his eyes. "You want to know why I went back into the Soviet Union?"

"For starters."

"Donald Harman was a Soviet agent working for General Borodin." It was a lie, but what else could he say?

"What about this Miroshnikov? Did you kill him?"

McAllister nodded.

"Why?"

"He got in my way."

Kingman sighed deeply and shook his head. "Well, Harman is dead, and so are Bob Highnote and his control officer Gennadi Potemkin . . . you killed him too?"

Again McAllister nodded.

"But your jaunt into Russia, I'm afraid, was a failure. Borodin has survived. In fact he was offered a promotion but he turned it down. Retired, from what I read."

"Sure," McAllister said, but he wasn't listening any longer. Zebra One, Zebra Two. He'd found Borodin, but who was Zebra One? Or would he never know?

"You're one amazing sonofabitch," Kingman said, not unkindly, and he was gone.

Gloria came later that morning, looking wan and drawn out. She kept trying to smile, and failing, and she couldn't seem to look him in the eye.

"I just came by to see how you were doing," she said.

"Are you all right?" McAllister asked.

"I'll get by."

"And Merrilee?"

"She took it hard, but she'll survive."

"I'm glad to hear it."

She hadn't bothered to sit down. She stood at the end of the bed nervously fingering the strap of her purse. "I just came to see how you were doing," she repeated herself.

"I understand," McAllister said. "I mean about that night in our house. You had no way of knowing."

She said nothing.

"What do you want to do now? I'll try again if you want me to."

She looked up, her faced screwed up in an expression of surprise and even a little disgust. "What are you talking about?" she said. "I came to apologize, but nothing more. Our marriage was over years ago. I can't take this insanity any longer. I was never able to take it."

"Maybe if I get out of the business . . ."

"No," Gloria said, holding up her hand as if to ward him off. "I've had enough. Get better soon. When you're ready we'll talk about a divorce. My lawyer says . . ." She stopped. "Just get better," she said, and she turned and left the room.

Over the next few days Kingman and others from the Agency began McAllister's debriefing. "We just want to cover the high points for now," the chief of security promised. The details would come later.

John Sanderson and George Mueller from the FBI stopped by for a brief chat, and when the time came for his formal debriefing they would be included.

But Stephanie had been strangely absent. They'd not given him a telephone so he could call her, even if he'd known where she was, and each time he asked that a message be sent to her, his request was received with a promise to do so.

He began to believe that like Gloria, she too had had enough of the insanity, and no longer wanted anything to do with him. And for that he couldn't blame her. He couldn't blame either of them. But he just wanted to talk to her. Tell her that he understood.

On the fourth day, the DCI, Howard Van Skike, showed up, his bodyguard stationing himself outside in the corridor, allowing no one else to enter the room.

"I have an extremely tight schedule this morning, so I can only stay for a minute or two."

"It wasn't necessary, sir," McAllister said. He'd only ever met the man a couple of times. Then as now he was impressed by the DCI's gentle but intelligent nature. Van Skike had been a power on the intelligence scene for a good many years. Unlike some of his predecessors on the seventh floor at Langley, he hadn't been a simple political appointment. He had worked his way up from the ranks. "The best man for the job," the President said, appointing him to head the Agency.

And he was. Everyone agreed with that. It was said that he was a man blessed with the "intuitive gift for understanding the Russian mind."

"How are you feeling?" Van Skike asked.

"A lot better."

"You'll be out of here in a month or two. Will you be interested in coming back to work?"

"I don't know," McAllister said. He hadn't faced up to that possibility yet.

"Well, just get yourself better, and when you're ready come see me. We'll talk."

"Yes, sir."

"Now, is there anything I can do for you? Anything you need?"

"As a matter of fact there is, Mr. Director," McAllister said. "Could you see to it that Stephanie Albright comes by to see me?"

"Why?"

The directness of the question was startling. "Because . . . because I want to thank her for saving my life."

Van Skike was watching him. "And?"

Again McAllister thought that the DCI's bluntness was odd. "I want to tell her that I love her."

The DCI smiled. "I'm sure that she'll be delighted to

hear that, Mac. She's waiting just out in the hall." His eyes narrowed a little. "She doesn't know about her father . . . what he really was. Let's keep it that way."

"Yes, sir," McAllister said. "Thank you."

"She's remarkable."

"Yes, she is."

"And so are you," Van Skike said.

There was nothing to say.

Van Skike remained standing at the end of the bed. He shook his head. "One last thing," he said.

"Sir?"

"I have a message for you. From Moscow. Zebra Two sends his regards and his thanks."

All of the air left the room. "You?" McAllister said, the word half choked in his throat.

Van Skike smiled but said nothing. He turned and went out of the room. Moments later Stephanie came through the door, a huge grin on her face, tears streaming down her cheeks.

Zebra One, Zebra Two.

It was truly over now, and as Stephanie came into his arms he thought that everything *was* going to be all right.